The Coven.

Part One - Koldunya.

Chapter One – Fun and Games. (Friday, 14th December. 1979.)

Garry sat on the couch and savoured the sight of Ann's naked body. They'd lived together for two years now but he still marvelled at what was on display. Ann was about five foot four, with long auburn hair and gorgeous hazel eyes. When she was aroused, as she was now, a wild, almost animalistic look came into those eyes. Garry loved that look and it always turned him on even more. Ann was breathing a bit raggedly and her lips were slightly parted. She knew a challenge was coming and her excitement was building in anticipation. She reveled in the lust her body awakened in men. She could see it in their faces and could almost feel their eyes as a physical touch on her skin. Even being naked in front of Garry, a longtime lover, still turned her on. But she knew something more was going to be asked of her – and that was good.

"When I say go," Garry told her, "I want you to go out on the verandah, without hesitation, and stand at the rail for three minutes. You've not to move, no matter what. I'll start timing you, once you're at the rail."

Their flat was on the second floor, so the verandah was no more than ten feet above street level. There was no concealment from anyone walking or driving past. Three minutes may not seem a long time but Garry knew it was relative. Standing naked and exposed to the sight of any by-passer was a test of nerve for anyone, even if you are titillated by the thought of being observed by some random stranger. Besides, it was a cold, frosty night. Too long and Ann would be frozen instead of horny.

Garry said the word and Ann stepped outside. He stood by the window to watch her as she carried out his instructions. It was about ten-thirty and the street was deserted. A few cars passed along the road at the end of their street but none turned in. There were houses across the street. Some of them were in darkness, the others had their curtains drawn. Maybe someone was watching from the darkened windows but there was no way of knowing. Garry kept one eye on Ann and the other on the second hand of his watch. It swept round twice – and still the street remained empty. The third minute ticked away. With only five or six seconds left, the headlights of a car appeared round the corner and started down the short street. Time would have been up before it drew level with the verandah but Garry chose to keep Ann where she was. For her to flee inside now, would smack of chickening out. If anything, she stood up a bit straighter as the car neared. It glided past and a startled man's face appeared at the side window. The car slowed for a moment and then sped up again, as the driver regained himself. God knows what he thought of this unexpected turn of events. Garry waited until the car turned the corner at the end of the street and then called Ann indoors.

Ann was shivering when Garry moved to embrace her. It wasn't entirely down to the cold. She responded with savage passion when he laid her on the couch and entered her. They'd only recently began experimenting with sex-games. It had begun with talking – a lot of talking. Ann was a very sexually motivated person and she'd given a lot of thought to this part of her nature. They had shared their fantasies. Ann's were all about ceding sexual control to someone else. Garry was taken aback when she told him her number one fantasy was to be tied naked to a bed and raped by a masked stranger. The idea of exhibitionism appealed to her greatly but only at the behest of another. Doing it of her own volition, she told him, would have felt wrong. She rationalized this by theorizing in this way. She had an almost overpowering wanton side but was, deep down, ashamed of it. If the responsibility was on someone else, then she was guilt free. This surrender, in turn, enhanced the thrill she experienced.

Garry didn't know how valid Ann's theory was but he was more than happy to indulge her. Her inclinations chimed very well with his own. Exercising sexual control over a desirable woman was a massive turn on. He knew that Ann loved the idea of inspiring lust in men through the power of her nakedness. He could share vicariously in that power and experience the same thrill, at second hand, by facilitating her fantasies. Neither of them had had a partner thus inclined previously, so they were experimenting with the reality of the matter. It was still more talking than doing, but that was fine. The exploration was fun also. They agreed, later that night, that doing things publicly on their own doorstep was unwise. They'd have to keep future adventures further away from home.

They had met a couple of years previously, when Garry was still with his wife. Ann had started work behind the bar of a club that Garry frequently drank in. He had cast a lustful eye on her at first sight. She was very pretty with a stunning figure. Garry knew that many of the male patrons spent time imagining her out of her clothes. He'd heard them say so. Garry took the bull by the horns and asked her out. She said no, but in a nice way. He was persistent though and eventually got her to agree to a date. After drinks and chat, he took Ann back to her flat. That's when he found out her naked body lived up to everything he'd imagined. She was full breasted, curvaceous and he thought her near perfection.

Garry was twenty-seven when they met. Ann was two years older. She was a divorcee who lived with her two daughters, Sandra and Karen. They were eight and nine when Garry got together with their mother. He'd moved in with her when his ailing marriage finally collapsed. It was meant to be temporary but two years later he was still there. They had only begun to tentatively enact their much discussed fantasies, late in the previous summer. They had gone for a jaunt in Garry's clapped out Ford Escort, one sunny afternoon. Ann's flat was in the Saint Ninian's area of Stirling. The plan was to drive from there a few miles to the Ochil Hills and take the road from the Logie Crossroads up to the Sheriffmuir Inn. Before they started their ascent, Garry stopped the car beside the Old Logie Kirk. He told Ann to take off her top and bra and said she was to stay that way, with her hands by her side, until they reached the top of the hill.

Ann did as he had instructed and placed the removed clothing down by her feet. Garry felt himself stiffening. He could tell that Ann was excited also. That look was in her eyes. They started off up the narrow road. At times there was only room for one car to progress at a time. At these points, there were little passing laybys, in case someone was coming the other way. For most of the ascent, despite their excited anticipation, it looked like they would be out of luck. Nobody walked the road and no cars came the other way. There were many twists and turns, which required careful and slow maneuvering. Two thirds of the way up was the most extreme turn. It was a proper hairpin-bend. The road actually doubled back on itself and required that you crawl round it, slowly and carefully. As they approached this, they saw a young male hiker standing at the apex of the turning, waiting to let them go past.

Garry felt a jolting thrill low in his stomach and he stiffened even more. They were about to give this random stranger an unexpected treat. He knew how gorgeous Ann's tits were. Any heterosexual male would be gratified by the sight of them. They drew closer and the young man's gaze fell on Ann's bared breasts. His jaw dropped . Garry noticed that Ann's hands twitched by her side. She was itching to cover up. It was a strange dissonance at work. Despite the fact that the whole point of what they were doing was to occasion just exactly what was happening, instinct and societal norms made it harder to go through with it than you'd expect. Nevertheless, Ann kept her hands where they were. They crawled past and the man's gaze never faltered from her nakedness. He couldn't have had a better view. At the slowest point of the turn, he was less than two feet from her. Then they were past and Garry accelerated. In the rearview mirror, he watched the young hiker gaping open-mouthed at the receding car. Ann was ecstatic. "Did you see his face?", she purred. That was the only encounter they had but it was enough — at least for the time being. They reached the top of the hill and Ann got dressed. Both of them had been titillated and aroused by this brief encounter, so Garry drew into a parking spot and they went into the woods to fuck enthusiastically. From time to time, Garry would hint that someone was watching them from the trees. This roused Ann to new heights of passion, as she moaned and bucked under him.

They had a few more adventures after that. Ann would get naked and go out onto the communal landing outside their flat door and lay down. Garry would let her lie there for a couple of minutes and then come out and fuck her. Anyone passing up or down the stairs would discover them. It was a risk — and that's what made it exciting. As it happened, no-one actually did, but it was still a thrill. With Christmas coming, they bought the girls polaroid cameras. To try them out, Garry took pictures of Ann, naked in a series of poses. Ann had a long dark green coat which covered her from neck to mid-calf. She would wear this and nothing else, apart from a pair of kinky boots. When the coat was fully buttoned, no-one could tell what was underneath. They took to going to pubs with Ann dressed this way. They'd wait for an opportune moment and Ann would open the coat. Garry would then snap a picture of her naked, while unsuspecting fellow patrons formed the background. They got a bit bolder. Going out of town, where they were less likely to be recognized, they did the same thing. Only this time, they made sure that there were men who could see what Ann was exposing. No-one ever objected and the two of them didn't hang around long after taking the pictures.

There was no coercion involved in these games. Ann willingly ceded control to Garry. In other facets of her life she was polar opposite. She was feisty and even a bit opinionated. She wasn't slow in standing up for herself. Garry was satisfied that he knew her mind. They talked often enough. He knew what turned her on and he was conscious of looking for her limits. So far, he hadn't found any. They were taking small steps. She was keen on a threesome with another man. That was certainly achievable, given a measure of discretion. She also had ambitions to perform a striptease for a roomful of men (having been ordered to do so, of course). This would be logistically a bit problematic – and would definitely have to be staged out of town. Ann had even worked out a routine. She showed this to Garry – and he was riveted. That was for the future but it would be an amazing spectacular if it could be achieved.

Later that night, Garry woke from a troubled sleep in the early hours of the morning. They'd gone to bed shortly after they finished their energetic session on the couch. They both had enough in the tank to go again. Afterwards they drifted off to sleep. Now he was awake. Something had disturbed him. He lay for a moment before he realised he needed to pee. That must be what had interrupted his slumber. He slipped out of bed and padded along to the bathroom. When he got there though, it was occupied. He could see the light was on through the frosted glass on the door. He made out the vague outline of someone inside. One of the girls, who'd been safely tucked up in bed before the adults had begun their games, must be answering the call of nature. Garry returned to his room and slipped on his boxers. He sat on the bed and watched the girls' bedroom door, which was directly across from his own. He'd see whenever the bathroom's current occupant returned to bed, then he could take his turn in the loo.

It felt to Garry like he'd been waiting for an inordinately long time. No-one could pass without him seeing. Eventually, he grew concerned. Perhaps one of the girls was unwell. He got up and went back through to the bathroom. It was in darkness. Puzzled, Garry pushed the door open. It was indeed empty. He relieved himself and went over everything that had just happened. He didn't understand. Leaving the bathroom he went to check on the girls. Both were sound asleep. How could one get past him without being seen? Perhaps it happened when he was putting on his pants, or maybe he'd dozed off briefly without knowing. Whatever the explanation, all was well. He was happy just to leave it as a minor, unexplained mystery. Without further speculation, he got back in bed and drifted swiftly off to sleep.

Chapter Two – Opportunity Knocks. (Saturday 15ᵗʰ December 1979 – 2.15 a.m.)

The streets of Stirling were all but deserted as Bill McQuillan made his way home. It was cold but he wasn't feeling it. His mind was occupied with self-recrimination. He'd managed to reach the final of the monthly snooker tournament for the first time. All the way to the final he'd been on sparkling form. The balls dropped with ease and his safety play had been immaculate. Even in the final, he had played well. His opponent was Tom Ingles, a tough prospect who had won the title multiple times.

With only the black ball on the table, Bill was four points clear. He had a shot to pot it and win the game. It was a fine cut but definitely achievable. At the last moment, he opted to play a safety shot. It seemed the most prudent course of action. His intention was to nestle the black against the top cushion and present his opponent with an awkward decision to make. Maybe it was tension, but Bill twitched as he made the shot. The black ball bounced big and came to rest in a position that gave Tom Ingles an easy shot, which he duly took. So near and yet so far.

Ah well. There was always next month. What he'd done once, he could surely do again. Next time, he'd take his chance. Bill turned into Wallace Street. He wasn't paying much attention to his surroundings as he walked. The other side of the street was lined with substantial, two storey houses. Suddenly, something caught his eye. A women was standing, watching him from the top window of the first house. It was an old-fashioned bow-window and she stood at the side section facing him. Her gaze was intense and a bit daunting. She seemed to be dressed in a long grey nightdress. A bit discomfited, Bill had paused briefly. Not knowing what to make of it, he started walking again. His eyes were drawn to the mystery woman as he went. She followed him and moved to the central section of the window. Once again, Bill paused. The woman's gaze never wavered. She continued to focus her attention on Bill. He turned to face her squarely. The woman never flinched nor looked away. She looked young and pretty with long dark hair. Was this some kind of invitation. Bill had heard stories of chance encounters like this leading to sex – women who selected random strangers to satisfy a need in them. He'd always dismissed them as fanciful, up till now. Bill pointed to himself and the woman nodded. She beckoned him with a graceful motion of her hand. Bill decided, nothing ventured, nothing gained. Opportunity was knocking and he'd answer the call. Perhaps he'd have a story to tell at the snooker club next time. Mind you, nobody would likely believe him. Bill crossed the street and pushed the door open to enter the building.

Chapter Three – Three's a Crowd. (Saturday 15th December 1979.)

It was just after seven o'clock when Garry entered the lounge bar of the Terraces Hotel. Janet was already there and had drinks on the table. Garry worked at Riverdale Day Centre, a facility for Physically Disabled Adults. Janet was a friend of one of his colleagues and he'd met her when she came along as a volunteer helper on a Centre holiday to Rhyl, in North Wales. The two of them got on well and hooked up in the latter part of the week. That had been last summer and they'd continued seeing each other on a semi-regular basis since.

Janet was a petite, pretty blond. She had lovely green eyes and wore her golden hair in a pageboy style. She knew about Ann, but Ann most certainly did not know about her. Garry was working "overtime" tonight, as he did every couple of weeks. He was well aware that he was being unfaithful and deceitful but this troubled his conscience not one bit. As long as Ann never found out, there was no harm done, at least that's what he told himself. He was ever alert for fresh fields to plough. Janet was by no means the first woman he'd strayed with, nor, he hoped, would she be the last. The fact that she was only nineteen helped feed his ego also.

Their date followed its usual pattern. They had a few drinks and chatted about inconsequential things. Garry liked her for more than her body. She was bright, witty and lively. He enjoyed her company and their drinks session was more than just a prelude to having sex. They spent a convivial couple of hours and then drove to the Centre where Garry worked. He was a key holder and it was a convenient place for some illicit philandering. Garry unlocked the door, disabled the alarm and they went in. He locked the door behind them, lest anyone wander in. They made their way through to the lounge area. Garry never turned on any lights. There were no curtains on the windows and they really didn't want anyone peering in and seeing them in action – which was quite ironic, given what Garry did with Ann. His relationship with Janet was much more conventional.

The ambient light from the streetlamps was more than sufficient for them to find their way about. There was a foam couch which folded down to a double bed. Garry prepared this and then guided Janet down on to it. He eased himself beside her and kissed her gently on the lips. From past experience, he knew that Janet was slow to kindle. He had to be patient and gentle. Rush her and she'd turn off and call a halt. Unlike Ann, she was not highly motivated sexually. In fact, she was a bit repressed. For instance, she absolutely refused to touch his dick, which he found strange. Given time and gentle persuasion though, she would come to the boil. And then she performed with reckless abandon. It was well worth the time and effort.

Their kisses became increasingly intimate as their tongues intertwined and probed. Garry began slowly unbuttoning her blouse. When it was fully open, he eased the ends clear of her skirt. Gently, he stroked her smooth midriff and then slid his hand up to push her bra clear of her breasts. Janet had a trim, almost boyish body. Her tits were small but they were firm and delightful. He caressed them and lightly tweaked her nipples. They were rigidly erect, which told him she was warming up nicely. He himself, was more than ready. His cock was straining to be set free. Strangely, having to exercise restraint, was enhancing his arousal.

Garry removed his lips from Janet's and kissed her on the neck. He lowered his head to her breasts. Taking her left tit in his mouth he teased the nipple with his tongue. Janet let out a low moan. It was time to step things up a gear. Garry brushed his right hand up her right thigh, pushing her skirt up as it went. She wasn't wearing tights. He slipped his hand inside her panties and began fingering her cunt. She was moist but not quite ready yet. Employing the lightest of touches, Garry manipulated and teased her clitoris. Every now and again, he slid his finger into her. Each time, he tried to gauge Janet's arousal and readiness . He increased the intensity of his ministrations by small increments. When he judged the time was right, he broke off and used both hands to remove her panties, discarding them on the floor.

Garry unzipped his trousers, undid his belt and pulled his trousers down to mid-thigh. He positioned himself between Janet's legs and pushed his cock into her. He had to pause for a moment. Given the prolonged build up, he was on a hair trigger. When the tight warm wetness of Janet's pussy engulfed his prick, he had to fight for control. When he was satisfied that premature ejaculation was no longer a threat, he began to move. He kept it slow and sedate to begin with. Janet needed time to get up to speed and anyway, it helped Garry fully master his come reflex. Janet was responding. Her hips were rocking back in forth in time with Gary's thrusts. Then, she suddenly went wild. She let out an ear-splitting scream and began to buck vigorously. Garry was amazed and wondered what he'd done right. She'd never reached this stage so early before. Then he abruptly realised that she was not seized with passion, but with terror.

Janet had managed to extricate herself from under Garry and was scrambling to her feet. "She was watching us - over there," she gasped, in a strangled voice. Garry looked where she was indicating. There was nothing and nobody there. "Who?" he asked, "There's no-one there. I locked the door behind us." Janet wasn't listening. She'd pulled her skirt down and was heading for the door. "It's a fucking ghost," she shouted hysterically as she went. "She was just standing there looking at us." "Janet wait!" Garry called to her. "You can't get out. The door's locked." She paid no heed but hurried on. Garry pulled up his trousers. He was slightly freaked by Janet's panic, but convinced himself that she'd been spooked simply by a trick of the light. The room was only dimly lit by the street-lighting. All sorts of shadows were thrown by it. That had to be what she'd seen. There was no-one here. He noticed Janet's panties on the floor. Picking them up he stuffed them in his pocket.

Garry caught up with Janet as she was trying to pull the doors open by brute strength. "Hold on", he said, "I'll unlock it in a minute." She cringed away from him. Puzzled, he unlocked the doors and Janet bolted. She was still in some disarray. Her blouse was wide open and her bra was poised untidily above her boobs. As quickly as he could, Garry set the alarm, exited and locked up. Janet was already turning the corner at the end of the road by the time he'd done this. He got into the car and went after her. She was walking, still adjusting her clothing, as he caught up with her. He stopped, but she just ploughed on, ignoring him. Garry leaned over and rolled down the window so he could talk to her. He caught up with her again. "For fuck's sake Janet," he shouted, "Get in the car. I'll take you home." He had to persist another few times before she finally relented and got in.

Janet was shivering, so Garry turned the heater full on. He noticed, for the first time, that tears were streaming down her face. She'd obviously had had a real scare. They travelled in silence for a bit. Eventually Garry said, "You look like you could do with a stiff drink. Want to go for one before I take you home? You can tell me what you saw." Janet hesitated for a moment and then gave a spasmodic nod of assent. A small sob escaped her lips as she did so. Garry drove back to the Terraces and Janet went to the Ladies' to tidy herself up, telling him to get her a large straight vodka.

When Janet joined Garry at the table, she was pale but much more composed. She'd obviously washed her face. She swallowed down most of her drink in one gulp. Garry went to the bar and got her a refill. When he got back to the table, he said, "Tell me about it." Janet took another swig of vodka, gathered herself and then spoke. "It was a woman," she said. "She was standing about six feet away, looking down at us. She had long hair and was wearing a full-length dress. She just stood there staring, with those horrible eyes. They were all white and glowing. I could feel that she hated me. She was pure evil. I'm never going back in that Centre again, not even in daylight. Never." Garry tried to be reasonable. "Do you not think it might just have been a trick of the lights and, you know, shadows?" he asked. "The street lights could have reflected off something, making you think it was eyes." Janet replied vehemently, "I know what I fucking saw, Garry. You'll not tell me anything different." "Ok, ok", he said, trying to pacify her. "Tell me something," he went on. "When I came to unlock the door, you looked scared of me. Why?" Janet hesitated again. "Ok," she said. "When I first saw her, I looked up at you. For a second or two, your eyes were the same as hers."

Chapter Four – A Day in The Life. (Monday 17th December. 1979.)

Garry crawled wearily out of bed. He'd hardly slept, that he could remember. When he did manage to drop off, he was forced awake by violent nightmares that he couldn't recall any detail of. He was still disturbed by how things had ended with Janet and felt fairly certain that his liaison with her had run its course. She couldn't get out of the car quickly enough when he'd eventually driven her home. As things stood, it seemed unlikely that he'd ever see her again. He had no idea what had actually scared the shit out of her but he was bloody sure it hadn't been a ghost. He even speculated that she was perhaps mentally unstable. She had certainly acted that way.

Ann was already up and about. She'd given up her bar job and was now working as a shop assistant at a department store in the town's Thistle Shopping Centre. Garry would drop her off there, on his way to work. As it was the run up to Christmas, she'd be working late. Unlike Garry's, her overtime was genuine. He was out of sorts, feeling jittery and anxious. Some of this, he attributed to the events of Saturday night. This surprised him somewhat. He was fond of Janet and loved her body, but she was hard work when it came to sex. If their time together was done, so be it. Doubtless there'd be someone else to take her place. He reasoned that it was more the manner of the affair's ending, rather than the ending itself, which was bugging him.

Ann was in the kitchen, making breakfast for the kids. Garry never ate anything first thing. He started the day with a ciggie and a black coffee. He lit up, walked to the living room curtains and pulled them open. Sitting on the verandah handrail, just where Ann had stood naked on Friday, was a large, black crow. It was peering directly at him. Normally, Garry quite liked crows. He kind of admired their intelligence and cheek. But this one irritated him, for some reason. Its unblinking gaze was unnerving him. For a moment or two, he tried to outstare the bird, to no avail. Then he lost patience and banged hard on the window with his open palm. His intention to scare the crow away failed. It stood there, unperturbed, for another few seconds. Then, seemingly in its own time, the bird spread its wings and flapped away.

Ann came through with a mug of coffee for Garry. "What was the noise?" she asked him. "Just scaring off a bloody crow," he replied. "Oh," was all she said. They got themselves ready and left for work. When they'd gone downstairs and exited the building, Garry couldn't believe his eyes. The fucking crow was standing on the bonnet of his dilapidated Ford Escort. It shot him a look and then winged its way skyward. Ann laughed. "Looks like it's out to annoy you," she said. Garry snorted but he felt uneasy and couldn't quite fathom out why. It was only a bloody crow for Christ's sake. They got into the car and set off. It took less than ten minutes to reach the back entrance to the Thistle Shopping Centre. Ann leaned across, kissed Garry and got out. He drove off and five minutes later arrived at his work.

As he parked at the kerb, his mate Jim Keenan came round the corner. Jim was a volunteer helper at the Centre. He was a former policeman but hadn't taken to the job. While he searched for something else, he'd decided to make himself useful by working with the physically disabled members of the Centre. Garry and he had hit it off and often went for a pint together, after work. As the two men greeted each other, a crow descended and landed on top of the rail fence in front of the building. Before it could settle, Garry ran at it, shouting and waving his arms wildly. The bird swiftly flew off. "What the fuck?" said Jim, taken aback. "That fucking crow's been bugging me all morning," Garry snarled vehemently. He recounted the story of the troublesome crow but Jim was unimpressed. "Jeez man," he said, "you're making a big deal out of nothing. You see hundreds of crows about every day. They're hardly a rarity and anyway – one crow looks exactly like every fucking other one. There's no chance it's been the same one every time. Are you ok?" Garry shrugged and gave a sheepish grin. "Been a tough weekend. That's all."

They went into the building. At that time in the morning, there was only staff present. The mini-buses bringing the clients in wouldn't arrive for another twenty minutes or so. It was a fairly small operation. In all, they had only twenty-three individuals on their books. Their conditions ranged from Cerebral Palsy, through Muscular Dystrophy, Multiple Sclerosis, Chronic Arthritis and several others. The Centre was a place where they could come and be looked after, whilst learning skills such as woodwork and a variety of craft skills. It also gave respite to the relatives and carers, allowing them the opportunity to work or simply relax. There were only four full-time staff members, of which Garry was one, and up to half-a-dozen volunteer helpers. There were also ancillary staff – a handy man, a cook and a driver and escort for each of the two mini-buses. Given what had happened the last time Garry had been in here, he felt a certain amount of trepidation as he went through the door. He didn't believe in ghosts, so he wasn't entirely sure what he was nervous about. It just seemed part and parcel of the general malaise he was feeling that morning. Whatever – the Centre was exactly the same as it had been every other time he'd come to work.

The staff gathered for a quick coffee before the mini-buses arrived. Michelle was lighting up a cigarette and offered Garry one. She seemed fine. Michelle was Janet's friend – the one who'd invited her to help out in Rhyl. She was well aware of what was going on between Garry and Janet. Apparently, she and Janet hadn't spoken over the weekend. Garry hadn't been at fault for whatever had freaked Janet out but that might not be the way it would be portrayed. Anyway – that was a problem for the future. For the moment, the status quo seemed intact.

The first of the mini-buses arrived and people started coming in. Some were in wheelchairs but the majority got about under their own steam. Fiona, one of two girls who had Cerebral Palsy, had recently been bought a powered wheelchair. Her erratic control of this, terrorised everyone in the Centre. So far, she hadn't actually injured anyone but it seemed just a matter of time. Fiona was determined though, and fully intended to master the necessary skills, no matter what mayhem ensued in the meantime. None of the normal activities were happening this week. Instead, everyone was working on transforming the lounge and craft areas into a "Winter Wonderland" for the Christmas party on the coming Friday evening. Following this, the Centre would be closed for a fortnight's holiday over the festive season.

Garry lost himself in working with the members and by lunchtime he was feeling much more like himself. He'd first become involved with the Centre, like his friend Jim, as a volunteer when he was unemployed. He found he had an aptitude for the work and this eventually led to a full-time job. He had no particular skills to impart but he was generally good with people – plus – he wasn't squeamish about some of the messier tasks that required doing. Before he could have his own lunch, he was assigned to help Kitty with hers. She was the other girl who had Cerebral Palsy. Kitty was a pretty and bubbly seventeen year old. She didn't have enough control of her hands and arms to feed herself and required assistance. When they were finished, Garry skipped his own lunch and went to the office to phone Janet. She was the receptionist at a local factory, so it was her who answered his call. She was very much on the cool side when she realised who she was talking to. When Garry asked how she was, she simply answered, "Fine." She then told him she was very busy just then and couldn't talk – and that was that. Garry replaced the phone. He decided that he'd leave it till after the holidays and then, perhaps, call her again. Maybe he should just let sleeping dogs lie.

Everyone went back to work. Given the physical difficulties, it was progressing slowly – but there were four more days to go and everyone was enjoying being involved. The afternoon passed quickly. Then it was time for everyone to go home. The staff relaxed with a final coffee then they too left. As he left the building, Garry scanned for crows. He felt an inordinate relief that there were none in evidence. Getting into his car, he drove home.

Chapter Five – Three's Company. (Friday 21ˢᵗ December. 1979.)

The Centre was looking great. They'd put the finishing touches to the décor that morning. The walls were festooned with tinsel, fairy-lights, fake snow and icicles. The short corridor between the lounge and the craft area had been transformed into a grotto, complete with elves and reindeer. The main party was planned for the craft area, where they had set up disco-lights. Tables and chairs were moved to the side to make room for dancing. A friend of one of the staff was coming with a disco deck and he would DJ for the night. A big turnout was expected, with the Centre's members, their families plus volunteers and other guests attending. People were to bring their own alcohol. It promised to be a lively evening. The Centre closed early that afternoon to allow everyone to go home and get ready.

Garry still wasn't sleeping well but he no longer felt so jittery, nor did he have any further unnerving crow encounters. The situation with Janet was still unresolved but he was letting that lie for the time being. Ann had managed to get the Saturday off work – no easy feat so close to Christmas. She'd negotiated to do a Sunday shift instead. She'd therefore be able to accompany Garry to the party without worrying about an early rise the next morning. Ann had to work late on the evening of the party, so they'd be a bit late getting there, but not by much. She did a quick turn around when she got home. Ann never wore much makeup – just a little eye-shadow and some lipstick. For the occasion, she'd bought an olive-green trouser and top combination. The trousers were one piece with the top and the whole thing was held up by a pair of thin shoulder-straps. Ann never wore panties. She said this was not a sexual thing but that she just found them uncomfortable. The nature of her ensemble was such, that a bra could not be worn with it. In effect, she was just wearing one garment. This titillated Garry immensely and he thought she looked stunning. The kids were off staying with their grandparents for the night, so they'd have the flat to themselves when they got home. Garry already had thoughts on that. Jim lived in Dunblane and there was no buses running there at the time the party was expected to end. Garry had suggested he come home with them and sleep on the couch.. He'd agreed.

The party was in full swing by the time they arrived. There were no near neighbours, so the disco music was loud. The room was already packed and the atmosphere was bubbling up very nicely. Garry put the bottle of whisky they'd brought onto the drinks table and then poured a couple of large ones for him and Ann into paper cups. The table was groaning under the weight of alcohol folk had brought in. It wouldn't run out any time soon. Ann was already attracting male attention. Garry wasn't surprised. She had to be the best looking women in the place by a long way. Then he caught sight of the divine creature standing chatting to the Centre manager, Marjory. The woman was wearing a black minidress which showed long, graceful legs and matched her waist-length jet-black hair. Marjory saw him looking and waved him across. "Hi Garry," Marjory said, "let me introduce my new neighbour Morgan. She's interested in volunteering here, so she popped in for a few minutes to see the place. Morgan this is Garry, one of my staff." Garry was enthralled. Close up, Morgan was even more breath-taking. Her facial features were regular and perfectly proportioned. She was the most beautiful woman he'd ever seen in real life. "Movie-star perfect," was the thought that sprung to his mind. It was her eyes which fascinated him most, They were actually violet in colour. He hadn't even known that was possible.

They chatted small-talk for a few minutes – and Garry couldn't remember anything that was said. Morgan eventually brought the conversation to an end. "Well, I must be off," she said, "I've got another function to be at." Garry thought her voice as delightful as the rest of her. She turned to him and said, "Nice to meet you, Garry. Maybe I'll see you again soon." He fervently hoped that this would be so. With that she left. Marjory had a knowing grin on her face. "For fuck's sake Garry," she said, "Pop your eyes and tongue back in, before you do yourself a permanent injury. She's way out of your class – and she's a friend of mine – which makes her off-limits. Understand?" Garry hadn't realised he'd been so obvious. He looked round guiltily to see if Ann had been watching the exchange. Fortunately, she was dancing with Jim on the crowded dance floor and paying no attention to what Garry was doing.

Garry saw how appreciatively Jim was eyeing Ann. He had a vague plan in mind and grew more committed to putting it into effect. Maybe an erotic fantasy could be fulfilled. The circumstances looked promising. The night wore on with much dancing and merriment. A lot of alcohol was consumed. By the time the party began to wind down, many, including Garry, Ann and Jim, were more than a little drunk. Garry decided to leave the car and phoned for a taxi. When it arrived, the three of them departed amongst many shouted farewells. Jim sat upfront with the driver, while Garry and Ann went in the back. As the taxi took off, he leaned across and whispered in her ear, "Do you think you can take two of us tonight?" She mumbled something, which he took to be assent.

When they got back to the flat, Garry was at a loss how to initiate his planned threesome. Just coming out and saying it, didn't seem right. Then he had a flash of drunken inspiration. He went to their room and got the polaroid pictures he'd taken of Ann. He brought them through and handed them to Jim, who was sitting on the couch. Jim looked at them and then did an almost comical double-take when he realised who and what was on the photographs. He began leafing through them. "Nice," he said, almost to himself. Garry was standing watching Jim peruse the pictures and Ann came to stand beside him. Garry had another inspiration. He turned to Ann and took hold of her shoulder straps. With a quick movement he pulled them clear and dropped her all-in-one garment to the floor.

Ann stood there naked and a little shocked. She hadn't been expecting this. Garry himself hadn't known he was going to do it, until the impulse took him. He took Ann by the hand and turned her to directly face Jim. "What do you think of the real thing?" he asked. Jim gave Ann a thorough up and down inspection. "Nice," he said again, but in a much huskier voice. Garry led Ann to the couch. He was already hard. Dropping his trousers, he sat on the couch beside Jim and pulled Ann on to straddle him. He pushed his cock into her and she began to move rhythmically. She had recovered from her initial shock and was now reveling in the situation. As she rocked to and fro, Garry said to Jim, "You ok with this?" "You keep shagging and I'll keep watching," he replied.

Jim couldn't take his eyes from Ann's hypnotically swaying tits. He reached up and cupped the one nearest to him, her right. Without losing her rhythm, Ann leaned over and pulled down Jim's zip. She fumbled his cock out and began stroking it. Jim was soon fully erect. For a few minutes they continued in this blissful condition. As they fucked, Garry couldn't help but picture Morgan's face. He'd only met her for a short time but she'd made a deep impression on him. How he'd relish doing to her what he was doing to Ann. He almost lost his control at the thought. His climax was only delayed for a little while though. Jim orgasmed. Garry looked down and saw Jim's cum running down Ann's hand. For some reason, this excited him so much that he came. His orgasm was massive and seemed to go on for a very long time. The brief period of mutual pleasure was over – all too quickly – especially for Ann.

Ann was not happy. Try as they might, the men were too drunk to get it up again. She'd tried manipulating their floppy dicks. She even took each of them into her mouth – all to no avail. Eventually she gave up in disgust. The prospect of a night of erotic adventure was gone. It had flared for a brief time quite intensely but came to a disappointing premature end. Garry and Ann went disconsolately through to bed, while Jim settled for the remainder of the night on the couch. Before Garry dropped off to sleep, Ann berated him. She reckoned his precipitate removal of her clothing had been a mistake. It hadn't allowed time for a sexual tension to build. A slow burn would have been better. She said that, if they ever tried this again, to make sure that both men were sober – and capable. Garry had some sympathy for her. At least he and Jim had orgasmed. Poor Ann was left unsatisfied. Nevertheless, he soon fell asleep – and slept better than he had for a week.

When they crawled out of bed, late the next morning, Jim was already gone. Garry picked up the discarded polaroids. He leafed casually through them, then did so again. Jim had taken one as a souvenir. Garry wasn't the least annoyed. The thought of Jim having a wank whilst looking at Ann's naked picture, pleased him quite a lot.

Chapter Six – Absent Friend. (Wednesday 26th December. 1979.)

Christmas Day had come and gone for another year. Garry had spent most of it in an alcohol induced euphoria. He always got a bottle of Grouse in his presents and it was the one day he allowed himself to drink in the morning. He managed to maintain his slightly tipsy state all day, by judicious whisky sipping. The girls had loved the bikes and polaroid cameras they'd received as presents.

All in all, it had been a pleasant and convivial day. Now it was Boxing Day and Ann was at work. The January sales began the day after Christmas. Matters had been somewhat fraught between Garry and Ann. It wasn't just how matters had ended with the truncated threesome, although that was probably the catalyst. Ann complained that they never just had sex anymore. It always had to be part of some game or another – something involving a third person – even if that person was some unsuspecting random. Garry hadn't been aware that, but when he thought about it, he realised that it was true. He resolved to do better in future.

Garry was feeling a bit bored and restless. He was actually looking forward to going back to work in just over a week. The kids were out on their bikes, playing with friends. He sat alone in the living room, smoking and watching telly. A knock came to the door. Garry got up to answer it, wondering who the fuck it could be. When he opened the door, two men stood there. One of them spoke. "Mister Wallace?" he asked. "Mister Garry Wallace?" "That's me," Garry replied. The man showed Garry a warrant card – as did his companion. "I'm Detective Sergeant McCall," the first man said. "This is Detective Constable Sneddon," he went on. "Do you mind if we come in and talk to you for a minute or two. We're conducting enquiries into a missing person's case and we believe you might have some information which could help us."

Garry was a bit taken aback but he invited the men in and conducted them through to the living room. The cops sat on the couch and Garry took his usual chair. The constable took out a notebook and the sergeant began to ask questions. "We're trying to find the whereabouts of a James Keenan. I believe he's a friend of yours." Garry nodded. The policeman continued, "We've had reports that he was seen getting into a taxi with you and your girlfriend, a Miss Ann Graham, following a party at the Riverdale Day Centre. He hasn't been seen since. His mother has reported him missing, when he didn't come home on Christmas. She's very anxious, as you'll understand. What can you tell us?" "Jim came home with us that night," Garry replied. "It was too late to get a bus to Dunblane and a taxi would have cost a fortune. He slept on the couch and was gone before we got up. That's all I can tell you."

The sergeant looked piercingly at Garry but his tone was still friendly enough. "Is it not a bit strange that he stayed the night but didn't wait to say goodbye in the morning.

"Not really. We were pretty late getting up."

"Have a bit of a skinful, did you?"

"Aye. We'd had a few."

"You know that heavy drinking can lead to violence?"

"Well it didn't."

"You didn't get into any kind of a fight with Mister Keenan? Did you?"

"Of course not. Jim's a mate. We had nothing to fight about."

"Maybe he made a pass at your girlfriend or said something out of turn?"

"No nothing like that. Like I told you. Everything was fine. Jim slept on the couch and was gone when we got up. That's honestly all I can tell you."

"So where do you think Mister Keenan might be?"

"I've no idea. Maybe he's with a woman somewhere."

"That's what his mother thought. It was only when he didn't show up at Christmas that she became truly worried. Tell me, did Mister Keenan have a girlfriend?"

"Not that I know of, but he could have met someone."

"Is there something you're not telling us Mister Wallace. I can't but help thinking that you're holding something back."

"No. Everything happened just as I said. I've no idea where Jim is but I hope you find him soon."

"So do we, Mister Wallace. Anyway – if you think of anything else, here's my card. Give me a ring."

When the police were gone, Garry heaved a sigh of relief. It had been an uncomfortable few minutes. He was concerned about Jim. It was completely out of character for him to vanish off the radar in this way. He didn't like the fact that the cop had suggested he might be, in some way, responsible for Jim's disappearance and that he'd guessed that Garry was holding something back. He reasoned that it had been just that – a lucky guess, or maybe just a standard police tactic. Fact was, he did hold something back. What they'd got up to that night, was none of the cop's business and was totally irrelevant anyway. Garry just worried that a lurid tale of a sex triangle would make the police more suspicious that something had got out of hand and foul play had taken place. Could it be that Jim was ashamed of what had happened and had decided to lay low? Maybe the anti-climactic ending was a factor. Garry turned this all over in his mind for a while and then concluded that it was unlikely.

Garry was in for another shock, later that evening, when Ann got back from work. Apparently, the police had gone directly from interviewing him to question Ann at work. He was annoyed and a little worried. They hadn't even hinted that this was planned. Were they really suspicious of him? It also made him wonder if it was normal for detectives to investigate a missing person. Would that not be a uniformed officer's job. Did the cops think something sinister had occurred. Garry's conscience should have been clear but he feared that he could be stitched up or that some miscarriage of justice might occur. Ann told him to relax. The police were just doing their jobs. There was no way anything could be pinned on them. They'd done nothing wrong. Anyway, she was sure Jim would turn up safe and well. Until then, they just had to sit tight and stick to their story, if questioned again. It was true, after all. Garry acknowledged that she was probably right but it didn't stop him worrying. He had a bad feeling.

Garry's low mood deepened even more later that night, with an item on the local television news. Pictures of Jim and another man appeared on the screen and the newsreader announced, *"Police are anxious to learn the whereabouts of two Stirling men who have gone missing in December. William McQuillan was last seen at a local snooker club, which he left in the early hours of Saturday the 15th. James Keenan was last reported at a friend's house on Friday the 21st. Neither man has been seen since. Anyone with any information on either of the men should contact Central Scotland Police."* She then gave a phone number to contact the police on. Garry didn't sleep well that night..

Chapter Seven – The Party's Over. (Monday 31st December. 1979.)

There was no further contact from the police and no news of Jim. Garry had begun to relax, though he did worry about his missing friend. The longer it went on the less likely there was to be a happy ending. He was due back at work on the Wednesday coming. It would be a blessed relief to get out of the house. The atmosphere at home was at best lukewarm. Ann was obviously pissed off and there didn't seem to be anything he could do to fix it. If truth be told, he couldn't be bothered trying too hard. She'd come out of it in her own time. It being Hogmanay, they planned to go to a party at the end of the street they lived on. It was being hosted by a friend of Ann's that Garry didn't know very well. Maybe some drinks and company would thaw Ann out a bit.

At about seven-thirty, Garry drove the girls round to Ann's parents, where they would spend the night. When he got back, they set off on foot for the party. The house was crowded with people Garry didn't know. Ann seemed familiar with many of them. She drifted away, leaving Garry on his own. He sought solace in drink. Somebody put some records on. It was about an hour, and several drinks, into the party, that Garry realised he couldn't see Ann anymore. Where the fuck was she? He set off to try to find her. If she wanted to abandon him, well he'd fuck off out of there. First he'd find her and tell her so. He'd had enough. There was no-one in the loo, so she had to be in one of the bedrooms. This did not bode well. The first door he opened, he found her. She was knelt on the floor with her shirt wide open and her tits on display. Three men were clustered close in front of her.

Stunned, Garry entered the room. That's when he saw that she had three dicks in her mouth – one from the front and one in each side of her mouth, supported by her hands. "Ann! What the fuck are you doing?" Garry called in a strangled voice. She didn't move for a few seconds and then she drew back and said, "Sorry. Couldn't answer. I had my mouth full." Garry bellowed, "What the fuck are you up to?" "Well," she replied, "I bet these guys that I could get all three of their cocks in my mouth at the same time. I won." "Why are you doing this?" Garry pleaded and he could hear the whine in his own voice. "What's good for the goose is good for the gander," was her reply. "I found the green knickers down behind your bedside table. A wee souvenir? Did you fuck her in my bed? Anyway. I've got work to do. I'm going to finish these guys off one by one. I've got a lot of spunk to swallow. You can stay and watch if you want. You normally like that kind of thing." With that, she seized the nearest cock and began to administer a vigorous blowjob.

Garry burned with humiliation. He was incandescent with rage but he wasn't a fighter. Besides – there were three men there. He could end up with a severe kicking. Garry turned on his heel and stormed out. He pushed blindly through guests that had spilled over into the corridor and left the flat. He'd picked up Janet's discarded panties when she'd freaked out in the Centre. He'd forgotten they were in his pocket until he discovered them as he undressed for bed that night. Quickly he stuffed them out of sight behind the bedside table, fully intending to get rid of them at the soonest opportunity. Then, he had once again forgotten them. He couldn't even claim that they were Ann's. She never wore the bloody things. He was caught, bang to rights. Ann's revenge was well out of order though. She'd deliberately humiliated him in front of three smirking witnesses. Well – fuck her. He was done.

Garry walked back to their own flat, seething. He'd pack his stuff and fuck off. It was early yet, so he'd try and find a hotel room and then go on the randan. Maybe he'd be lucky enough to find someone with which to fuck his anger away. It didn't take him long to pack his clothes in a couple of suitcases. There was nothing else he wanted, apart from the naked polaroids. He took them with thoughts of revenge. Ann would pay for fucking him over. Even though Garry was well aware that he was over the drink driving limit, he chucked the suitcases into the boot. Hopefully, the police wouldn't be out in force yet. Getting into the car, he drove into town.

The first couple of hotels Garry tried were fully booked. He could have gone to his parents', which he'd probably do tomorrow, but he wasn't in the right frame of mind for that yet. He drove to King's Street and parked at the kerb. When he tried the Kingsgate Hotel, he struck lucky. They had a room free and he paid cash in advance to take it. Better still, they had a bar in which lively festivities were going on. He intended to get blind drunk and search for a sex partner among the revelers. The suitcases could stay in the car overnight. With that, he went to the bar and ordered a large whisky.

Garry swallowed down three double whiskies in about five minutes. The alcohol soothed his feelings, leaving him pleasantly numb emotionally. It was time to see what else was on offer. There was a crowded, postage stamp, dancefloor and he turned his attention there. For a fleeting moment, he thought he spied Morgan amongst the crowd. Someone blocked his view for a moment. When the person moved out of the way, there was no sign of Morgan whatsoever. She'd never been there. He was getting seriously obsessed. Instead, on the spot where he imagined he'd seen her, was a woman looking directly at him. She smiled as she made her way towards him. As far as he could recall, Garry had never set eyes on her before. "You're here," she said, "I was worried you weren't going to make it." Garry was baffled. "I think you've mistaken me for someone else," he said. "You're Garry, aren't you?" the woman responded. Garry eyed her and decided she was quite a sexy looking little thing. She had pretty, green eyes and short brown hair. Her figure looked promising. Never one to look a gift horse in the mouth, Garry decided to play along. He was too befuddled by drink to understand what exactly was happening but he decided he didn't care. "It's me – Carole-Ann," the woman said, as if that should mean something to him.

Maybe Garry didn't have to do any hunting after all. Opportunity had presented itself , without him even trying. "What do you say, Carole-Ann," he asked her, "to a quick drink and then back to my room?" It was a clumsy approach and as soon as he said it he realised this. He might just have blown it. To his surprise and delight, she agreed. Ten minutes later he was undressing her in his hotel room. She had a lovely body. Her tits were a pleasing handful, with large brown nipples. Her torso was shapely with a neat little triangle of pubic hair. Garry was well turned on and ready to go. His cock was rampant and eager. He pushed her onto the bed and mounted her with no foreplay whatsoever. He was impatient to be inside her. Pushing his cock in, he began to fuck. It was all about him. He fucked her hard, going at full pelt right from the word go. Carole-Ann never complained. In fact, she matched his intensity. Garry was fueled by rage and took it out on Carole-Ann's cunt. He pounded away for what felt like hours, building to the point of climax. At last, it boiled over and he erupted into a juddering , forceful, never-ending orgasm. It was amazing. As he pumped his semen into her, Carole-Ann too climaxed, loudly and violently.

Garry rolled off Carole-Ann and fell back on his pillow. He felt great. He felt cleansed. He'd never fucked angry before and he found it amazingly therapeutic. Satiated, he closed his eyes and quickly fell asleep. When he awoke, it was daylight. For a moment or two, he couldn't remember where he was. When he came to enough, he was surprised to find that he was alone in the bed. Carole-Ann must have left while he slept. Pity. He would have welcomed another bout with her. He should have been hungover but wasn't. In fact, he felt energized and eager to get on with life. Ann was in the past now and he was happy to leave her there. It was time to seek new horizons and adventures. There were plenty more women out there and he would enjoy finding them and fucking them.

Chapter Eight – Morgan. (Wednesday 2nd January 1980.)

It was Wednesday morning and Garry was back at work. He was still feeling high and had done so since his encounter with Carole-Ann in the Kingsgate. He had moved back into his parents' house. He'd told his mother that he'd broken up with Ann and she was happy. She'd never liked Ann. Garry had done some thinking over yesterday. He had to admit that, had he arranged Ann's little oral exploit himself, he would have loved it. But he hadn't. She'd gone behind his back and obviously had hoped he would discover her in the act. If only he hadn't gone looking for her. His own infidelity did not figure much in his cogitations. That was altogether different. Anyway, it was over. Some of it had been good and some of it, not so much. He still harboured vague thoughts of getting even but nothing had yet come to mind.

He was working in the craft room that morning, helping five clients with their projects. Fiona was sitting at the same long table. She had a headband with a rigid rod projecting from it. She was using this to pick out her masterpiece on a portable typewriter. It was painstaking and time-consuming work but Fiona was determined. She just kept plodding on, writing the story of her life experiences, with the title, "A Lady in A Wheelchair". Every now and again, Garry had to move it to the next line for her, as she couldn't manage this herself.

The local newspaper came out on Wednesday. Someone always fetched one in and it would do the rounds from hand to hand. Garry always had a read of it, even though it normally was full of banal crap. This first edition of the year was to be different. On the front page was an article on a rash of disappearances in the town. Apparently, apart from Jim and the other bloke, another two men had gone AWOL over the last week. It certainly seemed to Garry that something weird was going on. Then again, for all he knew, dozens of guys went missing every week and it wasn't highlighted in the press. What he saw further down the page did shock him though. It was a picture of the woman from the Kingsgate. The text told how she'd died as the result of a tragic hit and run accident. If Garry had any doubts about her identity, the picture was captioned "Carole-Ann Dempsey". They'd fucked up the story though. They said she had died late on Christmas Eve. It should obviously have read "New Year's Eve". She must have left almost immediately when he'd fallen asleep and wandered out to meet her doom. It gave Garry goosebumps to think that someone he'd just screwed had died so soon after. Now, that was weird.

He was still contemplating mortality and the vagaries of fate when, around mid-morning, his day got a lot better. Marjory came into the craft room and by her side was Morgan. Garry actually felt his heart lurch. Despite being casually dressed, Morgan still looked like a million dollars. She was wearing jeans and a black T shirt. Her hair was loosely tied back, showing her incredible bone structure. Garry was almost drooling. Marjory shot him a warning look and then introduced Morgan to the assembled group. Morgan was going to be a volunteer helper, she told them. She was going to sit in on their activities, to get to know people and get a feel for the work. Morgan said hello and everyone said hi to her in return.

The rest of the working day passed very pleasantly for Garry. He managed to not embarrass himself by trying to impress Morgan. Instead, he did his best to be his normal working self, though he did spend a lot of time ogling her when she wasn't looking. As she spoke, Garry detected a slight underlying accent, which he couldn't place. Her English was impeccable but he thought it was probably not her first language. She, as it turned out, was a natural. Garry could see that everyone was charmed by her. She was helpful, without being pushy or intrusive. In particular, Morgan spent a lot of time in conversation with Fiona regarding her story. Fiona's speech was laboured and difficult to understand but Morgan was patient and intuitive. It was the best Garry had ever seen someone communicating with her. Garry was delighted. Morgan had a feel for the job. She seemed to be enjoying herself, so he reckoned she would continue to come to the Centre in future. This pleased him greatly.

At around three thirty, it was home time and people began to leave. For a moment, Garry was finally alone with Morgan but not for long. Michelle, who had been working in another part of the Centre, sought him out. Garry wasn't super-pleased to see her. Michelle had a message for him. She'd seen Janet over the holidays and had been asked to get Garry to phone her. She moved in closer to him and whispered, "She told me about the ghost. Spooky huh?" "There's no such thing as ghosts," he hissed back, feeling suddenly angry. "Whatever she thought she saw, it wasn't that." Whether his anger had made his voice too loud or whether she just had excellent hearing, Morgan, who was sitting a little distance away, heard him. "You don't believe in ghosts, Garry?" she asked with a playful smile on her face. "No I don't," he replied, "Why? – Do You?" "I believe in many things," Morgan said. "There are things unseen and not understood by humans. What a boring world it would be if all there was, was what we can see. I believe in Crystal Healing, I believe in Tarot Cards. I believe in Psychic Intuition and I believe in ghosts. I believe in many things.

Garry despised, what he thought of as, "New Age guff" but this was Morgan, so he didn't demur. He didn't want to alienate her. "Interesting," was all he said. "I see you're a sceptic," Morgan said. "Come. I myself read palms. Let me give you a reading now and see if I can open your mind." He saw no harm in humouring her, so agreed. Michelle sat down to watch the show.

Morgan came round the table to sit beside him and they turned their chairs to face each other. "Give me your hand," she said. He extended his right hand towards her, palm up, and she took it in both of hers. He felt an almost electric shock at the touch of her skin on his. Even this limited intimacy was causing his dick to stiffen. He ruefully and silently berated himself at this. He was like a teenage boy getting a hard-on, simply by holding a pretty girl's hand.

Morgan held his hand for a minute or so, peering at his open palm the whole time. "I see much," she said "and I am always truthful about it. Be prepared. I see, Garry, that my touch is causing you some sexual excitement." He was a bit shocked at this. Yes, he was partially erect but not enough to be visible through his trousers. Morgan smiled sweetly at him and her violet eyes sparkled. Then she went on. "You would very much like to add me to your conquests but you lack the confidence to do anything about it." Garry was feeling decidedly uncomfortable and wished that Michelle wasn't there. But there was more. "You are an experienced man and believe you know how to get the best performance from a sexual partner but I see that you are not as accomplished in this department as you think you are." Michelle was tittering under her breath. Garry was tempted to call a halt but that would mean letting go of Morgan's hand.

Morgan paused for a few seconds and then started in again. "You desire women for their bodies but you don't actually like them. They are simply a vessel on which you can expend your lust. You have dabbled in sexual dominance but your efforts so far have been insipid. It is easy to take control of a compliant woman. The real test, is to bend a strong unwilling woman to your will. This you haven't done." He really was at the point of crying mercy and stopping the torture. He didn't know how she was doing it but her pronouncements were too close for comfort. Then her tone changed. "The few things I've told you could be deemed character flaws and I see you don't like my reading. Remember, this is merely a preliminary session. I haven't gone too deep." Garry shuddered at what she might say if she did go deeper. "Anyway," Morgan continued, "what some may see as flaws, I see as markers of potential. With guidance and mentoring you have the seeds of a kind of greatness in you."

Garry was baffled by her last assertion, and he could see by Michele's face that she was too. "Anyway," Morgan said, "I promised Marjory that I'd have a coffee with her before I went home. I'll see you both tomorrow." She smiled at them both and then got up. As she did so, she leaned close into Garry and whispered, "If you want to talk more, meet my tonight at nine outside the Centre." With that she left. Garry sat there, wondering what the fuck had just happened. Michelle put his thoughts into words. "What the fuck was that all about?" she asked. Garry just shrugged. "What did she mean about greatness?" Again he shrugged. "She calls you for everything and then says it's all good. I'm not sure she's right in the head." Garry didn't disagree but he didn't care. Morgan was gorgeous, sexy and definitely intriguing. Even if she was as mad as a bag of frogs, he was enthralled by her. He would be there that night, come hell or high water. With that thought, he felt another delicious stirring in his loins. The hours couldn't pass quickly enough.

Chapter Nine – Beneath the Wolf-Moon. (Wednesday 2nd January 1980.)

Garry was outside the Centre twenty minutes before the allotted time. The evening had dragged, as the clock ticked slowly on. December had been stormy but tonight was calm and clear. The moon beamed down from an almost cloudless sky. It was nearly as bright as day. As he sat in the car anxiously waiting, Garry wondered what the night would hold. Would Morgan want to talk more pseudo-mystical bollocks or would something altogether more interesting ensue? Would she even turn up at all? He lit his third ciggie and looked at his watch for the umpteenth time. Then, at exactly nine o'clock, a shiny black Triumph TR7 appeared round the corner and parked in front of him. Garry didn't know a lot about cars but the look of it certainly fitted Morgan's exotic persona. She flashed her lights and beckoned to him through the windscreen. Feeling strangely apprehensive, Garry got out his car and walked towards hers.

Morgan leaned over and pushed the passenger door open. Garry got in and she said to him, "We'll take my car if you don't mind." He had no objection to that at all. Morgan was wearing a dark coloured mini-dress, possibly the same one as on the night of the party. As she drove off, he noted appreciatively how it rode up her thighs. "Where are we going?" he asked. "No questions," she answered. "Tonight, I want you just to live in the moment and focus your attention on experience. If there's anything you need to know, I'll tell you." Garry felt uncomfortable at that but he was enough under Morgan's spell that he didn't object. Ceding control in a tryst with a woman was beyond his experience. Perhaps the reward for doing so would make it worthwhile. His hopes were high.

Morgan drove back up through the town and over the river to the Causewayhead Road. She had been silent since admonishing Garry to ask no questions. Now she spoke. "That beautiful full moon up there is known as the Wolf-Moon, because it is the first of the year" she told him. "It's special to me. I wanted our first time together to be under the light of that moon." Garry was heartened by this news but with some misgivings. It seemed that Morgan was planning an alfresco liaison but it was January and freezing cold. To get with this stunning woman was worth some temporary discomfort, he decided. Morgan took them uphill and entered the carpark for The Wallace Monument. She parked there and turned off the engine. The monument stood on a wooded hill called The Abbey Craig, right on the edge of town. On this side, it was in unbuilt on countryside and isolated.

Morgan got out of the car and said to Garry, "Come." Here, where there were no streetlamps, he realised just how bright the moonlight was. She took his hand when he emerged from the car and once again he felt an almost physical jolt at the touch of her skin on his. They walked from the carpark to the narrow roadway which led up hill to the top. Garry was aware of a delicious anticipatory tingling low down in his abdomen. His cock was already rock-hard. It was darker in amongst the trees. At parts the moonlight would filter through dappling the surroundings in silver. As they climbed, Garry began to feel somehow dislocated. He had the sensation of unreality – like he was experiencing everything at one step removed – like in a waking dream. He didn't know when, but at some point he no longer felt cold. It wasn't that he was warmer, just that he no longer registered the below zero temperature.

Time had ceased to have any meaning. Garry didn't know how long they'd been walking when they left the road and moved into the trees. They emerged into a grassy clearing. The moonlight seemed even more intense here. Morgan conducted Garry to the centre of the clearing and laid him on the ground. He lay there gazing up at her beauty and marvelling. Morgan knelt down beside him and deftly unbuckled his belt. Then she pulled his trouser and underpants down as far as his ankles. Garry's freed cock sprang to attention. He didn't think it possible, but under Morgan's scrutiny, he felt it grow even harder. She stood up. Grasping the hem of her dress, she drew it up in one fluid motion and threw it aside. Underneath, she was completely naked.

For a moment or two, Garry couldn't breathe. Morgan stood there like some goddess come to earth and captured in glowing marble. Her body was even more exquisite than what he'd anticipated. Enraptured he studied her nakedness. Her skin shone in the moonlight. Morgan's tit's were neither too big nor too small. They were perfect. Goldilocks tits he thought, with vague amusement. Her aureoles showed slightly darker than the surrounding flesh and framed her even darker nipples. Her torso narrowed at the waist and swelled out gracefully to enticing hips. There was no little triangle of pubes between her legs. She was completely free of any hair on her body. Garry had never seen a hairless muff on an adult woman before. It was not the fashion at the time. He found it bewitching.

Slowly and sinuously, Morgan moved to stand over Garry, with one leg on either side of his body. He gazed up at her exposed snatch and his already intense arousal ramped up another notch. She lowered herself to her knees and took hold of his dick before inserting it deftly into her. Morgan descended completely and Garry's cock slid fully inside. Another random notion flitted across Garry's mind. If he could have designed a tailor-made cunt to service his cock, this would be the one. It was warm and wet – yielding but snug. It was heaven. Morgan began to undulate and gyrate as she rode him. She placed her hands behind her back, causing her breasts to thrust upwards and forwards. Garry watched, mesmerised. Morgan was performing an almost ethereal, erotic dance for him. There were times in the past, when Garry was shagging a woman for the first time, that the excitement of fresh conquest caused him to struggle with the spectre of premature ejaculation. Despite the fact that he was more excited at being inside Morgan than he'd ever been with anyone else, this spectre never remotely raised its head.

Garry marvelled at Morgan's majestic torso. He savoured the alternate tightening and relaxing of her abdominal muscles. Her boobs were too tempting. Garry reached up to fondle them. Immediately, Morgan stopped moving. She brought her hands from behind her back, took hold of Garry's wrists and firmly pushed them down by his side. "Don't move," she said commandingly but in a soft voice. "Lie still and surrender to the moment." Garry complied. There was never a thought of doing otherwise. Morgan re-commenced her dance. Garry's consciousness faded to focus on the sensations in his prick and the sights delighting his eyes. From time to time, Morgan spoke. Her voice seemed to be coming from a long way off and he couldn't make much sense of her words. It was jumbled in his head. There was something about power over others – that he'd have to exercise such to harvest more of it. She had her own way but his would be different. There was something about imbuing him with something from her and that he'd taken a big step that night but it was only a beginning. The words rattled about his brain with no real understanding on his part. There was a mission, apparently. What it was, he hadn't a clue.

Garry lost all conscious thought. He was adrift in a sea of pleasurable euphoria and he didn't seek rescue. He was jolted back to the clearing in the woods, when he and Morgan climaxed in unison. Hot vaginal fluid cascaded from Morgan over his cock and balls. He, in turn, pumped his own fluids in the other direction. It felt like his whole body was forcing itself through his dick and into her welcoming wetness. He was drained – seminally, physically and emotionally. Morgan stood up as Garry collapsed, almost comatose. He was vaguely aware that she had commenced a naked process around the perimeter of the clearing. Again, she struck him like a goddess or a wood-nymph come to earth. It struck him that she was parading her sublime nakedness for the benefit of unseen eyes amongst the trees. Whether or not these were human, he couldn't guess. It was almost like Morgan's body was radiating silver light, rather than merely reflecting that of the moon.

Garry couldn't remember getting dressed and only vaguely recalled the walk back to the car. He had a fuzzy memory of voices sounding from among the trees as Morgan enacted her imperious procession. He'd no idea whether they were real or not. Garry didn't know how long he'd been sitting in his own car before he came back to himself. He was still a bit numb as he drove home. By the next morning, it all felt like some surreal dream.

Chapter Ten – Spellbound. (Thursday 3rd January. 1980.)

Although Garry's memory of the previous night lacked clarity, he remembered enough to know it had been something special. He was feeling wonderful. His whole body seemed to vibrate with pent-up energy. The day abounded with myriad possibilities and he was eager to see what came along. Garry marveled at his positive mood. It was only a couple of days since he'd been humiliated by Ann and he found he actually didn't give a toss. She was out of his life. He'd had some fun with her and she was undoubtedly a good-looking woman, but the break-up was causing him no heartache whatsoever. Garry had never experienced such an easy end to a long-term relationship before – and two years to him was long-term. There were plenty more women around and besides – there was Morgan. He wasn't naive enough to expect anything long-lasting with her. She was so far above him. He determined to enjoy every moment she deigned to dally with him. He already had strong feelings for Morgan. This was not love though. There has to be some parity of status for love to take root. This was not the case here. Garry didn't love Morgan – he revered her.

Morgan arrived about half an hour after the mini-buses discharged their passengers. She was dressed casually again and looking as amazing as ever. She nodded to Garry but gave no further indication of anything between them. Fiona was visibly excited that Morgan was here. There certainly was a bond being forged there. They worked away as normal until morning tea break. Morgan put sugar and milk into Fiona's tea and set her up with her plastic straw. Then she asked Garry if they could have a private word. His heart leapt. On the corridor between the Craft Room and the lounge was the Therapy Room. This was small, containing only a chair and a therapy couch. Garry conducted Morgan to it. They wouldn't be disturbed there. She took the chair while he perched on the edge of the couch and waited patiently for her to speak.

"Last night," she said, "you probably most remember the sexual pleasure that you had. That's fine but it is the least important aspect of what happened. You don't understand it yet but last night I initiated you into a sacred and ancient order. Only someone with certain predispositions, which you have, would even be considered for this honour. I planted in you a seed, by gifting you some of my own power. You must take this seed, nurture it and make it grow. This will make you powerful too. It will give you command over women – to bend them to your will and make them do anything you desire – whether they want to or not. I know this chimes with your personality. In time, no woman will be able to resist you. You can have anyone you want – at any time and under any circumstances. No woman will be able to say no to you, even if they want to. Is that not every man's dream?"

"I don't understand, said Garry. "How can this be and why would you give me such a gift even if it was possible?" "Don't get bogged down in the whys and wherefores," Morgan replied, "Concentrate on what you can actually experience and forget the philosophy." Garry thought for a moment or two and then asked, "So, how do I do all this?" Morgan replied, "You cannot manufacture power. You have to take it from somewhere or someone else. In your case, every time you command a woman to your will, her power will decrease and yours will grow. You need to begin with relatively easy steps. For instance – you have a little friend called Janet. I heard you and Michelle talking about her. If, as I presume, you've been intimate with her, she will already be susceptible to you. Call her. Get her here and make her do something she would normally balk at – not by force or threats or anything – but by commanding her. Might I suggest you get her to give you oral sex?" "She had a bad experience the last time she was here," Garry said. "She told me she'd never come back in the Centre again." "Once she's in your presence," Morgan replied, "she'll do whatever you say. Think of it as a test. "Well," Garry told her, "she's always refused to even touch my dick with her hand. Putting it in her mouth might be a step too far – but I'll take your test." "Oh it's not my test," Morgan corrected him, "I know what you can do. This is to show you what you can achieve."

They went back to work. Garry wasn't exactly sceptical. He was inclined to believe anything Morgan told him. There was definitely something otherworldly about her. He just didn't understand it all. Why it would be the way she told him it was – and what caused all this in the first place. Nevertheless, he was intrigued and not a little excited. What if it was all true? He dared to dream. At lunchtime, Garry couldn't wait to get on the phone to Janet. She was still quite reticent when she answered. At first, she absolutely refused to see him that evening. She had plans. Eventually Garry persuaded her to meet with him for ten minutes. He just wanted to talk, he told her. They wouldn't even have to get out of the car and he promised to drop her off wherever she needed to go. Eventually, Janet relented and agreed to a brief meeting. Garry would pick her up outside her home at seven-thirty. He couldn't wait to tell Morgan, which he did on their way back to the craft room. "Good," she told him. "Remember, be confident. Use only your presence to command her. No physical force – no threats or intimidation. I think you'll surprise yourself."

Garry was bursting with anticipation for the rest of the day. Despite that, it passed quickly. He planned his campaign and that helped the time fly past. Janet was a couple of minutes late emerging from her front door but Garry was always confident she'd appear. She was looking very fine as she approached the car. She'd obviously put some work into her appearance. Garry doubted that it was on his account. He idly speculated that there must be another man on the scene. That was obviously was where she was bound for after she left him. Well – that's as may be. We'd see how things worked out before then. Janet got into the car. "Where do you want me to drop you?" Garry asked. "The Terraces," was her shamefaced reply. That had always been their trysting spot and she seemed a bit embarrassed about meeting someone else there.

Garry started the car and drove off. He waited a few minutes and then said, "We just need to go to the Centre for a couple of minutes first." Janet didn't respond immediately and then she said, in a small voice, "Ok." They didn't converse at all on the journey. Garry was perfectly comfortable with that. They arrived at the Centre and, still without speaking, he unlocked the door and they went in. As always, he locked the doors behind him. This time though, he led her through to the craft room, rather than stopping in the lounge. They could turn the lights on there, without danger of being seen from the street. If his plan came to fruition, he wanted to be able to see everything. The fact that Janet had set foot in the Centre at all, augured well.

Garry switched on all the lights as they entered the room. He took a chair from one of the tables and turned it round to face where Janet was standing, unsure what she should be doing. He regarded her, in silence, for several seconds. He felt immense. He knew he had complete control of another human being and could do with her as he willed. Even better, that she looked so good and had annoyed him so much in recent times. He'd heard it said that power was the ultimate aphrodisiac. Well, he was certainly well turned on by it. He reckoned nothing he could make Janet do would surpass the feeling of simply being able to make her do it. He'd once harboured a fondness for her but that was gone. All he saw now was a mere, albeit pretty, female, ready to be used and abused by him.

"Janet. Take your clothes off – all of them," he told her. He felt a lust induced catch in his throat as he spoke. He was almost trembling with it and his breathing was laboured. A look of consternation passed over Janet's face but then she started to comply. Garry watched avidly as she stripped off. He'd obviously seen parts of her body during their previous encounters but this had always been in poor lighting and he'd never seen her entirely naked before. Now she stood bare before him and he savoured the sight. Her body was as trim and delightful as he had anticipated. For the first time, he saw that her pubic hair was a few shades darker than that on her head.

Garry enjoyed the view for a few delicious minutes and then he stood up. "Come here and kneel down," he directed. Janet immediately moved to obey. Garry was almost bursting with arousal. He was actually struggling not to come in his pants. This exercise of power and control over another, was proving even more sexually exciting than even being with Morgan. He hadn't thought that possible. In a strangled voice he told Janet to pull down his zip and get his cock out. She must have understood him because she complied without hesitation.

The soft cool feel of her hand on his dick almost put him over the edge and triggered an orgasm. He managed to master himself and took it to the next step.

"Janet, take me in your mouth," Garry said. When she did so, he lost any restraint. Seizing the hair on the top of her head he began fucking her face. He pounded his tumescent cock into her mouth and felt it repeatedly striking the back of her throat. She was gagging and seemed to have difficulty catching breath. Garry didn't care. If she passed out, she passed out. Her teeth caught him a couple of times and he ordered her to keep them clear of his cock. He gloried in the thought that, not only was his the first prick Janet had ever handled, but also the first she'd ever had in her mouth. And his was the first spunk she would taste. With that in his mind, he finally let loose. Janet gagged and choked as semen cascaded into her throat. In the midst of his orgasm, Garry looked up and there was Morgan, standing behind Janet and watching the action. He'd locked the place up, so how she'd gotten in, he couldn't guess. Nor did he have any idea how long she'd been there. Morgan smiled at him, gave a thumbs up and turned to leave.

Janet collapsed to the floor, retching and gasping for breath. Garry looked down at her with contempt. He tucked his diminishing cock away and zipped up. Reaching down, Garry seized Janet by the arm and hauled her to her feet. He bent again to scoop up her clothes, except for her bra and panties. These he intended to keep as trophies. Ann had accused him of keeping the previous underwear as a souvenir. Well, this time, that's what he really was doing. He wished that he'd had the foresight to acquire a polaroid camera. Some choice pictures of Janet's humiliation would have been good. He could see that she was bleeding from the lip. His vigorous pummelling had inflicted this damage. Garry took hold of her upper arm and marched her through the Centre to the front door. Unlocking the door, he thrust her outside, naked as she was. He tossed her clothes out behind her. "Get dressed and find your own way to wherever you're going," he told her. She stood there with tears running down her cheeks and blood trickling down her chin. Garry closed the door on her and locked it again.

When he turned away, Morgan was standing next to him. "Well done," she said. "You passed the test. Putting her out on the street naked was reckless though. There are those who would seek to do us harm. It would not be good to alert them to our presence. Anyway – let's go and I'll show you how a blowjob should really be done."

Chapter Eleven – Uninvited House-Guests. (Friday 4th January. 1980.)

Detective Chief Inspector Donald "Donnie" Martin was feeling out of his depths for only about the second time in his career. His new case had all the hallmarks of a stinker. He had been drafted in entirely because of this. Given its potential for sensational media attention, the powers that be in Central Scotland police had required someone of senior rank and long experience to take charge. Donnie had been involved in numerous murder investigations and had led several successful ones. This one though, was no pub fight that got out of control or domestic assault that had gone too far. This was psycho, serial-killer material and promised to be a proper whodunit. A resident of Stirling's Wallace Street, had returned from an extended Festive Season break in Spain, to find two semi-naked and mutilated bodies lying in her living room.

The two dead men had already been named. Both carried identification and both were already on police books as missing persons. They were William McQuillan and James Keenan. Apart from his wallet, Keenan also had a polaroid photograph of a naked woman in his jacket pocket. The men had been decapitated, castrated and their hearts had been cut out. Their heads were placed between their spread legs and their hearts were stuffed into their mouths. Already there were whispers of "ritual killing" around police headquarters. The Press would have one spectacular field day when they got wind of the story. They were already sniffing about. The large police presence in Wallace Street had tipped them off that something big was afoot.

Martin hadn't even been to the crime scene yet. The case had only become his half an hour ago. What he knew, came from a brief appraisal that had been typed up for him. His first concern was to muster the resources that would be required for what promised to be a bitch of an investigation. His own Force was relatively small and manpower would be at a premium. Help was being requested from other Forces throughout Scotland and the Home Office had been informed. Donnie's forte wasn't brilliant deductive reasoning. He relied on calm, methodical and meticulous police work. He wasn't particularly "hands-on" in his approach but believed in delegation. Get the right people on the job and then allow them to do it, all the while keeping a watchful eye on proceedings but interfering only minimally.

The forensics people were still working over the scene and the bodies hadn't yet been removed for post-mortem examination. In the meantime though, certain routine actions were being set in motion. Door to door inquiries, spreading out from the central locus, were already underway. The families were being informed, of course, and a schedule drawn up to re-interview people from the initial missing person's inquiry. The backgrounds of the deceased would have to be thoroughly examined and everyone relevant interviewed. This alone, would generate a mass of information that would be a nightmare to manage – and that's before the press conference and an appeal for any witnesses to come forward. The scientific evidence would be crucial. Any coherent picture on that front would take days to emerge. The one wildcard, so far, was the naked polaroid found in Keenan's pocket. It might be significant and it might not. Nevertheless, priority would be given to identifying the woman in it.

Martin had one particular big nagging worry. He'd been informed that another three men, in the same age group as the victims, had been posted missing over the last couple of weeks. The worst case scenario was that more mutilated corpses would be discovered in the coming days. Given the violence and bizarre mutilations perpetrated on the murdered men, this was a credible concern. Still, that may not turn out to be the case. There were things to be getting on with in the meantime and there was no point expending energy on something that might never happen.

Donnie was on the point of leaving, at long last, for the crime scene, when he got a call to go to the Chief Constable's office. He was immediately ushered in when he got there. The boss started without preamble. "It seems your case has rung some alarm bells at the Home Office," he said. "They've reacted with uncharacteristic vigour. There's a couple of their people coming to join your team. They'll get here tomorrow. It seems they suspect that our perpetrator might be a serial killer they've been on the trail of for some time. Now, don't worry Donnie, this is still your case. You're still in command. I don't know exactly what remit these bods have but I'll be confirming it before they have any access to your team or the investigation. Don't look on this as an imposition, Donnie. Think of it as providing access to resources we don't have. I'll be here tomorrow to tie up any loose ends. Any questions?" Martin didn't know whether to be annoyed at this interference or whether it was a good thing. Nevertheless, any questions he did have could wait until tomorrow and he had a clearer picture of what was to be expected. He told the Chief Constable this and he nodded in agreement. Donnie got up and left. He had a crime scene to attend to.

Chapter Twelve – Workplace Sex Spree.   (Friday 4th January. 1980.)

Garry came to work filled with anticipation. He was in an adventurous mood and convinced of his own invincibility. That was a perilous combination. His exploits with Janet and then Morgan the previous night had left him elated and energised. That energy had carried on to this morning. A plan had formed in his mind and he was eager to put it into effect. His first target was Michelle. He'd always fancied her but she had rebuffed any flirtatious overtures he'd previously made. Well, we'd see about that this morning. While they were still at their morning coffee and Morgan hadn't yet come in, Garry told Michelle he wanted a word. He took her to the Therapy Room. Michelle looked a bit mystified but not in the slightest apprehensive. She thought that perhaps Garry wanted to speak about Janet.

Garry closed the door and told Michelle to lie up on the couch. She did so without question, even though she didn't understand why she was following Garry's instruction. He then proceeded to pull off her shoes, jeans and underwear, telling her to lie there and do nothing. Michelle complied. Garry pushed up her top and bra to expose her tits and stood back to savour the sight of her naked body. It was a view to be enjoyed. He was once again enthralled by his ascendency over the will of a woman. Without further hesitation, Garry climbed on top of Michelle and fucked her hard. She just lay there, unresisting. Garry was overjoyed by his new-found sexual potency and stamina. Whatever Morgan had done to him, he felt he could shag all day and every day. Even after orgasming, he could get it up again within minutes.

Garry could have gone on longer but he chose to climax. As always, his ejaculation was full, forceful and copious. He climbed off Michelle, tucked his dick away and zipped up. Michelle was instructed to get dressed and go back to work as if nothing had happened. She was looking distressed but made no protest. Garry went back to the kitchen to finish his coffee. When he got there, he found it was cold and undrinkable. Then his eye fell on Jenny, the Centre's cook and an idea kindled. He hadn't planned for her to be one of his targets but now he acted on impulse. Jenny was in her fifties and wouldn't normally be on his radar but she was far from hideous – and anyway – a ride was a ride. It would be something new – and that gave him a frisson of a sexual thrill.

Garry had climaxed only a few minutes ago but he already felt himself stiffening. "Jenny. Got a minute?" he asked and she assented. He led her to the therapy room. Michelle was just exiting as they got there. She shot Garry a poisonous look as they passed and seemed to be on the point of saying something to Jenny but decided against it before walking away. Garry repeated what he had done with Michelle. Jenny's body was much more appetizing than he had anticipated. It wasn't as firm and shapely as Michelle's but it wasn't repulsive either. After he finished with her, Garry admonished Jenny to go back to work and act normally. Once again, he zipped up and went back to work himself.

His original second target had been Ruth, a pretty seventeen year old volunteer helper. She didn't come in usually till mid-morning. He'd have to wait for an opportune moment to take her to the Therapy Room. He smiled at the room's name. It was certainly providing therapy for him – though probably in a way no-one had envisioned. Morgan would be in before he managed to have his way with Ruth but he didn't think she would object. After all – he was simply utilising the gift she had given him. It was about half an hour before lunchtime that Garry got his chance to invite Ruth to accompany him. Morgan simply looked at him, somewhat quizzically, as he led the young woman away.

Garry found this encounter the most exciting of his morning's recreation. Ruth had an almost perfect, smooth and milk-white young fresh body. It wasn't simply this that turned him on though. It was the young woman's innocence. He suspected that she was a virgin and thus his cock was the first to penetrate her. He had no difficulty doing so. She did cry out in pain but he told her to shut up and she did. He noticed a slight blood stain on the couch when he'd finished. That was something that could be cleaned up in the afternoon. Garry returned briefly to work. He was more than ready for his lunch now. He'd had a busy and strenuous morning. As he got up to head for the dining area, a short stocky man entered the Craft Room.

Garry didn't recognise the man but he seemed to know who Garry was. The stranger walked directly to him and he looked angry. Before Garry could say anything, the man kicked him square and hard in the balls. Garry's lower body exploded in molten pain and he felt ready to vomit. As he hunched forward in agony, the man unleashed two heavy punches to his face. Garry went down in a heap. The stranger kicked him several times in and about his ribs before bending towards him and shouting, "That's for Janet, ya cunt." The attacker had another couple of swift kicks before turning and storming off.

Garry lay on the floor, dazed, until Morgan came to assistance. She pulled him up and sat him on a chair. God, she was strong. Morgan had seen the attack coming and could have prevented it but decided that Garry needed taught a lesson. As it was, she'd still have some clean-up to do. She could scent three women on him and knew what must have happened over the morning. This wasn't good. Someone had alerted Marjory and she now appeared on the scene. She insisted that the police be called, even though that was the last thing Garry wanted. Morgan volunteered to take him to a bathroom and get him fixed up.

Morgan supported Garry as they made their way to the bathroom and again he marvelled at her physical strength. She'd picked up a first-aid kit on the way. Inside the bathroom she turned on Garry with barely suppressed fury. "You are moving too quickly and too soon," she hissed at him. "I understand that you want to test your limits but you're not ready. You have to rein yourself in. Very soon, you will desire stronger meat but you've not learned how to cover your tracks. You are drawing attention to yourself. I've told you there are people who would harm us. I wasn't kidding or exaggerating. They would chase us down and destroy us. We have to balance between indulging our desires and staying under the radar. You have to be more circumspect. Believe me Garry, I made you my kin when I initiated you but make no mistake. If you endanger me further, I will snuff you out, without hesitation and move on. Be warned!"

Morgan knew that she was being a tad hypocritical. Her taking of Garry's friend Jim had been on impulse. She had watched their brief threesome and its disappointing end. She needed a new victim and decided that Jim would do fine. It was a mistake. He had a connection to her chosen protégé and that was never prudent. Too late to worry about that now. Garry was surprised and a bit hurt by Morgan's anger. He thought she would have approved. After all, was he not exercising the gift she had given him? Her tone also scared him quite a lot. He really didn't want to anger her any further. Chastened, he vowed to do better and told her so. Before the stranger's intervention, he had contemplated further exploits that afternoon. Marjory, his boss, was the only other shaggable member of staff. She was his next intended target. It might lead to an uncomfortable work dynamic but he figured that ship had probably already sailed. After her, he could always go a second round with his previous conquests. Kitty, the seventeen year old with cerebral-palsy, was pretty enough though. So she had been put on his to do list. Given Morgan's reaction, those plans were put firmly on hold.

Twenty minutes or so later, the cops arrived. Garry spent an uncomfortable half hour answering their questions. He was pretty banged up and should probably have gone to hospital but dismissed this out of hand when it was suggested. He suspected that he might have concussion but decided he'd just rest up until it went away. The police wanted to know if he knew who his assailant was and why he'd been attacked. Garry was well aware that it was someone close to Janet – probably the person she was meant to meet up with after being with him. The last thing Garry wanted was for that connection to be made with the police – so he stonewalled – claiming ignorance and bewilderment. The police interviewed the several other witnesses to the assault, getting a variety of descriptions. They left, obviously suspicious and no doubt smelling a rat.

Garry was obviously not fit enough to return to work, so Morgan said she'd drive him home. When she got him in the car, she told him he was to pack a bag, that he was going to take next week off work and come to stay with her for that time. She'd stay home and look after him. When he raised the fact that she lived next door to Marjory and it might look suspicious, she simply said that she'd take care of it. When Garry got home, he had to spend some time allaying his mother's anxiety about his obviously beat up appearance. Eventually he calmed her down and went to pack some things, saying he was going to spend a week at his new girlfriend's. His mum told him to invite her in but he fobbed her off. His dad looked out the window at Morgan sitting outside in her shiny black TR 7. He whistled and said to Garry, "Punching above your weight there son." Garry didn't know whether it was the girl or the car that had impressed him most. He was off for a week with Morgan. This excited him but also scared him quite a lot.

Chapter Thirteen - Koldunya. (Saturday 5th January. 1980.)

Chief Constable Hector Moncrieff was presiding over the meeting in the conference room. Present were Detective Chief Inspector Donnie Martin and his second in command, Detective Inspector Joe Watson. From the Home Office was Major Tom Beresford and his colleague Gloria Garcia. She was an officer from Interpol. What Beresford's rank pertained to was unclear. He was very tall, perhaps six foot three or four, with steel grey hair and a military bearing. Garcia was petite and pretty with dark hair and brown eyes.

Moncrieff was finishing up his summation. "So, the powers that be," he said, "are concerned about this case and deem it serious enough to proffer assistance and advice. Major Beresford and Captain Garcia have been drafted in, by order of the Home Office. They will function strictly as observers and advisors – and will take no active part in the investigation. Nor will they carry any executive authority. That resides with Donnie here – and through him, ultimately to me. It seems that our perpetrator may have previously carried out similar atrocities in other parts of the world – and that authorities have been after him or her for some time. Perhaps you can tell us a bit more on this, Major Beresford?"

"Everything is in the report we furnished you with," Beresford said, "but I'll give you a brief summary. We believe that you are dealing with, what could best be described as, a cult. This centres on one woman. She goes by many aliases but is principally referred to by the name Koldunya. This seems to be a Russian word which roughly translates as witch. We don't know if this is a name or a title she has taken for herself – but it may point to her being a Russian national. She seems to be adept at changing her appearance. We have multiple descriptions in which she is a redhead, a blond or a brunette. The one constant there, is that her hair is always described as long or waist-length. We also believe that she uses contact lenses to change her eye-colouring. The other constant is that she is always said to be very attractive – indeed beautiful.

Anyway, when this individual appears on the scene, events always follow the same general pattern. Firstly, the mutilated bodies of men aged between twenty and thirty begin to turn up. The mutilations and posing of the remains, are identical to those you have discovered. The severed head is placed between the victim's legs and their heart is pushed into their mouth. The victims are castrated and the manner of this is striking. As your post-mortem will doubtless confirm, this is not accomplished, as you might expect, by using a sharp implement. The genitals appear to be chewed off. Your pathologist will find human teeth marks. Evidence indicates that this takes place while the victim is still alive. How she lures and overcomes these initial victims, we have no idea, but we're confident that she carries out these murders unaided. No trace of the missing genitals has ever been found. We speculate that there may be a cannibalistic element at play here.

Koldunya then seeks out a male apprentice. How she selects him is unclear but she seems to have a nose for discovering men with an innate hatred of women and a sadistic nature. Under her tutelage, he firsts embarks on a series of sexual assaults – none of which are reported to the police. They only become known, subsequent to the perpetrator being apprehended. These sexual assaults soon escalate into murders – which in turn escalate in their violence and cruelty. The torture and indignities visited on these women is truly hideous. Only someone sick in the mind and devoid of humanity could inflict them. For a time, the bodies of both male and female victims will continue to be found. Then, it appears that Koldunya moves on to a new location, leaving her accomplice to spread murder, mayhem and misery on his own.

Koldunya's personal killing spree usually accounts for between seven and nine victims, though there may of course be bodies that have never been found. Her accomplice just carries on killing until he is caught, which invariably up to now, they always have been. While she departs, the men continue to operate in the same geographical area until they are eventually apprehended. They are unrepentant of their crimes and speak of Koldunya in terms of awe and reverence and are grateful for the initiation – their word – that they received from her. There may be elements of some dark, perhaps Satanic, worship or devotion in these outbreaks. That is unclear and only a speculative theory. The motivation might only be pleasure in the deeds themselves. Over the last three years Koldunya has been active in Brazil, India and South Africa. It seems she has now come to Europe.

So you see, Gentlemen, why we are taking this matter so seriously. So far, you have two bodies. There will be more – probably many more. It's imperative that we do everything possible to bring this to an end and speedily. My colleague and I will do all within our power to assist – but this is a horrific situation – and it is likely to get worse. At least, if you take on board what we're telling you, you will have a head start on previous law enforcement investigations into these crimes."

There was silence around the table for a few moments. Then Chief Constable Moncrieff said, "A grim business. What's the state of play Donnie?" "Nothing significant from the door to doors yet," Martin replied. "We're in the process of re-interviewing everyone we've already spoken to during the initial missing persons' investigation. We're also identifying other of the victims' friends and associates as well as looking into their backgrounds. So far, we have nothing definitive from forensics – but it's early days yet. I'm expecting the post-mortem reports on my desk, later this morning. We have made one minor breakthrough which may or may not be significant. A polaroid picture of a naked woman was found in Mister Keenan's pocket. This was unusual enough to take our interest. We've now identified the woman in the picture. One of our Detective Sergeants recognised her as someone he'd interviewed during the missing person's investigation. She was part of the couple who had last seen Mister Keenan alive. He spent the night at their flat before he disappeared. She's being picked up, as we speak, for further questioning and we're bringing her partner in too. Other than that, we're waiting for the scientific evidence and to see if anything else is shaken loose by our routine investigations."

"Very good," said the Chief Constable. "As you say – it's early days yet – but keep on top of it. I want to be fully updated daily on any developments. If you need more resources – I'll do my best to furnish them. Perhaps our Home Office colleagues can be of assistance in that regard also." He glanced at them and received nods of assent. Moncrieff called the meeting to a close, having asked Martin to provide Beresford and Garcia with office space and get someone to show them the canteen etc..

When Beresford and Garcia were alone he said to her, "Do you think they bought it?" She shrugged and replied, "It doesn't matter. We have our own squad in place. As long as the locals share their data with us we've got a good chance of finally catching the bitch. We've never been on the ground so early in an investigation before. We can't let this slip through our fingers." "I wonder," said Beresford, "If we were more honest with them, maybe it would help them focus better on what we're actually looking for." "So we should tell them," Garcia said, "That we're pursuing a centuries old witch who draws power from ritually sacrificing her victims whilst munching on their balls. Do you think they'd take us seriously? Any chance of meaningful co-operation would be blown out of the water. Better that we tap into their investigation and use that to further our own." "I know, I know," Beresford agreed. "Let's hope we can get some momentum going before she abandons her local protégé and disappears. Identifying him is the key."

Chapter Fourteen – A Stay of Execution. (Saturday 5th January. 1980.)

Morgan had spent the previous night in some deep thought and soul searching. Her original plan had been to slaughter Garry that night. By indulging in a sex rampage on his own doorstep, he had compromised her. The Venatores were hot on her trail and getting closer. If they got wind of what had happened yesterday at the Centre it could have serious consequences. Garry had not even considered what the aftermath of his actions might be. He exercised control of the women while they were in his presence but this did not erase their memory of it. Nor did it stop them talking about it later. Janet had obviously done so. Hence the avenging angel coming to the Centre and administering a beating. Morgan admitted some culpability in that. She hadn't envisaged the savagery Garry had employed nor the total humiliation he had visited on Janet – who had only been selected because her previous intimacy with Garry gave him an opening to flex his incipient powers.

Morgan needed to make another kill soon. She was perfectly happy for Garry to fit that bill. Then she began to think. What if Garry wasn't a liability? What if, in fact, he was finally the one she was looking for? Perhaps if she persevered, her quest could finally come to fruition. Morgan's efforts had been continuously thwarted by the poor quality raw materials she had to work with. All the men she brought into her fold had failed miserably. Some had seemed to have promise but all had eventually descended into madness. The escalating nature of the deeds they found themselves carrying out, proved too much for their feeble psyches. This led to them making mistakes, which in turn led to them being caught. Sometimes they just simply handed themselves in to the police. She had never been able to achieve the degree of potency required to free Uzhas.

The Venatores were becoming more knowledgeable and thus more dangerous. Most, if not all, of their agents, were now warded against direct witchcraft. Morgan had captured one in Cape Town, prior to this warding being put in place. She had extracted much information from him before he died. The Venatores had no idea what her end game was, nor how she went about trying to achieve it. They were under the impression that she departed once she had set a male accomplice on his course. This could not be further from the truth. She stood, unseen, beside every atrocity that was perpetrated. That was where she harvested true power. Her own killings only served to prime the pump. Those of her proteges yielded exponentially more – and at a greater intensity. It was over a hundred and seven years ago that a Shastralabian High Priestess had trapped and bound Uzhas. It had taken Morgan (though that was not the name she used then) nine years to find him. Ever since then, she had striven to achieve sufficient power to shatter his bonds. So far, she had only met with frustration and failure – but she was patient and enduring. One day she'd find a suitable vessel.

Garry had surprised Morgan by his preciousness. None of her previous men would have had the gumption or confidence to embark on such a sex spree, without her say so. It had been ill-advised, arrogant and reckless. Nevertheless, the situation was probably not irretrievable. Perhaps Garry's very arrogance was what would see him through the trajectory he would have to travel and remain focused and functional. It was a risk – but Morgan was not averse to risk. Generally, she operated in as covert a manner as possible – but the very nature of what she did, required that certain chances had to be taken. Morgan decided that it was time to take a leap of faith. She would nurture Garry further – try to tutor him in how he should proceed to minimize the chances of being tracked down and apprehended. For the time being, Garry would be allowed to live and Morgan would use her craft to cover up his recent indiscretions.

Morgan had invested a lot of time and occult energy observing Garry before committing to recruiting him. She had visited the home he shared with the woman, Ann. Unseen, she had watched as they played their sex games. She had spied on him through the eyes of a crow. She was the ghost that Janet had seen while Garry was screwing her in the Centre. That was pure malevolent mischief. Morgan could easily have remained unseen – but she'd conceived a hatred of Janet and simply wanted to scare the shit out of her. She'd succeeded and also softened Janet up for Garry to take advantage of the next time they were together. In Morgan's opinion, the other three women Garry had fucked with, could be handled. She'd confirmed who they were with him, the night before. Janet, however, would have to go. It was also Morgan who inspired Ann to indulge in her multiple blow-job and made sure that Garry discovered her. She'd then given him the gift of a torrid interlude with the revenant of Carole-Ann. She'd been dead for a week before Garry fucked her. That had sowed the seeds of Morgan's dominion over him and prepared him for his initiation.

As part of her plan to ensnare Garry, Morgan had purchased the house right next door to Marjory, Garry's boss. It was in a new built are of Dunblane, just a few streets over from where Jim Keenan had lived with his mother. Marjory was lesbian and shared her home with her partner, Mary. It had been an easy matter for Morgan to seduce both women. Marjory had a pathological antipathy to the very idea of heterosexual coupling. The thought of being intimate with a man absolutely appalled her. Mary, on the other hand, had experimented with some male partners previously – until realizing that it was not for her and she embraced Sapphism wholeheartedly.

Garry had spent the previous night confined to a guest room, under strict instructions from Morgan not to stray from it. He was anxious, sensing that Morgan was displeased. He had no idea just how precarious his position actually was though. Now she had released him from that stricture and he was beginning to relax and hope all would be well. Morgan had invited Marjory and Mary for dinner that night. She had a test in mind for Garry. How he fared in it would determine whether he survived the night.

Chapter Fifteen – A Person of Interest. (Saturday 5th January. 1980.)

Beresford and Garcia hadn't been particularly interested in the naked polaroid found in Keenan's possession. They didn't see how it could relate to Koldunya. Nothing of the kind had shown up in previous investigations. The early warning system had done its job and the co-operation of the British Home Office had allowed them to hit the ground fast – while the case was still breaking. Now though, they'd have to wait for some kind of pattern to emerge. Something that would point to the witch's location. Inevitably, that meant more bodies. That is – until that afternoon's team briefing.

It was a packed room for the meeting. For the most part, Beresford and Garcia found it a waste of time. The investigation was well organized and methodical but it was centred on routine police work – not what was required for the case in question. It needed a different focus. The victims' backgrounds and associates were largely irrelevant – or so Beresford and Garcia considered. This changed when Detective Sergeant McCall delivered his update.

"We identified the woman in the photograph found on Mister Keenan, as being one Ann Graham," he told the assembly. "We brought her in for further questioning, this morning. She admitted straight away that the photograph was of her and she told us how Keenan had come into possession of it. Apparently, it was part of a series taken by her boyfriend, at the time – a Mister Garry Wallace. They were shown to Keenan as a prelude to a little steamy menage a trois. Miss Graham assumes he must have pocketed one as a souvenir. She insists that her and Wallace then went to bed and Keenan was gone by the morning.

As a matter of course, we attempted to interview Mister Wallace on this. It turns out that he and Miss Graham are no longer an item. He's gone back to live with his parents. He wasn't there when we visited a couple of hours ago. His mum told us he'd gone off with his new girlfriend. She doesn't know her name or where she lives. His dad said that she drives a fancy car – but he couldn't remember what type or colour. We'll keep trying until we get him – maybe when he's back at work on Monday. One other, possibly interesting, little snippet. Wallace's mum told us he'd come home early from work on Friday, before leaving with the girlfriend. She said he looked like he'd been in a fight. I did some checking and uniform attended a reported assault at Riverdale Day Centre on Friday afternoon. Apparently, an unknown assailant walked into his workplace and knocked lumps out of Wallace, before disappearing into the sunset. Uniform found the whole matter suspicious and were of the opinion that some kind of retribution was being meted out."

McCall's report certainly piqued some interest in the room but it was not seen as taking the investigation very much further forward. It would have to be followed up, of course. Something may come of it but in the context of the wider investigation, it didn't seem overly significant. Not so Beresford and Garcia. They were electrified – especially by the mention of a new girlfriend. Could this be a breakthrough? Had Koldunya made a slip? Whatever the case, this Garry Wallace had to be traced and put under surveillance. They would have to be circumspect though. If Wallace was their man, care would have to be taken not to alert his mistress. It would be best if the police were not too vigorous in their follow-up. They didn't want to spook their quarry. Beresford resolved to try and steer the locals on an alternative course. Meanwhile, he'd set his own agents on tracking down Wallace. Perhaps there was a chink of light at the end of the tunnel.

Chapter Sixteen – After Dinner Frolics. (Saturday 5th January. 1980.)

Morgan had been much more civil throughout the day. Garry began to believe that he was maybe out of the doghouse. He was a bit thrown when she told him that Marjory and her partner were coming to dinner. He'd worried about spending time with Morgan next door to his boss but now she'd been invited to join them. Still, he trusted that Morgan knew what she was doing. Then she dropped the bombshell. "I need to know if you have what it takes fulfill the role I have in mind for you," she told him. "This is important. It's another test. Pass it and we'll move forward together. Fail it and your time is done. If you come through, I'll explain the significance. If not, there'll be no need for explanations. Marjory is not a fan of the male anatomy nor the uses certain parts are put to. She would rather die than fuck a man. Your task tonight, is to inflame her with passion for you – so that she lusts after your body. I want you to screw her – and I want her to enjoy it. I'm not asking you simply to make her comply – that would be easy. You are not to issue any commands. You must only use your mind and the occult power you've accrued. Touch is allowed – but not in any overtly sexual manner – not until Marjory initiates it, anyway. Do not break the rules. I believe you can do it – but we'll see."

Garry admitted to himself that he was besotted with Morgan but also terrified of her. He hadn't taken time to reflect on the whirlwind that had ensued since he became involved with her. It was bizarre, yet he had unquestioningly forged on. He had simply accepted his strange new powers over women and indulged them wholeheartedly. His phenomenal, new-found sexual athleticism, delighted him but he'd never paused to wonder at it. In short, Garry felt that he was riding a runaway train and was perfectly on board with that. He had happily surrendered to Morgan and her madness. Now, he would do whatever she required to stay in her good books – no matter what. He also dreaded the consequences of letting her down.

Garry had sweated all the way through dinner. Morgan had been a towering presence. He hadn't joined in the conversation much, fearing that he might say something that could be construed as a command to Marjory. The trouble was, that he didn't have a clue how to accomplish the task Morgan had set him. He had strenuously tried to project his thoughts into Marjory's mind – all to no avail. The meal had been pleasant enough. Morgan had proved to be an excellent cook. There was plenty of wine available and everyone had imbibed freely. If the alcohol had lowered Marjory's inhibitions, Gary had seen no sign of it. She was an attractive redhead, somewhere in her forties. In truth, Garry had always found her a bit daunting. He had never seriously fantasised about her as a potential conquest – notwithstanding her openly lesbian orientation.

Marjory's partner, Mary, was more in Garry's preferred target group. She was younger, petite, blond and somewhat elfin – not unlike Janet, as it happened. She, he considered, would be more susceptible to any mind-control wiles that he was able to employ. Unfortunately for him, Marjory was the challenge he had been allocated and he looked doomed to failure. Time was running out. The guests were having one last glass of wine before departing. There was nothing particularly obvious in Morgan's features or demeanour, but Garry could tell she was majorly displeased. He didn't know what form her coming wrath would take but he feared it greatly. Again, he tried to beam lustful thoughts into Marjory's skull – and again, nothing happened. Then, it was too late.

Marjory and Mary got up to leave and Garry's stomach dropped. He stood up also, not really knowing why he'd done so. It was probably just nerves. As Marjory passed him, she staggered slightly. She had, after all, consumed a lot of wine. Garry instinctively put out a hand to steady her. Their hands met and a jolt ran through them, as soon skin touched skin. Marjory's demeanour changed in an instant. She looked at Garry quizzically for a couple of seconds and said, somewhat tipsily, "Why Garry. I'd never realised how pretty you are." Then she had a hand on either side of his face and her tongue was halfway down his throat."

What happened next was a blur which left Garry with only certain salient memories. He remembered being fascinated by Marjory's tits. Her nipples were the darkest shade of brown he'd ever seen on a woman. He remembered Mary looking shocked when Marjory kicked off, but Morgan had taken her by the hand and led her to the couch. "Let's just relax and enjoy the show," she'd told the young woman. Garry saw them sit down and Morgan's hand slip inside Mary's blouse to caress her tit. He remembered Marjory dropping to her knees in front of him and undoing his belt. Then his stiffened cock was in her mouth. For such a confirmed lesbian, she certainly knew how to suck dick. Getting to the next stage happened in a further blurred sequence. He was lying on the floor with his trousers at his ankles and Marjory was on top of him, naked. She was riding him in an ecstatic frenzy. He discovered that she was a squirter and on a hair trigger. Garry lost count of the times Marjory orgasmed. Each time, she drenched him in her hot vaginal fluids. Her climaxes grew more intense and closer together. At last, with a shuddering, juddering, screaming final peak, she collapsed on top of him. As she lay there, totally spent, he let loose his own prolonged and noisy ejaculation.

When it was all over and Morgan had set her guests straight, before packing them off home, she took Garry to her bed. "Will they remember what happened?" he asked her, as they climbed the stairs. "Of course they will," she replied. "I didn't do anything to mess with their memories. Don't worry though. They won't be put out by it. They'll simply accept that it happened and not dwell on it in any negative way. Trust me. I know what I'm talking about. Now – let's get into bed. I've got stuff to tell you." They both stripped off and climbed between the sheets. Once again, Garry was stunned by the perfection of Morgan's nakedness. No matter how many times he saw it, her body would never fail to enthral him.

"Now listen to what I have to tell you," Morgan said. "It's important." She looked stern and Garry felt himself tense up. "You came through tonight, Garry," she went on. "It was a close-run thing but you showed me you have what it takes. I am committing myself fully to you – and you must do the same for me. This is not something I take lightly. You have had some insights into my nature but know now who I truly am. I am a witch Garry. My name is Koldunya. My craft, in fact my entire existence, is all about human sexual energy and emotions – particularly lust, fear, pain, humiliation and despair. I draw strength and pleasure from the things I do and the things I make people do. I have a husband. Together we used to rampage throughout the world, spreading terror, degradation and death, in our wake. He has been taken from me and imprisoned. Since then, I've taken human surrogates. You are the latest of these – and I've come to believe, you may prove to be the best of them.

You have made mistakes – but these can still be remedied. When I initiated you, I gave you a gift – the power for you to have any woman you desired. To a man like you, that is something to be vastly cherished. You have embraced this more quickly than anyone has done previously – but you need guidance, or you will continue to make mistakes and be taken from me. You could fall foul of the police or be captured by the Venatores – a band of witch-hunters. That cannot be allowed to happen. Like anything in life, your gift is not static – nor is your attitude towards it. Things develop. Every time you exercise your gift you take a further step along an inexorable pathway. You become stronger in your craft – but simply fucking the woman will soon no longer be enough for you. You will crave stronger meat. In a short time you will seek to take the ultimate from your victims. Only their deaths will bring you sufficient gratification. You will kill – and you will exult in the killing. Then – even that will pale. You will have an overpowering need to inflict ever increasing pain, terror and degradation on your chosen. What do you think of that Garry? Does it appal you?"

Garry knew he should have been shocked and disgusted by what Morgan had just told him – but he was not. Instead – he felt a sexual stirring and sensed his cock stiffening. Morgan was not slow to notice this. She smiled and took hold of his hardening shaft. She had more to say. "While there is pleasure in abundance to be obtained from these things – that is not the sole reason for doing them. We seek power and inflicting misery on others is how we obtain it. Together we will feed on their pain and suffering. The more horror they experience – the greater our feast. That's why I set you a test with Marjory. Simply commanding a women to obey your instructions, brings a relatively low return for our needs. But – if you can make her lust after you – make her want you to visit indignities on her – then take that from her in the moments before she dies – imagine the degradation and self- loathing she will then experience. It adds a deal of substance and a piquant flavour to the feast. If you can trigger lust in Marjory, a woman totally antipathetic to male sexual attraction, you can do it to anyone – and your ability will only get stronger.

My husband is in chains but I know where he is. Together, you and I will accumulate enough power to break him free. Then, the three of us will cut a swathe across the nations of this world – taking whoever we want – and growing ever stronger. You will become, in time, a dark, malevolent and irresistible god. That's what your destiny could be, if you trust me and follow my instructions. That's the true gift I've bestowed on you. On Monday, I'll go to the Centre and amend the memories of the women you took on Friday morning. They will no longer be a problem. Your little friend, Janet, is another matter. She's obviously already blabbed to someone. You have to silence her. She will be your first kill. Phone her and command her to meet you. Have your fun with her and then snuff her out.

When these loose ends are tied up, you can then start hunting in the general population. Do not choose victims that know you in any way. You can pick women up in bars, buses and on the street – anywhere. It is easy to be discreet. You do not have to take them with you from where you've contacted them. Simply command them to meet you later at a suitable location. The only thing that can stop you, is if your mind proves too feeble to cope. I do not believe that this will happen to you. I will be with you at every kill. Together we will share the feast and the fun. Are you mine Garry? Do you and I have a future together?"

Garry didn't even have to consider his reply. "I'm yours – whatever you say," he told her. There was no more talking that night. It was almost dawn by the time they stopped fucking. Garry reached peaks of passion that he'd never experienced. He lost count of how many orgasms he had – and then went straight back to business again. Throughout the whole time, he enjoyed visions of Janet bleeding as she breathed her last. He found this more exhilarating than he'd ever thought possible. He was filled with hope and anticipation for the future.

Chapter Seventeen – The White Witch. (Sunday 6th January. 1980.)

The media was in full frenzy but the police had nothing new to report. The Press were not yet being critical of the cops but that would change rapidly, if more bodies started turning up. Chief Inspector Martin was still focussed on the plodding method of investigation that he favoured. He was happy enough to wait for the people employed at Riverdale Day Centre to return to work on Monday for them to be interviewed regarding events there and the possible connections to the disappearance of James Keenan. He did not consider this a priority, he didn't have home addresses of the employees and he had no idea where Mister Wallace currently was. All this could be resolved, come Monday morning.

Beresford and Garcia had other priorities. Locating Wallace was their urgent goal. Knowing what they knew, this looked like a lead that might finally take them to Koldunya. They were quite happy for the local cops to be focussed elsewhere. That way, there was less chance of them blundering in and spooking their quarry. If Koldunya disappeared, they would have to start all over again in another location and more people would die horribly. They had to hope that the witch had gotten sloppy. This had happened before but no-one had been in close enough pursuit to take advantage. Now was the best chance they'd ever had. They couldn't let it slip. Beresford would not wait until Monday to try to get a handle on Wallace. Small margins might make all the difference. He used his considerable authority to access Central Regional Council's records and obtain the home addresses of the staff at Riverdale Day Centre. Beresford had a dozen investigators, all accredited bona fide Special Branch officers. His best was his second in command, Gloria Garcia. He assigned her the task of interviewing the Centre's staff.

Gloria Garcia was a special lady indeed. Not only was she an accomplished investigator with a razor sharp intelligence, but she was also a White Witch. It's an unfortunate truth but White Witches can never be as powerful as the Black variety. Nevertheless, Gloria made full use of the gifts she had. Amongst these was her ability to project an aura of trust and empathy. People told her things they would never dream of telling anyone else and they would also believe anything she told them. This was invaluable in her investigative role. Gloria had a logical mind but she would trust to her intuition when it urged her to overrule logic – and that was the case now. Logic suggested that Gloria should interview the Riverdale manager, Marjory Craig, first. She would have an overview of her staff and should be a fruitful source of information. Instead,

Gloria opted to open her investigation with one of Wallace's co-workers – Michelle Wylder.

Accompanied by her apprentice, a young witch called Diane Hastings, Gloria arrived at Michelle's house just after 10 am on the Sunday morning. It was a small one-bedroom flat in the Cornton area of the town. Michelle looked a bit puzzled when they flashed their warrant cards but invited them in nevertheless. They made their way through to the compact, tidily kept living room. The two officers seated themselves on the couch and Diane produced her notebook while Michelle perched nervously on the edge of an armchair. "What's this all about?" she asked.

"We'd just like to ask you a few questions about a work colleague of yours – a mister Garry Wallace." Gloria told her.

"What do you want to know?"

"I believe Mister Wallace was assaulted on Friday at his work. Did you witness this?"

"Yes. I was there."

"What can you tell us about it?"

"He got off lightly. He deserved more."

"Why is that?"

"He did something terrible to a friend of mine."

"What was that?"

"She wouldn't tell me exactly – but I can guess. He raped her."

"Why would you think that Michelle?"

"Because she told me he's a monster……. And I think he raped me too."

"How do you mean – you think he raped you? Wouldn't you know for certain?"

Michelle hesitated – choosing her words. Then she said, "He asked me to go to the Therapy Room with him. I didn't think anything of it, so I went. When we got there, he told me to lay on the couch and undressed me. He didn't use force or anything. I wanted to say no – but I just couldn't. I just did whatever he told me. I wasn't able to resist but it wasn't because I wanted to have sex. I really, really didn't – but we had sex anyway. When he was done, he told me to go back to work – and I did. But I wasn't the only one. I saw him take Jenny, the cook, into the Therapy Room, a short time after. Then later, he did the same to Ruth. She's one of our volunteers – she's only seventeen. I don't know why any of this happened. He didn't threaten or force me – and I didn't see any of that with the other two. I've never fancied Garry. I would never have had sex with him - but that's exactly what ended up happening. I've felt dirty and disgusted with myself ever since."

Michelle collapsed back in her chair, sobbing. Gloria went and sat on the arm of her chair, to comfort her. "It's ok Michelle," she said. "It's not your fault. We believe Wallace might have drugged you with something that made you susceptible to hypnotic suggestion. There was nothing you could have done. You've been very brave to tell us this. We'll make sure that he gets what's coming to him. But you must help us just a little more. Will you – please? After a few further minutes, Michelle gathered herself. "What can I do?" she asked. "Tell us about your friend," Gloria replied.

"My friend's called Janet," Michelle said. "She was having an affair with Garry. He used to take her to the Centre for sex. He's a keyholder and it was a convenient place to go. One night, she got a scare. She thought she'd seen a ghost. After that, things went sour with Garry. I know they met up on Thursday night. That's when something bad happened. Janet's hardly come out her room since. She's in a terrible state." "Was that why someone attacked Garry?" Gloria asked. "Yes," came the reply, "but don't ask me who done it. I won't tell you. The bastard deserved it. I'd have cut his balls off." "It's ok," Gloria said. "We're not interested in getting anyone else into trouble – but we'll need to speak to Janet – for her own protection."

Michelle gave them Janet's address and Diane wrote it in her notebook. She'd felt a bit reluctant at first, but she trusted Gloria to do the right thing. "One more thing," Gloria said, "We hear Wallace has a new girlfriend. Have you heard anything?" Michelle thought for a moment or two. "Not that I know of," she answered. "He's only just split up with his long term girlfriend, Ann. She was nice. I liked her. Unless they're talking about Janet – but that's not the case. He has been making eyes at our new volunteer and she's a bit flirty with him – but she's way out of his league. I mean she's gorgeous – super-model gorgeous. I don't think there's anything going on there." "What's her name?" Gloria asked. "Morgan," said Michelle. "Do you know where she lives," was the next question. "Sorry. No idea," came the reply. "How did this Morgan come to be involved at the Centre, Michelle?" "I think she's a friend of Marjory's – our manager." "One last question, Michelle – does Morgan have long hair?" "Yes she does. It comes most of the way down her back. It's beautiful."

Gloria stood up. "Thanks Michelle," she said. "You've been very helpful. Now, I want you to pack a bag for a couple of days. We're going to put you in a hotel room. We fear that Wallace is dangerous and this is for your protection. We'll get Janet too and she can share the room with you. There'll be one of our officers with you." "What about my work?" Michelle asked. "We'll square that with your employers," Gloria replied. "It's only until we have Mister Wallace in custody. Hopefully that will just be one night – but we'll have to see." Michelle wasn't delighted by this but she nevertheless acquiesced.

As Michelle went to pack, Gloria went outside and got on the radio to Beresford. "Wallace is our man," she told him. "He's already exercising mind-control but it doesn't look as if he's killed yet. Koldunya is using the name Morgan and she's working as a volunteer helper at Riverdale. She seems to have befriended the Centre manager – Marjory Craig – so the chances are that she's been compromised. I've just interviewed one of Wallace's victims and I'm on the way to speak to another. The one I'm on my way to, was the motivation behind the assault on Wallace. I'm bringing them both in for protection and some further questioning. I suggest a room at our hotel. Could you send someone to pick up the first witness – and I'll bring the other one in when I've spoken to her." Beresford acknowledged her report and said he'd put arrangements in place. They'd talk further at the hotel later.

Half an hour later, Gloria pressed the doorbell at Janet's address. The door was opened by an anxious looking fortyish woman. This proved to be Janet's mother. She seemed reluctant to invite them in but eventually did so at Gloria's insistence that they needed to speak with her daughter. The woman went upstairs to fetch Janet, while Gloria and Diane waited in the hallway. It was a good five minutes before Janet and her mother appeared at the top of the stairs. The younger woman looked awful. Her face was pale and tear-stained with dark patches beneath her eyes. She was a picture of dejection with a haunted air about her. It took some assertive persuasion to finally detach her mother from Janet. She had wanted to be present while her daughter was interviewed but Gloria put her foot down. They wanted to speak to the girl on her own.

Eventually, the two officers were left alone with Janet in the kitchen. It took a long time and much of Gloria's talents to finally coax the whole story from the traumatised young woman. It was a shocking tale. Janet was totally repulsed by the things she'd been made to do. She couldn't understand why she'd so meekly complied. The violence Wallace had visited on her, compounded with the humiliation he'd inflicted on her, had left Janet feeling dirty, helpless and worthless. She was broken – especially as she'd used to really like Garry. Gloria seethed inside as the story unfolded. The sheer callous brutality employed by Wallace, absolutely disgusted her. Some thought that Koldunya corrupted the men she recruited. Gloria didn't share that view. She believed that the evil already resided inside them. True – it might never come to the fore without the witch's intervention – but given time, Gloria was sure they'd start down that path on their own. She resolved to spend healing time and energy with all Wallace's victims as soon as she could.

Janet seemed to have no fight or even free-will left in her. She made no protest at being taken away by Gloria and Diane. Her mother though, was a different matter. Gloria thought they'd have to use physical force on her, as she tried to prevent them leaving with her daughter. At length, Gloria threatened her with arrest if she continued to obstruct them. This finally worked and they succeeded in getting Janet from the house to their car, while her mother stood at the door wringing her hands. There was news waiting for them when they got back to the hotel. The bodies of three more butchered men had been found in a derelict warehouse.

Chapter Eighteen – A Day of Rest. (Sunday 6th January. 1980.)

Koldunya was running low on juice but was unconcerned. She was confident that she had enough in the tank to alter the memories of the three women at the Centre. She would do this tomorrow morning and then get an energy top up when Garry slaughtered that little bitch Janet. She didn't know why she so detested that girl. It was an irrational hatred – but Koldunya happily admitted to not being a rational creature. She was not, and never had been, human. Her kind held onto their grudges – and indeed nurtured them. Hatred was good and it was satisfying too. It was probably a risk targeting Janet – given Garry's history with her – but when she was seized by her vengeful nature, Koldunya was more than happy to waive good sense.

Koldunya knew she should have killed again yesterday – but she had been too busy experimenting with her new toy. She had a limited reservoir of occult energy, which was depleted with every magical act she performed. Even without enacting any witchcraft whatsoever, her primal metabolism continued to eat briskly into her reserves. She would stand with Garry as he committed atrocity on Janet and absorb her terror-stricken essence, to feed her witchy vitality – and all would be well. It would be a big leap for Garry. Normally, Koldunya's proteges developed to this stage in a progression, governed by their own personality. Garry would be jumping several steps – but she was confident that he could handle it. He had proved remarkably adept in everything he'd done so far.

In truth, Koldunya was in a vulnerable position. If things went wrong, she would currently be unable to flee. Her magic was completely location centric. When she arrived at her chosen locale, she had to invoke the powers inherent in that place to syphon off some for herself. This she did by ritually sacrificing male victims. The ritual provided her with start-up but also bound her to a perimeter centred on where the sacrifices took place. It took more power than she currently had, to break free and leave the area. Until her reserves were bolstered, she was stuck here, like it or not. It was not ideal – but that's how things worked. The scope of the perimeter varied, depending on what latent magic resided in the area in question. That was something that intrigued Koldunya, regarding her present location. There was something here she had never encountered before.

Koldunya had picked up ripples of an ancient presence when she made her first sacrifice. It was faint but it became more pronounced with each subsequent killing. It touched her most strongly on the night she'd initiated Garry under the Wolf-Moon. She was aware that the usual Boggarts, Spriggans, Wood-Nymphs and Wraiths were watching from amongst the trees on the Abbey Craig, as she rode Garry and then processed naked around the moonlit clearing. There was something unfamiliar there also. It was not unusual for some localised eldritch beings to be attracted to these occasions. Normally Koldunya paid little attention to them. They were no danger to her. This unknown presence felt different though. She sensed its hungry eyes following her every move. That did not unduly disturb her. She was used to hungry eyes on her body – in fact, she thrived on them. This felt different. There were echoes of something immensely old and immensely potent. Something slept nearby that it would be unwise to awaken. This wasn't what had been watching from the trees – but it was somehow connected.

With Uzhas by her side, Koldunya would have had no fear about disturbing whatever slumbered in or around Stirling. On her own though, she was vulnerable. She was therefore wary. That was partially why she had chosen not to make a further sacrifice and decided to wait for Garry to do his thing in order to augment her reservoir of power. She had poked the unknown entity five times, by tapping into the latent thaumaturgical energy of the area with her ritual killings – and once again with her ceremony on the Abbey Craig. There's only so many times you can poke a sleeper before it awakens. Something as strong as what she sensed this one to be, could well swamp and consume her, were it to arise. The transfer of power between her and Garry was a closed circuit. It would not impinge on anything or anyone else.

Whatever transpired, Koldunya was relaxed. The die was cast. She would rely on her bond with Garry and she intended to work him hard. They would mount a blitz like she'd never done before. Multiple victims could be taken every day. Starting with Janet tomorrow evening, they could build from there. The next day, Koldunya would have Garry attempt two killings. From there, they'd see what he was capable of. Her gut told her that he was a prodigy and several victims could be taken daily. She could be out of there and on her way to free Uzhas within a fortnight. It was ambitious and risky – but it was worth the attempt. Garry was like none of her previous men. He was a natural. She had faith in him. That was why she'd been guided to this location. Of that she was sure. The end of the quest to free her husband could well be in sight.

Koldunya felt mellow and relaxed. She had a plan and she had hope. That always made her feel good. Garry was her big hope. She wouldn't tell him that the first thing a risen Uzhas would do, is rip out Garry's entrails and devour them. He'd find out soon enough – or so she hoped. She'd never felt so positive before. Today, she would rest and dream of success. Garry would sleep alone in the guest room tonight. Koldunya wanted him at the top of his game tomorrow. She wanted him hyped up with sexual energy and his magically augmented libido craving satisfaction. Tomorrow would be a new dawn. It would be bloody and it would be fun. There was a little nagging doubt, that she was putting too much faith in this mere man – but Koldunya chose to dismiss it and didn't think of it again.

Chapter Nineteen – Neil. (Sunday 6th January. 1980.)

It was less than a week after her dramatic break-up with Garry and Ann was in a car with another man – heading for the town of Airdrie – a place she didn't think she'd been to before. Beside her was Neil, whom she'd met at that momentous New Year's gathering. Back on Hogmanay, Ann had buttoned up her blouse and made herself presentable, before exiting the room where she'd performed oral sex on three men. She was desperate for a drink, to wash the taste of spunk from her mouth. It was not a taste she was particularly fond of – but she did like the mechanism by which it was delivered. Ann loved cocks. They fascinated her. She delighted in how her touch could bring one from flaccid to engorged rampancy – changing size and shape. Ann loved to caress, fondle and even just look at erect penises. She was particularly enamoured by the convulsive spurting of spunk, at the point of climax. Looking at cocks, touching them and having them inside her – all gave her joy.

It was when Ann had returned to the living room, that her eyes first fell on Neil. She thought he was the most gorgeous man she'd ever seen. He was handsome and well proportioned, with short dark hair and dreamy brown eyes. He sat quietly in a corner, sipping at his drink. Their eyes met as soon as Ann came into the room and she'd felt an almost physical electric jolt. She was feeling a savage joy at how she'd shamed Garry. Her plan had worked out perfectly. She was surprised at herself for coming up with the idea in the first place and then having the nerve to see it through. She felt no shame. No-one had been forced to participate and everyone, except Garry, had left the room satisfied. The story was already beginning to circulate though. At least one of the men had shared it with other party-goers and it was spreading fast. Eyes began to turn towards Ann – the women with glowering hostility and the men with speculation.

At first, Ann had been inclined to brazen it out and just get drunk. It was, after all, still early. It wasn't even midnight yet. Then, all at once, she'd decided she wasn't in the mood anymore. It was time to go home. As Ann was fetching her coat from the hallway, she'd heard a voice behind her. "Leaving so soon?" It was a pleasant voice. The accent was Scottish – but with an unusual lilt to it. She'd turned around and there was the gorgeous man from the living room. He'd introduced himself as Neil and offered to walk her home. Had it been anyone else, Ann would have refused – but there had been something about this handsome man that had made her accept. It hadn't simply been his looks that had influenced her. There was something else about him. He had a presence that Ann had found compelling.

They'd walked briskly the short distance to Ann's flat. It was freezing cold. "Don't let small-minded people, like those back there, get you down," he'd told her, as they went. "Ah – so you've heard the story," Ann had said, "Are you shocked?" "Not in the slightest," Neil had replied. "As long as it's between consenting adults, there's nothing sexual that is wrong. At least, that's what we believe, where I'm from" "Do you think this makes me an easy mark then?" Ann had asked next. "Maybe you are and maybe you're not," Neil had said. "That's entirely up to you – but I'm not trying to pick you up for sex. Would it be so bad if I was?" Ann didn't reply. Neil's voice was soft and reassuring. His gentle lilt was pleasant to her ear. She found that she felt safe and relaxed with him. When they'd got to her place, she'd invited him up to her flat.

As it happened, they'd not ended up having sex, though they'd talked plenty about it. They'd sat and drank vodka, late into the night. Ann had opened her soul to Neil like she'd never done before. She'd told him all about Garry and their break up. She'd spoken of the sex games they'd played and how much she'd enjoyed them. Neil had been interested in everything Ann had to say. He had been an excellent listener. Ann had poured her heart out to him. She'd told him how much she was turned on by the lust her naked body inspired in men – how she enjoyed their voracious eyes upon her. It was at its most intense, she had explained, when they were strangers – seeing her for the first – and the last time – a moment of mutual animalistic arousal.

Ann had shared her fantasies with Neil – telling him how she preferred being dominated sexually – how this let her pretend to be doing things against her will, when most of the time, the opposite was true. She had explained her theory that this was a mechanism to assuage her guilt at her own lewd nature. If someone else was making her do it, then it wasn't her fault. Ann had spoken of her unfulfilled, as yet, fantasies – being tied naked to a bed and raped by a masked stranger and being forced to do a striptease for a roomful of men. Ann had poured all this out – and never for a moment wondered at what she was doing. It had all seemed perfectly natural to her. Telling this complete stranger her innermost secrets had not seemed odd at all.

Neil had, for the most part, simply listened. He did ask a couple of questions about Garry but didn't comment until Ann had finished her discourse. She'd asked him where he was from and what he did. He'd answered that he was from around here but that he travelled a lot. He'd said that he was a trouble-shooter. His job was to deal with problems and stop them getting bigger. He'd said that he was considered ruthless but at times, on a whim, he liked to help people. Now was one of those times. He had decided to help Ann. She had accepted this without question, though at any other time she'd probably have found it quite patronising.

"I'll start with some advice," Neil had said. "It's not good to always be submissive in sexual matters. It's a slippery slope and can lead to grief. What if someone makes you do something you really don't want to do? It's better if you assert yourself sometimes. Take responsibility. Have fun doing things that you want The more you do that, the more you'll enjoy it and the more confident you will become. You don't need anyone else to ease your guilt. There doesn't need to be any guilt. With the fantasies you spoke of – forget the masked stranger tying you to the bed. Those scenarios rarely end well. I can help you with the striptease. You described your routine and it sounds marvellous. I can provide a venue for this to happen – but it has to be because you want to do it. It has to be your decision. I'll park below your window at 7 pm on Sunday. I'll honk my horn and wait exactly five minutes. If you don't come down in that time, I'll just drive away and no hard feelings. If you do decide to come, you can call off at any time. There's no pressure on you whatsoever. If you go ahead, it will be because you and you alone have decided to do so. Whatever you decide – the responsibility will be entirely yours."

Neil's words had had more of an effect on Ann than she would have credited. She took them to heart. For whatever reason, she'd found that she'd trusted him. So – when Neil sounded his horn on Sunday evening, Ann had been ready and waiting Within a minute she was getting into his car. He told her that they were heading for a hotel in Airdrie. The manager owed him a favour and had agreed to put on a men's night. There would be a comedian and three other strippers. Ann was scheduled to go on just after the comedian. She would be the first of the strippers, if she chose to go through with it. Neil reckoned that the audience would be at their most receptive then. He reasoned that they would become more sated, and perhaps even a bit jaded, as the night wore on.

Ann was excited and nervous. She'd been preparing all week. She'd even gone shopping for suitable clothing – including a matching black bra and panties and a black suspender belt. As a rule, she never wore panties – but her routine required them. They'd only be on for a short time anyway. Ann was a very good dancer and this was part of her planned performance. Getting naked was the prime purpose of the exercise – but Ann wanted to achieve this in as provocative and artistic manner possible. She had made a tape of the music she wanted to perform to. From start to finish, her routine lasted for just over eleven minutes. Ann had rehearsed her moves during the week, after the kids went to bed. She just hoped that she wouldn't freeze on the night.

They got to the hotel and parked. There hadn't been much conversation on the journey. Ann was too wound up by nerves for any small talk. It was another cold night so they hurried indoors. It looked like a nice place and Ann was a wee bit relieved. She had been apprehensive that the venue might turn out to be some sleazy dive – not that this would necessarily have stopped her going ahead. Neil conducted Ann across the foyer and showed her the function room where the show was to take place. They looked in through the door. It was already beginning to fill up. There was a small dance floor – brightly lit – in the middle. Around it were tables – in relative gloom. There must have been a couple of dozen of them – each with room for six people. Ann felt herself go a bit weak at the knees. If the hall filled up, there would be well over a hundred guys watching her.

Neil told Ann that she had about an hour before going on and took her back through the foyer and upstairs to a room on the first floor. "I'll leave you here to get ready," he told her. "Remember – it's entirely up to you whether you go ahead or not. I'll let you know when it's five minutes before your time." With that, he left her alone. Ann was not entirely sure she could go through with it – but she started to get changed anyway. She stripped naked and then put on the matching black bra and panties. Then it was the black suspender belt – to which she clipped sheer dark stocking. Ann had spent some time replacing the buttons on her white blouse – so they would easily rip apart. The blouse had a red rose embroidered on the front of each shoulder. She then slipped on a dark blue skirt which was split to the thigh on either side. She'd altered the stitching on that too. Last was a pair of shiny red high-heels. They could wait until it was time to go.

Ann lost count of how many times she went to the loo while waiting for Neil to come back. She didn't have a watch, so had no idea how the time was going. She'd put on some bright red lipstick and a light dusting of blue eyeshadow. She seriously considered just going downstairs and telling Neil she was calling it off – but this was a chance that might never come again. It was something Ann had fantasised about for a long time. This was different to the scenario she'd had in her head. No-one was compelling her to do this. If she was ever going to fulfil this fantasy, she needed to do it while she still had a great body. Leave it too long and things would begin to sag. Ann nearly jumped out of her skin when a knock at the door broke into her thoughts. It was Neil. The point of no return, was the thought that flashed in Ann's mind. It was now or never. She decided it was now.

Neil escorted Ann downstairs to the function room. They stood at the door and looked in. It was jam-packed. Not only were all the tables full but there was a sizeable knot of men at the bar – standing or on barstools. Ann's heart was pounding. It was fear rather than excitement. The comedian finished his last few gags and then said, "And now gentlemen, for your entertainment, please welcome, the lovely Ann." Neill whispered, "Good Luck'" and it was time. The room erupted with boisterous acclaim. There was clapping, stamping of feet, shouts of encouragement to get them off and loud whoops. Ann started forward on shaky legs. Somewhere between the door and the dancefloor her apprehension turned to anticipation. She had a moment of revelation. This was empowerment. She could give these men what they wanted – or she could withhold it. Either way – she had them in the palm of her hand. Their full attention was on her and would be for the next eleven and a half minutes.

Ann took up position in the middle of the small dancefloor. The applause had died down but there was still frequent shouts and whoops. She felt confident and in control now. Her tape began to play over the sound system. The first song was "I feel Love" by Donna Summers. And stood stock still for the first few seconds – and then she began to dance. She stepped and swayed to the compelling rhythm – running her hands over her body as she did so. The men from the further away tables had all gotten up and moved in close, to get a better view – as had those at the bar. The dancefloor was completely surrounded by a wall of avid spectators. Ann loved it. She was in the moment and realised she was in her element also.

Ann began a strutting and whirling progress around the perimeter of the dancefloor. When she whirled, her skirt flew out and flashed her thighs. The song lasted eight minutes. She intended being naked by the time it finished. After she'd completed one full circuit, Ann started the next by tearing open her blouse. The weakened button stitching did its job and the garment ripped wide, exposing Ann's bra and torso. There was a loud roar at this mingled with whistles and some shouted sexual profanities. Ann continued her circuit – still dancing as she pulled the blouse off, whirled it a couple of times around her head and then threw it into the spectators. There was another roar of approval at this.

The atmosphere was growing more and more erotically charged. Ann could almost taste the testosterone in the air. She could practically feel the men's gaze on her skin – like hot little kisses. Before she completed that circuit, Ann tore off her skirt – and that went flying into the crowd too. The shouting was constant now. Hands clapped and feet stamped. Ann was loving every moment. She was so turned on that she could hardly believe it. Kicking off her shoes, Ann now moved to the centre of the floor. She unclipped her right stocking and rolled it gracefully down her leg. This too was hurled into the gathered spectators. There was a scramble to see who would catch it. Ann followed suit with the other stocking and then wriggled out of the suspender belt. This, she danced over and handed to a shy looking young man who was sitting at one of the nearest tables.

It was down to the nitty-gritty now. Ann's excitement was hard to contain. She wanted to hear the explosion of sound she knew would occur when she removed one of the final garments. She could feel the lust and desire radiating from the spectators. They were captured in a hungry frenzy of sexual longing. All they wanted, at that moment, was for Ann to remove the last of her clothing. They were desperate to see her nakedness. The clamour coming from the crowd was raucous, continuous and rising in volume. Ann was reaching new pinnacles of arousal. Each time she thought it had peaked – it surprised her by going up a notch. She was very wet – and wondered if it was showing through her panties. Not that she really cared.

Ann slowed her dancing and moved sinuously to the back of the floor. She reached behind her, as if to unclip her bra. The shouts of encouragement grew even louder – only to morph into groans of disappointment when she brought her hands back round to the front. Ann judged that there was only a couple of minutes left of Donna Summers's song – so it was time to move things along. Once again she reached behind her – but this time the bra came off. There were cheers and whistles stamping of feet and whoops. Ann whirled the bra around her head and launched it into the crowd. She savoured the feel of a hundred and thirty pairs of male eyes focussed on her tits. They were good tits and she was proud of them. The spectators obviously agreed with her.

Time for the coup-de-grace. Ann stood stock still and then slid her panties slowly to the floor. The crowd went mad. It didn't seem that they could have got any louder – but they did. Ann stood there – completely naked – locked in mutual lust with all these men. Then she bent down and picked up her panties. She noticed, in passing, the damp patch at the crotch. Ann dangled her underwear from one finger and began to walk slowly on one last circuit of the dancefloor. Men were begging for her panties as she passed them. She let the clamour grow – and then handed them to an old guy who looked like he was having the time of his life. He now had a slightly soiled souvenir of the evening. It would give him something to sniff later.

It appeared that the audience thought the performance was at an end. The applause was loud and rapturous. But – Ann had other plans. "I Feel Love" faded out and there was no music for a few seconds. Then Anita Ward's "Ring My Bell" began. Ann danced slowly and sinuously back to the top of the dancefloor. As she did so, she ran her hands over her naked body – fondling and caressing. Ann stood – still writhing and swaying on the spot. With her left hand she played with her tits while, with her right, she began to masturbate. She did this elegantly and with precision. Her wrist was angled gracefully and she used only her extended middle finger to stimulate her clit. The audience were enthralled. For the first time, they fell silent. The erotic tension was palpable. Ann had intended to finish with a simulated orgasm. She didn't have to. Her climax was swift, almost overpowering and completely genuine. There, in full view of a hundred and thirty odd men, she came loudly, forcefully and convulsively.

Ann was weak at the knees again – but for a totally different reason this time. She later reflected that perhaps her's hadn't been the only orgasm in that moment. She was sure that several of her audience had come in their pants at the same time. The noise from the crowd eclipsed even the volume it had reached previously. Ann gathered herself and began walking to the door. The men parted to allow her passage. When she reached the door, Ann turned to face the crowd once more. She spread her arms wide and bowed. The crowd responded with even more vigour. Ann turned and left. Naked as she was, she walked through the foyer and upstairs to her room – much to the surprise of several guests, sitting or standing around. Their heads had all turned to the noise and were greeted by the sight of a beautiful naked woman striding across to the stairway. Maybe there were complaints – but Ann never found out.

When Ann got into the room, she collapsed on the bed. She felt euphorically happy – but physically and emotionally drained. She lay there, still naked, hoping that Neil might come in and fuck her. A good shag would recharge her batteries. As time passed, she realised that this was not going to happen. Ann got dressed and went down to find Neil sitting waiting for her in the foyer. He got up to greet her. "You were magnificent," he told her. "The other girls will be an anti-climax after that performance. Did it live up to your expectations?" "It was better," Ann replied. "Good," Neil said. He reached into his pocket and brought out a fine gold chain with, what looked like, an amethyst teardrop on it. He went to Ann and fastened this around her neck. "This is a little memento of your triumph," he said. "Wear it. It will bring you luck." Ann loved it and thanked him.

Ann was chattier on the return journey. It seemed to pass much more quickly than the drive to get there. She invited Neil up when they arrived – but he politely declined. He promised to be back in touch – but that he travelled a lot – so he didn't know when. Ann thanked him again and got out of the car. Neil drove off. He smiled when he thought about Ann and her splendid and explicit performance. He liked this human. She'd provided him with enough information to get a fix on his quarry. The opportunity to fulfil her fantasy was his thank you to her. Besides – he'd thoroughly enjoyed it himself. She did have a wonderful body and an interesting mind. Maybe he'd see her again. It all depended on how quickly the current situation could be resolved. Perhaps Ann would have a further part to play in this. His intuition told him that this might be the case – though he hoped he was wrong. Time would tell.

Chapter Twenty – The Best Laid Plans. (Monday 7th January. 1980.)

Monday morning brought disappointment on a wide front. Beresford moved in on Riverdale Day Centre, before it opened. The plan was to scoop up Wallace the moment he showed up for work. They would then wring from him Koldunya's whereabouts. They had ways of doing this that were fast, efficient and clean. Afterwards, he was to be terminated. Garcia and Hastings were inside with the Centre manager, Marjory Craig. They suspected that she may have been compromised and they didn't want her warning their targets. There were two teams of four in cars nearby – ready to move in to give support.

All the victims of Wallace's recent predation had been taken into protective custody. Beresford had drafted in extra bodies to babysit them. He had considered this a prudent move. Analysis of Koldunya's previous forays, had shown that many of the female murder victims had previously been sexually assaulted by the witch's current attack-dog, before he returned, to torture and murder them later. If they didn't get Wallace locked down today, these women could be in great danger. Everything was in place – only – Wallace didn't show. He hadn't turned up at the time he should have started work.

Garcia was in the office when the phone rang and Marjory Craig answered it. They hadn't alerted her to the suspicions they had about her. They'd only said they were here to interview her staff. She was warned not to alert anyone that they were there. Marjory wasn't aware yet, just how few of her staff had turned up. Garcia and Hastings had kept her isolated in the office. They could only hear one side of the telephone conversation but it was clear that Wallace was on the other end. "Hi Garry," she said. "Ok, thanks for letting me know. It never rains but it pours. Give me a ring when you know how long you're going to be off for." She hung up. "That was Garry Wallace," she told Garcia. "He was assaulted on Friday and isn't fit to work today." "Oh," Garcia replied, "We believe he's with his girlfriend. Someone called Morgan, who is a friend of yours and volunteers at the Centre here. Where does she live?" Marjory gave an unconvincing little laugh. "I'm afraid I don't have Morgan's home address. I only know her through her volunteer work. Besides – Garry and her aren't an item. He's a nice enough guy but Morgan's way out of his league."

Garcia left the office and immediately got on the radio to Beresford. "Wallace is a no show," she told him. "He phoned Craig moments ago to tell her – but I'm sure she already knew. She used the phrase "it never rains but it pours" when she spoke to him. I believe that was a code to alert him that we were on to him. This changes everything. Koldunya will be on the move now. We may have lost her." "Ok," Beresford replied. "I'm putting things on an emergency footing. I have the authority, from the Home Office, to take full command of the police operation. I'm doing so now. Bring Craig in and we'll find out exactly what she knows. I'm not giving up just yet. I'll put out a general alert for Koldunya and Wallace. Let's see what turns up."

Meanwhile, in the Koldunya household, all was not rosy. The day had started with high hopes and spirits. As per their plan, Garry had phoned Janet's work. The intention was for him to instruct her to meet with him later in the day. His hold over her was such, that she'd be forced to obey. He was surprised when it wasn't Janet who took his call. She was the receptionist and it was always her who'd answered previously. The voice was unfamiliar and when he asked for Janet, he was told that she hadn't come to work that morning. Next, Garry tried calling her at home. He didn't have that number and had to look it up in the phone book. There was no answer. Alarm bells were beginning to sound for Koldunya. She told Garry to phone Marjory – ostensibly to inform her he wasn't coming into work that day. That's when Marjory had used the agreed warning phrase. Someone – the police or the Venatores – were waiting at the Centre. Garry had obviously been identified as a suspect – and with him, the woman they would know as Morgan. It was time to get out of town.

Koldunya was more furious than afraid. Their enemies could only have found them so quickly because of Garry's reckless rutting with his work colleagues. She briefly thought of simply slitting his throat and leaving him behind – but she needed him. Her lifeforce was too depleted for her to survive outside the perimeter to which she'd been tethered by her tapping into the latent magic that resided here. Starting over from scratch, was out of the question – given how close the pursuit was. She needed Garry to garner more power for her – and she needed it quickly. The current turn of events was not entirely unanticipated. Koldunya had, of course, made contingency plans. She had another house ready as an emergency bolthole. That's where they would go now and re-evaluate the situation.

There was no need to pack. Everything Koldunya needed was in a hold-all bag. She picked this up and told Garry, "Come on. We need to leave right away." They left the house and got into the TR 7. It was a distinctive car but Koldunya had no fears that it would be recognised. There was an enchantment on it. Anyone seeing it, would immediately forget the make and even the colour of the vehicle. Garry had travelled inside the car, so he was now immune to the enchantment. He was a worried man. It was obvious that Morgan (he still thought of her by that name) was more than a bit annoyed – and probably with him. As she drove, Koldunya fumed aloud at not getting her hands on Janet. "That little bitch is a burr under my skin," she told Garry. "I won't feel whole until we snuff her life out. Her screams and pleading will be music to my ears." Garry didn't know exactly why Morgan had developed such an extreme hatred of Janet. He didn't really care though. He too, would relish the torture and murder of someone for whom he used to have an affection.

"I need a killing soon," Koldunya said. "If we can't track Janet down, we'll need to find another victim." "I've got one in mind," Garry replied. "I want payback on that whore Ann. She humiliated me and has it coming. I've still got the key to her flat – and there's a bonus. Her two girls should be there as well."

Koldunya's spirit soared. The rape and murder of a mother and her two daughters would generate a massive volume of anguish, pain and horror. It would be a sumptuous feast. Just what she needed. Had Garry's identity remained undiscovered, Koldunya would not have contemplated Ann as a victim. Even the ordinary police would not have failed to see the connection between her and Garry. But that ship had sailed. Desperate times need desperate solutions. The prospect excited her. "Do you think you could go through with it?" Koldunya asked. "With pleasure," Garry replied. "And the girls too?" was her follow up question. "You've no idea how much I'll enjoy doing those two," Garry said. "I've had my eye on them since I first moved in with Ann. It'll be delicious." Koldunya was delighted. Garry was turning out even more depraved than she had hoped. He was definitely something special. Her optimism rocketed. All might still be well.

While Koldunya and Garry were settling into their new abode, Beresford was sailing stormy waters. He had presented his Document of Authority to the Chief Constable and been met with incredulous fury. At first Moncrieff had blustered and refused to accept the Document's validity. When Beresford informed him that failure to comply would lead to his dismissal and prosecution for obstruction, he got on the phone to the Home Office. He was ashen faced and trembling with supressed anger when the call ended. He refused to even look at Beresford but sent immediately for Detective Chief Inspector Martin. Donnie entered the office and took a seat. "We have orders from on high," The Chief Constable told him, "That we have to cede control of your investigation to Major Beresford here. There will apparently be dire consequences if we refuse. Now – I'm not too sure how legal all this is. I'll be consulting our lawyers." "There's no time for any delay," Beresford interjected. "I expect all your available officers to meet with me in the canteen in half an hour. This matter is bigger than your egos. Do not make any decisions that will irrevocably damage your careers." With that, he got up and left to gather his own personnel.

Beresford didn't know how effective his high-handed approach would prove to be – but he didn't have the time for gentle persuasion. Lives depended on them taking Koldunya and Wallace down – either here or wherever the witch moved to next. The Venatores had chapters in many countries worldwide. Beresford was merely head of the British one. He dearly wanted to wrap this case up on his watch. Gloria Garcia had interrogated Marjory Craig under a truth spell. They now knew where Koldunya had been based. They had dispatched a squad to the house in Dunblane – but – as expected – the house had been abandoned. Koldunya and Wallace were in the wind. They had to be found – and quickly.

There were about twenty or thirty local officers present when Beresford, Garcia and three of their colleagues entered the canteen. The babble of conversation died immediately they came in. The silence felt hostile – which was to be expected. Nevertheless, like it or not, they would do as they were told. Beresford needed feet on the ground and eyes far and wide. The more complex and perilous operations he would trust to his own staff. The local officers would be vulnerable to Koldunya's powers and thus endangered. His people were protected. When the fugitives were located, it would have to be the Venatores who took them down. The reasons for this could not be explained to the locals – so it would, no doubt, appear as arrogance to them. So be it.

Beresford spoke. "Good afternoon, ladies and gentlemen. Some of you already know me. I am Major Beresford. I am an official of the British Government's Home Office Special Crime Squad. By the authority of the Home Office, I am assuming command of your current investigation. This is no reflection on your work nor on that of Detective Chief Inspector Martin. He will continue as my liaison with yourselves. I'm merely changing the focus of your operation. Our only priority will be to locate the two prime suspects. The first is one Garry Wallace – a local man who is already known to some of you. A recent photograph of him will be distributed to you when I'm finished talking. The other is a foreign national we know only as Koldunya. A description will also be distributed. It's pretty vague. She is said to be very attractive, about five foot four, with waist length dark hair and violet eyes. The eyes colouring might seem to be a very distinctive feature – but we believe she uses coloured contact lenses to change her appearance. So – bear that in mind.

Earlier today, we took into custody Marjory Craig, who is the manager of Riverdale Day Centre, where James Keenan – one of our murder victims – worked as a volunteer. Mister Wallace is also one of her staff. She recently recruited Koldunya – going by the name Morgan – as another volunteer. It turns out that Koldunya had bought the next door house to Ms Craig in Dunblane – and that's how they became acquainted. Craig is facing charges of aiding and abetting, obstruction and accessory to murder. Let me emphasise – our two fugitives are extremely dangerous. They are not to be approached under any circumstances. Locate them and I'll send in a specialised squad to take them down. I want covert surveillance on the house in Dunblane. It's unlikely they'll return there but we have to cover that base. I also want surveillance on Wallace's parent's home and on the home of his ex-girlfriend – Ann Graham. I cannot emphasise this too much – it is imperative that these people are traced. Innocent lives depend on it."

The meeting concluded without any questions. Beresford couldn't tell how diligently his instructions would be carried out. He'd left DCI Martin to work out the nuts and bolts of the surveillance operations. Rather than have his own officers sitting around doing nothing but wait, Beresford sent them out, in teams of two, to patrol the town and nearby villages in cars. They were all in constant radio contact – ready to respond the instant something came up. There was nothing further Beresford could do now but wait and hope something shook loose before Koldunya disappeared into the sunset.

Chapter Twenty One – In The Land of The Fey.

"So tell me, Neil Mac Mannanan, what you have discovered about who it is that disturbs the sleep of the Adversary," said the King. "Yes King Feargas," replied Neil. "It is a woman. The humans – namely the Venatores – consider her simply a witch – but she is more than that. She is, in fact, of our kindred – though from a distant and dark branch of it. She does not seek deliberately to awaken the Beast under The Hill. What has happened, comes about as an accidental consequence of her upsetting the balance of magical energies around her resting place.

The woman's whole essence is centred on sexual depravity, enslavement, horror and murder. She taps into the intrinsic occult reservoir of a place, through ritual human sacrifice – and draws power from it. This is a double-edged sword, as far as she is concerned. It makes her powerful but it also binds her to the environs from which she has drawn her strength. Whilst she remains there, the latent magic sustains her life-force. Should she leave – her life-force burns away at a phenomenal rate – and thus she perishes. In order to move on, the woman requires to build up her personal reserves of energy. This is a problem for us. It means that she is obliged to perform further acts in order to acquire more power. This – in turn – brings the possibility of awakening the Adversary. She must be stopped before this can be allowed to happen.

"What more do you know of this woman?" the King asked. "Can you kill her, Neil Mac Mannanan?" "I believe she was the female half of the Nasilnik – who left a trail of rape, murder and devastation across Central and Eastern

Europe centuries ago. I don't know what happened to the male – but it seems the female is still in business. In the present situation, she has taken a male accomplice – a piece of scum called Garry Wallace. With him, I believe she will carry out more atrocities against the human population. Whilst human lives are of no consequence to us – the repercussions could be dire. The Venatores – no friends of ours – are close on her trail. They may be able to end her – but I do not have faith in their ability to do so. It falls to us to handle this matter – and thus it falls to me. I'm confident that I have the skills and strength to defeat and kill this menace. I don't yet have a fix on her location – but I'm close. I simply need your permission to proceed." "You have that permission, Neil Mac Mannanan," said the King. "Go and deal with this matter – and do so as quickly as you can."

Chapter Twenty Two – A Killer Comes To Call. (Monday 7th January. 1980.)

All was peace and harmony in the Graham household. This was not always the case. Ann's daughters, Sandra – aged eleven and Karen – aged ten, were close – but were also known to bicker for no apparent reason. Ann had worried about how her break up with Garry would affect the girls. He had been in their young lives for the last two years. A long time – given their ages. So far she hadn't noticed anything detrimental in the girls' behaviour. Tonight, Ann had hired a video – "Pete's Dragon". Garry had taken them all to see it in the cinema, a couple of years previously. This was near the start of Ann's relationship with him. The girls had loved the film the first time round. Ann just hoped that, two years on, they'd still find it enjoyable.

Ann had decided to make a night of it. As well as the video, she had brought home crisps, sweets and a bottle of Irn Bru. These were now on the coffee table, next to where all three were sitting, on the living room couch. Ann had treated herself also. She was sipping at a glass of white wine. She didn't normally drink alcohol when she had work the next day – but tonight, she was making an exception. Besides – she could handle one bottle of wine and still be fine the next day. Ann was still bathing in the afterglow of the previous night's performance in the Airdrie hotel. It had been exquisite. She mused on the possibility of doing something similar again. Perhaps a repeat performance would prove a disappointment. She doubted that she could ever reach those heights again. Everything had been perfect. Recreating that, might just not be possible.

They put the video on just before seven. Ann tried to concentrate on the movie but found her thoughts now straying to Neill. He was undoubtedly dreamy and had that air of mystery. He'd not made any move on her – a fact Ann regretted greatly. Maybe she'd see him again. Fortunately, the girls had quickly become engaged with the movie. They'd talked about it a lot, after seeing it in the cinema. They now were having fun recreating their memories of that first time. They'd each poured themselves a glass of Irn Bru and were tucking into the snacks. Ann put her thoughts to one side, relaxed and began to enjoy the video herself.

Just after Ann and her daughters began watching the movie, a couple of miles away, in the village of Bannockburn, Koldunya and Garry left their new hideaway and got into her car. Before doing so, Koldunya had given Garry a wicked looking knife, from the bag she'd brought with her from the house in Dunblane. It had a nine inch long, razor-sharp blade. Garry attached its sheath to his belt. He was already in a state of high arousal. The anticipation of what was to come was delicious. A night of savage, bloody pleasure beckoned and he was more than ready. The journey to Ann's would only take a few minutes – and then the fun could begin. As they drove, Koldunya gave Garry his final instructions. "As soon as you take control," she told him. "Command them to stay silent. We can't have their screams alerting nosey neighbours. You should do the children first. That will maximise the anguish. I will be with you – but not in body. It's easier to show you than to explain. You'll see shortly. We're almost there."

Koldunya pulled into the kerb just around the corner from Ann's street but did not stop the engine. She rolled down her window and sat in silence for about half a minute, before a crow appeared from the dark, night sky and perched beside her. She touched the bird on the head with a finger and then it flew off again. "I'm using the bird's eyes to scout ahead," Koldunya told Garry. "When you go into the flat, the crow will go with you. My physical body will remain in the car but I will project myself fully into the bird. Its form amplifies the psychic energy generated from the fear, pain and degradation you will release from the victims and helps me maximise the pleasure and nourishment I glean from it." She broke off from her explanation. "There are watchers," she said. Koldunya had spotted the two men sitting in a car, just up the street from Ann's flat. She brought the bird in for a closer look. They had to be police or Venatores. The former wouldn't be a problem but the latter would mean they had to abandon their plans. Koldunya landed the crow on the car's bonnet.

Through its eyes, she saw one of the men point and say something. She projected her magic through the crow and the two men promptly fell asleep. They were merely ordinary cops. The plan could go ahead.

Koldunya drove round and parked beside the car with the two sleeping cops. She knew Garry was excited and she was too. No matter how many times she did this, she never lost the thrill of anticipation. The crow had come back to perch beside her, at the open window. Koldunya squeezed Garry's hand. "Go and have fun," she told him. He got out of the car and looked up at Ann's window. The curtains were drawn but the lights were on. As he stood there, the crow flapped across and landed on his shoulder. Garry looked around quickly to see that no-one had witnessed this unusual sight. The street was quiet and empty. His heart pounding – and with a prodigious hard-on, Garry entered the close and climbed the stairs to Ann's flat.

Garry slipped the key into the lock and eased the door open. He could hear sounds from the living room. The television was on. There was a song playing that he didn't recognise. This was good. The music helped mask Garry's stealthy progress along the hallway. The first the three females knew of his intrusion, was when Garry opened the door and stepped into the living room. Ann was startled and bemused by the sight of her ex-boyfriend standing there with a large, black crow on his shoulder. She wasn't particularly alarmed to begin with – just surprised. Garry spoke. "Hi ladies," he said. "Just sit there and don't move. No matter what happens – none of you is to make a sounds. Not a word – not a whimper – not a scream. You'll want to do all three – but you will remain silent."

Garry stood silent for a few seconds, savouring the feel of three lives in his hands. "Now to business," he finally said. "The three of you stand up." Ann and her two daughters immediately obeyed. "Sandra and Karen, go over and stand in front of the tv. Oh – and switch it off. It's annoying. Ann – stay where you are." The two girls did as they were told. "Right girls," Garry went on. "I want you to undress. Take everything off." Ann stood helpless. She was baffled and fearful. She couldn't understand what was happening. Then she saw the lustful way Garry was watching her girls undressing. Fury erupted inside her – but it was impotent. She couldn't move. Garry glanced at her. He must have seen the fear and anger in her eyes. "To start with, I'm going to fuck those two and you get to watch," he said. "Then I'm going to carve them up. But look on the bright side, Ann – at least your daughters aren't going to die virgins. Oh – and don't worry about their pussies being too small. I've got a way of making them bigger." With that, he drew the knife from his belt, held it up where they all could see it and waggled it about. The crow flapped from his shoulder and settled on the back of the couch. It's eyes seemed to shine with a feverish, unnatural light.

Ann felt like she was in a terrifying nightmare. What the fuck was happening? Only a few minutes had passed but it seemed like an eternity. The girls were naked by this time and standing as if uncertain what to do next. Garry was staring at them with a hungry look on his face. For some time, Ann had been vaguely aware of a tingling on her skin, where it was touched by the pendant Neil had given her. This had been low in her awareness. Other, more distressing matters, were occupying her mind. Then the sensation strengthened at an accelerated pace. Suddenly Ann was free. She no longer felt the overwhelming compulsion to comply with Garry's orders. Ann's fury was abruptly given free rein. She snatched up the Irn Bru bottle from the table and swung it, with all her might, into Garry's face.

The sturdy glass of the bottle did not shatter on contact. Not so, Garry's nose and cheekbone. He felt both crack as he reeled back in shock. Ann pressed home her attack. She rained frenzied blow upon blow on Garry. Some of these, he managed to ward off with his left hand and arm – but some got through to his face, head and shoulders. He was stunned and panicked. Blindly, Garry lashed at Ann with his knife but missed by a distance. The bottle had finally broken and Ann was now using the jagged end to stab at any part of him that came into range. Koldunya was shocked at this totally unexpected turn of events. She resolved to intervene and subdue Ann, the same way as she'd previously done to the police in their car. Only – it wasn't working. There was a strange light emanating from the pendant Ann wore. It grew and grew in intensity, till it felt like it was searing her eyes. Suddenly and shockingly, Koldunya was precipitated back into her body as the crow's head exploded.

The erupting crow's skull probably saved Garry's life. It distracted Ann, long enough for him to break off and make his escape. He was badly hurt – feeling near collapse and bleeding from several punctures and lacerations. He turned and, with a shambling run he made it along the hallway and out the door. Ann recovered from her momentary surprise and set off in pursuit. She didn't follow Garry outside. Instead, Ann slammed the door shut and pushed the snib up, so it couldn't be opened from outside by the key. She then rushed back to the living room to comfort her distressed children. They were hysterical, confused and in tears. Ann calmed them as best she could – but she couldn't spend much time doing so. Help had to be summoned, in case Garry came back. "Listen Girls," Ann said. "I want you to get dressed now. I've got to phone the police. It's important. It won't take long. It's over now. We're all safe. It'll be ok. I promise."

Ann picked up the phone and her heart sank. It was dead. There was no dialling tone. She fought down the incipient panic that threatened to engulf her. "The phone's not working," she told the girls. "But don't worry. I'll wait till someone's passing outside and get them to phone the police. Just sit tight. It'll be alright." She said these words to reassure her daughters but wasn't sure she believed them herself. She went to the window and pulled back the curtains. There was no-one about. After a bit, Ann opened the door and went out onto the veranda. Still no-one around. She scanned the street in both directions. There was no sign of Garry or his car. There was a vehicle parked a bit up the street which seemed to have two people in it. Ann waved frantically to try and attract their attention – but they were either ignoring her or they weren't looking in her direction.

Time was passing and Ann was anxious. The longer it took for the police to become involved the longer it would be before they could go after Garry. She'd messed him up pretty badly. She began to worry that she herself might be labelled as the aggressor, if Garry got his word in first. The girls had calmed a bit but were still very much on edge. They hadn't spoken yet about what had just happened. Ann didn't know how to start. She was having trouble processing the events herself. She really didn't understand what had happened and why she had initially been so submissive to Garry. It hadn't been the threat of the knife he had. She was already obeying him before she'd even seen it. A car passed on the street but Ann was back indoors and was too late getting out on the veranda to wave down the driver. Eventually Ann made a decision. "Listen girls," she said. "I'm going to go upstairs to use the Kirkwood's phone. I'll only be a few minutes and I'll lock the door behind me." The girl's anxiety flared up. They didn't want Ann to go – and then they wanted to go with her. They didn't want to be left alone. It took some time to calm them again – but eventually they subsided enough that Ann could risk leaving them for a few minutes.

Ann unsnibbed the door and cautiously edged it open. The landing was clear so she stepped out. The Kirkwoods lived one flight up from Ann. She just hoped that their phone wasn't out too. Then her heart skipped several beats, when she realised there was a figure coming up the stairs from street level.

She almost screamed – and then she recognised Neil. She was relieved and astonished in equal measure. "Ann – are you alright? He asked. "Not really," she replied. "Garry was here. He was going to harm me and my girls. My phones not working, so I'm going to a neighbour's to phone the police." "I don't think that's a good idea," Neil said. "I can help – more than the police can. Let's go back inside. We have to talk."

Chapter Twenty Three – A Throw of The Dice. (Monday 7ᵗʰ January. 1980.)

Koldunya was livid. She dearly wanted to vent that anger on Garry but she grudgingly had to concede that the fiasco that had just transpired was not his fault. There had been magic at play – powerful magic – possibly more powerful than her own. Where had Ann found that amulet? The witch considered, not for the first time, snuffing Garry out – but he might yet be of some use. Now was not the time for precipitate and irrevocable actions. She felt the situation was becoming more and more desperate. Mistakes had been made. Undoubtedly, Garry's sex spree at the Centre was one – but she too had made some. She should have kept a tighter rein on him. She had also let herself be seduced by the prospect of a banquet of pain and torment with Ann and her two daughters. They could, instead, have picked up and feasted on a couple of random victims already.

Despite her witchcraft, Koldunya had very few skills when it came to healing. It had never featured much in her hierarchy of needs. Garry had lost a lot of blood – much of it in her car. Ann had really done a number on him. When they got back to Bannockburn, Koldunya made a concoction that she slathered on his wounds. This solidified into an artificial skin that stopped his bleeding. She then mixed a potion that killed most of his pain. None of this was done out of mercy. She had the inkling of an idea that would require him to be at least basically functional. When her anger had subsided a little, weariness had washed over her. She was very old and her glory days were long in the past. She missed Uzhas and ached to set him free but the last century had consisted of a succession of raised hopes that were all doomed, sooner or later, to end in crushing disappointment and failure. Each time, Koldunya had picked herself up and started over. She wasn't sure she could do so again. Her hopes for Garry had burned very brightly – but those too were now dashed to pieces. Perhaps it was finally time for Slavnaya Smert – a glorious death.

Koldunya could feel the pursuit closing in on her. As things stood, she was trapped in this locality, with nowhere to run. The debacle earlier that night had cost her in spirit and energy. The magical amulet that Ann had been wearing was a development in her enemy's powers. Either the Venatores had learned new tricks or there was a different player in the game. The latent thaumaturgical energy Koldunya had sensed in and around Stirling, was potent indeed. Perhaps she had trodden on the toes of some other otherworldly entity. She had no doubt that such creatures were a distinct possibility in this neighbourhood. Anyone who possessed or fashioned an amulet of such power, could well be able to track her by magical means. Whatever and whoever was coming after her, Koldunya was not going to go quietly. If she was going down, she was not going to go down alone. She would settle scores and take as many as possible with her. Her first thought was Janet. That little blond slut had somehow gotten under her skin. Her hatred wasn't rational – but that didn't matter. It was an itch she had to scratch.

In order to enact her fury on Janet, Koldunya first had to find her. It was time for some scrying. Garry was not required just now, so she had told him to eat something and then lay on the couch to rest. He was weak from loss of blood and she would need him mobile when she was ready to make her move. Koldunya knew she was low on energy herself but the things she planned were all fairly low-level magic. She was confident that she had enough juice – though, if matters developed favourably, a top-up would soon be on the cards. The witch went to the kitchen and filled a mixing bowl with water. She placed this on the dining table, turned the light off and sat down. Koldunya took a pinch of powder from a small pouch sewn inside her dress, put it in the bowl and then stirred the water with her index finger. A few seconds passed. As it swirled around, the water darkened. When it finally came to rest, it was fully opaque. Koldunya hunched over it and concentrated. She conjured an image of Janet in her mind. Nothing happened for some time and then a picture began to form in the dark water. It was a building with a sign above the door saying "The Golf Hotel". The picture zoomed in further to the interior of a hotel room. There sat Janet, watching tv and beside her was Michelle.

Koldunya explored further and discovered Jenny and Ruth were also in the hotel. They were obviously there under protection – probably by the Venatores. The witch was delighted. Perhaps her luck was changing for the better. All four women had already succumbed to Garry's control. That would make them susceptible to further manipulation. All it would take, would be the sound of Garry's voice. This night could yet turn out to be spectacular. Koldunya went to the living room and roused Garry. "Do you know where The

Golf Hotel is?" she asked. "Yeah," he replied. "It's up near the King's Park."
"Get some more rest," Koldunya told him. "We'll be going there later tonight."

Chapter Twenty Four – A Friend of The Fey. (Monday 7th January. 1980.)

Despite her agitation, Ann agreed to go back into her flat with Neil. She felt reassured by his presence. As they did so Neil said, "There's a blood trail on the stairs – Garry's?" Ann nodded. "I attacked him with a broken bottle," she said. The girls were still standing, huddled together in the living the room. They looked relieved that their mother had come back so soon but a bit wary of the stranger who was with her. Neil noted the dead crow as soon as he entered the room. It was lying behind the couch, where it had fallen after its head had burst open. There was blood spattered everywhere. Some of it from the bird but most of it, obviously, from Garry. Neil looked closely at the two young girls. "I don't know exactly what has happened here," he said. "But before you tell me, I can see that your daughters are severely traumatized. Some things can scar for life. If you'll allow me, I can do something about that." Ann didn't understand but tentatively nodded. Neil stepped to the girls. He touched each briefly on the forehead. "I think it's time for bed," he told them. Sandra and Karen both smiled and nodded assent. They said goodnight to their mother and went off to their bedroom. "They'll sleep now," Neil said, "and in the morning they'll have no memory of what happened tonight. It's for the best."

Ann wasn't sure what to make of what had just happened nor the assertion Neil had just made. Before she could seek an explanation, Neil asked her to tell him what had happened earlier. Ann took a deep breath and recounted what had happened when Garry had stepped into her living room. She remembered everything with clarity – even though, for a time, she seemed to have no will of her own. She told Neil how Garry was threatening to rape and murder her children – but she had done nothing to stop him. Then – she had seemed to snap out of whatever was holding her and she'd attacked him with a glass bottle – injuring him and driving him out.

Neil listened attentively. When Ann had finished, he considered for a moment or two and then spoke. "I'm going to tell you some things," he said. "They may well sound crazy to you – but – If you're the person I think you are, then you will know that I speak the truth – not necessarily with your logic but at a visceral level. Ok – here goes. I am not exactly what you might call human. I belong to the Fey. My people are what are often called the Fair Folk or even – Faerie. As you see, we do not have gossamer wings and our physical stature is similar to your own. My full name is Neil Mac Mannanan. I am Sherriff of the lands that include this town of Stirling. I hold this commission from the King of The Fey. Part of my job is to keep watch for magical irregularities that could lead to truly dire consequences. Such an anomaly has occurred here. It was occasioned by the incursion of a witch from the dark side of my kindred. I've recently learned that she goes by the name of Koldunya."

Neil paused to see how Ann was taking it so far. She said nothing, so he continued. "This witch is particularly nasty. She thrives on murder and the pain of others. Her nature is depraved – even by Fey standards. To aid her in her efforts, she seduced your ex-boyfriend – Garry. He is not a good man. Even without the witch's influence he would have come to do you harm. Neither would your daughters have been safe with him in the house. He fully intended to rape and murder all three of you tonight. The witch has endowed him with a magic that gives him the power of mind control over women. That's why you couldn't resist him. It was the amulet I gave you that broke his hold on you and allowed you to fight back. Its activation also alerted me that something was wrong and I came here as quickly as I could. The amulet was also responsible for killing the crow that Garry brought with him. The witch was using it as a vehicle – and that means I can use it to track her.

I know this is a lot to take in. Magic is real. Witches are real – and faeries are real. I don't have time now to go into more detail. I must get after the witch. You damaged her tonight and she won't forget that. She will also be weakened and vulnerable – for the moment. She is liable to do something drastic in her desperation. I need to stop her. In the morning, you'll see that your daughters do not remember the events of tonight. If you doubt what I've told you, perhaps that will convince you. I would advise you not to contact the police. It would also be good if you could clean up the blood, so the girls are not alarmed by it. I'll take the crow with me. You have a decision to make. I can offer you the same as I've done for your daughters. I can erase the memory of Garry's attack on your home. You will sleep and forget. Or you can remember – and become what we call – a Friend of The Fey. It's an exclusive club – not many humans belong to it. It's your choice."

Ann thought for only a few seconds. "My head tells me," she said, "that what you've told me can't be true. But, what I experienced tonight is unbelievable too – so my gut tells me to believe you. I would rather remember. There's something about you that inspires trust – so I do trust you. Besides – being a Friend of The Fey sounds exciting." "So be it," Neil replied. "I must go now but I'll return to tell you how things work out and perhaps to answer questions you will have." He left then, taking the dead crow with him. Ann sat for a while, pondering. Then she roused herself and set about cleaning up as much of Garry's blood as she could. The world had suddenly become much more strange and frightening.

Chapter Twenty Five – Frustration Therapy. (Monday 7th January. 1980.)

Gloria Garcia and Tom Beresford had spent hours in the police control room, waiting for something to break. They had as many eyes and ears on the street as they could muster. The urge was there to do something more – but neither could think what that might be. It was frustrating and increasingly boring. Just after nine, Beresford said to Garcia, "Take a couple of hours off. Go back to the hotel, have something to eat and relax for a bit. If anything breaks I'll call you on the radio." Gloria was only too happy to comply. It looked like being a long night and a little break would help re-charge the batteries.

It only took Gloria about ten minutes to drive to the hotel. It wasn't a large establishment. There were only twenty-one rooms and the Venatores had booked all of them. As a senior officer, Gloria didn't have to share. She popped her head into the small bar as she passed it, to see if any of her colleagues were there. The little room was empty – apart from one guy sitting at the bar. He looked round as Gloria entered – and she was smitten. He was absolutely gorgeous and ticked all her boxes – at least as far as looks go. Their eyes locked for a couple of seconds and Gloria felt a delicious thrill course through her body. As far as she could make out, she'd had a similar effect on him. "Hi," he said, "buy you a drink?" Gloria made a snap decision. "I'm in room three," she told him. "Give me five minutes."

Gloria walked from the barroom without another word. She was confident the stranger would follow her shortly. It would be nice if she could say that she never usually did things like this – but, if truth be told, the vast majority of her sexual encounters followed a similar path – chance and brief encounters in bars and restaurants. Her busy life did not leave space for elaborate courtship. She was rarely in one place long enough to allow such a thing to unfold. Besides – she wasn't looking for romance. All she wanted was a good fuck, to blow away the cobwebs. With any luck – the guy in the bar would know what he was doing and be able to give her a good time. Unfortunately – all too many of her liaisons resulted in disappointment – even when they looked as promising as the present guy did. Well – you took your chances. Gloria felt no shame in her approach to sex. She enjoyed it. If your luck was in – two people had a brief interlude of fun and pleasure. If not – well she wasn't ever going to see the man again.

Gloria had wanted five minutes in order to divest herself of the Ruger 9mm she wore in a concealed shoulder holster. It wasn't prudent to let that be seen by strangers. She took off her jacket, removed the holster and stowed it in her bedside cabinet, before unclipping the radio from her belt and laying it on top of the cabinet. Might as well hurry things a long a bit, she thought. There was the distinct possibility that a call might come through at any time from Beresford to interrupt her planned recreation – so every second might count. Gloria stripped down to her bra and pants. It maybe wasn't very classy – but she didn't want any romancing or the time-consuming rituals of seduction. She just wanted an uncomplicated fuck – no foreplay required. Her thinking was almost masculine in this regard. The physical act was the imperative. Anything else was just window-dressing.

A knock came to the door and Gloria opened it. Her new friend stood there. He ran his eyes over her body and she could tell he appreciated what he was seeing. Gloria was confident in her body. She knew it looked good. She was petite and compact with a slim waist and toned midriff. Her boobs were full, firm and shapely. Her hips swelled out just right and her legs were smooth, slender and well formed. Gloria knew that the full package presented a pleasing sight. She took the man by the hand and led him across the room to the bed. Without preamble she pushed his jacket off and dropped it on the floor. Reaching behind her, Gloria unclipped her bra and sent it to join the jacket – followed almost immediately by her panties. She fell back on the bed – pulling the man with her.

The man had been passive up to this – simply following where Gloria had led. Now he got with the programme. He undid his belt and pushed down his trousers and pants. Gloria reached up and grasped his already stiffened prick. It wasn't huge but more than adequate for her purposes. The man was obviously on the same page as Gloria. He didn't waste any time mounting her and pushing his cock in. He began to rhythmically thrust deep into her. As he did so, Gloria opened his shirt and slid it from his shoulders. His torso was lean and muscled just enough for her taste. Gloria was far from passive. She met each of his thrusts with one of her own, as she run her hands over his naked chest and stomach.

The pace and vigour of their exertions escalated rapidly. The man pounded away while Gloria bucked and writhed beneath him. There was no finesse to their coupling. It was primal and verging on brutal. Gloria had lost herself in the moment. She felt herself beginning to build towards orgasm – and hoped fervently that this man would not reach his before her. What an anti-climax that would be. He seemed to know what he was doing though. The tension low in her belly built and built. She was, unusually for her, becoming vocal. She was emitting short high-pitched yelps that increased in volume and frequency by the second. And then – suddenly – Gloria orgasmed – violently and very loudly. The man took his cue from her and achieved his own release a few seconds later.

"Wow," Gloria said, as she lay back breathless. That had been just what the doctor ordered. Her fidgety frustration had fully dissipated and the tension headache she had been nursing for the last three hours was totally gone. "Wow indeed," said the man, who was already standing up re-arranging his clothing. "I usually like to be more subtle in the sex act – but I sensed your need was urgent – so I tried to give you what you wanted. I also sense that you're a witch – but you're outmatched by the one who's coming against you." Gloria was stunned. "What did you say?" she asked incredulously. The man repeated his previous statement word for word. Gloria too was on her feet now and she was scrambling, with scant dignity, to get into her clothes again. "Who the fuck are you?" she shot out. "My name is Neil Mac Mannanan – and I'm of the Fey. I believe your people have heard of us."

If Gloria was stunned before – she was even more so now. She froze in mid-scramble. If the man was telling the truth, she'd just had amazing sex with a supernatural being. Gloria pulled herself together and finished dressing. "Ok," she said when she was done, "why are you here and what do you want?" "I'm here," he replied, "to give you information and enlist your co-operation. I intended to simply introduce myself – but I like your method of introduction better. Anyway – the witch, Koldunya, has been spying on this hotel. She was scrying earlier and knows the secret you thought hidden from her. I believe she will move against you sometime tonight. There are things you need to know and I'm here to tell you." "I need to contact my boss," Gloria said. She picked up her radio from the bedside cabinet and called Beresford. He responded almost immediately. "Tom, I've got a man here you really need to talk to." "Bring him in then," Beresford replied. "I can't say too much on the air," Gloria said, "but I think it's urgent that you come back to the hotel – and probably recall our units here also. I've got new information and the situation could be getting a bit tricky."

Chapter Twenty Six – Council of War. (Monday 7th January. 1980.)

They gathered in the hotel's barroom. Beresford and Garcia were there, along with their eleven other warded operatives. The hotel staff had been sent elsewhere. It was coming up to ten thirty by the time they were all there. Neil, the self-proclaimed Fey, sat calmly, a little apart from the assembled Venatores. Beresford got proceedings underway. "So you say your name is Neil Mac Mannanan and that you're Fey. How do we know you aren't lying? The Fey are notoriously uncooperative with human authorities." "Which part are you having a problem with?" asked Neil, "me being Fey or my cooperation?" "Frankly – both," Beresford answered. "Perhaps a little magic trick will convince you I am Fey," said Neil. "It always seems to impress you humans."

With that, a couple of bottles floated from the shelf behind the bar and came to rest, suspended in mid-air, just below the ceiling and above the centre of the room. Neil hadn't moved in any way. There hadn't been any dramatic hand gestures or anything. He just sat there – seemingly completely relaxed. The bottles hung motionless, about five feet apart, for a few seconds. Then they rushed violently together. They crashed into each other and shattered. Broken glass and booze rained down. Before any of the debris could fall on anyone, it suddenly froze and just hung there above their heads. Then the liquids coalesced together and the broken glass re-assembled itself around them. The seemingly unscathed bottles then floated serenely back to their positions on the shelf.

"So – as you can see, I'm Fey," Neil said. "Now I'll address your scepticism regarding my co-operation. We have a mutual desire to bring down the witch, Koldunya. I have information you are not aware of – and I also need your help." "But I don't believe we need yours," Beresford said. "We are perfectly capable of dealing with the witch ourselves." "No doubt," Neil told them, "but you must not kill her. She too is Fey. At her core is a magical essence. A sudden and violent death would cause this to detonate. The explosion would cause no physical damage. You probably wouldn't even be aware of it – but its repercussions would be cataclysmic. Koldunya has already caused disruption to the ambient magical energies of this area. Her death might well precipitate the awakening of something that would best be left undisturbed. I can say no more on this – but believe me – the consequences would be far worse than if you let the witch live. In order to safely deal with her – I must consume her life essence as she dies. That is why you need my help."

"Ok," said Beresford, "even if we accept all that as truth – what help do you need from us?" Gloria was listening very carefully. She knew that the Fey were reputed to have the gift of the Golden Tongue. This meant that they could be very persuasive to humans – sometimes against the human's own best interest. She was trying to filter Neil's words with this in mind. "First let me tell you what I know," Neil said. "I have learned things recently. Earlier this evening, Koldunya and Garry Wallace mounted an attack on Ann Graham at her home. Don't worry. Ann is well. I befriended her a little while ago and gave her an amulet of protection. This helped her resist the attack. She turned on Wallace and – by the amount of blood he left behind – mauled him severely. The witch was not physically present. She inhabited the body of a crow and travelled with Wallace in that guise. It's an old trick. It keeps the witch's own body safe from harm and the corvid's form acts as an amplifier for the absorption of the psychic energy that feeds Koldunya. The bird died as a result of the amulet's power. The amulet also alerted me. I retrieved the bird's body and managed to link myself through it to the witch.

Incidentally, Koldunya put two of your policemen to sleep prior to the attack. They should be waking up anytime now. She intended that Wallace would rape and murder Ann and her two daughters – but Ann foiled them – with some help from the amulet. Now – Koldunya is very old – even by Fey standards. Like many Fey, she has become obsessive in her old-age. She has a burning hatred for one of the women you have concealed in this hotel – the one called Janet. The witch will gladly kill all four – but that one is the focus of her twisted vengefulness. To that end, through scrying, she searched for Janet and found her here. That's why I believe Koldunya will come here tonight. Her lust for this girl's life is so intense that she will risk facing you and your people to achieve it. She is resigned to death – but doesn't want to die alone. Janet must go – and anyone else Koldunya can take with her. She is not at full strength but is still formidable – especially given that she no longer seeks to escape alive. That is a dangerous combination of circumstances. I am masked from her at present – but I must get close in order to snuff out her life. She will sense my presence once I'm near. You can help me by keeping her distracted until I'm close enough to overpower her. That's the only way this business can be brought to a satisfactory conclusion."

Chapter Twenty Seven – A Final Fling. (Tuesday 8th January. 1980.)

It was just before two in the morning when Koldunya parked next to the King's Park. All was quiet. There was no-one around. The Golf Hotel was about half a mile away. Garry sat beside her in the car. He was not doing so good. Koldunya had dosed him with another pain-killing potion but he'd lost a lot of blood and was probably suffering from concussion. He was conscious but not very communicative. The witch was confident though, that he'd be able to play his limited part in her plans.

Koldunya reached out with her mind and took control of a crow roosting in a nearby tree. She sent it to sweep the streets around the hotel. There was nothing to raise her suspicions. Nobody lurked in parked cars. She took the bird further aloft. There were a handful of cars moving through the night streets of Stirling but none seemed connected to or circling the hotel. The witch abandoned the crow and quested inside the hotel until she discovered the small presence she was looking for. Through the eyes of the mouse she checked out the corridors and reception area. All were empty. No-one stirred. The hotel was asleep. It looked suspicious to Koldunya – as if they were trying to entice her in. Surely the Venatores were not so complacent as to not post sentinels. She had felt a tugging at her consciousness earlier. It was brief but someone was undoubtedly spying on her. The Venatores were forewarned and no doubt lying in ambush. Well – she had no intention of entering the hotel.

Koldunya got out of the car and told Garry to come with her. All she needed from him now was his voice. The two of them entered the park and walked along, just inside the railings, until they were about a hundred yards from the Golf Hotel. There, they concealed themselves within a large clump of tall shrubs. Koldunya took both of Garry's hands in hers. "I'm going to project your voice into the minds of the women in that hotel," she told him. "I want you to call each of them by name and tell them to come directly to the park. They will obey your voice. Just say the words and I'll send them. Bring them to me – and this time I will wield the knife myself. Do this for me Garry. It will be your last act in our time together." Garry did as he was instructed. Koldunya was silent for a few seconds and then said, "Good – they're on their way." With that, she pushed the knife into Garry's lower abdomen and slowly drew it across, until his intestines spilled out. In his weakened state, Garry died quicker than she would have liked – but she still managed to harvest some power from his suffering.

Gloria Garcia and Tom Beresford sat in the hotel room they had set up for surveillance.. In front of them was an array of tv monitors. They had installed cameras to cover all the approaches to the hotel. There was also one showing the entrance foyer. As the night had worn on, the nervous tension had given way to boredom. They had begun to doubt that anything at all was going to happen that night. There were no cameras however in the corridors – so the first they knew that anything was amiss was when Janet, Michelle, Ruth and Jenny were seen crossing the foyer and leaving by the front door. The women were all in their night clothes, with nothing on their feet. "Koldunya's got into their heads," Gloria blurted. "She's not coming for them – she's making them come to her. We've got to stop them." Beresford put a hand on her arm as she stood up to go after the women. "Wait," he said. "This is our chance to finally get the witch." He spoke into his radio. "Units two and three," he said, "converge on the park. Look out for the women we've been protecting. They are being drawn to the witch. Move in when you see them. Shoot to kill, as soon as you have sight of the witch."

"What about what Neil told us?" Gloria asked Beresford. "We can't pay too much attention to some nebulous warning about undefined consequences," he shot back. "We may never have a better opportunity to kill Koldunya. We can't pass that up." "But we're putting those women's lives in danger," Gloria protested. "I can't be party to that. I'm going after them." "Ok – ok," Beresford said, "go after them – but hold back long enough to see where they're going." Gloria did not acknowledge his words. She was out of the room before he could say anything else. The Venatores had vehicles with two person teams circling the hotel at a distance. They followed an erratic course and were ready to go quickly to wherever they were needed. Those were the units Beresford had ordered to converge on the park. The rest of his team had remained concealed in various hotel rooms. These Beresford sent to flank the women on parallel streets with the intention of getting in front of them and waiting in concealment, to pick them up and follow them when they arrived.

Neil was already in the park. He had his feelers out and had located the witch as soon as she'd arrived. Now he was stalking her. He was trying to get as close to her as possible without giving away his presence. That way, he'd be able to rush in when, as he hoped, the Venatores did something to distract her. That hope was dashed. "I feel your presence, brother," Koldunya said. "Stop sneaking about and show yourself." With the hoped for element of surprise blown away, there was no point in further concealment. Neil uncloaked himself and stepped forward to confront Koldunya. "Why is it," she asked him, "that you side with humans against one of your own kind?" "I side with no-one," Neil replied. "Your actions here in my Sheriffdom, sister, have endangered the occult equanimity of my lands. It has to stop." "So have you come to kill me Sheriff?" "It does not have to be that way, sister," Neil told her. "Come with me now to the Realm of The Fey. There's a place there for you. What you've done on this plane will not be held against you. Human deaths are of little meaning to us. Come now and live out your last years in peace and companionship with your own kind. Here – only death awaits you."

Koldunya seemed to consider Neil's offer. "Very well," she finally said, "I could do that – but I've a task to complete first. You see those women," she pointed with her still dripping knife at her approaching intended victims. "I'll spare three of them – but the little blond one – I will not. Once I've gutted her, then I'll come with you. After all – human deaths have little meaning to our kind." "I cannot allow that," Neil responded immediately. "It would cause further disturbance. Come straight away or my offer is revoked." "So be it," Koldunya replied calmly. She pulled an amulet from inside her blouse and held it up for Neil to see. He was shocked. It was a Dibirt Na Siog. He hadn't thought that any still existed in this world. He made ready to rush the witch – but before he could, she held the amulet towards him and said a word of power. There was a blue flash and both he and the amulet were gone.

The women were approaching the small gate that gave access through the iron railings. Koldunya hefted her knife and left the cover of the shrubs which had been concealing her. She stalked along parallel to the railings and towards the gate. Gratification was only minutes away. Two cars slewed to a halt on either side of the group of women. People were getting out with guns in their hands. The women just continued to make steady progress – their faces devoid of any expression – belying the churning terror they were experiencing internally. Koldunya could do nothing directly against the encroaching Venatores. They had warding against witchcraft – but if they thought that made them safe – they were very much mistaken. The witch hurled one car and then the other into the people who'd just exited them – crushing out their lives in an instant.

Koldunya was very low on juice now. Half a dozen more Venatores had appeared from the side streets. The witch hadn't enough power to stop them. She needed a kill and she needed it fast. Her plan changed quickly. She would quickly rip open the bellies of the first two women to reach her. Janet, she would retain until she had time to deal with her properly. A quick infusion of energy would see her through – at least until she could deal properly with the object of her hatred. In another few seconds, her victims would be close enough. The women were blocking the Venatores from having a clear shot at the witch. It would buy her precious time.

Gloria was coming up rapidly behind the women. She had her gun out – but like her colleagues – she couldn't take a shot for fear of hitting one of the innocent women. They were bunching up as they moved to enter the park at the gate. Koldunya was just a step or two away – and she had a nasty looking knife in her hand. The witch was looking ropey. She stumbled a little but regained her footing quickly. Gloria sped up and shoulder barged her way through the four women – knocking Janet and Ruth to the ground in doing so. Koldunya was exposed and Gloria squeezed off a shot. It must have hit her somewhere mid-body but she did not go down. The witch moved quicker than Gloria would have expected. She lunged and Gloria felt a burning pain as the knife scored her hip.

Garcia tried to bring her gun to bear for another shot but Koldunya seized her wrist and diverted the weapon away from her. Gloria, in turn, got a grip on the wrist of the witch's knife wielding hand. The two women wrestled face to face and toe to toe. The witch was surprisingly strong physically. She twisted Gloria's wrist so violently that the gun went flying from her grasp. Koldunya snarled in fury and erupted forward. She dropped the knife and locked both hands around the other woman's throat. Her grip was unbreakable. Gloria struggled to free herself it but to no avail. The witch bore her backwards until she went down beneath the fury of the attack. Koldunya rode down with her. She pressed Gloria to the ground and held her there with her superior weight.

Gloria struggled frantically but could do nothing to free herself. She was beginning to lose consciousness and could only hope that some of her colleagues would arrive and put a bullet in Koldunya's brain before it was too late. When all seemed lost, the pressure suddenly disappeared from Gloria's throat. She felt a dead weight on her body and hot liquid cascaded over her face. She looked up blearily – and there stood Janet, with a dripping knife in her hand.

Chapter Twenty Eight – Unfinished Business. (Friday 18th January. 1980.)

Tom Beresford was pleased with himself. He'd been in charge of the successful mission to bring down Koldunya. Gloria Garcia was less sanguine.

Yes – Koldunya and Garry Wallace were dead – but so also were four of their colleagues. Perhaps, in the grand scheme of things, this was a favourable outcome.. Numerous innocent lives had doubtless been spared as a result of their mission. Gloria was sickened though, by Beresford's callousness and doubted she could ever work with him, in good conscience, again. He had been only too ready to risk the lives of the four women who were under their care and he'd shrugged off the deaths of his own people with apparent ease.

There had been a great deal of cover up to do, regarding the events in and around the King's Park. A story was put in place and then made public. Two suspects had been identified as the perpetrators of the grisly murders that had rocked the town – and further afield – a Miss Morgan Jones and a Mister Garry Wallace. As the police closed in on them, they had formed a suicide pact. Both suspects were dead and the police were not looking for anyone else in connection with the crimes. There were days of lurid headlines in the media but they and the public had accepted the concocted account. The police themselves were puzzled by what was being said but had been warned that any breaches would be severely punished under the Official Secrets Act. In time, the story would die down.

Beresford and Garcia were in their office at police headquarters, preparing to leave for the last time. Gloria had only been seconded to the British Venatores for the duration of the mission that had just ended. "So that's that then," Beresford said. "The job's finished. Are you going back to Spain?" Gloria was still having difficulty speaking. Koldunya had seriously damaged her throat. "No," she croaked in reply "I'm going to do some more work with Janet. She's a mess. Hardly surprising, after what she's been through. She did save my life after all. If the fall hadn't jarred her out of her trance, I wouldn't be here today." Beresford nodded. Gloria felt an obligation to help the young woman. Apart from that, she was convinced that Janet had potential to be more than passable as a white witch. Channelling her energies in that direction might help her deal with the traumas she'd recently gone through. "Besides," Gloria went on, " I want to stick around in Stirling to see if anything comes of the warning Neil gave us." "Ah, our tame Fey," Beresford said. "I wonder whatever happened to him. Didn't show when the chips were down."

Gloria didn't respond. Personally, she feared that Neil had come to harm at the hands of Koldunya. He didn't seem the type to disappear when the going got tough. True, she hardly knew him. Their first encounter had been spectacular to say the least – but other than that, he'd struck her as sincere in what he'd said. She intended to monitor the situation for a while. Just in case. She also hoped that Neil might resurface for other reasons. He'd told her that he liked to be more subtle in the sex-act than how he had performed for her that first time. She was curious about what that might be like.

Part two - Harbinger.

Chapter Twenty Nine - The Magnificent Seven. (Friday 15th May 1980.)

It was just after seven o'clock and the lounge bar was filling up. The pub was in converted farm buildings and the décor reflected that. There were stools in the shape of sheep and some of the animal stalls had been retained to provide convenient alcoves for the patrons. In one of these alcoves was a group of seven women. The women had been brought together by Gloria Garcia in the aftermath of the hunt, she and other Venatores had conducted for the witch, Koldunya. Four of the women were survivors of sexual assault by Koldunya's male stooge, Garry Wallace. The other three were Gloria herself, her apprentice – Diane Hastings and Ann Graham – the former live-in girlfriend of Wallace. The group had been assembled almost accidentally – but had coalesced into something special.

Gloria hadn't initially set out to bring the women together. When the witch and her male associate were dead, the Venatores' interest in the matter was concluded. The officer in charge of the mission, Tom Beresford, had no interest in the victims of the wicked creatures they pursued. His entire focus was on hunting down and destroying the evil-doers. Gloria had to admit that he was very good at this – but his approach lacked humanity in her opinion. During Koldunya's recent brief reign of terror, women had been sexually assaulted and brutalized. Men had also been victimized. Five had been brutally and ritually murdered. The women though, did not understand what had happened to them. They had been made to feel compliant in their own abuse. Wallace had employed mind-control magic to bend the women to his will. The murdered men were beyond help – but the women had questions that needed answered. Otherwise – how could they ever be able to heal. Gloria had stayed on in Stirling for a variety of reasons. One of these was to offer some solace to Wallace's innocent victims.

These victims had been held in protective custody at the Venatores' hotel without any clear explanation of why it was happening – other than that Wallace was dangerous. Whenever the women sought an explanation of why they had complied so easily with Wallace's instructions – even though they really hadn't wanted to – they were met with avoidance and obfuscation. Then it was all over and the women were abandoned to return to their everyday lives, with not a clue about why things had transpired the way they had. Gloria was a white witch as well as a Venatorc officcr. As such, her empathy was finely tuned. She had begun working with Janet right from the start, as she was severely traumatized, having been brutalized sexually by Wallace. It was, in fact, Janet who had finally killed Koldunya, by jamming the witch's own knife into her throat. Gloria had picked up on a kernel of magic within Janet. She thought the young woman had potential for becoming a white witch like herself.

Gloria had reached out to Michelle Wylder, Jenny Tait and Ruth O'Hanlon one by one. She wanted to give them some context into why they had complied with Wallace's sexual assaults on them without protest. She spoke to Michelle first and found it hard going – until she decided to skirt Venatore protocols and tell the truth. It was a risk speaking, to civilians about The Shadow World. Magic might well have been seen as an outlandish and perhaps insane explanation for what had happened – but Michelle seized on it and accepted it right away. It actually made sense of what had happened. Michelle immediately felt better in herself. The sexual assault had still happened and that continued to make her feel dirty but at least she could stop blaming herself for not resisting. It was a start. Gloria adopted the same approach to the other two women, with more or less the same result. She did have an aura about her that made people inclined to believe what she told them.

The six women, including Diane, began meeting up regularly. They were able to share their experiences safely and with people who understood what they were talking about. Bringing Ann into the fold was a bit more problematic. Janet had, after all, been shagging Ann's boyfriend, Garry Wallace, behind her back. It was finding a pair of Janet's knickers that had first alerted Ann to the fact that he was two-timing her. Ann had briefly succumbed to Wallace's mind control, when he had come, intent on doing harm to her and her two daughters. She had broken free, with the help of a magical amulet and had attacked him – almost killing him, a few hours before Koldunya actually did. Gloria had spent time with the four other women, prior to approaching them. Ann was a stranger to her – but she still felt it was important to speak to her. It turned out that Ann had more knowledge than the others, having been befriended by Neil Mac Mannanan – one of the Fey and the person who had given her the amulet.

Janet was apprehensive about meeting Ann. She feared her wrath. As it turned out, she needn't have worried. Ann proved to be a wonderfully warm and empathetic person. She assured Janet that there was only one scumbag in this situation – and it wasn't her. Wallace was the only one to blame. It was hard for Ann. Wallace had turned out to be a despicable and depraved individual, yet she had spent two years with him and shared a home and bed. Now he was dead. It was a lot to process. Nevertheless Ann responded graciously to Janet. She actually took the younger woman under her wing and they became friends.

As Gloria got to know the women better, she came to realise that Michelle, Jenny and Ruth also had that kernel of magic inside them – just like Janet. Now the incidence of this occurring in the general population was very small. The chances of four women in such a tiny group exhibiting a similar characteristic was extremely remote – astronomically so. Gloria had to assume that it was connected to their experience at the hands of Garry Wallace. It was like he had somehow infected them with magic. Something residual had been left with them. None of the known victims from Koldunya's previous forays had survived – so this phenomenon had never been observed before. Gloria was duty-bound to report this to her superiors – and she did so. They were very interested and allowed her to stay on in Stirling to observe the women and see how things progressed. As the magic used against the women was evil in nature, there was an obvious worry that the women might become corrupted. Over the ensuing months, Gloria saw no indication of this happening. It still required monitoring though.

Gloria was not a particularly powerful witch. Belonging to the white branch of witchcraft, precluded the use of many powerful amplifiers on ethical grounds. The black branch had no such compunctions. The women acted primarily as a support group for each other but they also indulged in some experimentation in witchcraft. Ann was not excluded. The amulet she wore seemed to have endowed her with some magical efficacy also. They found that working together, their power was boosted exponentially. These experiments help bond the women even closer. In truth, they became a true sisterhood. They even began jokingly referring to themselves as the "Seven Sisters". But now, their companionship was coming to an end. Their gathering in the pub was in the nature of a farewell get-together. Gloria was being recalled to Spain and Diane was being assigned a new mentor in London.

Chapter Thirty - A Bad End to The Night. (Friday 15th May 1980.)

Pat Turner was angry. She'd just witnessed her boyfriend snogging his ex. She had been severely tempted to confront them – but she was not a lover of drama. Making a public scene was not her thing. Instead, Pat opted for getting her coat and storming out of the club. She resolved never to see the cheating scumbag again. It was a pleasant enough night weatherwise. There was still plenty of people and cars about – so she felt perfectly safe. Kirkcaldy was not regarded as a particularly dangerous place. There was a taxi-rank down on the esplanade and that was her destination. It was early enough that the pubs were still open. On impulse, Pat decided that she needed a stiff drink before getting a taxi. She diverted into the lounge-bar of the first pub she came to.

The lounge was quite busy and Pat felt a bit exposed, being the only unaccompanied female in the place. Nevertheless, she made her way to the bar and ordered a large Jack Daniels and coke. She perched on a barstool, regretting her decision to come in here. She dreaded someone trying to pick her up. She was in no mood for any such hassle. In consequence, Pat gulped her drink down rather hastily. She had a nasty itch between her shoulder blades – as if someone was watching her. A quick glance round didn't seem to confirm her gut-feeling. No-one was paying any attention to her – as far as she could see. Still – she felt spooked. Pat rationalized that her uneasiness just stemmed from being upset by what had gone previously. Quickly, she finished her drink and left.

Outside, Pat felt easier. She set off briskly for the esplanade and the taxis. It would take about five minutes – if she stayed on the main thoroughfares but there was a shortcut that eliminated much of the distance. It was a narrow alleyway that led directly from the street Pat was on, downhill to the waterfront. The passageway was dark but only about twenty to thirty or so paces long. Had it been a greater distance, Pat would doubtless have avoided it but she would traverse it in less than minute, so that was the route she chose to go. All she wanted now, was to be in the taxi and home as soon as possible. Her thoughts turned to what she'd witnessed at the club and her anger flared again. With a quick glance around – and seeing nothing untoward in her vicinity – Pat entered the alley. With only a few steps until she reached the end of the alley, Pat suddenly felt a sting on her neck, just below her left ear. Seconds away from safety, she collapsed to the ground.

Pat came back to consciousness, with a bitter liquid being poured into her mouth. Reflexively she swallowed but some of the liquid spilled from her mouth and ran down her cheeks. Spluttering, Pat tried to sit up but found she couldn't. Her hands were somehow secured above her head, as she lay prone on the ground. Then she discovered that her ankles were also tethered. Panic swelled in her, as her head began to clear and she realised the perilous nature of her situation. It got immediately worse. She was naked. "Ah – you're awake at last," someone said. The voice was soft, mellow and sounded kind. Somehow, that made it even creepier. "I've given you something to keep you awake while we conclude our business together," the voice went on. "Can't have you passing out on me. That ruins the fun."

Pat strained at her bonds, frantically trying to get her bearings. Unbelievably – she was still in the alley. She could see the street, a matter of only a few feet away. A car went past and she could see and hear people walking and talking. She filled her lungs and screamed desperately for help. No-one responded – even though she continued to plead at the top of our voice for what seemed a long time. All the while, Pat struggled with her restraints – twisting and writhing in an attempt to break free. Her captor was above her head and out of her line of sight. Eventually he spoke again. "Calm down, pretty," he said. "You're just wearing yourself out. No-one can hear you – and nobody will come into this little alley while we're busy. We won't be disturbed. So – let's get to work – eh?" Pat stopped screaming but found herself whimpering instead. "I'm not going to rape you," came the voice. "I know your thoughts have probably strayed in that direction – but my appetites are somewhat different."

Pat sensed movement and finally her captor revealed himself to her. She screamed again. He was wearing the most hideous and lifelike mask. It had grey warty skin, a long hooked nose that protruded far from the face and a cruel, thin-lipped slash of a mouth. Yellow, shining eyes completed the horror of this apparition. "My name is Keranrodai." The thing said. "It means – the one who goes before. You have the honour of being my first human in centuries." He knelt down on the ground beside the terrified woman. She held her breath – fearing whatever would happen next. All the while she was aware of people and cars passing in the street below. All were completely oblivious to her plight.

The man produced a small, vicious looking knife and held it in front of Pat's horrified eyes. She cried out in pain when he lowered the knife and cut into the front of her left thigh. He made one slow incision and then another parallel to it. It was agony – excruciating and prolonged. Pat was screaming now – loudly and non-stop – but still no-one in the nearby street paid any attention. This had to be a nightmare. Surely she'd wake up soon. Her tormentor was holding something else in front of her eyes. It was about six inches long and dripping blood. With a jolt of extreme horror and terror, Pat realised that this was a strip of her own flesh. The creature leered at her, tilted his head back and dropped the morsel into his mouth. Slowly he chewed, with a blissful expression on his face as he savoured the taste. This was not a nightmare – at least not the sleeping kind – and it had only just begun.

It was perhaps an hour and a half later that the woman finally expired. She had bled out from the many pieces of flesh that had been sliced from her body. Keranrodai was replete. He had relished the taste of her – particularly enjoying the cheeks. The drink he'd administered to the woman, had kept her from going into shock or fainting. It had kept her awake, alive, kicking and screaming throughout his feast. It had been ever such a long time since he'd enjoyed such a meal – or indeed so much fun. For centuries he'd been incorporeal – gliding through the world – seeing much but unable to effect anything. He had flitted amongst the trees, watching, when Koldunya had enacted her erotic display, with her pet human on the hill. He'd known then that his time was coming. Now, he had a body and a mission. He had to prepare the way for the Mother.

Keranrodai regarded the lifeless body at his feet. The woman's body was drenched in blood. He thought she had never looked so beautiful as she did now. There was no actual word for the kind of being he was. Perhaps, demon came closest. He looked with affection, one last time on the mutilated woman. She had given him sustenance and entertainment – and for that he was grateful. He had to build his strength. There was much to do. Keranrodai shifted into his human disguise – a fairly nondescript youngish man – and removed the spell that had kept the alleyway free from human perception. The bloody corpse would be discovered soon enough. That was good. Part of his mission was to spread fear, alarm and paranoia through the human population. He left the scene discretely. It was time to be about his Mother's work.

Chapter Thirty One - A New Mission. (Saturday 16th May 1980.)

Gloria awoke to the strident ringing of her hotel room telephone. She struggled reluctantly awake – not best pleased. It wasn't often she let her hair down but she'd certainly done so last night. Much alcohol had been consumed. It had been fun but sad also. The women in her little group (or coven – as someone had described it last night) were the first friends she had made in some considerable time. She would be sad to leave them behind. Gloria glanced at her watch. It wasn't even eight o'clock yet. Who could be calling her at this time on a Saturday morning? She'd intended to have an easy day today – recovering from her hangover. Tomorrow, Gloria was meeting with the girls for a farewell bar lunch and on Monday, she was flying home to Spain.

Gloria fumbled the phone to her ear. "Hello," she croaked. Her head was thumping. "Hi Gloria," said the voice on the other end. "You're sounding rough. Heavy night?" Gloria was in no mood. The voice sounded familiar but in her disorientated state, she couldn't place it. "Who is this?" she said, snippily. "It's Tom Beresford. Sorry to disturb you on the weekend but there's something we'd like you to check out. It's more or less on your doorstep." Gloria composed herself. "Ok – what is it?" she said – more civilly this time. "There's been a rather grisly murder in Fife. Kirkcaldy in fact. Now that wouldn't necessarily be of interest to us – but – there's also been a series of animal mutilations over a period of three days – starting near Stirling and progressing daily into Fife. Now, if they are connected – then we may have a problem. You still have your Home Office accreditation, so I've set up a contact meeting for you with the police in Fife. It's a D.I. Boyle who's heading the investigation but your contact is a D.S. Brunton. He'll liaise with you and fill you in on the details. They'll be expecting you around 1100. I'd appreciate it if you could give me a call back this afternoon with your gut feeling about whether it has any supernatural connotations or not."

The last thing Gloria wanted was to work with Beresford again. She found the man callous and oblivious to the human beings devastated by the monsters the Venatores hunted down. Nevertheless, he was effective – so perhaps, on balance, he did benefit innocent lives that would otherwise fall victim to the threats Beresford eliminated. Besides – what he was presently asking, was merely a fact-finding expedition. Gloria wasn't much in the mood for a drive that day but she was a Venatore and duty called. Her stomach couldn't face food just yet, so she decided to skip breakfast. Instead she phoned reception and had them deliver a pot of strong ,black coffee. She swallowed down a cup when it arrived and then went for a shower. After the shower and another coffee, she was feeling a bit more focussed, but not yet at her best. The drive to Kirkcaldy would take about an hour – maybe slightly more , so she decided that she had a little time to kill before she needed to set off. Diane was in a room, just along the corridor. Gloria decided to share the misery and include Diane in her little road trip. She had just got to her feet to go and knock on her apprentice's door, when a knock came to her own.

Gloria opened the door, half expecting to see Diane there. Instead it was Neil Mac Mannanan. Gloria was stunned. "What happened to you?" she eventually blurted out. "Where the hell have you been?" "It's a bit of a long story," Neil replied. "Can I come in?" "Give me the short version," Gloria said stepping aside. Neil entered the room and sat on the only chair. Gloria followed and perched on the edge of the bed. "Ok. Spill." She said. "I didn't abandon you that night," Neil began. "I confronted Koldunya in the park but she had a banishment amulet – a Dibirt Na Siog. It is particularly effective against Fey. Anyway – it threw me into a hell dimension – populated with multitudes of demons and even a handful of dragons. It took me quite some time, to fight my way clear."

Neil paused for a moment but Gloria maintained a poker face. She was wary of the Fey's gift of the Golden Tongue and didn't want to accept anything at face value, until she had time to evaluate it. "Anyway," Neil went on. "When I got home my King was not best pleased. He did not accept the banishment amulet as an excuse. The bottom line is that I had failed. He removed me from my post of Sheriff and appointed a distant cousin of mine in my stead – Brigid Nic Lyr. I have no official standing here – but I'm worried. There's a new tone in the magical harmonies of this place. Something disturbing. I believe it to be linked to the energy released on the witch's death – as I warned you previously. That's why I've come to see you. I want to help. There could be something nasty on the loose. By working together, we may be able to do something about it. There, that's the short version."

Gloria reflected for a moment or two and then said, "Ok – fair enough. You might well be right. If you've got a couple of hours, there's something I'd like your opinion on." Neil agreed immediately and Gloria filled him in on the bare details that she knew of the animal mutilations and the murder. All she could say about the latter was that there must be something significant about it, to have attracted attention from the Venatores. She was bending the rules to involve an unauthorised outside person in official business but she found that she actually genuinely trusted Neil. He did seem keen to help and he would doubtless have insights into the supernatural that mere humans wouldn't.

Half an hour later, they set off for Kirkcaldy in Gloria's car. "I've got a question for you," she said. "Is it normal for Fey to give magical artifacts to humans? Surely it could be dangerous if it fell into the wrong hands?" "Ah," Neil replied. "You're no doubt speaking of the amulet I gave to Ann Graham. A remarkable woman by the way. Well – the amulet was attuned specifically to her. So – no-one else could use it for any purpose. I did have to enter her mind in order to seek her signature vibration though." "Did Ann know you were doing it?" Gloria asked. "No – I hadn't revealed myself to her at that point. I suspected that trouble might be coming her way but I couldn't be certain. I also thought she might be instrumental in helping me track the witch, given her connection to Wallace. So I sought her out and had a long conversation with her. She had an ambition she wished to achieve and I helped her enact it. Most of what she experienced that night wasn't real. It was an idealised form of what she had in her own mind. Doing this, gave me the opportunity to find what I needed to tune the crystal."

Gloria was appalled. "You invaded a person's mind without her permission and used her as bait to try to trap Koldunya. I find that all very unethical – and in fact downright wrong." Neil shrugged. "Ethics has never featured much in my people's thinking," he said. "Success or failure are the only two criteria we factor in. What I did was successful and saved Ann's life – as well as her two daughters. All's well and all that. Besides, my people have been doing that kind of stuff to your people since we first came into contact, many centuries ago." "Doesn't make it right," Gloria said. "If you ever try that on me – I swear I'll kill you. Wait a minute……. did you use that on me the night we met." "No," Neil replied. "That was all me. Still – it's nice to know you thought it was that good." "Don't be getting big in the head," was Gloria's reply. "Any cock would have done that night. Yours just happened to be available." Despite their words and different viewpoints, Gloria found that she liked Neil and that worried her. Was it real or was it something he was doing to her?

They completed the journey pleasantly enough. They confined themselves to neutral subjects and idle chit-chat. After a couple of wrong turns, Gloria eventually found the Kirkcaldy police station. She asked for D.S. Brunton at the front desk and after only a couple of minutes, he appeared. He was a tall, dark-haired man in his late forties. Gloria identified herself and presented her credentials. She introduced Neil as a civilian consultant. Brunton got straight down to business. "The victim was Patricia Turner, aged twenty-three," he told them. "Her body was found just after eleven, by a group taking a short-cut down a dark alley, leading to the taxi rank on the waterfront. She was naked, lying on her back and her clothes were beside her. The victim had more than a hundred strips of flesh cut from her body. The excisions were all over the front of her body and face. Most of them were about six inches long, an inch across and an inch deep. None of the excised pieces were found at the sight. Our best guess, just now, is that the cause of death was blood loss due to the many wounds inflicted on her. The post-mortem will probably confirm this. Evidence suggests that she was murdered where she was found – yet, so far, nobody seems to have seen or heard anything. It's the weirdest and most disturbing murder I've ever seen. I don't know what kind of sick bastard could do such a thing."

When Brunton had finished his concise report, Gloria asked if it was possible to see the body. The policeman assented and conducted them to the mortuary. Gloria's stomach was still queasy from last night's festivities. She hadn't had anything to eat yet that day. The sight of Patricia Turner's body, almost tipped her over the edge. She'd seen many a gruesome sight in the course of her duties but this was the worst thing she'd ever encountered. It took all her will power not to throw up – not that there was anything in her stomach to do so. She was looking pretty green around the gills by the time they left the police station. She'd held herself together long enough to thank D.S. Brunton and make a dignified exit. She was grateful to be out in the fresh air again.

Gloria and Neil found a café and went in. She still couldn't face anything to eat but had a coffee. "So – what do you think," she asked Neil. "The murderer was definitely not human," he replied. "I caught a whiff of something hellish from the body. My guess is that it was some kind of ritual cannibalism. I suspect that something was feeding on the mutilated animals and has graduated onto humans. Believe me – there will be more." At the mention of cannibalism, Gloria lost interest even in her coffee. She just wanted to get back to her hotel room and curl up in bed.

Chapter Thirty Two - Secret Friends and Allies. (Sunday 17th May 1980.)

A good night's sleep and Gloria felt much better. There was also an idea taking root in her mind. She'd reported back to Beresford the previous afternoon. He had sounded distinctly unimpressed. "I'll probably send a small team to Fife," he had told her. "They can investigate further and see if there's anything of interest to us." Gloria hadn't been fully honest with him. She'd left out any mention of Neil. She wasn't sure why. Anyway – it wasn't her case. She was going back to Spain after all. She'd worked with the British Venatores for three years – as part of a Europe-wide exchange scheme, being chosen for her fluency in English. That time was now at an end and she had no desire to work under Beresford again. Nevertheless, she'd been annoyed at how dismissive he'd been of her report.

Neil had given Gloria his phone number when he'd left her last night. Apparently, he had a cottage a few miles outside Stirling. Diane was leaving on the Sleeper that night, to take up her new assignment in London. The group was meeting up for a bar lunch later. It was the last time they'd all be together for the foreseeable future. Gloria phoned Neil and invited him to meet her in her hotel later that evening. There was something she wanted to discuss with him. He agreed. Then she phoned her people in Spain and spoke to her superior requesting a fortnight's vacation time. She had it – and more – due. Besides – Gloria was a well-respected Venatore officer. Her superior didn't hesitate in granting her request.

The women enjoyed a convivial lunch and there were tearful farewells and hugs when it was over. Gloria didn't tell them about her change of plans – and felt extremely guilty about it. She planned to go off grid – to follow up on the horrific murder in Kirkcaldy in her own way. But first – she had to enlist Neil's aid. She needed the Fey's insight and knowledge. Her intuition told her that he knew more about what was going on than he'd yet told her. She also suspected that it was all tied into what Neil had told the Venatores whilst they were hunting Koldunya. There was something that scared him and she had to find out what it was.

Neil duly arrived, just after seven and Gloria got straight down to brass tacks. "Look," she said. "I'm not satisfied that Beresford is taking Patricia Turner's murder seriously enough. I also know he won't involve you in any way. He doesn't trust the Fey. Well – we're here on the ground and you know things that are relevant – even if you're reluctant to talk about them. So I propose that you and I team up and see if we can track this killer down. I won't be constrained by Venatore rules or protocols and we have a head start on any team that Beresford might send. So – what do you think?"

Neil looked amused. "You're going renegade?" he said. "Not exactly," Gloria replied. "I've just got a feeling we need to act quickly and between us, we might just have what it takes to do the job. Let's face it – the Venatores don't trust you and I don't think you trust them. I'm suggesting we trust each other." "Well," Neil said, "I'm already a kind of renegade. When my King took away my Sheriffdom, he ordered me not to return to the human realm – on pain of permanent exile. As you see, I defied him – so I can never go back to my homeland. It's ok though. I like humans and don't mind living amongst them – and anyway, things can change over time. You see – I feel responsible for not suppressing Koldunya in time to stop her doing the damage I fear she has. So that's why I'm here – and yes – I would be happy to go renegade with you, though I fear that things might already have gone too far for anyone to rectify."

Gloria was relieved. She knew that Neil's help would be invaluable. "Great," she said. "Now I know you have an idea what's going on. So tell me." Neil took a deep breath. "Ok," he said. "All I can tell you is the legend that's known to my people. Much of it is shrouded in mystery but my people take it very seriously. So this is the story. Over two millennia ago a child was born in land to the north of here. Her birth was heralded by terrible and ominous portents. The local people were terrified. In those days there was a Druidic settlement where Cambuskenneth Abbey now stands. The Druids had been alerted by the disturbances they had sensed in the ether but before they moved to investigate, the people came in a deputation to them, bringing the child.

The Druids examined the baby and what they found was dire. When she grew to adulthood, she would unleash War, Famine, Plague and Pestilence. Her nature was unequivocally malevolent and destructive. A faction among the Druids wanted to kill the child there and then but their chief, an individual called Caradoc, refused to countenance this. Instead he undertook to raise the girl himself and see if he could bend her undoubted power from evil to good. For a time, it seemed that Caradoc's approach was going to work – but then, in the girl's fourteenth year, her true nature came to the fore. Villagers from the nearby settlements visited the Druid's enclosure, bringing produce and seeking aid or healing from the Druids. One group somehow offended the girl. No-one knows what the offence was – but she ripped seven of them to pieces without laying a finger on them. She simply used the power of her mind.

The Druids were appalled. Two of them tried to intervene and were similarly obliterated. The girl stormed from the Druid's settlement and nobody dared get in her way. Caradoc was saddened but he was a powerful mage. He knew he could not overcome the girl face to face but that night he tracked her down with six of his brethren in attendance. He cloaked them from the girl's attention until she finally went to sleep. There, amongst the trees, Caradoc put a spell on her, that would keep her asleep during the many centuries to come. The Druids picked the girl up and bore her to the Abbey Craig. That's the hill on which the Wallace Monument now stands. Caradoc had a magical key that opened a passage to a chamber deep within the hill. They deposited the girl there and departed. Caradoc closed the entrance to the passageway and locked it. He then sent the key far away.

Caradoc was a friend of the Fey. My people visited him often. He shared the story with them and asked them to keep it in their memory – because there will come a time when the spell wears off. His hope was that, by that time, the Druids would have found a way to control her. Unfortunately, the Druids are now all gone and if they ever did find a solution, they didn't share it with anyone else. They never committed anything to writing either. So – when the girl eventually does awaken, there is nothing and no-one to stop her. My people have been monitoring the situation for centuries now. We have become aware recently that there are stirrings within the hill. We do not know if the girl was ever given a name. We know her only as the Adversary. Our fear with Koldunya was, that her invasive method of extracting power from the intrinsic ambient magic of a place, was disturbing the sleep of the Adversary and hastening her awakening. The shockwave of energy released by the witch's death, might just have been the final straw.

Caradoc said that the nature of the rock surrounding the prison chamber was such that its occupant could not use her powers to break free. In order for her to escape, the passageway would have to be opened by Caradoc's magical key. That is why he sent it away. Where it is hidden nobody knows. Unfortunately, that won't prevent the Adversary from liberating herself. Caradoc foretold that, once she is awake, the Adversary will project her psyche to ensnare one of the many incorporeal entities that hover and dance through the ether. She will endow it with a body and send it to locate and recover the magical key that secures entry and exit to the hill. It is possible that the perpetrator of the animal mutilations and the foul murder – presuming it is one and the same being – is that entity. If so – this is the harbinger of the coming terror and the Adversary is awake. That's why I said, it may already be too late."

Chapter Thirty Three - Alfresco. (Sunday 17th May 1980.)

John Hanson drew the car into a shrub surrounded layby, next to some university buildings and parked. It was a secluded nook and the vehicle would be mostly concealed from casual eyes. He and his passenger, Ann Graham, got out of the car. They were in the grounds of Stirling University. It had to be one of the most picturesque campuses around. It had a very rural wide-open feel to it. The University buildings were loosely scattered around a small body of water, called Airthrey Loch. The loch itself was surrounded by gently sloping, broad grass lawns. A single track road led past the layby where John had parked his car.

The couple crossed the road and stepped onto the grass. They had only been seeing each other for about a month and John was very much intoxicated by Ann. She was a fascinating woman – funny, passionate and with an amazing body. Their lovemaking, to date, had been fairly sedate and conventional. John had no complaints – in fact, he hadn't even realised this until Ann had suggested they might want to spice it up a bit. John hadn't been offended. On the contrary, he had been intrigued and excited. Ann wasn't planning anything terribly outrageous. She didn't want to fall into the same trap as she had with Garry – where they only had sex in the commission of some voyeuristic act. All she had proposed was, doing it outdoors.

Ann was well versed in the preparation required to carry out such an operation smoothly. She'd dug out the long dark green coat she had utilized for various sexcapades with Garry. When buttoned up, it covered her from neck to calf. Wearing only a pair of boots, Ann put on the coat. No-one could tell that she was naked underneath. Thus attired, they had set off for the University. It was a pleasant mild evening. They had waited till after it was full dark to embark on their jaunt. There wasn't much of a moon, so visibility was low. There was no-one around at that side of the loch when they arrived. They walked a short distance onto the grass and found what they agreed was a suitable spot. After a quick look round, Ann took off her coat.

Ann's nakedness immediately aroused John. Being out in the open made it doubly exciting somehow. Ann laid her coat on the grass and told John to lay down on it. She knelt beside him, undid his belt and tugged his trousers down. His member immediately stood to attention. Ann leaned forward and took him into her mouth. Holding the base of his dick with her hand, she slide her lips slowly down its length and then back up again. John groaned with pleasure. He began to relax. He'd been tense in case anyone should chance upon them but had reasoned that their line of sight was unobstructed and they would see someone coming before they were spotted themselves. Another couple of lengths from Ann's soft lips and John was no longer caring.

Ann kept up her oral ministrations on John's cock for a couple of minutes but stopped before he shot his load. She wanted some genital stimulation herself, so she moved over and straddled the prone man. Positioning his prick at the entrance to her vagina, Ann pressed down and took him inside her. She began to rock to and fro. As she got into her rhythm, Ann began to gyrate as she rocked. John was absolutely enthralled. Her body was always entrancing but seeing it in this form of motion was the most erotic thing he'd ever witnessed. He reached up to fondle her breasts and lost himself in the visual and physical pleasure of the moment. John was transported. The sexual bliss grew and grew and John lost all track of time. The pressure mounted more and more within him and then it released in a mind-blowing orgasm.

Ann had enjoyed the experience well enough but it hadn't hit the heights for her. Maybe John would get better – given patience, time and some coaching. He was a nice guy though and he treated her well – so she wasn't considering getting rid of him just yet. Sex wasn't everything, after all – but it did figure quite highly in Ann's needs. She was a sexual person. A fact she freely admitted to herself. They disentangled themselves and got to their feet. Ann put on and buttoned her coat. John pulled up his trousers and buckled his belt. Once they were both ready, they walked back towards the car, hand in hand.

When John and Ann were about twenty feet from the car, a figure emerged from the shadow of the surrounding shrubs. It was a campus security man. How he'd got there unseen, Ann couldn't fathom. True – his dark green uniform blended into the background – but even so – he must have been stealthy in his approach. Ann had no doubt that he'd been spying on them – which didn't particularly bother her. He was a big guy – tall and burly. "Do you know it's illegal to park here after business hours?" the security man said. "I'm very sorry – we were just leaving," John said in a conciliatory tone. The couple had stopped where they were, the moment the man had appeared. "You better co-operate or I'll call the police," the security man said. "I'll tell them I saw you breaking into premises also – unless you do as I say. You miss – unbutton your coat."

John uttered a protest but Ann put a hand on his arm to still him. This was just the kind of scenario that Garry would have manufactured. Ann would probably have relished it – being ordered to expose her naked body by an authority figure – and one in uniform at that. Her hands moved to her coat and she began to undo the buttons. It was almost like she was on automatic pilot. Then – Ann stopped. It was her body and she would only show it when she wanted to – and then – it would be as much for her own gratification as for whoever was watching. Besides – she didn't like this guy. There was very much the stench of a bully from him. "No," she said, "we're going now. So get out of our way."

The security man's face contorted in rage. "You'll do what I say," he snarled. "You're going to give me what you've just given him." He started forward, menacingly. John was much smaller but, to his credit, he gamely stepped in front of Ann and confronted the other man. The big guy punched him hard – then taking hold of the front of his shirt – punched him twice more. Ann cringed at the hollow sound of the blows landing on John's face. John collapsed in a heap and the big man turned his attention fully on Ann. She was on the verge of panic. To her extreme alarm, he rushed her. He never got within six feet. Ann threw out her hands, palms forward, in an attempt to ward him off. The large burly man was stopped in his tracks and hurled backwards – to crash violently into the shrubs, ten to fifteen feet away.

Chapter Thirty Four - The Fey Detective. (Monday 18th May 1980.)

First thing in the morning, Gloria and Neill set off for Kirkcaldy again. Gloria had used a hire-car, paid for by the Venatores while she was based in Stirling on official business. Now that she was going temporarily off the books, she'd had to return it. Likewise, with her hotel room. She could, of course have paid for these things herself but that might well have alerted Venatore officials to what she was doing. She'd intended to move to a hotel in the Fife area but Neil had offered her his spare room and she'd accepted. He had a country cottage in a little hamlet called Pitgabhar – about fifteen miles outside Stirling and not far from Fife. Gloria had been initially surprised at how spick and span the cottage was – not something she expected from a single man living on his own. Then, she remembered – if you could use magic, housework was easy.

They had sat late into the night talking. Mostly, they discussed the case and how to go about pursuing it. Later though, Gloria had told Neil about the group of women she'd grown close to. He was intrigued by her description of the magic she had sensed inside them. It was not totally unheard of, he told her. Such a transference of magical potential usually came from something that was given from one to the other – the amulet he'd given to Ann, for instance. Any magic she had, would be down to that. With the other women, it had to result from Wallace's ejaculation inside their bodies. The magic must have been carried in his semen. It seemed that magic could be a sexually transmitted disease.

Gloria had agreed that, after they were finished with their present task, she would introduce him to the women of her group. He was interested in evaluating them. First though, they were on their way to Kirkcaldy in Neil's red Ford Capri. Gloria wasn't quite sure why. Neil had said he wanted to interview witnesses. When she pointed out that there were none, he simply said that, in fact, there were most likely many but that not everyone could speak to them. He was being mysterious and Gloria decided to humour him. When they got to Kirkcaldy, Neil drove along the waterfront until he located the alleyway where the murder had taken place. He parked the car next to it. "Ok," he said, "there are many things in this world that humans are unaware of – sprites, pixies, dryads and assorted spirits of the air etc. They are everywhere – and everywhere invisible to mortals. I can summon those who were in the alley that night and question them on what they saw. It's a Fey thing. Wait in the car I won't be long."

Gloria didn't know if Neil was winding her up. Was this some kind of Fey humour? But she'd seen many fantastic things in the course of her work. Her knowledge of the Fey was not extensive. After meeting Neil previously, she'd looked up all that the Venatores had on them. It didn't amount to much. The main message had been that the Fey were not to be trusted. They could worm their way into your confidence and make you believe the most outlandish things. Was that what was happening to her? She didn't fully understand why she was doing what she was doing. Going off the books was distinctly frowned upon by the Venatores. If she was found out, it would seriously damage, or even end, her career. Gloria was ambivalent about this. She appreciated having the logistical support of the organisation but there were many restrictive elements also. She also felt that the wrong people were being promoted to senior positions. They lacked humanity and empathy, in her opinion. It all seemed to be about acquiring power and furthering careers. Tom Beresford was a prime example. Anyway – her gut told her she was doing the right thing and that she could trust Neil. Time would tell.

Time went by and Gloria began to get impatient. She was on the point of going to look for him, when Neill emerged from the alley and came back to the car. He got in and sat for a moment or two without saying anything. Gloria's impatience kicked in. "Well," she said," did you get through to them? What did they say?" "Sorry," Neil replied, "I was thinking. The spirits don't communicate in words as such. They share sights, sounds, smells and tones. So this is what I gleaned from them. The murderer is a shapeshifter of some kind. He can present as a human male but his underlying being is goblin-like. He brought his victim down with a potion dipped dart from a blowpipe. While she was unconscious, he stripped and shackled her. Then he waited for her to come round, before giving her another potion to drink. This, I believe, was to keep her conscious throughout the rest of the ordeal. When she was awake, the shapeshifter cut a strip of flesh from her and ate it. This sequence was repeated many times until the victim finally expired."

"That more or less confirms what we thought happened," Gloria said. "It doesn't take us any further forward." "Not so," Neil responded. "We now know that we are looking for a shapeshifter – and the spirits shared his tone with me." "What's that?" Gloria asked. "Everything, animate or inanimate, has its own vibration," Neil answered. "It's as individual as human fingerprints. It means I will recognise this shapeshifter, if we ever encounter him. It also means that, if we get relatively close to him, I'll be able to track him. I haven't told you the most interesting part though." Gloria waited but Neil was obviously enjoying the drama and wanted her to ask the question. "Ok," she eventually said. "What's the most interesting part?" "I wasn't the first to summon the spirits regarding this matter," he told her. "Someone else did so yesterday." "Another Fey?" Gloria asked. "No," came the reply. "This is the interesting bit. It was a human man. I didn't think that was possible."

"So – are you annoyed that a mere human can do a Fey thing?" Gloria asked. "Not at all," Neil replied. "I'm intrigued, is all. It seems someone else is hunting the same quarry as us." "You see," Gloria said – determined to get an answer to something that was bothering her. "You are Fey – with all these powers – able to do wondrous things. Why have you taken up with me – a mere human? It's not as if I can get you access to Venatore resources. You don't really need me." Neil reflected for a moment. "But you're not a "mere human" – are you? You're also a witch and a Venatore officer. You have skills. Besides – I like you. I liked the way you introduced yourself to me. Mostly though – my intuition tells me that you have a crucial part to play in this matter and I'm famed for the accuracy of my intuition." "It wasn't particularly accurate when it came to handling Koldunya – Was it?" Gloria rejoindered. "She blew you into a hell dimension, after all." "Well – it's not an exact science," Neil smiled.

"So, what do we do now?" Gloria asked. "I suggest we go back to my place," Neil said. "I've got maps there – some very, very old. I think we should look for ancient Druid sites. Perhaps we can find a place where Caradoc might have hidden the key. Once we determine the Harbinger's direction of travel, it might give us an idea where he is going. I assume he has some means of detecting the key's whereabouts." "How do we determine his direction of travel?" Gloria asked. "I'm afraid," Neil said. "Our only course is to wait for another mutilated body to be found." Gloria did not like this answer at all. "Can you not track him using your Air Spirits?" "It would take too long," Neil said. "Communing with them takes a lot of energy. I can only do it, at most, once a day. It would take weeks to even find the general direction he took after leaving the scene of the murder. Unlike in the alley, which is a confined area, we wouldn't have any focus to work with. It's impractical and I'm afraid he will kill again soon. It is deeply unfortunate and dreadful but I don't believe there's anything else we can do." Reluctantly, Gloria had no choice but to agree.

Monday night was Group Night. Even though Gloria and Diane were gone, the women fully intended to continue meeting. This was the first night with just the five of them and all of them had something to say. Janet kicked proceedings off. She'd had a phone call from Gloria, right before she'd left for the Halfway House. They used a back room in the pub, just outside Stirling, for their gatherings. Gloria had told her of a change in plans. She had not gone home to Spain but was temporarily working with the Fey, Neil, on a pressing new investigation. Gloria wanted to let them know she was still in Scotland and that she was thinking of them. Neil – and indeed the Fey – had been discussed extensively in the group, given his involvement with Ann and Gloria herself. Neither woman had wholly divulged their dealings with the good-looking Fey. He had facilitated a powerfully erotic opportunity for Ann to indulge her predilection for exhibitionism and he'd provided Gloria with a therapeutic, rugged fuck, minutes after meeting her. These two episodes had been strategically left out of the women's accounts.

Ann spoke next. She told her friends about what had happened at the University – how she'd hurled a large man for yards, without even touching him. "I think I might have killed him," she said. "I looked in the papers this morning but I didn't see anything about it." "Maybe be in the local rag this Wednesday," Michelle suggested. "I wouldn't worry," said Janet. "It sounds like he got what he deserved. God knows how many women he'd molested previously." There was a general murmur of approval. "It's not just that," Ann said. "I don't know how I did it and I'm afraid I might do it again without meaning to. It's a bit worrying."

"I had something weird today also," Michelle said. "I wasn't really sure it had actually happened at the time. I was having lunch and reading. I had a can of coke on the table. I was about to reach for it and suddenly it was in my hand. I swear I hadn't moved. It freaked me out a bit." "Has anyone else had any strange experiences?" Janet asked. "I have," Ruth said. She was only seventeen and was usually fairly diffident in group meetings. The loss of her virginity to Wallace's vile depredation had hit her hard. All the women had suffered by Wallace's actions. Their reactions to this varied.. Some were recovering quicker than others. Ruth was probably having the most difficulty coming to terms with the situation she'd found herself in. "I know it's silly, but I've got a phobia about spiders," Ruth went on. "I'm terrified of them. Anyway – I was watching tv last night, when I saw a spider running along the arm of my chair. It was coming towards me really fast. I know they can't hurt me but I freaked. Then – it just kind of exploded. I wasn't going to say anything. I thought there must be some explanation but after what's been said, I think I must have made it happen."

There was much consternation around the table. No-one was quite sure what was going on. They were obviously aware of the magic within them. They'd experimented with it under Gloria's tutelage but they had never managed to do anything individually, remotely as powerful as the recent occurrences. Any true manifestations had only happened when they were working together in unison. The women ventured theories but couldn't reach any satisfactory conclusions. They hadn't enough knowledge of the subject to do so. Eventually Janet said, "Gloria said that we should keep what she's doing private – just between ourselves. If anyone came asking about her, she would like us to say that she'd gone home to Spain – as far as we knew. She gave me a phone number to let her know if anyone was asking questions. If you like, I'll go and phone her just now, to see if she has any advice?" Everyone seemed relieved at Janet's suggestion. Gloria had only been gone one day but they were already feeling a bit lost without her. Janet went off to the payphone, while the others sat back and waited to hear what Gloria would say.

Chapter Thirty Five - The Vagaries of Magic. (Monday 18th May 1980.)

Gloria's conscience was bothering her at several levels. Firstly – she felt guilty about deceiving her friends. It was one thing being less than truthful with the Venatores but the women in her group were close to and trusted her. Gloria knew she wasn't being totally logical. She questioned the logic for what she was doing with Neil. She couldn't totally shake the idea that he was controlling her in some way. He was Fey after all. Nevertheless – her gut told her she was doing the right thing and she had learned to trust her gut over the years. Besides, what did Neil have to gain from any subterfuge? That particular pang of guilty conscience was easily assuaged by a phone call to Janet.

Far harder to shake, was Gloria's unease at waiting for another person to be cruelly murdered. It didn't sit well with her at all and she'd argued this out with Neil. Surely there was something more proactive that could be done in the pursuit of the killer? Were they even sure there would be another murder? Her trusted gut was of the opinion though, that there almost definitely would be and she thought it their duty to try and prevent this. She did manage to wring some concessions out of Neil. Tomorrow, they would go back to Fife and scout the area around Kirkcaldy, to see if Neil could detect the signature, as he put it tone, of their quarry. Perhaps, by chance, they may come close enough to the murderer for the Fey to sense him. During his time as Sheriff, Neil had built a network of human informants. This was extensive, as his fiefdom stretched south as far as the borders and north to include Angus. He had put out word to this network to be on the alert for unusual occurrences, especially nasty murders. None of Neil's informants had the ability to sense the killers presence. That was a Fey thing.

Gloria had other questions, If they did catch up to this shapeshifter, how would they deal with it? Could it be killed? Neil reckoned he had a special blade that would do the trick – but that would involve getting up close and personal. He did say that ordinary bullets might suffice, admitting that he didn't really know for sure. Pure iron and silver projectiles were also worth considering. These two metals were often anathema to eldritch beings.

Another big red flag for Gloria in this situation was the paucity of information regarding this, so called, Adversary. Where did she come from? Who were her parents? Surely she had been given some name other than what she was known as now? Gloria was quite disturbed that an infant could be judged and labelled as inherently evil. It seemed precipitate and unfair to her. Nowhere in the story was anything from the girl's side. Why had she killed the seven people? Had they done something vile to provoke her? It was hard to see what it was but perhaps she'd had a good reason to do what she did. Gloria had little doubt that the girl would indeed be hostile now. If she'd been put to sleep and imprisoned underground for millennia, she'd be pissed off too. If they truly believed she would bring death and destruction, why hadn't they killed her when she was vulnerable? Why kick the problem down the road for others to deal with – others who were Ill-prepared and didn't know nearly enough to handle the situation.

Neil could not enlighten Gloria any further. All he knew was the story that had been handed down to him. The Druids never wrote things down, he reminded her. It was actually a relief when the phone went and Neil answered it, to tell Gloria it was Janet and she wanted to talk with her. She took the phone and Janet quickly told her of the events that had worried the group members. Gloria, initially didn't feel there was anything too much to be concerned over. She had other priorities at the moment – but then she reflected – magic was new to these women and the incidents that had happened were actually quite disturbing. "Santa Maria," she said. "I leave you for one day and you start getting up to all sorts of mischief. Ok – I'm quite tied up at the moment. I don't know when I'll be free in the next few days but we're at a bit of an impasse at the moment – so I can come across right now. Give me half an hour or so. Oh – and I'll be bringing Neil with me. He has knowledge of magic that might be useful."

When Gloria hung up and told Neil what had happened, he gladly agreed to drive her to Stirling. It would be a blessed relief from her constant questions and agonising. It took them just over thirty minutes to get to the pub. When they entered the private back room, both Gloria and Neill immediately felt the latent magical potential from the assembled women. Gloria was particularly amazed. How could things have progressed so much in the short time since she last saw her friends. They sat down with the rest of the group and listened, while Ann, Michelle and Ruth recounted their stories once again.

When they had finished, Gloria asked Neil for his opinion. She was a witch but Neil was Fey. What had happened was outside Gloria's experience. Neil paused for a few seconds. Then he spoke. "Let me say, right from the start – magic is not a science. Not even the Fey fully understand it and all its nuances. Gloria has told me your history. Ann – the magic in you comes from the amulet I gave you. Each of us has a unique vibration – what I call a tone. The amulet was tuned to your own personal vibration. Even so – I'm surprised that the magic inside you seems to have grown. Something else is at play. The rest of you – I'm sorry to be indelicate – but you were *infected* with magic when Wallace assaulted you. It entered your bodies with his ejaculation. It's not totally unheard of but it is far from common. It has something to do with the chain of transference. Koldunya passed power to Wallace. He, in turn, inadvertently passed it on to you. It's not known whether this phenomenon happened with any of the other men Koldunya recruited. As far as we know, all the victims they sexually assaulted were murdered shortly after the initial assault. Maybe Wallace was something special or unusual. I'm afraid, nobody knows.

Anyway – it looks like the magical energy has been growing within you. As it does so – it is effecting other changes. By my reckoning, there are subtle changes being made to the very fabric of your bodies. Your personal vibrations are synchronising. They are moving into harmony with each other. I know these changes must be very scary for you all. You no doubt have a worry that, given its source, the magic may turn you to evil. Magic is neither good nor evil. It's simply magic. How you choose to use it, is what determines your future development. I believe you have all been getting stronger without realising it. I also believe that you will get stronger still. Learning to control your abilities is the key. Two of you were triggered by fear and alarm. That is a powerful motivator. Your incident Michelle was an unconscious act. Until you master your skills, try to be very deliberate in what you're doing. That lessens the chance of inadvertent manifestations.

The most exciting thing for me, is the harmonisation that is taking place with your *tones*. It means that together you will form a very powerful coven. Given that there are different sources and varieties of magic spread through the group, this is truly remarkable. Ann's is pure Fey. Gloria's is harder to read – but she seems to be the unifying factor in all this. She is the catalyst for the changes that are taking place. You have a unique and potent bond – the makings of an amazing coven."

"Why has this only come to light now?" Gloria asked. "I felt the increase in power the moment I entered this room. It wasn't like this yesterday." "I believe there was another member of your group," Neil replied. "Yes," Gloria said, "Diane – she was apprenticed to me for a year. She's been reassigned now." "My guess," Neil went on, "is that this Diane was a disruptor." There were murmurs of protest from around the table. Diane had been lovely, Everyone liked her. "I'm not saying anything against her," Neil assured them. "It's not something she was doing on purpose. Her inherent magic was not on the same wavelength as the rest of you. It's like when a radio signal is being jammed. When you are stronger, her influence won't have any effect on you but in your early development, she was inhibiting your progress."

There was more discussion and certain reassurances – particularly from the Fey. Both he and Gloria taught the others a few mind-focussing techniques. They both assured the women that, once they were free of their current mission, they would work with them to help develop and control their burgeoning powers. Gloria noted that none of her friends seemed to want out of this strange and undoubtedly scary trajectory they were now experiencing. In fact, some of them asked if there was anything they could do to assist her and her Fey friend in what they were presently engaged in. Gloria thanked them but said it was too early for them – maybe somewhere down the line but not yet.

Gloria and Neil left the women, satisfied that they'd done all they could in the short time available to them. If they could conclude their hunt for the Harbinger – and if they even survived that hunt – there was work to do with Gloria's Coven. Somehow, on the drive back, the subject of sleeping arrangements came up. Neil suggested that Gloria move into his bed. They'd already had sex, he pointed out and it would be a good way of unwinding. Gloria told him that sexual relations between colleagues was unprofessional. Neil responded that they weren't really colleagues – just friends who were pursuing a common interest. Gloria wasn't actually averse to the idea but she didn't want to agree too easily. As it happened, the decision wasn't required that night. The phone was ringing when they got into Neil's cottage. He answered and listened for a few moments. Then he turned to Gloria and said, "It seems there might have been another attack in Fife – only – the victim's still alive this time."

Chapter Thirty Six - Curiouser and Curiouser. (Monday 18th May 1980.)

They were in Neil's Capri again – heading for Fife. "Are you sure this is another attack by this Harbinger?" Gloria asked, "Not entirely – yet," Neil replied, "but the victim was mutilated." "Yeah – but the victim was left alive – that's not the same as last time," Gloria said. "We'll find out for sure in a bit," was Neil's reply. Before leaving, Neil had phoned a couple of his informants, one of whom worked for the police in Fife. As far as could be ascertained, there had been no contact made by the official Venatores – not even about the first murder. Beresford had obviously judged it not to be of interest. Gloria had suggested alerting to alert him to what they suspected was really happening. Neil was opposed to this. He reckoned there was nothing they could usefully do and they might just get in the way. Gloria wasn't convinced – but she agreed to hold off for the time being.

"Burntisland though," Gloria went on, "it's only a few miles away from the first murder. Surely he'd have moved further than that in three days?" "Who knows?" Neil replied. "Perhaps he's searching for the key in that area." I would have thought Caradoc would have sent it further afield than that," Gloria said. Neil just shrugged. "Ok," Gloria continued, " the Venatores aren't interested at the moment but what's your new Fey Sheriff doing?" Neil shrugged again. I don't know," he replied. "Probably not very much. She'll most likely just have a watching brief. I was more hands on and Koldunya, being Fey, was considered something we should deal with. Our people will not engage with the Adversary unless and until she becomes a threat to Fey interests. I don't think they want to provoke her." "So – it's just us," Gloria stated. "Not entirely," Neil replied. "There is the human that consulted the air spirits at the first murder site – though how he fits in, I don't know."

They were on their way to Victoria Hospital in Kirkcaldy. That's where the victim, a young woman by the name of Mary Douglas, had been taken. Her injuries were said to be severe but not life-threatening. Gloria and Neil had no firm plan on what to do when they got there. They would decide when they assessed the situation. Whatever they did would have to be covert, as Gloria had no official status in the matter. The police were keeping a firm wrap on details regarding the murder of Patricia Turner in Kirkcaldy. The press hadn't yet got wind of the horrific nature of her wounds. Inevitably that would leak out. Someone would tip off some reporter and then it would be plastered all over the papers. Tonight's attack was different. It was already public knowledge, to an extent and the press were besieging the hospital, seeking salacious morsels to feed their readers. This would make an unobtrusive entry difficult.

There were police at every entrance to the hospital – checking people's legitimate reasons for entry. No doubt, there would also be others posted outside the victim's ward. Neil suggested it was time for some Fey magic. He could enter unseen and reconnoitre the situation. Gloria should wait for him in the car. They were parked in a dark corner of the carpark – well away from the hospital's main door. Gloria watched as Neil crossed to the entrance and then winked out of sight. No-one seemed to notice anything untoward at all. She settled down to wait – wondering what exactly her role was in this partnership. Anything useful seemed to be coming from Neil. After about half an hour, she was getting impatient. Their journey here had taken an hour or so and she was fed up sitting in the car. Time to stretch her legs a bit. Gloria got out of the car and began pacing up and down. She was sorely tempted to go to the hospital and see if her Home Office warrant card would gain her entry. As she was contemplating this, Gloria suddenly felt a sting on the back of her neck. Unconsciousness followed quickly thereafter.

Neil returned to the car a few minutes later. At first, he wasn't alarmed to find Gloria not there. He simply assumed she had gone off to follow some initiative on her own. Inside the hospital, he'd found the victim easily enough. She was in a private ward and heavily sedated. He ghosted past the policeman on the door and entered the room. Mary Douglas would not be regaining consciousness for several hours but that was no obstacle to a Fey. He entered her mind and accessed her memory. Mary had left the chip shop and walked back to her car. As she got in, there was a sharp pain, just behind her right ear. She felt herself slumping in the seat and then darkness.

Mary awoke to a bitter liquid being poured down her throat. She was naked and manacled by her wrists and ankles. A whimper of fear escaped her lips as she saw the hideous creature that loomed over her. She tried to pull away but she was held fast. Her ordeal was about to begin. The goblin spoke – his voice jovial. "Ah. You're awake pretty. Let me introduce myself. I am Keranrodai – the one who goes before. The drink I gave you, will keep you alert and awake while we have some fun. You are fortunate. I will not totally extinguish you – but I will hurt you. You are to carry a message to those that pursue me – so remember well. I will feed every second day from now on, while I seek what my Mother sent me for. Catch me if you can before others die. I won't roam far. What I want is right here."

Mary was aware of people and vehicles passing close by – but no-one seemed to see her or hear her anguished cries for help. The goblin produced a small knife. He inserted this into Mary's left eye socket and adroitly popped her eyeball out. He chortled happily as she screamed in pain and horror. Severing her eye from its nerves, he popped it into his mouth and began chewing – obviously savouring the taste, before swallowing. "Don't worry," he said. "I'll leave you the other eye. I'm not a monster." "Eyeballs are tasty," he went on, "but a bit squishy. Now we need something with a bit of crunch." With that, the horror cut off the little toe on Mary's right foot. This too went into his mouth. He chewed the toe, bone and all, without any difficulty. The goblin repeated this process for all the toes on that foot before proceeding to do the same with her other foot. When he swallowed the last toe he said, "All done. See – that wasn't too bad – was it?" The goblin smiled a hideous leering smile and then simply walked away. Suddenly people could hear her screams and they came running. Then she mercifully passed out.

Neil had to take some time to steady himself after sharing Mary Douglas's memories. As a Fey, he was somewhat inured to human suffering – but the sheer cold-blooded horror of it had left its mark on even him. Back at the car now, he began to grow anxious. He waited and waited for Gloria's return – which never happened. Eventually, Neil summoned the air-spirits and discovered for certain that Gloria had been taken.

Chapter Thirty Seven - Dream a Little Dream. (Tuesday 19th May 1980.)

Just after three in the morning, the women of Gloria's Sisterhood, simultaneously began to dream in graphic detail.

Jenny.

Jenny Tait was a married woman with two grown-up children. At fifty-six, she was the oldest of the group. If you asked her, she would tell you she was happily married. She loved her husband, Archie but this hadn't stopped her having a string of affairs over the years. She preferred young men. What they lacked in technique, they tended to make up for in enthusiasm. Of all the women violated by Garry Wallace, it sat lightest upon her. That's not to say she wasn't troubled by it. She was – but unlike the others, she felt no shame regarding the incident. Had things been different, Jenny might well have entertained Garry as a sexual partner. She had found him attractive but he had taken her without preamble and without permission and when she was powerless to say no. Any shame in this matter, she attributed solely to him.

It was night and Jenny was walking along a beach. The sea was to her right and a cold wind was blowing in from it. To her other side, someone walked along with Jenny. She didn't know who it was but somehow she was afraid to look. That was not the only thing she feared. A knot of anxiety was growing inside. Jenny didn't know why. Her heart was pounding and she could feel herself on the verge of panic. It was dark but there was some sporadic moonlight as the clouds flitted overhead. Up ahead, Jenny could vaguely make out a shape lying on the sand with a figure looming over it. She walked on – fear rising in her. As Jenny got closer, she could see that the shape on the ground was a naked female. The woman was chained hand and foot – and standing over her, knife in hand, was a horrific goblin-like creature.

Jenny wanted to turn and run but something compelled her to keep moving forward. The woman on the ground was straining at her bonds. She lifted her head from the ground and turned towards Jenny. With a heart-lurching shock, Jenny realised it was Janet. A voice sounded in Jenny's left ear. "I couldn't finish the bitch," it said, "but the Harbinger will." Startled, Jenny turned towards the voice. There beside her, her unseen companion was Koldunya. The witch threw her head back and began to cackle with maniacal laughter. Jenny sat up in bed – covered in a cold sweat – her heart hammering in her chest. It took a long while for Jenny to calm down – but she slept no more that night.

Michelle.

Michelle Wylder was twenty-three and unattached. She hated Garry Wallace with a profound passion. He had taken something from her that she would never have given willingly. He had defiled her body. Michelle still struggled with the self-loathing she felt for complying with him. The fact that she now understood the compulsion she'd been placed under helped – but there was still a way to go yet before she fully forgave herself. Him – she would never forgive. Michelle had been moderately sexually active, prior to his rape. Since then, sex was something she just couldn't face. The burgeoning magic within her was a mixed blessing. It gave her something to focus on and experiment with – but it was also a constant reminder of how it had gotten there in the first place. It had been Michelle who'd first brought Janet into contact with Wallace. That was another source of regret and guilt.

Michelle was well aware that she was dreaming – but even for a dream, it was weird. She seemed to be a passenger and spectator in someone else's body. She had no control over anything. Somehow, Michelle was piggy-backing on another's reality. The person was in some kind of cave or tunnel. The walls and ceiling seemed to be cut from living rock. Michelle was picking up echoes from her host's mind. She sensed anger, frustration and a thirst for bloody vengeance. The host was seeking to break free from where she was currently imprisoned. Michelle somehow knew that it was a woman's mind she was trapped in.

The host seemed to become aware of Michelle's presence in her mind and was not happy with the invasion. She seemed to be actively trying to eject her. This suited Michelle completely. She herself was straining to escape. Neither had any success initially. Michelle could feel her host pushing harder and harder and becoming more and more annoyed. Suddenly, with a disorientating rush, Michelle popped clear. She was catapulted from the stranger's mind and into the Therapy Room at the Centre where she worked. To her horror, Garry was standing there looking at her. "Lie up on the couch, Michelle," he told her. Unbelievably, Michelle began to obey. She seemed to be reliving the nightmare all over again. The torment would renew and be continued. Michelle felt anger welling up inside her. At first, this was directed against herself. How could she be so weak again? Then – something else kicked in. Michelle experienced a moment of perfect clarity. Her anger turned to something else. It was an icy focussed fury. Whirling round, Michelle threw her hands out in Garry's direction. A bolt of fury coursed through her body and exploded towards her tormentor. Wallace was blown to pieces and splattered all over the wall behind him. Michelle woke with a start. After a few minutes reflection, she settled down again and, feeling satisfied, slept the sleep of the just for the rest of the night.

Ruth.

At seventeen, Ruth was the youngest of Wallace's victims. She was also the most conflicted. Ruth's problem arose through the fact that she had enjoyed parts of what had happened to her. She totally abhorred the way it had come about but her body had responded to the physical stimuli of the sex act. For a brief time it had been pleasurable – and this caused her no end of guilt. She had chastised herself about it ever since. Ruth had been a virgin before Wallace had taken that away from her. She was sexually quite naïve – but the guilt she felt was not new to her. The incident with Wallace held many echoes of an experience she'd had in the past and it reawakened the angst she'd been dealing with since then.

One summer, when Ruth was ten, she'd been playing in a swing park with some friends. Her Aunt had come on a surprise visit and they'd sent Ruth's cousin to fetch her home. His name was Tom and he was fifteen at the time. On the way home, the two cousins took a shortcut through the woods. Tom took Ruth in amongst some bushes and told her to lie down. Just as she had with Garry, Ruth had done as she was told. Tom knelt beside her, put his hands up her skirt and pulled down her knickers. He then began to touch, what she'd called at the time, her flower. Ruth knew this was wrong – but it felt nice. She'd never realised up till then that this part of her body could give her pleasure. She'd been frightened, ashamed and titillated in equal measure. Tom had kept this up for some time. Then he had taken his penis out. Ruth had seen a penis before and even knew its proper name. She had a younger brother. This one was different though. It was huge, hard and angry looking. Ruth was scared. Tom made her touch it and then stroke it, till white stuff had spurted from its end. Tom had put his penis away and told Ruth that what they'd done was a secret. She could never tell anyone about it or the police would come and take her away. She never did tell anyone. Her cousin's family moved away to England shortly thereafter and she'd never seen him again.

Ruth had been terrified but intrigued. Over the coming weeks, she'd began experimenting with touching herself. It became a guilty secret and pleasure. She never really connected it with the sex act. It was something to be done alone in private. Of course, as Ruth got older, she learned the facts of life and the mechanics of sex – though she'd never experienced it until Garry had penetrated her. Then, with a resurgence of her guilt, her body had betrayed her. There was pain initially and then, God help her, there'd been pleasure. Ruth had never admitted this to anyone – not even her new circle of friends. It continued to eat at her and made her hate herself. What kind of horrible person was she?

In Ruth's dream, she was having consensual sex for the first time. She was with Gloria's friend, Neil – the one they said was a Fey. Both of them were naked and he was inside her. This was marvellous. It was natural and the way it was meant to be. Ruth was sure she'd feel no shame over this. Maybe she could put her demons to rest. The past was the past and in the future, Ruth intended to be her own person. No more being the victim. Neil had done wonderful things to her with his hands. He'd elicited responses from her body that she'd never experienced before. The Fey had been gentle with Ruth but now things were growing more frantic as they mounted towards a crescendo.

Ruth felt herself building to the first orgasm she would have that didn't involve her own fingers. She closed her eyes and surrendered to the delicious growing tension, low in her body. Suddenly, Ruth screamed in pain, as the cock inside her grew to gigantic proportions. It mangled her cunt and split the flesh above it. Ruth's eyes opened in alarm and saw that the handsome Fey had morphed into a hideous goblin. With a scream of pain and horror, Ruth sat up in bed, She sat for a long time sobbing. Like Jenny, she slept no more that night.

Ann.

Strictly speaking, Ann Graham had not been a victim of Garry's predation. She almost had been though and so had her daughters. Neil's amulet had helped her save both herself and her girls. She'd been delighted to see Neil earlier that evening. It was the first time she'd seen him since that fateful night back in January. She hadn't had a chance to talk much to him but hoped she would see him again soon. Unlike her new sisters, Ann's magic was directly Fey in origin. Neil had invested her with it through the amulet and it had struck a resonance within her. Ann held the conviction that this magic would grow and become stronger – especially in conjunction with the other women of her group. Ann did have her demons though. She had willingly allowed Garry into her home and into her bed. Unforgivably, Ann had placed her children in harm's way. She hadn't seen the darkness in Garry until the night he'd shown up intent on rape, torture and murder. She'd pandered to his predilection for exercising sexual control of her. Well – that would never happen again. Ann was much more comfortable with her own sexuality. She'd learned to be responsible for her own actions and foibles.

Ann dreamed she was on a nighttime beach. A deep foreboding filled her and hammered at her heart. Something was coming – something very bad. Ann cast about her to try and discover what was causing her unease. Then, out to sea, she saw an ominous sight. A massive wall of water was rushing towards shore. Ann stood for a moment, transfixed with horror. Then – she snapped out of it and turned to flee. In her panicked state, Ann could not get up any speed. The sand was deep and she sank into it with every step. It soon became clear to her that she was never going to escape the furious tsunami that was rushing upon her. Ann turned at bay and tried to stop the wave with her magic. It was a forlorn hope. The raging water would engulf her and everyone she loved. If only her friends were here with her. Together, they might have done something. The wall of water came on relentlessly. It rolled over Ann and she was borne away. The shock woke her up. Ann lay on in bed but sleep was a long time coming.

Janet.

Janet Clark was all but broken by Garry Wallace. It wasn't just the brutality with which he'd treated her – though that was extreme enough. It was also the way he'd abruptly changed from a seemingly kind, considerate and caring man, into an arrogant, sadistic abuser and rapist. She had really liked him and had thought he liked her. But Garry Wallace didn't break Janet. She had a core of steel that she hadn't realised that she had. It was Janet who had picked up Koldunya's discarded knife and jammed it into the witch's throat – saving Gloria's life. Gloria had, in turn, helped Janet through the initial stages of her recovery. There was a way to go but Janet's strength was growing and it showed. The others looked to her for leadership when Gloria wasn't present – despite her being the second youngest in the group.

Janet had sensed Koldunya's hatred of her right from when she'd mistaken the witch as a ghost when making love to Garry in the Centre. This overpowering hate had been confirmed after the witch's death by Gloria. It had been a big factor in the errors of judgement Koldunya made that led to her apprehension and demise. Perhaps the witch had somehow sensed that Janet's would ultimately be the hand that took her life. The magic that now resided inside Janet was strong. She was convinced that when she killed Koldunya, some of the witch's essence had been absorbed into her – boosting what had been placed there through Garry's actions. Janet abhorred the source of her magic but her conscience was clear in making use of it. Unlike some of her sisterhood, Janet felt no guilt over what had happened to her. She put the blame firmly on the perpetrators.

Janet found herself in a nighttime street. She did not recognise the location. A young woman had just exited a nearby pub. Janet's eyes were drawn to her and she felt compelled to follow. Just as she did so, a man also exited the pub. There was nothing distinctive about this man but Janet felt a deep foreboding. The man set off determinedly after the woman. It seemed obvious he intended to do her harm. Janet tried to shout out a warning but no sound came from her mouth. She ran past the man, who paid her no attention at all. Janet caught up with the young woman, just as she entered a narrow and darkened alley – but when she laid a hand on the woman's shoulder, it passed straight through. Janet was aware that this was a dream – and she quickly realised that her role here was spectator. There was nothing she could do to influence whatever was going to happen next.

It would have been easy for Janet to turn away. She was sure something nasty was about to happen and it wouldn't be pleasant to witness. She was made of sterner stuff though. This was being shown to her for a reason and she wouldn't balk at seeing it through. Janet didn't understand yet what she was bearing witness to but it must be important. The man had entered the alley just behind the woman. He produced a blowpipe from his jacket and sent a dart into the woman's neck. She collapsed within seconds. The man immediately morphed into a grotesque creature like nothing Janet had ever seen before. She was sure this was an actual transformation and not just one of those weird switches that can happen in dreams. Janet watched in growing horror, as the creature stripped, shackled and then sadistically tortured his victim to death – consuming her flesh in the process. She knew intuitively that what she watched was real – something that had happened or would happen in the future.

Mercifully, the scene faded to grey and disappeared. Janet stood in nothingness for a while – expecting that soon she would awaken – but it wasn't to be. A new scene began to coalesce. It was still night but now Janet found herself on grass covered land. There were park benches, swings and a roundabout. The man from earlier now had another young woman in his power. Janet watched in dread as he transformed again and proceeded to mutilate his victim. This time, he didn't kill the woman though the things he did to her were horrific. Once again, the creature ate the body parts that he'd cut from his victim. Janet was sickened to the very depth of her soul. The only thing that gave her the strength to endure was the burning conviction that she herself would avenge the indignities visited on the women by this creature from hell. It was yet another perpetrator of violence against women and would have to die. Why else were these visions being shown to her – if not to allow her to intervene.

Once again, the vision faded to grey. Janet didn't know how much more she could take – but once again a new location came into view. This time she was on a darkened beach. This was different though. It seemed fuzzier somehow and more shadowy. Janet also became aware that she was holding a knife in her right hand. It was the same one with which she'd killed Koldunya. Perhaps, she reasoned, this was something which hadn't yet happened. Which meant the first two had. The man was a few yards in front of her – stalking yet another woman. The woman was walking, seemingly deep in thought, and completely oblivious to the coming menace. Something drew Janet's gaze to her left – the side away from the sea. There was a small bus station and a cluster of buildings – a chip shop and an amusement arcade amongst them. The sign on the arcade said "Leven Beach Family Amusements." For the first time in her dream, Janet could identify a location. This had to be the reason for her visions. Surely she was meant to save this woman's life and destroy the evil murderer. Janet didn't have the knife. She'd thrown it into some bushes after killing the witch. She'd no idea whether it had been recovered afterwards. There had been a lot going on – so perhaps it was still there. If it could kill Koldunya, surely it would be sufficient to slay this creature. It was as if everything had clicked together in Janet's mind. She knew what she had to do now. As this scene faded to grey, Janet slept again – but she'd remember everything in the morning.

Chapter Thirty Eight - Enemies or Allies?. (Tuesday 19th May 1980.)

Gloria awoke to find herself handcuffed. She was on a chair and fully clothed, so she reasoned that her captor wasn't the Harbinger. Who it was, remained to be seen. Gloria was furious at herself. She couldn't believe she'd been sloppy enough to let someone close enough to put a dart in her. There was still an itch in her neck from where it had penetrated. She had the presence of mind to feign continued unconsciousness, as she tried to assess her situation. Her mind quested for the mechanism of the handcuffs – but before she could affect any movement in it, she was slapped very hard across the face.

Gloria was so startled her eyes flew open. She looked around her surroundings, squinting against the bright light that shone in her face. She was sitting on a wooden chair with her hands handcuffed behind the back rest. A man stood in front of her – obviously the person who'd struck her. Gloria was aware of another two figures standing behind him but they were beyond the light and she couldn't make them out properly. The light itself, was some kind of industrial lamp that was angled to shine directly into her eyes. They seemed to be in a large indoor space – possible a disused factory or warehouse. The man spoke. "I knew you were awake," he said. "Now we have your attention," he went on, "we have questions."

"Where is the Shadow-Man's lair?" the man asked. "We know he has to sleep through the day. So where is it?" Gloria was still trying to gather her thoughts. "What?" was all she could say.

"The Shadow-Man – the Harbinger – we know you are his companion."

"I've no idea what you're talking about."

"We saw you with him in the hospital carpark. We saw him cloak himself in shadows to enter the building unseen – no doubt to finish his latest victim. Tell us where he sleeps and we'll set you free."

"I still don't know what you're talking about."

The man slapped her again. "One way or the other," he said, "you will tell us what we want to know." Despite the questioning and the slapping, Gloria had managed to engage with the mechanism of the handcuffs. She threw out an aura of defeat and dejection. She wanted her captors to believe she was beaten and ready to spill the beans. Gloria began speaking – letting the volume of her words decrease as she did so. "Ok," she began, "I'm afraid of him. He makes me help him. During the day……." The man leaned in closer, the better to hear. Gloria snapped the handcuffs open. As they dropped to the floor, she launched herself from the chair and headbutted the man squarely in the face. Gloria heard a satisfying crunch when she made contact. The man staggered back and Gloria followed him. She delivered a precision punch to his solar-plexus and then a strike with the heel of her hand directly to his nose.

The first man went down and Gloria bowled on past him. She kicked the second man in the balls and then kicked him there again. The third of her captors reacted more quickly than the first two. He sidestepped Gloria's charge and elbowed her in the back as she went past. She recovered quickly. Swivelling, Gloria kicked the man behind the knee, buckling his leg and taking him to the floor. She followed up with a stamp to his groin and another to his face. The man stayed down and lay still. Gloria scanned to see that all of her captors were incapacitated and there was no-one else around. Now that the light wasn't shining in her eyes, Gloria could see her gun lying on the table next to the lamp. The magazine had been ejected and was beside it, along with her wallet. Gloria had filled that clip with alternating iron and silver bullets. Neil had told her that either of these two metals might prove inimical to the creature they were hunting. She quickly retrieved the pistol and slid the magazine back in. The bullets would suffice to take humans down as well.

Gloria surveyed her fallen captors. The first two were beginning to recover somewhat. The third, still lay inert. There was every chance that she'd severely injured that one but they had forcibly abducted her and the consequences were entirely on their own heads. Now she had to decide what to do with them. Obviously, Gloria could just leave but she wanted to find out who they were and what they were up to. The first man, at least, had some knowledge of the Harbinger. How could this be? She took command of the situation. Both men were on the ground within a couple of feet of each other. Gloria's second victim was already sitting up and the other was pulling himself into a similar position. She covered them both with her gun. "Stay on the ground and keep your hands where I can see them," she told them. "Now – who are you and why did you kidnap me?." The men sat where they were and made no reply. They wouldn't even look in Gloria's direction.

"I am a Government official," Gloria went on. "You saw my I.D., it's in my wallet. So you must know you're in a lot of trouble. So, what do you know about this Harbinger you spoke of?" The men sat in stolid silence. Gloria tried one more time. "Look," she said. "My companion and I are hunting this Harbinger. If you are too, then we're on the same side. Maybe we can help each other." She didn't say anything about Neil being Fey. That wasn't her secret to reveal. The man who'd been questioning her looked briefly in her direction and then returned his gaze to the floor. His lips remained sealed. Gloria was at an impasse. As she was considering her next move, the third man began to come round, with much groaning. So, at least he wasn't dead. Just then, Gloria stiffened at the sound of a door being opened. She probed the darkness with her eyes but was unable to see who the new player was. She was uncomfortably aware of being exposed in the only well-lit part of the space they were in.

A voice rang out. "Don't shoot. It's me. I've come to rescue you." Gloria relaxed as Neil emerged from the surrounding gloom. "How did you find me?" she asked. "We have a connection," he replied. "If we take up the sleeping arrangement I suggested, I'll be able to find you even quicker." He looked at Gloria's captives. "I recognise this one," he said, indicating the man who'd been interrogating Gloria earlier. "He's the human who summoned the Air Spirits in Kirkcaldy before I did. They showed me his face. I knew he was one of your abductors when I summoned those in the carpark, after I realised you were gone."

"So – what do we have?" Neil asked. "Don't know," Gloria replied. "They refuse to talk." Neil turned to the man they perceived to be the leader. "I am Neil Mac Mannanan," he said, "And I am Fey – if you know what that means. I can enter your mind and know all your secrets – or you can simply tell us who you are and what your interest in us is. I will know if you speak truth. The choice is yours." "How do I know you are what you say you are?" the man said. "How do I know you are not the Harbinger of the Adversary?" "You summoned the Air Spirits at the first murder sight. You must have seen that I am not he." "The Harbinger is a shapeshifter. He can put on any face he desires," the man insisted. "Not so," Neil said. "Most shapeshifters only have two persona. That is their core and they cannot deviate from that. But surely you can sense my tone. That is unique and cannot be mistaken."

The man looked baffled. "Ah I forgot," Neil said, "You are merely human, after all. Well – enough stalling. Speak now or I enter your mind." The man seemed to make a decision. "I am Michael," he said, "and my companions are George and Mathew. We are Druids." "How can this be?" interrupted Neil, "There are no true Druids now." "Not so," replied Michael, "The Order of Caradoc has existed, in secret, through the many ages. It is a small but thriving community. Our mission is to be ready to deal with what is now in motion – the coming of the Harbinger. I am sorry that, in our eagerness, we have wronged you. Nevertheless, I can divulge no more of our Order's secrets. I beg you to forgive us. I also beg you not to take from my mind information that is not mine to divulge. We may not be able to be allies but we are not enemies."

Neil looked at Gloria. "He speaks truth, as far as he knows it," he told her. She thought for a moment or two and then said, "It's a pity they don't see fit to co-operate – but as long as they don't interfere with us again, I'm happy to leave them be." Neil nodded. "You heard her," he said to the three men. "Stay out of our way and we won't have a problem." "You better get that guy some medical help," Gloria said, indicating her third victim, who was now sitting up but looking decidedly wobbly. With that, she holstered her pistol and left with Neil. Outside the building, Gloria saw that they were in an urban industrial estate. "Where exactly are we?" she asked. "This is Dunfermline," Neil replied. His red Capri was parked nearby, next to a white Ford Transit, which Gloria assumed had been used to bring her here. She glanced at her watch. It was a little after 1 a.m..

As they drove back to Neil's cottage, he told her what he'd learned at Mary Douglas's bedside. Gloria digested it for a moment or two. "How much do you trust this?" she asked. "To be honest – not at all," was his reply. "It doesn't make sense for this Keranrodai character to give us so much information," Gloria said. "It could simply be misdirection," Neil replied, "or he could just be taunting us – holding the spectre of more attacks and atrocities over us. If, as he says, he will continue to focus his attention on this particular area, he is either lying or supremely confident that we can't catch him." They eventually decided that they would treat the information with healthy scepticism. Nevertheless, they thought it would be wise to move their base of operations to the Kirkcaldy area. They'd go back to Neil's cottage tonight but find a hotel in the coming day. It was time to be more proactive. The two of them would patrol during the nights. It was a fairly forlorn course of action. The chances of encountering Keranrodai were remote – but perhaps Neil could pick up his Tone, if they happened to come close enough. With that slender plan, they went home to bed. At the same time as her sisterhood were having their various dreams, Gloria discovered what subtleties Neil brought to the sex-act.

Chapter Thirty Nine - A Journey of Discovery. (Tuesday 19th May 1980.)

Janet awoke with a sense of purpose. She had no idea that what she'd seen in her dream, was the case that Gloria and Neil were currently working on. Her feeling was that she'd been given an insight to help her save a life. The whys and wherefores, she didn't understand but she was convinced that what she'd seen was real. Janet hadn't decided on a firm course of action yet. She wanted to check some things out before involving anyone else. She'd passed her driving test about a year previously and for her twentieth birthday, a month ago, her grandparents had surprised her with a ten year old, green Hillman Imp. It was her pride and joy. Skipping breakfast, Janet got into her car and drove to the King's Park. She hadn't been back to work since the events at the turn of the year, so she had plenty free time. Her doctor had signed her off with stress.

Janet had steered well clear of the park since the night she killed Koldunya – so it was with some trepidation that she approached it now. There was a hard knot of anxiety in her stomach but she persevered. She parked the car next to the small gate where Gloria had barged her over and broke the trance she'd been in. Janet did not in the least regret killing the witch. Nevertheless, taking a life was no small thing – no matter how justified. As she'd stood there in the aftermath, with warm blood dripping on her hand, she'd been filled with a sudden revulsion. On a reflex, she had thrown the knife from her in disgust. It had fallen into a nearby clump of Whin Bushes. Janet had no idea if anyone had witnessed this. There was so much more to draw their attention. There were the four dead Venatores and the wreckage of their cars. There was the dying witch and an injured Gloria and there was the disembowelled body of Garry Wallace.

Janet entered the park. In the daylight, everything looked different. She tried to picture where she'd been standing on that night. It wasn't easy. Everything had been in turmoil and her recollection was hazy, to say the least. The clump of Whin Bushes was easily identified though. It was the most extensive of the three that were in the immediate vicinity. The knife might still be in there – or perhaps not. Obtaining a weapon was only part of Janet's motivation. She had seen herself, in the dream, carrying this particular knife and wanted to test the veracity of her vision. Now that she was actually there though, she wasn't at all sure that she really wanted to find the weapon. Still – she had to know. The bushes were very prickly and Janet found it difficult to get amongst them. Gingerly she pushed aside the vegetation and began to search. With practically the first movement she made, the knife was dislodged and fell to the ground. Janet felt herself being swept away in an overwhelming wave of predestination. It scared her.

After a moment's hesitation, Janet reached in and lifted the knife. Its nine-inch blade and part of the hilt was covered in dark, dried blood. Once again, she was filled with revulsion but fought it down. Quickly looking around to see if she was being observed, Janet pulled a plastic carrier-bag from her pocket and concealed the knife in it. She desperately wanted to speak to Gloria but was loath to disturb her, knowing she was busy. Janet needed time to think. She went back to her car and drove home. Once there, she took the knife to the bathroom and washed away the blood in the washbasin. Drying the blade off, Janet replaced it in the bag and concealed it in her room.

In her dream, Janet had seen a sign for "Leven Beach Family Amusements". She figured she had to find out if that was a real place and if it corresponded to what she'd observed in her vision. Janet had heard of Leven but wasn't entirely sure where it was. Getting her Dad's AA road atlas she looked it up and discovered it was on the east coast in Fife. Janet decided to check that out first and then she would try to contact Gloria. She jotted down a route from the atlas – noting which roads she should follow to get to Leven. Janet had a bite to eat before setting off on her journey. She felt a bit daunted. Leven wasn't that terribly far but it was further than she'd ever driven before. All of her recent excursions had been in and around Stirling.

Janet navigated to Leven without any great deal of difficulty. It did take her quite a while though, almost two hours to reach the little town on the North bank of the Firth of Forth. She was not confident driving on unfamiliar roads. Once Janet reached Leven it was fairly obvious how to reach the beach and there were street signs pointing the way, just in case. She drove until she reached the Promenade and followed it with the water on her right. She didn't have far to go. Very soon the bus station and other businesses came into view. It was exactly as she'd seen it in her dream. Although she had more than half expected it, Janet's stomach lurched. She pulled into the kerb and stopped the car. Whatever the source of her dream, wherever it had come from, it had shown Janet a place she'd never seen before in her life. The vision had indeed, it seemed, been predictive.

Janet had to sit for a time before she felt able to drive again. There was a weight pressing on her and she was filled with a sense of foreboding. Although she was an initiate into the world of magic and the supernatural, she was far from totally comfortable with it. Janet had rallied a lot from her lowest point but there was still a fragility to her. She needed advice. She needed to speak with Gloria. Janet drove home. As soon as she got in she dialled Neil's number. Unfortunately, he and Gloria had already departed for a hotel in Kirkcaldy and there was no answer.

Chapter Forty - The Sheriff. (Tuesday 19th May 1980.)

Gloria and Neil hadn't slept at all in the night just gone. They had been busy doing other things. It was their intention however, to find a hotel in the Kirkcaldy area and sleep through the day – so that they could patrol through the night. Gloria had found Neil an amazing lover. He seemed to know just what to do to please and excite her. She wasn't sure whether he was just gifted in that department or whether he was delving into her mind to extract her desires. This made her uneasy – although not while they were engaging in it. It was an ongoing theme for her. Gloria had an innate distrust of Fey mind-control and ethics. She hadn't been particularly happy at Neil probing Mary Douglas's memory while she was unconscious, though she had to admit that sometimes the end justified the means – particularly if it led to them eliminating Keranrodai before he uncovered the key or tortured and killed again. Gloria was also uneasy that sleeping with Neil was hardly professional behaviour. She justified this to herself by reasoning that he wasn't really a work colleague. What they were doing was off the books and thus not official. Even to herself, this argument felt thin.

They were having a leisurely breakfast, before setting off, when Neil suddenly let out a groan. "What's wrong?" Gloria asked. "We've got company," he replied. The front door led directly from the living room, where they were sitting, to the garden. Neil looked at it and it swung open. "Come in cousin," he said, "What a pleasant surprise." The most beautiful woman Gloria had ever seen walked through the door. She was tall with a mane of flaming red hair and startlingly blue eyes. She carried herself with a haughty demeanour, moving with self-assured grace.

Neil made the introductions. "Gloria, this is Brigid Nic Lyr, appointed by King Feargas as Fey Sheriff of these lands. Brigid, this is my friend and colleague, Gloria Garcia, a captain of the Venatores. So – to what do we owe the honour of this visitation?" It struck Gloria that their unexpected visitor looked vaguely familiar – and then she realised why. She'd only seen Koldunya once – and that was when the witch was depleted and looking a bit the worse for wear – not to mention her features being contorted in a murderous rage – but her beauty still shone through. Brigid was like a younger and better looking version of the witch.

"I am here at the King's command," Brigid said – her tone supercilious. "He is concerned by matters in this realm." "I should think he would be," answered Neil. Brigid went on, "He is displeased at the increasing number of humans you are revealing your Fey identity to. He orders you to cease and desist forthwith. You are forbidden from active involvement in human affairs. You are to live quietly and in an unobtrusive manner. There is to be no more rutting with this human female, lest a hybrid child be conceived. This is your King's command." Brigid had looked at Gloria with withering contempt as she delivered the last part of this diatribe.

"Feargas forfeited the right to my obedience when he spoke the words of banishment to me," Neil replied. "He is my King no longer. What I do here is none of his concern. It would be better if he took some action against the catastrophe that is unfolding here. Does he think that the Realm of The Fey will be unaffected by the Adversary risen. That is what he should be concerned with – not trivial matters of isolationism and secrecy – and most definitely not of my love life. Go back and tell him that." "You do realise," Brigid said, "that if you do not comply, the King will send his Sealgaire Glas after you." "Then few, if any of them, will return to him," Neil replied. The two Fey glared at each other for several seconds until Neil said, "You may go now cousin, you are no longer welcome here. You, or any Fey who approach me with hostile intent, will be swiftly dealt with. Now go."

Gloria expected more argument, or even that Brigid would flounce off. Neither happened. The beautiful Fey simply turned and walked serenely back out of the door, which closed gently behind her. "Wow," said Gloria. "Are you in trouble?" "Not for the first time," answered Neil with a smile. "Who are the ones she spoke off? I can't remember the words she used." "The Sealgaire Glas – it simply means the Green Hunters. They are the King's supposedly elite bodyguards and assassins. I don't fear them." "It's a bit of a complication though," said Gloria. "having to dodge Fey assassins while hunting the Harbinger." "It probably won't come to that," Neil told her. "So get your gun and let's be on our way." "Just out of interest," Gloria asked him, "are you armed?" "Yes," he said, winking at her "I always carry a concealed weapon." Gloria made a face at him. "Oh no," Neil said, "I wasn't making an inuendo. I really do have a concealed blade. It's magical and I can summon it at need – whether against Keranrodai or the Sealgaire Glas. Gloria sighed, went and got her shoulder holster and put it on. Then they departed for Fife.

Chapter Forty One – The Coven. (Wednesday 20th May 1980.)

Janet was dog-tired. She'd kept vigil all night by the beach in Leven, little knowing that Gloria and Neil were patrolling just ten miles away in Kirkcaldy. Neither she nor they had encountered anything untoward. Janet had been terrified but nevertheless she'd felt duty-bound to do something – to possibly save a life and eradicate the vile creature that was torturing women. Through the long and lonely watch of the night, she had come to realise how foolish she was being. The task she had set herself was beyond her capabilities. She was way out of her depth. Janet had more experience of the eldritch than most and had been imbued with a measure of magic as a result – but to try to take on a denizen of the night, one on one, was foolhardy. Loath as she was to endanger anyone else, Janet had friends – friends who had also been endowed with magic and were growing stronger in it, seemingly day by day.

Janet wasn't one of those who believed that everything happens for a reason but she did wonder why she and her friends had been given their magic, if not to do something good with it. She had kept herself awake with the help of a thermos of strong, black coffee. That was now long gone and weariness engulfed her. Still, Janet had to face the lengthy drive home. When she got there, she intended to sleep for a few hours and then phone round the others, to set up an emergency meeting as soon as they got off work. She would also try, once more, to contact Gloria.

As she left Leven at first light, it was still early when Janet got home. Her parents were in the kitchen having breakfast before going to work. She had told them that she was staying at a friend's house overnight. They were quite surprised to see her home so early. When Janet popped into the kitchen to say hello, her Mum told her that Jenny had phoned last night and wanted her to phone back. Janet promised that she would but she was going to bed for a bit first. Janet set her alarm clock for two o'clock. That would give her time to phone round. Ann worked in a department store, on the floor, and couldn't be reached by telephone – so Janet would have to drive in to see her face to face. As it happened, Janet was having a coffee just after getting up when Jenny phoned again. She'd already set up a meeting for five o'clock. It was Ann's half day, otherwise they would have had to schedule the meeting later. Jenny hadn't managed to get hold of Gloria. Nobody knew where she was. She wouldn't elaborate on why she'd called the meeting, other than to say it was important.

Janet fretted through the rest of the afternoon but she was relieved that she'd be able to talk to the others regarding her vision. She fully expected to be given a hard time for her actions the previous night – actions, she now admitted to herself, had been reckless and dangerous. Janet got to the Halfway House at quarter to five and discovered that the rest were already there. As Jenny had called the meeting, she kicked-off the proceedings. She told them of the vivid dream she'd had two nights ago. This was prophetic – of that Jenny was convinced and it scared her. She told them that she'd seen Janet naked and shackled, with a goblin-like creature looming over her. Janet's stomach turned over at these words. She knew that the thing Jenny described was the same vile beast she had seen in her own dream.

Before anyone else could comment, Janet recounted her own prophetic vision and then told them of her vigil the previous night. As expected, her friends were appalled and proceeded to chastise her on her idiocy. Michelle was the first to intervene and spare Janet further grief. She told the group that she too had had a vivid dream on that same night. At that, the others chipped in that they too had experienced dramatic and graphic nightmares on the night in question. It seemed that something significant had occurred but what it was, they didn't have a clue. Each of the women recounted their dream in turn. All of them went into detail except for Ruth who just told them it had been frightening and disturbing. There had to be a big picture but the women didn't have enough information to work out what it was. Perhaps Gloria would have had some idea but no-one knew how to contact her.

After a few minutes of discussion, Janet had a suggestion. "Neil told us," she said, "that our magics are all in harmony and that Gloria was the key that brought it all together. Maybe we could try to contact her by combining our magic in some way." "How would we do that?" Ann asked. "I don't know," Janet replied, "We're all new to this. Maybe we could join hands in a circle and try to focus our minds on Gloria." "A bit like a séance?" Michelle asked. "Yes," Janet agreed, "but instead of trying to contact the dead, we try to contact the living." The five women gathered round a table. They hadn't reserved the back room that night but it was early and there were no other customers present. They linked hands and closed their eyes. For two or three minutes nothing happened. "Don't try too hard," Janet counselled her colleagues. "Just relax and let it happen. Visualise Gloria's face"

Another couple of minutes elapsed – and then something began to bloom. They all felt a growing degree of synchronisation. None of the women could have put it succinctly into words but each of them began to feel the presence of the all others in their minds. This sensation grew more intense and focussed until each of them began to lose their sense of self. For one sublime moment, there was a complete melding of five into one. The image each woman had of Gloria in her mind suddenly flared brightly and then the connection sundered and they were all back in the room. "Did it work?" Ruth asked. "Well something happened," Ann said. "Whatever it was." There was a bit of hiatus as the women reflected on what they'd just experienced.

It was Janet who drew them back. "So, what do you think we should do about my dream?" she asked "Are you absolutely sure that it was a genuine vision?" asked Ann. "Well I saw the beach and the amusement arcade in Leven and I'd never been there before. It was exactly as I saw it in my dream. But more than that – I just feel in my gut that what I had was a vision of things that had actually happened and things that were going to happen. That's all I can say. I fully intend going back to Leven tonight, unless anyone has a better idea." There was a lot of head scratching as the women tried to come up with some satisfactory course of action. They were in the midst of this and getting nowhere when the landlord came into the room. "Would one of you ladies be Janet Clark?" he asked. When Janet identified herself he told her, "There's a call for you on the payphone. Someone called Gloria."

Immediately, there was a hubbub of excitement around the table. It seemed their effort had worked. Janet got up quickly and went to the phone, which was situated on the wall in the corridor connecting the lounge to the game's room. Gloria told her that she'd had a vivid vision of the group, gathered round the table in their usual meeting place and had rightly assumed they were trying to make contact. Janet gave her an edited account of what had been happening, trying to include all the salient points. Gloria was astonished and then went on to astonish Janet in turn, by telling her that her vision had tapped into the case she and Neil were currently engaged in. The goblin was a character called Keranrodai and he was guilty of the things Janet had seen. There was reason to believe that he would be hunting in the coming night. If Janet's vision was indeed prophetic, they could lie in wait for him and end his predation. Janet agreed to meet with Gloria and Neil in Leven, to show them the location her vision had revealed. They would rendezvous in a couple of hours.

There wasn't time to share everything over the phone, so Gloria promised to meet with everyone in the next couple of days. She told Janet the hotel she was staying at, in case they urgently needed to contact her again. Janet was mightily relieved that the whole burden of stopping this monster was no longer on her shoulders. She went back and told her friends what had been said. The mood amongst them lifted considerably and many expressions of relief were voiced. No doubt, Gloria and Neil would know how to handle this Keranrodai. It could all be over tonight.

Chapter Forty Two – On The Beach. (Wednesday 20th May 1980.)

Keranrodai strolled nonchalantly along the beach. It was dark now but he could see clearly. He was well aware that he was being stalked but that did not trouble him in the slightest. There were three of them. Only one had any significant power – but not enough to worry Keranrodai at all. The other two were negligible. He would kill the two weaklings and retain the stronger one for his evening entertainment. Keranrodai was still in his human form. It made no difference. His magic was powerful in either persona. He only really adopted the more eldritch shape in order to intimidate and terrify. Perhaps these particular stalkers would not be terror struck by what they saw. He would shift at the right time nevertheless. His goblin aspect might just throw them off balance.

The moment of truth was coming rapidly. The stalkers were closing in. Keranrodai readied himself. Three loud reports suddenly rang out. How can they be clever enough to find me yet stupid enough to use a gun? the creature wondered. Each bullet found its mark but passed straight through, doing no harm whatsoever. Keranrodai never even felt any discomfort. He shifted to goblin mode, whirled round, charged five yards, taking another bullet to the chest, and ripped the shooter's throat out with his wickedly clawed right hand. Keranrodai easily avoided a desperate knife lunge and seized the attacker by the head. With a savage twist he wrenched it round to face all the way backwards.

As the two human's bodies dropped lifeless to the beach, Keranrodai's final opponent hit him with a binding spell. It was pathetically inadequate to hold a creature such as he. Keranrodai normally liked to use a blowpipe to subdue his playmates but that wouldn't work at close quarters. There was no time. The Goblin had a dart concealed in his left hand and with blinding speed he rammed it into his opponents neck. It worked almost instantaneously and the last of the stalkers fell to the ground. Keranrodai preferred female victims. He found their flesh tastier and more tender but the male form held certain anatomical delicacies – so an occasional change was alright. It was time to get to work.

Chapter Forty Three – A Dish Best Served Cold. (Thursday 21st May 1980.)

Malcolm Brown was a bully. He knew he was a bully and was perfectly comfortable with it. In fact – he revelled in it. But Malcolm wasn't some unthinking thug. He was selective in how he exercised his propensity. Work colleagues, for instance, thought he was a great guy – the salt of the earth. In their company, Malcolm was careful to treat everyone with courtesy and respect. He would only indulge his natural tendency when his victim was isolated and he was in a position of power. Malcolm was a big man – physically imposing and intimidating. Women were his preferred prey and sexual molestation was his favourite pastime. He worked security at the Uni and this gave him many opportunities for harmless fun. Pretty female students, young and naïve, fell victim to him – but only when there were no witnesses around. None of them had yet dared to come forward to accuse him – so his reputation was intact and his predation unchecked.

A favourite ploy was the random drugs search. Usually at night and always with a lone female. Brown could quickly determine how far he'd be able to go with any given individual. If the student seemed to be clued up and knew her rights, he'd back off. Those that were unaware of the rules would often submit to intimate searches – including hands in their bras and even, at times, their pants. Even if they later discovered that this was not allowed, they'd always been too embarrassed and ashamed to report it. On the relatively few occasions when Malcolm actually did find drugs, it opened whole new vistas of opportunity. He'd tell his victim that the University had a strict no-drugs policy and that immediate expulsion was the penalty for being caught in possession. There was, of course, no such rule but most accepted his word and were worried. Brown would then trade his turning a blind eye for sexual favours – up to and including intercourse. Again, he was calculating in how far he could go with each women. He rarely got it wrong.

Emboldened by his successes, Brown had even taken his predatory approach into the outside world. It had happened quite spontaneously and he'd taken a big risk but it was an experience he treasured and thought about a lot. He intended repeat it, with better planning and preparation, in the future. It was a Sunday in late November. Malcolm had been watching a football match on the telly at a friend's house in Stirling. By the time he left to go home, at about six o'clock, he'd had a few cans and a couple of generous nips. Brown wasn't terribly drunk – but just enough to be uninhibited enough for risk taking. It was already dark as he left his friend's home. On his way to the railway station, to catch a train back home to Falkirk, Malcolm passed a bus stop. It was behind the Thistle Centre and very little pedestrian traffic passed that way. There was a shelter, which tended to hide those waiting for a bus from passing vehicles. It also shaded the interior from the street-lights, making it relatively dark. Standing at the bus stop, was a pretty teenage girl, who was in conversation with a couple of even younger looking boys. Malcolm got the impression that they were strangers to each other and just passing time while they waited.

On an impulse, with no actual plan in mind, Brown chose to dally at the bus stop. He would wait to see what developed. It wasn't long before the boys boarded a bus and left Malcolm alone with the girl. He struck up a conversation with her. She seemed friendly enough and completely unwary. Turns out she was waiting for her boyfriend, who was late. Malcolm heard opportunity knocking very loudly. He decided on a variation of his random drug search routine. Brown showed the girl a photo-identity card that he had for his work and told her he was a cop. If the girl had looked closer, then his story wouldn't have held up – but it was dark – and most people wouldn't know what a police warrant card looked like anyway. She swallowed his story – he was on a drugs stake out and she matched the description of a suspect. He'd have to search her.

Adjacent to the bus stop was an open, people-sized entrance to the lower floor of the carpark. The vehicle entry was closed at that time of night. Brown took the young woman in there. She, trustingly, went with him. Malcolm told her to stand still and he went behind her. He put his hands over her shoulders, down the front of her top and into her bra. As he did so, to keep her off balance, he asked her name and age. She was Louise Coletti and fifteen. Malcolm took his fill of her tits and then moved on. Louise had stoically endured his fumbling in her bra but when he put his hand down the front of her trousers and pants and touched her genitals, she reacted. The girl pulled away and demanded to see his ID again. Malcolm stepped forward and grabbed a handful of her hair. There was no pretence anymore. The unfortunate young woman was alone in an isolated location, with a man twice her size – and he was going to have his way.

Holding her captive by her hair, Brown warned the girl not to cry out. She was terrified and only wanted to make it out of there alive. He turned her round, pulled her trousers and pants down, bent her over and raped her. When he had sated his lust, Malcolm zipped up. He warned Louise to stay where she was until he was gone. He left her there, sobbing, trembling, with her trousers and underwear around her ankles. Brown left the carpark and made his way quickly to the station. He was careful not to attract attention. Once on the train, Malcolm began to worry. Had anyone seen him? Would the girl go to the police? Would they arrest him when he got off the train at the other end? Brown made it home un-arrested but for the next week or so he was twitchy and then he began to relax. Perhaps Louise hadn't even gone to the cops.

Malcolm re-visited the memory of that evening a lot over the ensuing months. He fully intended to replicate it at some point but to take fewer risks while doing it. He had a sidekick called Bob Montgomery. Bob held Malcolm in awe. He was a small man and seemed to both fear Malcolm and desperately crave his approval. Bob would be a willing and even enthusiastic accomplice in any scheme Malcolm devised. He would do whatever he was told unquestioningly – and Malcolm had, just now, come up with a mission for him to undertake.

There were a few times when Malcolm visited his attentions on members of the general public who came into his grasp. These always happened on the night-shift. People would come onto the University grounds for a variety of nefarious purposes. Sometimes, theft or burglary was the motive. Catching any of those, provided Malcolm with a lot of leverage – provided of course that their number included a shaggable female. Others though, found the grounds ideal for a bout of outdoor sex. If the boyfriend could be intimidated, then these too provided ripe pickings. Last Sunday, just such an opportunity had arisen. Malcolm had enjoyed watching the slut riding her wimpish boyfriend. She had to know she was being observed. Why else be totally naked and displaying herself for all to see? As a connoisseur of the female form, Malcolm had greatly approved of what he saw. Her body was wasted on the little runt she was pleasuring. Malcolm decided that she'd soon be accommodating him instead.

Everything was going to plan. The runty boyfriend was easily dealt with. The female was looking like she was planning to be awkward but that wasn't a big problem. What happened next was a mystery to Malcolm. He suddenly found himself, bruised, baffled and humiliated, amongst the bushes that he'd earlier been hiding behind. The boyfriend must have blindsided him somehow. The thing was – he recognised the woman. He'd seen her somewhere before but couldn't place where – that is until today. In the Thistle Centre, shopping with his wife, he'd spotted her through the window of Donavon's Department Store. That's where he'd seen her before Malcom held a grudge and believed in getting his own back. He thirsted for revenge and also for the use of that body. Now that he knew where she worked, Malcolm would set Bob onto stalking her until he found out where she lived and anything else he could discover. The possibilities gave Malcolm a warm glow.

Chapter Forty Four – The Morning After. (Thursday 21st May 1980.)

Janet was disappointed and a wee bit mortified. She had been convinced that her dream had been prophetic. Gloria and Neil had confirmed that the first two attacks that she'd seen had actually happened. Yet they'd staked out the beach at Leven and Keranrodai hadn't shown. Janet felt guilty, because the chances were that the Goblin had tortured and killed another victim, elsewhere that night. Gloria had tried to console her by saying that, as there was no way of knowing a timescale, her vision might yet come true. Janet found this scant comfort. Neil said there was nothing that could be done about it now – but he felt it important that they all put their heads together – the three of them and the rest of the women in their group. There was a bigger picture to be puzzled out and they needed to co-ordinate their knowledge and insights. It seemed that, for whatever reason, they all had a part to play.

Janet would go home and get some sleep. Gloria and Neil would go to their hotel for the same reason. Then they would all assemble in Stirling, early that evening. When Neil got back to the hotel, he phoned his contacts in Fife to find out if there had been another murder during the night. There had been – but this one was different. Three bodies had been found on the beach below Ravenscraig Park in Kirkcaldy. All of them were male. Great violence had been visited on them all but only one had been mutilated in a similar fashion to the women who'd been attacked. On a side note – the Home Office was sending someone to Fife. It seemed The Venatores were finally becoming engaged.

Keranrodai was not following any clearly identifiable pattern, other than the frequency of an attack on each second night. Gloria and Neil were working on the assumption that he had to feed one night and then spent the other one searching for the key. The last three attacks had varied in terms of outcomes, gender of victims and number of victims. They really needed more information. With the Venatores on the scene, it complicated matters somewhat. Gloria felt guilty. She was, after all, a Venatore officer. She had information not known to her British colleagues. Beresford and his staff would be playing catch-up. It would be difficult though, sharing what they knew without exposing that Gloria had been working off the books – a big no-no. That was a dilemma Gloria and Neil decided to park for the time being.

To find out what had happened, Neil said they had two options. They could go to the murder site and he could try summoning the air spirits – or he could adopt his unseen state and visit the mortuary. He couldn't remain unseen and do the summoning at the same time – so was liable to attract police, or even Venatore, attention. They opted to grab a few hours' sleep and then visit the mortuary. Hopefully the bodies would have been taken there by that time. So at about two in the afternoon, Neil parked a few streets from the Police Station. Gloria would remain in the car while the Fey would adopt his unseen mode and seek entry to the mortuary. As Gloria watched, Neil shifted. To her, he looked transparent – but she could still see him. If that was how he appeared to everyone else, it would do more than attract a little attention. When she told him, he assured her that it was only because they had an intimate connection that she could see him thus. He could never be totally invisible to her now.

Neil wasn't gone long – no more than about ten minutes. "It's our three friends, the Druids," he told Gloria. "Either Keranrodai hunted them down, or they tracked him and he proved too much to handle when they found him. One of them had his throat torn out and another had his head twisted backwards. The leader, Michael I think he was called, was the one who provided Keranrodai with his dinner. All his fingers and toes were gone. His genitals had been consumed, along with his eyes, nose tongue and ears. It looked to me like his liver and heart had also been taken. Keranrodai was obviously powerful enough to take out all three without breaking a sweat." "To be fair," Gloria said, "I took out all three without breaking a sweat – and I'd been drugged and handcuffed." "True," Neil acknowledged.

"I don't know where this takes us," Gloria said. "Well," Neil said, "It seems likely that somehow they managed to track Keranrodai down. I'd like to know how they did that." "Unless we can find their van," Gloria said, "The only place we know that they've been was the building in Dunfermline that they took me to. Maybe it would be worth swinging by there before we go to Stirling. I don't expect to find much but it's the only lead we've got at the moment. Do you think you can find it again?" "No problem," Neil answered. They set off and reached Dunfermline half an hour later. Neil drove unerringly to the industrial estate and parked outside the empty building where they'd encountered the Druids.

The door Neil had used previously was locked this time. It didn't take him more than a couple of seconds to manipulate the mechanism and open it. As they stepped over the threshold and into the building, Neil put his hand on Gloria's arm. "Careful," he whispered. "There's someone in here." They looked around the large open space. The table was still there and the chair where Gloria had been handcuffed. On the far wall were windows that looked into office spaces and large, industrial-sized doors which probably led to storerooms or some such. The office windows were grimy and difficult to see through but Gloria and Neill clearly saw movement behind one. Not knowing who or what it was, Gloria put her hand inside her jacket and put her hand on her gun. The dimly seen figure moved to the door and opened it.

A young dark-haired woman emerged. Gloria judged her to be in her mid-twenties. "Hi," she said in an Irish accent. "I'm Sharon Kelly of The Order of Caradoc. You must be the Fey and the Venatore. I've been expecting you." "We are," Gloria answered. "I'm sorry to tell you that the three members of your Order that we met before have all been killed." "I know," said the young woman. "I located the Harbinger for them but I warned them not to go after him last night. Michael was my superior and overruled me. I'm a seer, though no seer gets everything right. Michael chose to gamble and lost. I just got here yesterday and brought this." The woman was carrying a thin book bound in a tanned leather cover. She held it up and said, "This is The Codex of Caradoc. It is believed to contain all he knew regarding the Adversary. Unfortunately, we can't read all of it. Some of it's in a script that we cannot decipher. We suspect it may be an obscure, ancient Fey notation. Since the events of last night, I've been authorised to give you access to it. Our Council judge that you are now the best – and perhaps only hope of containing this crisis."

"I thought the Druids never put anything in writing," Neil said. "Caradoc chose to make an exception in this case," Sharon replied. "He thought it a matter of great importance – and as I said, it is hardly accessible to just anyone. I've been instructed to co-operate with you – if you'll have me. A word of caution though – we do not want the Codex in the hands of the Venatores. Our Order does not trust them. You, Miss Garcia, we are prepared to trust but not your organisation." Neil spoke to Gloria. "She speaks truth," he told her. To Sharon he said, "You located the Harbinger – who we know as Keranrodai. Can you do it again?" "He's gone from me," the young woman replied. "I believe that he learned of me last night from Michael – whether through torture or directly from his mind. It seems that he is now shielding himself from my view."

Gloria and Neil excused themselves and drew aside to confer. "Do you trust her?" Gloria asked. "I know that what she's told us is the truth," Neil replied. "I think she has skills that could help us – plus, I'd be interested to have a look at that book. I'd say, let her in but it's not my decision. You'd have to consult with the rest of your coven. I feel they are integral to this matter." They went back to speak with Sharon. "Where are you staying?" Gloria asked. "I'm camping here at the moment," she replied. "Do you have any skills in interpreting dreams – verifying or refuting prophetic visions?" Neil asked next. "Some," the young woman replied this time. "It's not an exact science – unfortunately." "Would you come with us now?" Neil said. "I have a room you can use for a time – but there are other people we have to speak to regarding your involvement with our mission." "Understood," Sharon said. "I'll get my things together." As the woman left to gather her belongings, Neil said to Gloria, "She has a reservoir of magic in her and her tone harmonises with yours. Did you know – seven is the ideal number for a white coven? Just saying."

Chapter Forty Five – The Coven Complete. (Thursday 21st May 1980.)

The women had pushed two tables together and the seven of them gathered in a circle around them. Neil sat off to one side. He was not part of this but he was a keen observer. The Fey could feel the air thrum with magical potential. Whereas Gloria's old apprentice, Diane, had been an inhibitor, Sharon Kelly seemed to be a catalyst and amplifier. As far as Neil was concerned, she completed the circle. For some reason, these women had been brought together. Some higher power seemed to be at work – whether for good or ill, remained to be seen. This group of women, this Coven, already commanded much magical power. In Neil's opinion, they would only get stronger.

Sharon had been asked to sit through in the Bar while Gloria and Neil had briefly spoke to the other women. They laid out an outline of the mission they'd been pursuing, how it seemed to connect to them as a group and how Sharon came to be part of it. The women, without exception, assented to asking her through to join them. They would see how she fitted in and whether they wanted to trust her further. Immediately Sharon entered the backroom, Neil sensed the atmosphere heightening dramatically. The others seemed to feel it too. As the women gathered in a circle, Neil moved aside. He'd had a chance to have a look at the alleged Codex of Caradoc. It was indeed written in Fey runes – but of an archaic form that Neil was unfamiliar with. He reckoned that, with the help of some of his lore books and a deal of puzzling, he should be able to decipher the script. Whether it would be worth the effort, he didn't know. They didn't have much more to go on though, so he would give it a try.

Gloria ran through the bare bones of the story so far, so that everyone was mostly up to speed. Then she asked Sharon to address the matter of the dreams that seemed to have visited five of the women simultaneously. Gloria was the only one who hadn't experienced a dream at the same time but she hadn't been sleeping at that particular moment. "Please forgive me, Sharon said, "If I say things that you've already concluded or that seem obvious. I'm only trying to be methodical." There were nods all around the table. "I think," Sharon went on, "That we have to look at the dreams in a block and also individually. In general terms, when simultaneous dreams or visions occur there are three reasons. Some higher or outside power is trying to send a message, some similar type of power is launching a psychic attack, or the group has inadvertently tapped into the ether. This last can happen when a group who share a close psychic bond, like you do, unconsciously connect and communally quest into the psychic realms. Before I can try to read the nature of your dreams, I need each of you to describe what you experienced."

All the women told their stories in turn – all that is except Ruth. She refused to speak of hers and the others respected her right to be private. Sharon listened closely to them all. "Some," she said, "Seem to be obvious in interpretation. Michelle, it appears, was channelling the Adversary. Perhaps she was the source of the visions. Michelle realised some of her own power by how she dealt with appearance of Garry Wallace in her dream. The other three visions seem to be prophetic. Ann's symbolises the coming of an overpowering force – and we can see how that fits the current situation. Janet and Jenny's prophetic visions appear to be different views of the same event. There is a warning in them. Remember, because something is prophetic, it doesn't mean that things will work out as they are shown. It is only one version of what might come to pass.

To my inner eye, I believe Janet and Jenny's visions to be the real thing. Keranrodai will stalk the beach at Leven and Janet will try to destroy him. We must ensure that she does not do this alone – so that Jenny's vision of Janet captive, does not come to fruition. I guess what I'm saying is that Janet's vision feels true to me and that Jenny's flows from this. I still urge caution. What's been shown might not tell the full tale. A lot depends on where it came from and who or what is responsible for sending it. The other imponderable is timescale. There is nothing in Janet's vision to nail this down – other than it takes place at night. Unless she can recall something new or has a further dream – then it could happen anytime."

When Sharon was finished, the conversation moved on to what to do next and Neil was invited to join the women. He warned them that already things might be moving away from them. It was certain that the Adversary was awake and seeking a way out of her prison. If the Harbinger located the key, then she would be liberated quickly. Perhaps, if they could foil him, the Adversary might be held for a time – but it would probably only be a delay rather than a solution. He told them that he was not being defeatist but simply sharing the facts with them. Sharon, from her Druidic background, confirmed Neil's reading of the situation. "Perhaps," she said, "If Neil could decipher the Codex, some course of action might be discovered." Finally, they arrived at a broad plan. They would continue to monitor the beach at Leven and in the meantime, Sharon would set up a small group to work with her in trying to locate Keranrodai again. She told them that three was a good number and invited Michelle and Ann to join with her. They would seek to combine their consciousnesses and search the ether for their quarry. Sharon sensed that Ann and Michelle were most in tune with her and the women agreed.

It had been quite an intense meeting and now that business had been concluded, as far as it went, they all relaxed and general conversation ensued. There had been no formal invitation or acceptance but everyone took it as read that Sharon was now part of their Sisterhood. The Coven was once again "The Seven Sisters." During the earlier discussion, Neil had noticed that Ruth was glancing at him from time to time. This was especially noticeable when she was demurring on recounting her dream. At the first opportunity, he drew her aside. "Was I in your dream?" he asked her but she just shrugged and said nothing. "It's really important that you tell me," he said. "You can trust me, no matter what it was. It could be significant and might make a difference – maybe even save lives."

Ruth still hesitated – but Neil had an aura that inspired trust. It was part of his Fey persona. He wasn't doing any kind of mind-control. It was just part of who he was. Ruth relented. As Ann had done in January, when she first met the Fey, Ruth opened up and shared her most intimate secrets with him. She told him about the sexual assault by her older cousin and the guilt she harboured at feeling physical pleasure during it. Similarly, her body had betrayed her during her rape by Garry Wallace. There had been pleasure then – even though she knew it was wrong. Then she got to the most embarrassing part – but carried on nevertheless. Ruth told Neil that, in her dream, they'd been naked together and having sex. In the midst of the pleasure she was feeling, he suddenly transformed into a hideous creature, that she now thought was Keranrodai. His member had grown massively and had ripped apart her genitalia and lower abdomen. The pain had been awful. Neil thanked her for her honesty and courage in telling him. He promised to talk to her further, to see what might be done.

The gathering broke up. Working to Keranrodai's two day cycle, they agreed that Gloria and Neil would pick up Janet and go with her to Leven, the following night. Sharon, Michelle and Ann would meet up to see what they might achieve. Jenny and Ruth would hold themselves in reserve until needed. Sharon went with Neil and Gloria. She would have the use of Neil's spare room, for the time being. When they were alone, Neil said to Gloria, "It seems I might have to have sex with Ruth." Gloria, at first, thought he must be joking but he assured her he wasn't. "What are you talking about?" she asked him. "I can't tell you," he replied. "It's not my secret to share – but I feel it's necessary for her future well-being." "Neil, she's only seventeen," Gloria protested. "Are you saying she's too young?" Neil responded. "Well, she's much younger than you," Gloria said. "You're more than a hundred years younger than me – and it hasn't stopped us," was Neil's reply. Gloria hadn't really thought about Neil's age. Being Fey, she knew his lifespan was different to humans – but a hundred years!! She considered for a moment or two and then said, "Look – you're a free agent – so you can do as you like." "I wasn't actually asking permission," Neil said. "Then why did you tell me?" "Ruth is part of your coven. I thought you should know if something was affecting her. I can't tell you exactly what it is - but I'll ask her to speak to you about it. Trust me." Gloria sighed and said, "Whatever you think's best."

Chapter Forty Six – A Close Encounter. (Friday 22nd May 1980.)

First thing in the morning, Neil took Gloria and Sharon into Stirling, so they could both hire cars. They needed to be able to travel independently. Sharon and Michelle would be assembling with Ann at her home, after work that evening. They would attempt to join together and try to find Keranrodai. Gloria was driving to a Venatore storeroom in Glasgow. All such facilities opened with the same key – and as an officer, Gloria had one. She was going to "borrow" some of the handheld radios that they used. The settings could be changed to avoid the Venatore's frequency. Sharon reckoned that Keranrodai wouldn't be able to hide from her when he uncloaked to carry out his next murder. If they could pinpoint him and inform Gloria and Neil – perhaps they could get to him in time to save his victim. At the very least – they would have a chance of destroying the eldritch creature.

Neil had set up a meeting with Ruth, before they left the pub the previous night. While Gloria and Sharon went their separate ways, he set off to keep his assignation. Ruth was waiting by the Black Boy Fountain in the Allan Park district of Stirling when Neil drove up. Neil had a proposal to put to her. He'd considered the ethics of what he had in mind. Being Fey, his moral compass was, on the whole, different from most humans. Nevertheless he tried to examine his plan from all viewpoints. Neil genuinely liked humans – unlike most of his kind. He'd lived among them for a long time. When it came to women, Neil preferred human women to the bland perfection of the Fey. He thought that Gloria was the most exquisite creature he'd ever met. Ruth was also an attractive young woman – but that was not a motivation for what he intended. He came to the considered opinion that his motives were altruistic. His actions, he thought, would do massive good for little cost.

Ruth got into Neil's car and they sat there to talk. He spoke to her about what she'd told him of her dream and her actual sexual encounters. "Your experiences of sex have both been abusive in nature," he said. "That is not your fault. Neither is the fact that you experienced some physical pleasure during these acts. That was just a physiological response. Certain nerves were stimulated and sent messages to your brain. There is no shame in that. The way your dream ended shows a fear you now have of sexual pleasure. The guilt you associate with the sex-act triggered the horror and pain you experienced in your dream. I've no doubt that Keranrodai influenced what occurred. He tapped into your insecurity and manipulated it. This gives him a hold on you. I know of a way to undo this – but you have to consider it carefully. In what I'm about to propose – consent is a necessary prerequisite – your consent."

Ruth had an inkling about what Neil was about to say. She was a shy girl and could feel her embarrassment growing. She had a crush on Neil but never saw it going anywhere. He was with Gloria after all. Neil was well aware of Ruth's crush. He had a well-tuned sense of such things. It was part of his Fey nature. Ruth wasn't the only woman in Gloria's coven to have such feelings. All of them, apart from Sharon, harboured lustful feelings for him. He also knew that, given his relationship with Gloria, none of them would ever take it further. Neil gave Ruth a moment. Then he went on, "I'm suggesting that you and I have consensual sex. It would be a one-time only thing. By giving you a true experience of how it can be, it will ease some of your anxieties. I promise that the ending will not be at all nasty. As two consenting adults, there will be nothing to feel shame or guilt about. I've spoken with Gloria – so you will not be betraying her. I hope to give you such an experience as will sweep away your insecurities and give you a healthier viewpoint on your own sexuality."

Ruth still said nothing. "I know you might find this difficult," Neil said. "You don't have to say anything right now. Go home and think about what I've said. I'll be here at two o'clock tomorrow afternoon. I'll wait for exactly ten minutes. If you do not turn up – I'll not bring up the subject again. I won't be angry, disappointed or insulted. If we do this – it's got to be because you want to." Ruth looked at him and managed a smile, though her face was flushed. "Ok," she said and got out the car. Her mind was racing as she walked away. Could she actually do this? She knew she wanted to but wasn't sure her nerve would hold. Would she really feel no shame afterwards? Ruth had a lot of thinking to do.

The plan for the coming night was quite simple. Gloria, Janet and Neil would travel together to Leven. They knew that Keranrodai was powerful and that it might well require all of them to overcome him. One of Gloria's "liberated" radios would go with them. Sharon and her team would have another one. If Keranrodai showed up in Leven they would be in position to take him down. Sharon's group would have a map of Fife on a table between them. If they got a whiff of Keranrodai they would try to pinpoint his position and immediately radio the Leven group – who would then rush to try and intercept.

During the day, before they left for Leven, Neil worked on The Codex of Caradoc. It was written in archaic Fey runes but he had several lore books that should help with deciphering it. Despite his best efforts, Neil was getting nowhere. He couldn't get the script to make any sense. It was either written in a language he didn't know or was in some kind of code. Neil had an extensive knowledge of languages, both ancient and modern but this one had him baffled. The words he was translating just seemed to be meaningless gibberish. Neil even resorted to trying magic on the puzzling script but with no success. He had a lot of endurance but even he ended up with a headache. Neil put the book aside for the time being.

In the early evening, Gloria, Janet and Neil set off for Leven in Neil's car. When they got there, they took up station at their usual spot and settled down to wait. Nothing happened for a couple of hours. Just when it was getting dark, a car, with a man and woman inside, crawled past and Gloria slithered down in her seat. "Those are Venatore officers," she told her companions. "I don't think they saw me." "What about me?" Neil asked. "Would they recognise me?" "No," Gloria replied, "Those two weren't in the hotel when you were there. It looks like Beresford has sent out patrols." As a precaution, Neil moved to a carpark from which they could still monitor the beach. He didn't want to be in the same spot if the Venatores came back. It would probably raise their suspicions. Both Gloria and Neil had radios, so Gloria switched hers to the Venatore's channel in order to monitor their communications.

Beresford had indeed sent several units on patrol of the coastal towns in this part of Fife. The radio traffic was routine stuff – units checking in with nothing to report. Over the next two hours, the same car from previously crawled along the promenade twice more. It was full dark now. Suddenly, both their radios sprung into life, almost simultaneously. Sharon's call was slightly ahead. "Keranrodai has uncloaked," she said. "He's in a place called Dysart – just a few hundred yards from where he killed my friends." Seconds later, on the Venatore frequency, an urgent call went out. "Unit six reporting a code red – repeat code red. We have sight of a strange creature at Dysart harbour. Definitely not human – possibly goblin." Almost immediately, Beresford was on the radio. "All units, converge on Dysart," he said. "Unit six, keep eyes on the creature. Do not let it escape but try not to engage until backup arrives. That should be no more than a few minutes. Shoot to kill!"

Gloria looked at Neil. "Why aren't we moving? Those operatives won't be able to kill Keranrodai unless they have specialised weapons. They won't know what they're dealing with. We need to get there – quick." "Wait," Neil replied. "There's something not right. Keranrodai would not be seen by humans if he didn't want to be seen. Remember he carried out a brutal murder, yards from passing people in Kirkcaldy. No-one saw or heard anything. This is a diversion. He means to attack elsewhere – maybe even here. We should wait. Even if this is not a subterfuge, the presence of so many Venatores complicates matters. We're liable to be arrested on suspicion or shot." Gloria wasn't convinced. "Maybe it's time for us to co-operate," she said. "To pool our knowledge and help each other. This is too big for petty rivalries. We can use the Venatores and their resources." "You'd be as well signing your own resignation," Neil said. "Beresford will happily take your badge." "My future is of lesser importance than nailing Keranrodai," was Gloria's reply.

Neil started the car. He was reluctantly about to comply with Gloria's wishes when Sharon spoke on the radio. "Keranrodai's disappeared again," she said. "There's no trace of him now." The hubbub on the Venatore frequency was almost frantic. The two officers who'd spotted Keranrodai were dead and their quarry was nowhere to be seen. "We've missed our chance," Gloria said. "Not necessarily," Neil replied. "I've got a hunch. I suspect Keranrodai is going to double back. I think the next attack will be back in Kirkcaldy. He's diverted attention to Dysart. He's playing with the Venatores. It's only twenty minutes from here and close enough for Keranrodai to get there quickly by foot." Gloria shrugged. "We've nothing to lose," she said. "Go for it."

Traffic was light on the road and Neil put his foot down. They made it to the outskirts of Kirkcaldy in less than fifteen minutes. It was only a couple of minutes later that Neil stopped the Capri on the town's promenade. He turned to Gloria with a smug smile on his face. "Never underestimate Fey intuition," he said. "He's here. I hear his tone. He is close." The three got quickly out of the car. They were opposite the alley where Keranrodai's first atrocity had been committed. "He's in there," Neil told his companions. " You two should flank me but stay slightly behind me. It would be a good time to ready your weapons." Despite the fact that there were people and cars around, Gloria drew her gun and Janet pulled her knife. Neil raised his hand over his right shoulder and suddenly, from nowhere, drew forth a shimmering sword. The blade seemed insubstantial. The body of the weapon was almost mist-like – with shifting shapes swirling within it. The edges though, were sheathed with a thin but solid silver, glowing outline. "Clayfansolas," said Neil "The Sword of Light."

They moved towards the alleyway. Their weaponry was beginning to attract the attention of passers-by. Most seemed amused – thinking it was some kind of stunt. Neil's sword didn't appear real. It looked like some kind of fancy light-sabre. Neil, Gloria and Janet paid no heed to the spectators. They had more important things to occupy them. As they approached the alley, Gloria keyed her radio and called Sharon. As there had been no communication the other way, she had to assume that Keranrodai was still cloaked. That wouldn't stop Neil being able to track him. Gloria told Sharon that they were locked onto their target and that she and her companions could stand down for the night. She'd let them know how matters worked out.

At the entrance to the alleyway, Neil stopped. "I can sense his magic," he said. "He's cloaked but he's also in unseen mode. He'll be visible to me but not to you two. It would be foolish for you to go any further. The first you'd know of Keranrodai would be when he ripped your throat out. You should either wait here or go back to the car." Gloria protested but Neil insisted. "I'm a warrior of the Fey," he said, "One of the best – and I have Clayfansolas. I can handle this." Gloria was professional enough to know that Neil was being prudent. Going against a powerful, invisible enemy was not a wise move. Reluctantly she acquiesced. Neil entered the alley and Keranrodai was waiting for him.

"So", said Keranrodai, "Finally – the Fey who has been searching for me – and getting nowhere close." "Until today," Neil replied. "I see you have a magical sword," the Goblin went on. "And here's me – totally unarmed. Is that a fair fight for a Fey warrior? Where's your honour?" "Was it a fair fight when you tortured and murdered a defenceless woman in this very alley?" Neil said.

Keranrodai shrugged. "She was only a human," he said, "They are way below the likes of you and me. By the way – I like the looks of your two companions. I wager they'll be delicious. When I'm finished with you I'll go after them."

Neil had had enough of talking. He hefted his blade and rushed to the attack. Keranrodai threw out a percussive spell but Neil had been expecting some such and resisted it with his own magic. He swung Clayfansolas at the Goblin's head but Keranrodai was lightening quick. He ducked and swerved past the Fey. As he did so he smashed a fist into Neil's face. The Fey was jolted but recovered quickly. He whirled round and went on the attack again. Keranrodai proved to be a slippery opponent. Pursue him as he may, Neil couldn't close with him. Gloria was watching from the bottom of the alley. The lighting was poor but she could see Neil well enough, due to his glowing sword. She couldn't see his invisible enemy though, so she didn't know how well the combat was going.

Gloria was tempted to squeeze off a couple of shots but without a visible target she held fire for the time being. Neil kept up his pursuit in a flurry of sword strokes but Keranrodai dodged and jinked, staying out of reach. The fight was edging down the narrow alley, coming ever closer to the bottom. Finally, Gloria could resist no longer. She began to move slowly and cautiously towards the half-seen combat – with her gun raised in front of her. She was looking for her moment and then it arrived. Neil was facing across the breadth of the alley and Gloria realised that Keranrodai must be facing him. She squeezed the trigger four times, aiming in a pattern where she surmised the Goblin to be. Her pistol was loaded with alternate silver and iron bullets – in the hope that these metals would prove inimical to Keranrodai. As soon as the shots were fired, the Goblin winked into view. She'd obviously hit him and the impact of the bullets had knocked him out of his unseen state. He turned his gaze on her with a venomous rage-filled stare. Neil did not hesitate. Taking advantage of his enemy's distraction he thrust Clayfansolas towards him. The blade only encountered empty air. Keranrodai was gone.

"Where is he?" Gloria asked. "Is he dead?" "I don't think so," Neil replied. "He's got more tricks than I gave him credit for. He is gone. You've hurt him but I think he'll go off and nurse his wounds. Who knows how quickly he'll recover. He has transported himself somewhere else. We're going to have to reconsider our approach to this. Just locating him is not sufficient. We have to find a way of holding him in place until he can be killed. There's nothing more we can do tonight. Let's get out of here before the gunshots bring the police."

Neil sheathed his sword which winked out of sight and they trooped disconsolately back to the car. Once more, Keranrodai had come out on top – but at least, this time they'd injured him.

Chapter Forty Seven – An Unexpected Peril. (Friday 22nd May 1980.)

Sharon, Michelle and Ann relaxed a bit when Gloria told them that Keranrodai had been found. They were still on edge though, waiting for word on how matters transpired. Sharon turned to Ann with a serious look on her face. "Ann," she said, "There's a problem I need to tell you about. Someone is planning to harm you. I saw it when we were working together." Ann was shocked. "Who?" she asked. "It's a man called Malcom Brown," Sharon replied. "He works security at the University." Ann immediately knew who Sharon meant. Her mind went back to the incident on Sunday night and the man she had reflexively hurled into the bushes with her magic. He had been intent on having sex with her and she was having none of it.

Sharon went on. "This is a bad man. He is a serial molester and rapist. He takes advantage of young women he encounters through his work – but he has also attacked an underage girl in a multi-storey carpark. He pretended that he was a police officer and lured her away from a bus stop. Then he groped her, terrorised her and eventually, savagely raped her. The girl is a wreck and scared to go out. Brown relished this incident and plans to repeat it in future. This man will one day go further and end up killing some innocent woman. I fear that you might be that victim. He is fired with a thirst for revenge against you, for resisting him previously. He does not know exactly how he was bested by you but he feels humiliated and aggrieved. He has a friend – a little weasel of a man – who has followed you home from work. They know where you live now. Brown is inflamed by lust and the desire to hurt you. He plans to stalk and rape you. He is a danger to you and perhaps even your daughters."

Ann was appalled and not a little scared. "What can I do?" she asked in consternation. "You have to deal with him before he gets to you," was Sharon's reply. "Are white witches allowed to harm people?" was Ann's next question. "Magic is magic," Sharon said. "There is no real distinction between white and black. The line comes between what practitioners of either branch are prepared to do to accomplish their wishes. I was raised in the Druidic tradition. We have no compunction about killing our enemies. We are involved in trying to destroy Keranrodai. This Brown is just another kind of monster. He will continue to harm women until he's stopped. He won't do it of his own accord."

At that moment Gloria came on the radio to say that Keranrodai had eluded them again and that she and her companions were on their way home. Everyone in the room was deflated but also relieved that none of their friends had been hurt. Ann returned to the subject of Malcolm Brown. "Could we not go to the police?" she asked. "I don't think they would accept the word of a Seer as evidence," Sharon replied. "Well, what can I do?" "That's entirely up to you," Sharon said. "You could wait for him to come to you – but that could prove messy. Or, you could go after him – with the help of your friends. Using force to defend you and yours is perfectly acceptable. It depends on whether you trust my word or not. He is a dangerous man."

Ann did in fact trust Sharon implicitly. She just found it difficult to imagine herself acting aggressively. True – she had attacked Garry and viciously beat him when her children had been under threat – but this felt different. Sharon waited in silence for Ann to reach a decision. Ann thought back to her brief encounter with Brown last Sunday evening. She had sensed a nastiness in him then. He certainly had a forceful personality. Ann had almost found herself complying with his orders. Part of that was probably due to the conditioning she had undergone during her time with Garry. Brown had been brutal in his treatment of John – beating him mercilessly. Ann could only imagine that level of violence being visited on a woman. She had wanted to take John to the hospital that night but he had demurred. They were no longer an item. Ann wasn't too upset by that. His sexual technique left a lot to be desired – literally. Ann remembered the fear and anger she'd felt that night. The thought of Brown coming after her in her home and possibly harming her girls was terrifying. It was the possible threat to her daughters that finally decided her. "Let's go get him," she said.

Sharon smiled and nodded. "I think that's wise," she said. "I know where he's going to be in just over an hour from now. I'm sure three witches like us can handle him." Ann's daughters were already in bed, so she went upstairs to her neighbours, the Kirkwoods, to see if their teenage daughter would sit in the flat for a couple of hours while she popped out on urgent business. Fifteen minutes later the three women were in Sharon's hire car heading for the University. Given Sharon's prescience, they were able to make their dispositions undetected when they got there. Ann and Michelle secreted themselves in the very bush covered alcove where Brown had concealed himself on Sunday evening. Sharon would play the part of a lone female and see if Brown accosted her.

Sharon had got her timing spot on. Right on cue, Malcolm Brown appeared. Ann and Michelle were not particularly under cover but it was dark and they were fairly well concealed. Sharon began to walk along the single track road that wound its way through the rural University grounds. She timed her progress so that Brown encountered her right in front of where the other two women were hiding. Brown reacted true to form. "Excuse me Miss," he said, "Can I ask what you're doing here?" "Just walking," Sharon replied. "There's been reports of a woman matching your description attempting to break into University buildings," Brown said. "Wasn't me," said Sharon. "Trying to get money for drugs – were you?" "No!" "So you say. I'm afraid I'm going to have to search you." "Can you do that?" "Yes. Under section 12 of the Criminal Justice Act – sub-section c, I have the power to detain you on suspicion and carry out a search of your person."

This was all nonsense, of course. Brown had simply made it up. He had a set of handcuffs in his jacket pocket that he'd recently purchased. He was eager to try out his new toy and this seemed like an opportune moment. Once the cuffs were on, he could do just about anything he wanted. Brown took them from his pocket and moved towards Sharon. "Put your hands out in front of you, Please Miss," he said. Sharon stood her ground with her hands by her sides. She looked small and vulnerable next to the hulking Brown. Ann decided it was time to intervene. "Hey!" she shouted. "Leave her alone." Brown was momentarily startled, having thought he was alone with his intended victim. He spun round in the direction of Ann's voice as she and Michelle walked from their hiding place. His face twisted into a vicious snarl as he recognised who it was.

"I hear you've been looking for me," Ann said. Brown could only assume that Bob Montgomery had somehow sold him out – but he wasn't one to look a gift horse in the mouth. She was here now. Quickly Brown looked around – making sure there was no-one else lurking in ambush. The prospect of taking on the three women did not trouble him. He was perfectly prepared to use overpowering violence on them. If there were any repercussions, he could swear that he'd apprehended them up to no good and that they, in fact, had attacked him. He spoke to Ann – his voice menacing. "Thanks for making my job easier," he said. "You and I have got business to attend to." He looked at

Sharon and Michelle in turn. "You two can leave," he told them. "It would be best for you, if you did. She's staying."

None of the women made a move. Brown decided it was time to seize control. He took a couple of steps and lunged for Ann. Suddenly – he was held immobile. Strain as he might, he couldn't budge an inch. The three women had moved to stand in ring around him. Each of them was holding their right hand towards him, with the palm forward. The women hadn't actually planned this far. They were acting purely on instinct. Connected to him as they were, they could clearly see the murderous darkness that he nurtured inside. He would take what he wanted from anyone that he wanted to and they would face the violent consequences if they resisted – and maybe even if they didn't. With one accord, the women crushed his black heart and he dropped down dead.

Chapter Forty Eight – Sexual Healing . (Saturday 23rd May 1980.)

Ruth was a nervous wreck. Her sleep had been troubled the previous night and not because of any disturbing dreams. She very much wanted to take Neil up on his offer of a sexual assignation. Ruth had had many lustful thoughts about the good-looking Fey – of which she was ashamed. She was sexually naïve but eager to experience the sex act properly. Ruth already knew that her body responded with pleasure to stimulation of her genitals, despite her only encounters being abusive in nature and short in duration. She had explored herself and enjoyed the pleasure of masturbation but dearly longed for the opportunity for intimacy with a man. Technically, Ruth was no longer a virgin, due to her rape by Garry Wallace but she considered herself as such. Her next sexual encounter would, in fact, be her first, as far as she was concerned. In Ruth's opinion, Neil would be the ideal person with which to surrender her virginity.

Things were not straightforward though. Ruth worried about how weird it would be afterwards. Neil seemed to be of the opinion that they could have sex and then go back to normal. Perhaps for him, that would be the case but Ruth doubted it would be so for her. In fact, the way he'd talked about it, it had seemed more like a therapy session or a visit to the doctor. It was not couched in any kind of romantic way. Ruth had definite feelings for Neil. She was honest enough with herself to realise that this was in the nature of a crush rather true love of any kind. Ruth wrestled with her desire to experience, what she thought of as, the wonder of sex, against her misgivings of what the consequences might be. In the end, Ruth decided that having a liaison with Neil was not a good idea. With regret, she opted to let the opportunity pass.

By mid-morning, Ruth had changed her mind. She still wasn't fully committed but was edging towards it. As lunchtime arrived, she was far too nervy to eat anything. Ruth began her preparations. She was totally unsure of herself. After showering, Ruth examined her naked body in the bathroom mirror. Was she desirable? She couldn't tell. Ruth now began agonising about what she should wear. All her underwear was functional rather than sexy. Unfortunately, there was nothing she could do about that now. She selected her best pair of white cotton pants and a matching white bra. Most of the time Ruth was a jeans and tee-shirt girl but she did have a nice little black mini-dress that she wore for social occasions. Ruth always thought it looked good in it – so she decided to wear that. She hadn't experimented much with makeup – a fact she regretted now – so reluctantly Ruth opted to go without. She did know enough to put a little dab of perfume behind each ear. She didn't want it to be overpowering. Then she was ready – and promptly decided she wasn't going after all.

Unlike Ruth, Neil had no doubts whatsoever about what he intended. He was growing more and more certain that Gloria's Coven – The Seven Sisters – had a big part to play in the matter of the Adversary and her Harbinger. Ruth was an integral part of the Coven. She needed to be functioning at her best to play her part. Doubt had been planted in her mind, by either Keranrodai or by the Adversary herself. Advantage had been taken of Ruth's sexual naivety and guilt engendered by the abusive encounters she had previously endured. All this served to undermine her confidence. Neil knew it could be argued that he was also planning to take advantage of Ruth. After all, he was planning to have sex with naïve young woman that had a massive crush on him. There would undoubtedly be sexual pleasure for him in this. Ruth was an attractive woman but Neil saw no contradiction in enjoying himself whilst performing what he saw as an altruistic act.

Neil never used magic to influence women to have sex with him. He had the natural charisma of the Fey and of course, their fabled good looks. His innate empathy allowed him to do what would best please any sexual partner. He had, however, manipulated Ann's mind to help her fulfil a dream. She had imagined that she was doing a steamy striptease to a room full of men, when, in actual fact, only Neil had been present. The whole experience was geared to Ann's perfect fantasy. To her, it was real and was immensely cathartic. It helped her realise her own power and to take responsibility for her own actions and desires.

Neil was astounded at how quickly the women of the Coven were growing in power and the ability to wield it. When Sharon had returned home last night, she'd told them of the whole episode regarding Malcolm Brown and what she, Ann and Michelle had done. Gloria was shocked at first. She called it murder but Neil thought it justifiable homicide. Gloria spent some time quizzing Sharon regarding how her gift as a Seer worked. Sharon told her that it wasn't a perfect science. Sometimes she could focus on a specific area where information was required and meet with success. Other times, things just came to her unbidden. It was only because she'd been in communion with Ann the previous night that the matter had come up in the first place. Gloria asked Sharon how much she trusted her own insights. She replied that sometimes they were vague enough to warrant circumspection – but at other times they were very strong and clear. These latter ones, she trusted implicitly. Last night's had fallen into that category. Asked if she knew everything that was going to happen, Sharon replied, "not at all." Neither could she see anything to do with her own personal future – though she could, at times, see that of friends and acquaintances. In the end, Gloria accepted that The Venatores often terminated people without due process, so perhaps the women's actions could be justified – as long as they didn't make a habit of killing people.

The Codex of Caradoc was proving a source of unending frustration to Neil. He was getting nowhere with it. There were Loremasters in the Land of The Fey who could probably have helped him but to go there would mean instant death to him. He did not fear the Sealgaire Glas in this realm but over there, they would come at him in overwhelming numbers. If only the King would change his policy of turning a blind eye to the whole business of the Adversary. It would end up biting the Fey sooner or later. An afternoon with Ruth would prove to be a welcome distraction from his frustrations. He didn't know if that thought was unworthy. The Fey had a very relaxed attitude to sexual matters. Just about anything was tolerated. Be it straight sex, homosexuality and even incest – it was all fine. Monogamy was not valued at all in their society. Necrophilia was frowned upon and rape was punishable by death – as was sex with anyone under the age of twelve. Neil couldn't help sharing some of that ethos but he had adopted much of the human approach to matters sexual. That was why he told Gloria of his intentions towards Ruth. He didn't know if she believed him or even understood what he meant but at least he'd been honest with her.

Neil was surprised when he drove up to the meeting place and Ruth wasn't there. He'd been fairly certain that she would come. He could also understand why she might not show up. He had promised her he would wait for ten minutes – so that was what he'd do. After seven minutes, Ruth appeared. She was hurrying and looking anxious. A smile appeared on her face when she saw him there. She gave Neil a wave and he reciprocated. Ruth was looking good. She was a pretty girl with short black hair and pale-blue eyes. Ruth had a pale complexion which was framed by the blackness of her hair, giving her a striking appearance. Neil reckoned that Ruth didn't realise just how attractive she was. The black mini-dress she was wearing, perfectly complemented her natural colouring. In her short life, her experience of sex had been unfortunate, to say the least. Neil intended to remedy that today – if that was what she truly wanted.

Ruth got into Neil's car. He could see how nervous she was. Neil leaned over and kissed her on the lips. It was the briefest of contacts but it made Ruth feel much better. Perhaps, she thought, there might be an element of romance in their assignation – rather than the sterile therapy session it had threatened to be. Ruth thought that Neil was the most perfect man she had ever seen. He was about five foot ten tall with dark blond hair and dreamy grey eyes. Apart from the dream she'd had about him – which of course ended disastrously – she often imagined his face when she was pleasuring herself alone in bed at night. Despite her earlier vacillation, it had been almost inevitable that she wouldn't pass up the chance to be with him. Part of this was her yearning for a fulfilling sexual encounter. Like many young people, who hadn't yet truly participated in sexual intimacy, it had assumed a greater significance than it possibly would have if she'd been more experienced.

Neil drove off and Ruth chattered away – inconsequential things and probably a sign of her nervousness. Their destination was The Royal Hotel in Bridge of Allan. Neil had booked a room there. He parked in the hotel carpark and they went inside. They picked up the key from reception and then proceeded directly to the room. Ruth's stomach was full of butterflies. Her nerves were jangling but there was a delicious anticipatory pressure in her lower abdomen. Excitement was her overriding emotion. "This is really happening," she told herself. When they got to the room, Ruth hadn't a clue what to do next – never having been in such a situation before. She would have liked to behave with sophistication and seductiveness but knew she couldn't pull that off. Instead she waited to take her cue from Neil.

They both removed their jackets and put them on a chair. Neil had arranged to have a bottle of white wine waiting for them in the room. He took it from the ice-bucket and poured them both a glass. Neil sat on the bed and Ruth sat next to him. They sipped their wine in silence for a few minutes. Ruth felt the butterflies in her stomach settling down. Her nerves were calming but her sexual anticipation was growing. Being close to Neil and alone in the room with him was arousing her – even though nothing had happened yet. Neil finished his wine and laid his glass on the bedside table. Ruth followed suit, a few seconds later. He put an arm round her shoulders and leaned in to kiss the corner of her mouth. It was a very gentle touch and he repeated this twice more. On the third kiss, Ruth turned her head and met him full on the lips. For a moment or two they kissed, almost chastely and then their lips parted and their tongues entwined. Ruth had obviously heard of French kissing and always thought it sounded kind of gross but the reality was different. It was a whole level of intimacy that she had never experienced before or thought possible.

After a time, Neil broke off and stood up. He began to undress. Taking her cue from him, Ruth did the same. She slipped off her dress and let it fall to the floor. Standing there in just her bra and pants, Ruth suddenly felt very self-conscious. Nevertheless, with just the briefest of hesitations, she unhooked and discarded her bra. There were conflicting feelings competing in her innards – a knot of anxiety offset by a powerful and visceral sexual excitement. Fearing that any delay would make her lose her nerve, Ruth quickly removed her pants and stood naked. Neil finished his undressing and Ruth gazed on his nakedness. She had never seen a man fully naked before and she thought it was perfection. Neil's body was well proportioned and firm with defined muscle tone. There was no hair at all on his torso – apart from a nest of dark blond around his pubic area. His cock was already fully erect. Ruth remembered thinking that her cousin's erection looked angry when she first saw it all those years ago. She knew it was foolish to ascribe attributes to a mere appendage but Neil's didn't look angry. It looked eager.

Neil, in his turn, savoured the sight of Ruth unclothed. He had suspected that she would look good but the reality surpassed his expectations. Her body, though fully mature, was obviously youthful. It was firm and toned. Her breasts were not large but well-formed and shapely – with pale areola and small pink nipples. It was the whiteness of her skin that he found most striking. It was almost like marble but no marble had ever been so vibrant. The effect was stunning. Only the pinkness of her nipples and the small triangle of black pubic hair broke the uniform alabaster of her body. The rich blackness of her pubes was a fascinating contrast to the rest of her form. Neil was captivated.

At first, Ruth was embarrassed by Neil's contemplation of her body but as she saw his obvious approval, she began to enjoy the moment. Neil moved to her and they kissed again. As their tongues encountered each other once more, Neil cupped Ruth's breast and she was electrified. He guided her towards the bed and she lay down. Neil got onto the bed with Ruth and began to work with his hands. In her dream, Ruth had imagined Neil doing delicious things to her with his hands. Well, now he did all those things and several more that she hadn't even thought of. He caressed, stroked, kneaded and tweaked – all the time kissing her deeply. Neil worked his way down to her cunt and began to manipulate Ruth's clitoris. He seemed to know exactly how much pressure to apply and the optimal frequency with which to elicit the most thrilling response. Ruth mounted towards orgasm. She found herself emitting vocalisation that, to her own ears, sounded like a chimpanzee. This briefly distracted her but Neil's ministrations swept her away and she no longer cared. Her sounds grew in intensity, volume and frequency until they culminated in a long, screaming orgasm. This was the first she'd ever had in congress with someone else. It was also the best and most powerful that she'd ever experienced.

It was only after she'd come, that Ruth realised she had a hold of Neil's dick and was vigorously wanking it. Neil knew of the disastrous ending that Ruth had experienced in her dream. He had feared that she would freeze if he brought her near orgasm whilst penetrating her. The fear might prove too much for her and that would be very damaging. He intended to make sure that she was fully relaxed and in the zone before he actually entered her. So now, he went to work on her with his mouth. Neil started at her neck, shoulders and throat. He kissed, sucked and tongued her. This was totally outside anything Ruth had even thought of. Neil worked his way down her body and Ruth shuddered with anticipation of his final destination. He reached her tits, where he nibbled, sucked and licked her nipples – whilst caressing and stroking with his hands. Neil moved down to Ruth's belly-button. She had never realised that this part of her body could be so sensitive – as Neil darted his tongue into it – licking and sucking.

Ruth's hands were on Neil's head – grasping handfuls of his hair. Then – to her joy – Neil brought his head down between her thighs. His lips and tongue sent shivers of pleasure through her. Neil knew exactly how to maximise her sexual gratification. He worked her clitoris – sucking on it, licking it and nibbling on it – whilst darting his tongue into her cunt and tasting her juices. Ruth's grasp on Neil's hair was becoming more intense and her gasping grew frenzied once again. Then, Ruth climaxed for the second time – and – unbelievably – it was stronger and more intense than the first one. Ruth was not normally a squirter but this orgasm was so forceful that she sprayed Neil's face with hot vaginal fluid. This came out in three convulsive and prolonged spasms. Half an hour ago, this would have mortified Ruth with embarrassment but now she simply revelled in the joy and pleasure of it.

Neil had expected to experience pleasure from this encounter but he had never anticipated just how much. He'd told Ruth that this would be a once only liaison. Now he wasn't sure that he wouldn't want to come back for more. It was time. Neil positioned his body between Ruth's legs and inserted his cock into her. She gave a little gasp of pleasure as she felt him inside her. They began to move – rocking in rhythmic unison with each other. At first their motion was gentle and sensual but it gradually grew in speed, intensity and forcefulness. Neil totally lost himself and fucked Ruth harder than he'd ever fucked any human. She responded with equal vigour. Her fingernails raked Neil's back and this roused him to even greater endeavour. Both of them were loudly vocal in their exertions – something that had never happened to Neil before. Then, Ruth reached her third climax of the afternoon and Neil cut loose his own. His semen exploded from him and pumped into Ruth's cunt. His ejaculation was long and prodigious – an extended moment of pure pleasure.

Neil and Ruth collapsed, spent, onto the bed. Tears of pure joy were coursing down Ruth's cheeks. This had been all and more than she had hoped for. She felt fulfilled and ecstatic that she was no longer a virgin. She knew that she would never find another lover as skilled and sensitive as Neil but that was alright. For the time being, she just wanted to bask in the memory of what had just happened. They lay for a while entwined on the bed. After a while they talked. Neil suggested that Ruth should speak to Gloria about her dream and her past history. He thought it important that she do so. Gloria was the leader of her coven – their sisterhood. Neil was an outsider to this and it was important for the sisters to be honest with each other. Their survival might depend on it. He'd told Gloria of his intentions with Ruth – so it wasn't a secret. How awkward things might turn out, remained to be seen.

They lay in companionable silence for a while and then Ruth reached for Neil's cock and began to manipulate it. It leaped to attention almost immediately. Neil lay on his back and manoeuvred Ruth astride him. This was something she'd never even thought of. Neil pushed his cock into her once more and she began to ride him. She liked this. It was her who was in control and she relished it. Neil had no complaints as he viewed Ruth's wonderful body while it undulated to and fro. Their coupling began sedately as before and, as before, it grew more and more urgent until it ended in a frenzy of orgasmic force and vocalisation. Both were totally spent and replete. Neither had any doubt that this would not be the last time they would be together like this.

Chapter Forty Nine – Planning the Endgame. (Saturday 23rd May 1980.)

Gloria summoned the coven to a meeting at Neil's place. Their reactive approach to finding Keranrodai was bearing no fruit. At any moment, the Harbinger might finally locate the key and The Adversary would be set free. They needed to be more proactive and that need was growing increasingly urgent. The one fixed point they seemed to have was that they believed Keranrodai would walk upon Leven beach at some time in the future. Establishing when that would happen could be the key to success. Gloria's time was running out. She only had just over a week before she'd have to report for duty in Spain. Gloria was not at all sure that she wanted to resume her career in the Venatores. That was a decision she'd have to make and soon.

Neil had come home in the late afternoon and told her he'd been with Ruth but would tell her no more. He said that was Ruth's to do if she so chose. Gloria was not bothered by whatever Neil did or who he slept with. She did not consider herself in a relationship with him, in the sense it was usually meant. He was good in bed and that fulfilled a need in her. Less than ten minutes after they had first met they had been having enthusiastic sex. Gloria wasn't a heart and roses kind of girl. She had no desire for a steady relationship. A no strings attached situation was ideal for her. When she'd voiced concerns about Neil having sex with Ruth, it had simply been because of Ruth's comparative youth and vulnerability. Gloria did trust Neil for the most part. He would not have embarked on such a course of action without having a good reason – at least in his own perception.

Gloria was tired of spinning their wheels. They seemed to just go off on one wild-goose chase after another. Not only that but when they finally did track Keranrodai down, Neil had been unable to finish him off. Gloria had shot and injured him but how badly was unknown. She'd no doubt that he would recover and be back to plague them. What she wanted to do tonight was explore what the coven might be able to do. That's why she had chosen to have the meeting here at Neil's cottage. The back room of the Halfway House wasn't private enough. Neil would absent himself while the women met. He'd go to his room and continue puzzling over The Codex of Caradoc. Janet would bring Michelle and Ann while Sharon drove in to pick up Ruth and Jenny.

As soon as Ruth came in, Gloria saw the change in her. The energy emanating from her was fizzling. Whatever she and Neil had got up to, it had certainly seemed to work. There was a confidence about her that had always seemed lacking before. Gloria doubted that it was simply down to the joys of sex. She'd often heard men imply that all a woman needed was a good fuck to sort out their problems. In her opinion, finding a good fuck wasn't all that easy. Anyway, Ruth seemed to have laid some ghost to rest – possibly as she'd also laid Neil. Ruth was still as sweet as ever but her characteristic diffidence seemed to have evaporated.

The women gathered in Neil's living room. Gloria asked Sharon, Michelle and Ann to tell the others about their dealings with Malcolm Brown. All of them thought that their sisters had done the right thing. Gloria did counsel though, that taking a life should never be undertaken lightly. What Gloria was most interested in was how the three women had pinned Brown to the spot before they finished him off. She wondered if the combined power of the coven could do the same to Keranrodai and perhaps kill him in the same manner. He had powerful magic at his own disposal but maybe the combined might of the Seven Sisters could overcome this. It would be a perilous course of action and much could go wrong but each of the women's magic had increased manifold and their combined talent was greater than the sum of its parts. If they could pull this off, they might even be a last hope of combatting the Adversary.

The women gathered in a loose circle. Sharon had a small hand-drum which she had used in Druidic rituals. It was a way of focussing a group's consciousness. She began to beat out a rhythm and intoning a three word chant which she'd taught to the others. The others joined in and they chanted in unison. It was slow in coming but gradually the women became aware of their sisters' minds impinging on their own. Each could feel all the others as a presence in their psyche. The level of attunement continued to grow until the coven became a singular entity with one group mind. Each woman was still aware of their own being but their identities merged and overlapped. The magical energy in the room fairly crackled. Neil, in the next room, felt it strongly. There was no adequate test for taking on Keranrodai but each of them felt the power they could call upon as a collective. If they could get him in their sights, maybe it would be enough. After a few minutes, Gloria signalled to Sharon and she stopped her drumming. It took several minutes before the women reverted to their normal selves. Gloria was impressed by the power she'd felt at their disposal but she had no idea how effective it would prove against Keranrodai. She would put her mind to working out a more realistic test. Perhaps Neil could suggest something.

There was a bit of a hangover following the intensity of their bonding. There was also the fact that, it was one thing to have great potency, it was quite another to know how to wield it effectively. This was something none of them had experience in. Having said that, Michelle, Ann and Sharon had acted purely on instinct when dealing with Malcolm Brown. Perhaps they would know exactly what to do when finally called upon to act. The beach at Leven might well be the site where this would be put to the test. Apart from the two Venatore officers in Dysart, Keranrodai hadn't killed the night before. As far as they knew, he hadn't feasted on human flesh. How this would bear on his usual two-day cycle of depredation they didn't know. Would he hunt again tonight or would it be tomorrow? Gloria was monitoring Venatore radio traffic to get a heads up if anything should occur. She was able to deduce that Beresford had taken control of the police operation – just as he had done in Stirling at the turn of the year. There was a heavy Venatore presence all along the Fife coast – augmented by local police.

If it could be established just when Keranrodai was going to be on Leven beach, they could set an ambush for him. Sharon was still convinced that Janet's vision, where she'd seen him hunting in Leven, was a true sight. The when of this was the unknown. Sharon proposed to go with Janet to Leven in the morning. There, on the actual site, she would trance and seek to unlock when Janet's vision would come to pass. With this information, a trap could be laid. Gloria asked everyone to be ready to move at a moment's notice should it be necessary. Until then, there wasn't much more to be done.

Neil was called through from his room and he told them of the power surge he'd felt when they melded their minds. It was far stronger than he would have thought possible. He approved of the plan for Janet and Sharon to go to Leven the next day. He thought that being in the actual location might be the key to discerning the timeline of Janet's vision. Speaking of keys, he told them of his difficulties with translating The Codex of Caradoc. He could decipher all the runes but the words they revealed were in no known language. They were gibberish – nonsense syllables. It had to be a cipher – and there had to be a key to this somewhere. Neil questioned Sharon if she knew of anything that would fit this description. She good think of nothing. Neil was at the point of giving up on the book. He didn't even know if there was anything in it that would help them. His intuition told him that matters were fast approaching a climax. He just didn't know how that climax would fall out.

Chapter Fifty – The Sealgaire Glas. (Sunday 24th May 1980.)

Gloria and Neil had gone to bed when the others left. She saw no reason to stop sleeping with him just because of his dalliance with Ruth. As they undressed she had noticed the scratch marks on his back. "My, you did show Ruth a good time," she had commented. Neil had simply smiled and said, "As she did me. Are you Jealous?" Gloria had snorted and replied, "It's not a competition, you know." They had stopped speaking then and let their bodies do the talking. Relaxed and fully satisfied they had then settled down to sleep.

It was coming up to one in the morning when both of them awoke – fully alert. The door to their room had just opened. Each of them rolled from their own side of the bed to the floor. Gloria snatched up her gun from the bedside table and Neil drew forth Clayfansolas. Silhouetted in the doorway was Sharon. She ignored their nakedness and said urgently, "There are Fey hunters coming to kill you both." "How many and how soon will they be here?" Neil asked tersely. "There are seven and they'll be her in less than fifteen minutes." Was her reply. As Gloria and Neill began pulling clothes on, Sharon told them what else she had seen. "The Adversary has sent an emissary to the King of The Fey, offering him an accord. If he has you two destroyed, she will grant his Realm amnesty, when she is finally free. He has agreed to this. His Sherrif's complaints against you were merely a pretext for this action. It seems the Adversary must fear you."

Neil was livid. "The treacherous bastard," he said. "When this is done, I will chase him down and end him. He has instituted a blood feud." "How can I kill them?" Gloria asked. "Either your iron or your silver bullets will work – but you must hit either the brain or the heart. Anything else will just make them more annoyed. But – if you kill a Fey, you will be part of the blood feud and they will hunt you down." "Well – they're already wanting to kill me – so what's the difference?" Gloria said. "How can I help?" Sharon asked, "I've got a gun but only standard bullets." "What calibre is your weapon?" Gloria asked. "9 mm," came the reply. "I've silver and iron bullets to spare. They should fit," Gloria told her. "I suggest you get on to loading up some magazines."

As they readied themselves, Neil quickly briefed them. "Seven is a formidable force," he told them. "Even I would have no chance against that. We must ambush them. They won't know that we are expecting them and that's our only hope. These are elite hunters and they can detect you by the beating of your heart. I will use magic to cover your actual heartbeats and make it seem they are coming from the bedrooms. They cannot enter from the rear of the house. There are no windows large enough for them to get in. I believe they will come through the front door – trusting to stealth – and they are very stealthy. You two should hide yourselves here in the living room on either side of the door – making sure not to be in each other's line of fire. As soon as you see someone, start blasting and don't stop till you hear from me. Be careful. There will be archers. I too am an archer. I'll be outside, hiding in the trees and I'll take them from the rear." With that, Neil went to a closet and took out a bow which he quickly strung. He hung a quiver of arrows on his belt. "These are deadly to Fey," he told them. "What if they go unseen like you do?" Gloria asked. "They won't," Neil replied. "It wouldn't work on me and they don't know you know they're coming – besides – they do not fear mere humans. Their mistake." Neil grinned and said a quick "Good luck," before slipping out the door and into the night.

Gloria and Sharon quickly disposed themselves around the living room. Gloria hunkered down beside a sofa. It was scant cover but there wasn't anything much better. Sharon took up position in the doorway to her bedroom. She too hunkered down, keeping as low a profile as possible. They settled down to wait. Not a sound pervaded the room apart from the loud ticking of the wall clock. Gloria had experienced combat situations before but this one scared her a lot. She feared the Fey and the powers they had at their disposal. She only hoped that the benefit of surprise would work in their favour. Sharon too was tense. She'd never done anything like this before. Druidic breathing techniques helped Sharon still the erratic beating of her heart – but not by much. With a sense of resignation, she commended her soul to the afterlife. Survival seemed unlikely.

Neil had glided silently through the darkness and now he was ensconced in the branches of a tall Ash tree. This offered him the concealment he needed and gave him clear line of sight to his front lawn and the door to his cottage. He crouched there, immobile and barely breathing. The least movement could alert his deadly foes. Even Neil's acute hearing detected no sound as the seven figures appeared from the treeline and onto his lawn. One of them had actually passed under the tree where he was hidden. Neil recognised them all. Before his spell as Royal Sherriff, Neil had belonged to the Sealgaire Glas himself. Those stealing through the night towards his home were the best the King had at his disposal. He was certainly serious about seeing Neil and Gloria dead. Moving with infinite slowness Neil nocked and arrow to his bow.

Inside the cottage, the two women heard nothing. Each of them tried to fight down the growing dread that blossomed in their chests. Then, without warning, the door swung silently open. Gloria's heart missed a beat and she had to suppress a gasp. A few seconds later, a dark figure entered the cottage, carrying a bow with an arrow already on the string. He paused just over the threshold and peered around. Immediately he spotted Sharon and raised the bow to fire on her. Gloria had taken a bead on the intruder's head and now cut loose. She put three rapid shots into her target and he went down. Sharon was blasting away also now – even though no-one else appeared through the door. Then a figure fell into the room with an arrowhead protruding from the front of his throat. As he collapsed to the floor, the shaft of the arrow could be seen sticking out from the back of his neck.

Neil's first shaft had been the one that had killed the Hunter who fell dead into the cottage. Before that arrow had even reached its target, Neil had launched another one, that took a Fey through the heart. With the release of his second arrow, Neil threw himself from the tree. Three arrows thwacked into the tree trunk a second later – just where Neil had been hiding before he'd leapt to the ground. The Hunters now knew where he was. More arrows sped in his direction but Neil weaved and jinked, spoiling their aim – though some came uncomfortably close. Three of the remaining Hunters went after Neil, as the greater threat. The other proceeded towards the cottage to snuff out the mere humans within.

Gloria slid a fresh magazine into her gun. She didn't know what was transpiring outside but instinct told her it was time to move. She scuttled to the door, keeping low. Gloria poked her head around to look out and realised she'd made a terrible mistake. A Fey Hunter was standing a few yards away with a drawn bow. Such a skilled archer couldn't miss from that range. He released the arrow and it sped towards Gloria. It would take her square in the forehead. Suddenly, everything seemed to go into slow-motion. Gloria stood up and held her hand towards the arrow's flight. The projectile burst immediately into flames and fell in ashes to the ground. Gloria took careful aim and shot the Fey through the heart. Her knees buckled, at realising how close death had come to her. She almost collapsed to the ground but steadied herself in time. Gloria had no idea what had just happened and how she'd done what she did. It had been instinctive and unpremeditated – and totally inexplicable.

Neil was playing hide and seek among the trees. He'd discarded his bow and drawn Clayfansolas. In the thick woods, a bow was no longer a viable weapon. One of the Hunters hadn't realised this yet and paid the price when he couldn't bring his weapon to bear in time to stop Neil cutting him down. The sound of gunfire from the cottage had ceased. Neil hoped it was not for the worst of reasons. He had lost sense of where his enemies now were and hoped they had similarly lost him. He laid his back against a tree trunk and stood stock still, senses questing for any hint of his foes. A single gunshot rang out, momentarily distracting him. An undetected Hunter burst from the cover of the trees and rushed him with a sword, similar to his own, raised aloft. The Hunter brought the weapon crashing down towards Neil's head. With lightening reactions, he brought his own sword up to parry the strike. The blades clashed and a brilliant white flash illuminated the surrounding woodland. Twice more the swords rang together and twice more the eye-searing flashes lit the night. Then the Hunter lunged a stabbing thrust towards Neil's body. With a breathtaking economy of movement, Neil twisted aside just enough to avoid the deadly weapon and with a backhanded swing, took off the top third of his opponent's head.

The single combat had been brief and swift but Neil knew it would have alerted the remaining Hunter to his position. Keeping low and treading carefully he circled to his left. He worked his way back towards the edge of the treeline, anxious to see how matters stood with his two human companions. The cottage was in darkness and the door still stood open – but there were four Fey bodies visible. There had been only three when he'd fled to the trees. At least one of his companions was still alive then. Neil almost jumped out of his skin when three rapid gunshots rang out, close at hand. This was followed by a crashing thump as a body hit the ground. The remaining Hunter had climbed into a tree and had been waiting in ambush for Neil to show himself. He had been taking aim when Gloria had shot him off his perch. So much for underestimating mere humans – something Neil was often guilty of himself.

Gloria showed herself and Neil went to greet her, just as Sharon emerged from the cottage. Unbelievably, an entire squad of elite Hunters had been destroyed with no casualties on the other side. There was no time for swapping stories at the moment. There was much to do and there'd be no more sleep that night. They gathered the Fey bodies and Neil disposed of them by means of magical fire. It wouldn't do to leave them lying about to be found by the police and eventually the Venatores. The cottage was no longer safe. It was time to move elsewhere. They gathered whatever they thought they'd need and set off. Neil had another property, just a few miles away, in the Ochil Hills. He had kept it secret against the eventuality of needing an alternative hiding place. They set off for this and the chance to regroup. The others would have to be warned that they too might be in danger. Given what only two members of the Coven had achieved tonight, all seven assembled would be formidable to say the least. It seemed that the Adversary thought so too. Neil reminded himself never to get on the wrong side of The Seven Sisters.

Chapter Fifty One – Leven Beach – Part One. (Sunday 24th May 1980.)

After the drama of the night just gone, there was some discussion of postponing Sharon and Janet's trip to Leven. Sharon was adamant that it go ahead. The attack by the Sealgaire Glas had been traumatic and a worrying distraction. Nevertheless, there was still a job to be done. Gloria was concerned over the security of her friends. The King of The Fey had targeted herself and Neil at the behest of the Adversary but that didn't mean that the other members of the Coven were safe. Neil doubted that the Fey would mount another attack so soon but he couldn't rule it out completely. In Sharon's opinion the risk was small. No-one would know exactly where she and Janet were. Gloria eventually agreed. The risk, in the meantime, seemed small but they'd have to consider the implications for their future safety. It was a complication that they could well do without – considering that things had not been going so good anyway.

As it was Sunday and she had no work that day, Michelle had decided to accompany them. Janet had been her friend for a long time and they rarely saw each other now, outside of Coven meetings. It would give them a chance to catch up. Gloria was happy with this. She reckoned the extra body would increase their security. Gloria also insisted that Sharon take her firearm with her – loaded with silver and iron bullets. Janet, of course, was never without the knife she had used to kill Koldunya. It was a fine morning when they set off and looked set for sunshine throughout the day. Sharon hadn't had much sleep during the night, so they chose to take Janet's Imp, so she didn't have to drive. The plan was for Janet to show Sharon where she had seen Keranrodai in her vision. Sharon would then employ her skills as a Seer in the hope that proximity to the site would aid her in eliciting information. Perhaps they could finally track down and destroy their murderous quarry.

Despite the gravity of the overall situation, the women enjoyed a light-hearted journey to Fife. There was a lot of laughter, banter and joking. They got to Leven just before mid-day and decided on a quick bar lunch before getting down to business. It was partially an attempt to prolong the feel-good of their journey. They did limit themselves to soft drinks only. There was still work to be done. After lunch, Janet drove to the esplanade and showed Sharon where she'd seen Keranrodai in her dream. Sharon sat down cross-legged on the beach and began to meditate. The other two women went for a stroll along the beach to give Sharon space to do her thing. When they returned, twenty minutes later, Sharon was getting nowhere. She was exhausted from lack of sleep the previous night and the stress of the attack from the Sealgaire Glas. Sharon reckoned that what she needed was a short nap to regain some energy. They returned to the car and Sharon got into the back while Janet and Michelle sat in the front. Soon, Sharon was snoring loudly. She'd made her friends promise to wake her in no more than an hour.

Michelle and Janet sat for a while in silence, not wanting to disturb their sleeping companion. It was a warm day and they'd rolled down the car's windows for coolness. Janet began to feel her eyelids drooping. She was growing drowsy. It surprised her, as she'd slept fine the night before. Nevertheless, she was slipping towards sleep. Janet gave her head a shake to waken herself up and glanced at Michelle. Her friend was already deep in slumber. Janet felt a momentary stab of misgiving – but an increased weariness washed over her and soothed away her anxiety. It was still early and a little nap couldn't do any harm. Janet gave way to her torpor. She relaxed, closed her eyes and soon was fast asleep.

Chapter Fifty Two – Finding a Key. (Sunday 24th May 1980.)

Ever since her almost religious experience with Neil at The Royal Hotel, Ruth had felt on the brink of some revelation – but couldn't quite bring it to the fore. Then, while she'd slept, another dream – once again vivid in nature – had come to her and she understood. As soon as she was up in the morning she tried to phone Neil and Gloria but there was no answer from them. Twice more she phoned but with the same result. This was a little worrying. Ruth felt there was something wrong, though she didn't yet know of the attack on Neil's cottage during the night. A psychic link had been established, or strengthened, between Ruth and the Fey during their sexual congress. Through it, she saw something that he had missed in his frustration with translating the Codex of Caradoc. Ruth paced the floor, as her anxiety grew. This was important. She had no transport of her own. Michelle, Janet and Sharon would be away in Fife, whilst Ann and Jenny didn't have cars either. Getting to Neil's cottage was all but impossible by public transport.

Ruth resolved to try the phone one more time. If that was unsuccessful, she'd get a bus as far as possible and then walk the last five miles or so to the cottage. Though, if they weren't answering the phone, the chances were that they weren't there. There was no answer when Ruth tried again. As she was on the point of leaving, her own house phone rang. Ruth answered and was relieved when she heard Gloria's voice. Gloria briefly described the events that had taken place overnight. She was intending to drive in and pick up Ruth, Jenny and Ann. The women who'd gone to Fife would join them later. In light of the Sealgaire Glas attack, Gloria told her, they'd have to work out how to guard against further raids from that source. All their lives were in peril and they had to be aware. Ruth was more relieved than worried about what Gloria said. She told her that she had been shown something in a another graphic dream and she'd explain when they were all together.

An hour and a half later, the four women and the Fey were together in the cottage in the hills. Ruth was bursting with excitement and couldn't contain herself. Immediately, she asked Neil to fetch The Codex of Caradoc. He brought it out and placed it on the kitchen table. Ruth explained that she had seen the book in her dream. She examined it now. The book was bound in thick brown leather. Around the edges of the front and back cover were decorative stitches. These were probably once golden in colour but had faded to be almost as brown as the covers. Ruth got a sharp knife from the kitchen drawer and sliced the stitching at the top of the front cover. What had seemed like a single thick piece of leather, turned out to be two thin sheets held together by the stitches. This is what Ruth had seen in her dream. She pulled the rest of the stitching clear and revealed a thin sheet of parchment sandwiched between the leather. She extracted this and handed it to Neil. It was covered in double columns of runes. Neil saw at a glance that this seemed to be a key to transposing one set of symbols for another. Quickly, he tried it on the first group of runes in the Codex and it gave him a word he understood. It was in an ancient form of the Brythoneg language and said the word "know".

There was great excitement around the table. Here was the key to deciphering the Codex and hopefully finding something of use in its contents. Neil said it would take him some time but he'd get right on it. He took the book through to the living room and placed it on a coffee table before fetching a notepad and pencil. The others busied themselves in the kitchen making a pot of tea and some sandwiches. Gloria popped in briefly to see Neil. "Ruth's on fire," she said. "What on earth did you do to her?" Neil just shrugged. "Maybe," Gloria went on, "I should get you to shag all the others, to see if it has the same effect." "Yes," Neil replied with a straight face, "I think that would be a very good idea. I have been considering it." Gloria looked at him. She couldn't tell whether he was being serious or not but he would say no more. She rolled her eyes and went back to help the others in the kitchen.

Despite the many problems that crowded them, the mood was upbeat for the rest of the afternoon. It only began to dissipate when afternoon turned to evening and the group from Leven hadn't returned. There were many mundane reasons that could account for their lateness. Something could have happened to the car. Traffic could be heavy. There could be roadworks. Nevertheless, given the current situation, it began to be worrying. Surely, if anything transport related had been a problem, Sharon would have phoned. She had taken the number here before she left. More time went by – and still nothing.

Chapter Fifty Three – Leven Beach – Part Two. (Sunday 24th May 1980.)

Janet awoke, feeling groggy and disorientated. For a moment or two, she couldn't remember where she was. Then she sat bolt upright. It was dark outside. Just how long had she been out? Michelle was sound asleep in the passenger seat and Sharon still slumbered in the back. Janet reached over and urgently shook Michelle. No matter how hard she did so, Michelle could not be roused. Janet knew Michelle was alive. She was clearly breathing quite normally. With rising panic, Janet turned round in her seat and tried to awaken Sharon. This too, proved fruitless. Janet was momentarily stumped. She also had taken the phone number of Neil's new bolthole. She'd find a phone box and call for help. There was something unnatural going on here. It reeked of magic – and that could only mean Keranrodai.

As Janet readied to exit the car, a familiar looking women passed and walked towards the beach. With a shock, Janet realised where she'd seen her before. The jolt of recognition momentarily paralysed her. It was the woman from her dream. Janet watched in disbelief and then her nightmare was confirmed. At a distance behind the woman, Keranrodai appeared – stalking her. As if still in her dream, Janet found herself opening the car door and getting out. She lifted the knife, with which she'd killed Koldunya, from the receptacle on the door and gripped it in her right hand. Knowing that she was probably making a grave mistake, Janet set off after Keranrodai. She felt compelled and could do nothing to resist it. It was Déjà vu and could not be opposed. Full of fear, Janet pressed on.

They were now walking along the beach, with the water to their right. Keranrodai was in his hideous, Goblin persona. Janet knew that, by rights, she shouldn't be able to see him. He must be letting himself be seen. This was ominous and Janet was terrified. She was being drawn into terrible peril. Keranrodai made no attempt to close with the woman he was following. Janet realised that the woman was just a lure. She herself was the actual target. Keranrodai slowed and then turned to face his true target. He stood still and waited for Janet to approach him. She wanted to turn and flee but was unable to do so. The Goblin stood with a hideous grin on his face. He managed to look gruesome and smug at the same time. Repulsed as she was, Janet continued to approach. Eventually, she managed to still her progress and stopped about twenty feet from the Goblin.

For a moment or two, they stood facing each other. Then Keranrodai shook his head and said, in a disparaging tone, "Silly little girls – playing at being witches. They think their magic is so strong but their defences are thin – ever so easy to put them to sleep. Still – you look like a tasty treat. I promised the Fey that I'd go after his companions, the last time we met – and I always keep my promises. I might be a despicable wretch – but you can't say I'm not trustworthy. Well – I'm ready for my feast. Shall we get down to business?" Janet broke her inertia. With a despairing cry, she gripped her knife more firmly and charged. As she did so, Keranrodai raised a blowpipe to his lips and puffed. Janet felt the sting of the dart as it hit her throat. Then the sand of the beach was rushing up to meet her. She was unconscious before she landed.

Chapter Fifty Four – Into Thin Air. (Sunday 24th May 1980.)

Something tugged at Michelle's sleeping mind. It irritated her and caused her to stir in her seat. The feeling persisted until it brought her reluctantly awake. She could hear someone moving close at hand and then Sharon said, "What the fuck?" Suddenly, Michelle came fully awake. She couldn't even remember falling asleep. Both women were confused. How come it was dark? And then they realised – where was Janet? Alarm brought them fully alert. "Something sent us to sleep," Sharon said. "My guess is Keranrodai. I think he's got Janet." This filled them both with dread. They knew what he did with his victims. The thought of Janet enduring that fate was almost too much to bear. "We've got to find her," Michelle said and Sharon nodded in assent.

Quickly, the two women got out of the car. They hurried towards the beach as the most likely place to find their friend. Visibility was low owing to the darkness of the night. Somehow, that seemed unnatural too. Frantically, the women hurried along the sand, calling out Janet's name. The beach was deserted. People were walking on the esplanade and cars passed on the road – but not a soul moved on the beach. Sharon and Michelle searched for at least half an hour but not a sign of Janet could be found. They knew that Keranrodai could cloak himself and his victim. If he didn't want to be seen, then he wouldn't be. Michelle was in despair. She'd been Janet's friend for a long time. She broke down and began sobbing uncontrollably. Sharon took her by the shoulders and shook her fiercely. "That won't help," she said. Michelle controlled herself with an effort. "Let's get to a phone and ask the others for help," Sharon said – although she thought this was a forlorn hope. "They must know we're overdue."

It took them only a few minutes to find a phone box – but there was no answer when they called. Sharon worried that Keranrodai had a long reach. Maybe he had somehow managed to harm the rest of the Coven. He was a terrifying enemy and they didn't really know the extent of his powers. Sharon feared that they were outmatched. She too felt herself slipping into despair. Janet was gone – and there was nothing they could do to save her.

Chapter Fifty Five – Leven Beach – Part Three. (Sunday 24th May 1980.)

Janet awoke with a bitter liquid being poured into her mouth. She choked and spluttered and reflexively swallowed. Her stomach lurched with fear as she recalled how she came to be here. Janet could feel the sand beneath her naked body. She was spreadeagled, arms and legs wide, with shackles on each wrist and ankle. Her first reaction was to wrench on her arm restraints but these were immovable. They could only be anchored in loose sand but might as well have been set in concrete. Keranrodai loomed over her. "Welcome back, lovely," he said in an oily voice. "My little drink will give you the strength to endure. Can't have you dying before I've had my full measure of fun."

Janet's head was clearing rapidly, although it was almost overwhelmed with terror. She knew that hideous torture and a slow death lay in store for her. She became aware of her name being shouted somewhere close. "Listen," her captor said, "your friends are awake and searching for you. Let's enjoy their despair for a while." The voices grew closer and closer. Janet turned her head to the right and there were Michelle and Sharon passing, a few feet away. Michelle even seemed to glance directly at her but showed no sign of seeing anything. "You're in my little bubble," Keranrodai told her. "Mortals cannot see or hear anything from it – unless I allow them to." He mimicked Janet's friends. "Janet! Janet!" he called out in a loud falsetto voice and then burst into merry laughter. "So you see – a daring rescue just isn't going to happen. They're moving away. How sad." He laughed again. "Your friends have abandoned you. Earlier tonight, this place was crawling with those hunters I played with a couple of days ago in Dysart. Maybe they could have saved you – but I've set them off on a wild-goose chase, further down the coast. Never mind – eh?

Keranrodai surveyed Janet for a moment or two. His gaze made her skin creep. "I must say, I'm a bit disappointed," he told her. "You're frightful skinny. Not a lot of meat on those bones. Still – there are a few choice morsels. Those nipples look tasty and your eyes will no doubt be delicious. Then there's always the liver, heart and lungs – but you'll most likely be dead by the time I get to them. Anyway – enough talk. Let's get down to the feasting and screaming. I'm going to start by excising your cunt. It'll be a nice chewy snack while I'm choosing which part to take next." He knelt in the sand between Janet's legs and produced a small knife. Keranrodai held this up, so Janet could get a good look. She writhed and struggled to try and get free but couldn't overcome her bonds. This made Keranrodai laugh again. He was having a wonderful time.

Janet tensed and waited for the onset of pain. The Goblin delayed – no doubt to intensify his captive's terrified anticipation. Janet could hear her heart beating very loudly in her head. This grew louder and then slowed – falling into a regular rhythm. Janet felt her fear begin to dissipate. Calm flowed through her. She realised that her heartbeat was now synchronised to the beating of a nearby drum. Voices began to impinge on Janet's consciousness. They were chanting a three-word phrase in time with the drum. It took her only a moment to recognise it as the chant she and her sisters had employed the night before in Neil's cottage.

Janet began reciting the words aloud – matching the cadence of the voices in her head. Immediately, she felt her sisters all around and inside her. Power seemed to fill her up. Effortlessly, Janet snapped the bonds that had held her immobile. She stood up and could see the rest of the Coven emerging from the darkness in a circle of which she was the centre. Further out, Janet saw Neil pointing with his magical sword towards Keranrodai's bubble. His Fey eyes were able to direct the mortal witches to where the Goblin was hiding himself and his intended victim. Janet felt energy surge inside her. She looked at her tormentor. Now it was his turn to be held in thrall and unable to stir. Janet saw her possessions lying in a heap, next to where she had been chained. She walked to them now. Ignoring her clothing, for the time being, Janet retrieved her knife. It felt good in her hand. Swiftly moving to Keranrodai, she drove it into his throat.

Black blood cascaded from the Goblin's throat – but the knife was merely a knife and could not kill him. Nevertheless, the wound broke his spell and the whole scene became visible to the mortal onlookers. Despite his perilous situation, Keranrodai began to laugh. His voice was distorted by the knife which Janet had left sticking into him – but his words were clearly audible to all. "I have done my Mother's work," he cried exultantly. "My task was to spread pain and terror – and have I not done so? But more than this – I drew the eyes of you fools to where it was of least use. You thought I searched for the key with which to set my Mother free – but I am the Harbinger – the one who goes before. I heralded the advent of my Mother. I am not the one to procure the key. My Mother always knew its location – in lands beyond the sea. She sent another of her children to fetch it – and now she is free. So tremble, fools. In this moment of your supposed triumph, you are met with ultimate defeat."

Keranrodai's disturbing words, momentarily jolted the collective mind of the Coven. Their control faltered and the Goblin broke free. He leapt to his feet and tore the knife from his throat. Janet was his nearest target and he rushed on her, intending to take her into death with him. She reacted quickly and managed to sidestep the Goblin's charge. This gave Gloria a moment's grace to draw her gun. She stepped forward and emptied her full magazine into Keranrodai's head. The hideous creature collapsed on the sand. Neil strode to the corpse and decapitated it with Clayfansolas. "Best to be certain," he said. No-one quite knew what to do now. Janet went to her clothes and got dressed. When she was ready, Gloria said let's go back to the cottage and work out what we have to do now. We'll need to make a stop and buy some booze on the way. I don't know about the rest of you – but I could use a drink. The Harbinger was dead but – if what he'd told them was true – they were in even more trouble now.

Gwendolen Y Lleuad.

Free at last. This world was very different from the one Gwendolen had left millennia ago. For centuries she'd slumbered in unnatural sleep – unknowing, as she grew to maturity. Since she had awakened, she had probed the minds of mortals and learned their changing ways and technologies. This world held no fears or surprises for her. She had much to do. There was vengeance to be wreaked and havoc to be sown. But first – a worthy mortal man would have to be found. She required impregnation. Then her reign of terror could truly begin in earnest.

Part Three - The Adversary.

Evil magic turned to good,

Will fertilize a Sisterhood,

And Seven Sisters shining bright,

Shall face the coming of the night,

Then one brave Sister will arise,

And through Her awful Sacrifice,

Shall heal the Rent and close the Veil,

So Gwendolen cannot prevail.

Chapter Fifty Six – The Codex of Caradoc.

Know then that I commit these words to parchment, in contravention of the customs and strictures of my Order. I am Caradoc of Yestre Felyn – High-Druid of these lands. My hope and belief is that these writings will find their way to where they are most needed and the people who can best use them. I have committed them to cipher, that only one of the wise might find their meaning. I hope that they might provide hope and guidance in a troubled time.

Fifteen summers ago, two nights after the Beltane Fires, the Moonchild was born. Her mother was Gwenefyr and father Madoc, a chieftain of the Maetae. For a twelvemonth prior to the birth, evil portents and ominous signs abounded. A gigantic fiery dragon was seen traversing the night skies for a full month, accompanied by many falling stars. Ravenous wolves attacked travelers and even invaded isolated homesteads. There was pestilence, crop failures and monstrous births amongst livestock. On the night the child was born, the chieftain's village was surrounded by a horrific storm of howling. Some of it was undoubtedly wolves but it seemed to be interspersed with more eldritch, darker voices. The villagers spent the night huddling in fear and dread. In the light of the morning, they went in deputation and demanded the baby be taken to the hills and left exposed to the elements until dead. Gwenefyr vehemently refused. For a time the situation was fraught and bloodshed seemed imminent. The village wiseman, a minor bard, intervened to propose a solution. The child would be brought to us, the Druids, for judgement and disposal.

My brethren and I were obviously cognizant of the many portents. We had mulled them over and come to the conclusion that an aberrant birth was imminent. Who, where, when and why, we could not ascertain – but expected to hear of it soon. Madoc's village lay only half a day's easy journey from our compound, Pentref Derwyddon. He installed his wife and new child onto a cart, cushioned by a stack of sheepskins, and set off with a mounted escort of his House-Warriors. They planned to reach us well before darkness came and fell creatures were abroad. Our compound is extensive, lying between the River Voritia and the nearby Hill of Morden. This hill is important to what follows. Nine years previously, when I was installed as High-Druid, I also became the Keeper of The Key. This was a magical artifice that gave entrance to the extensive tunnels within the Hill of Morden. No-one knew who had delved these tunnels – nor what their intended purpose was. They are believed to be immensely ancient and the work of unknown beings with powers way beyond our own.

The deputation from the village arrived late in the afternoon. When I was informed, I gathered my Council of Druids and summoned the parents and child to my quarters. We felt the power as soon as they entered. The babe's aura was intense and redolent of evil potential. The child was asleep but there was no doubt that her birthright was ominous. Then she awoke and opened her eyes. Even my stoic Druids were shocked. The baby's eyes were a vivid yellow, with no whites and their black pupils formed a vertical shape – broad in the middle but tapering to a point at top and bottom. They were the eyes of a serpent. My council immediately clamoured for the child's instant death. It was undoubtedly a disconcerting sight. I was not convinced. The child might well have a sinister destiny but I judged her to be no more deserving of death than any other newborn. It mattered not what my Council advised. In matters of doctrine and governance, I was deemed infallible – by virtue of my high office. I ruled that we would take the night to consider and re-convene at first light in the morning.

I did not sleep that night. Now that I had a focus, I had investigations to make. I studied the heavens. I cast the bones, several times and I communed with The Spirits of The Air, The Spirits of The Woods and The Spirits of The

River. By morning, I had gained great knowledge of the peril that threatened the world of humans. Gwendolen – for that was the name the child's mother had given her – had been born to be Queen of Demons. There are many Hell Worlds wherein dwell hordes of Demonkind. Some cosmic conjunction had occurred that caused the Moonchild's birth to tear a rent in the veil that separated one of these worlds from that of human kind. Even now, multitudes of fell creatures were streaming through. If this horde ever made it to the realm of humanity, the result would be cataclysmic. Mankind would be devastated and subjugated – and maybe even obliterated. This was the disaster, Gwendolen was destined to reign over.

All was not lost – at least not yet. Although they were escaping their own hellish dimension, the horde had not yet reached the surface of the Earth – and they would not, until Gwendolen summoned them. The lifeless surface of the Sacred Moon, was being used as a staging post in the Demons' journey. The Infernal throng was spreading across the face of that planet, unseen and unseeable by mortals. There, they would impatiently await their Queen coming into her own. In order to exercise her dominion over these creatures and bring them to her side, Gwendolen had to commit a vile and unspeakable atrocity. She must bring forth a child and sacrifice her newborn in a fire ritual, within a day of its birth.

Reading this, you may well think that the obvious thing to do, was to snuff out the Moonchild's life and end her threat. If only it were that simple. As I cast the bones in the night, I asked for guidance from Cerridwen – the Goddess of The Moon. It was she who warned me against slaying Gwendolen. The veil had been rent and the Demons had spilled through. They would not come until their Queen summoned them and she would not have the power to do that until old enough to give birth. If she were to die prematurely though, there would be nothing to stem the onrush of the Demon Horde from the Moon to ravage the face of the Earth. Paradoxically, while she lived, Gwendolen would act as a gatekeeper. Her subjects would not dare to risk her wrath by coming to our world unbidden. This was a dilemma. All I could do was delay the impending doom until I could discover a solution. Gwendolen must not be allowed to die – nor must she be allowed to procreate.

I delivered my ruling in the morning. I did not share all that I knew with anyone else. That was my burden alone to bear. Gwendolen would be allowed to live but as my ward. She would dwell in the Druid's compound and I would oversee her upbringing. My Druid brothers and sisters protested my decision but I was Chief and my word was law. Gwenefyr and Madoc acquiesced to my edict. Gwenefyr was distraught but also relieved that her daughter was not to be killed. Madoc simply seemed relieved. I had certain plans. There are potions that can be given to a woman, after she'd had her first flow of blood, that would render her barren and unable to conceive. It was my intent to deceive the girl. It was not noble but I judged it expedient – but I would later discover that Gwendolen was well able to practice deception also.

I appointed Blodeuwedd, a high ranking Druidess, to be the girl's guardian. She would be responsible for Gwendolen's day to day care but I would keep a keen eye on matters. I charged Blodeuwedd to inform me when Gwendolen had her first bleeding. I did not tell her why but I did warn her to be vigilant. The Moonchild was not as other females and there was no telling at what age this might occur. I allowed that the parents might come to visit their daughter – but no more than four times a year. Gwenefyr duly did so for the entire time that Gwendolen stayed with us. The Father never did. The child grew and developed as any child would. Were it not for her chilling eyes, she would have been considered comely. She was well-formed in body and limb with lustrous hair of a pale blond that verged on silver. In fact – as she matured towards womanhood – she promised to become a great beauty. Her only blemish, as I've said, was her serpent eyes. Even I, versed in all manner of the occult, had to suppress a shudder when I looked into them.

I modified her name and henceforth the girl was known as Gwendolen Y Lleuad – Gwendolen of The Moon. As she grew, Gwendolen was always demure and biddable. At first I was suspicious of her demeanour, suspecting that she was dissembling – but over time, even I was deceived. I always sensed that Gwendolen harboured a deep reservoir of occult power but she never manifested this as she grew up – at least not when anyone was watching. By the time she did, fortunately, I was still the stronger. Another year or two – then who knows. My hope was that, by keeping her ignorant of her destiny and treating her with kindness, we could turn her from her diabolical potential. On reflection, perhaps Gwendolen did not see our treatment of her as kindness but as restriction. She had no-one of her own age to play with. No other child lived on or even visited our compound. Even most of the adults avoided her. Nevertheless, Gwendolen was never rebellious or disobedient. She seemed cheerful enough, in a kind of detached way.

I must admit, that over time, I was beguiled by the Moonchild – but I did not totally let down my guard. It was to become clear that Gwendolen was more informed and devious than I had realised. She knew of her destiny and what she had to do to achieve it. I had informed no-one of the knowledge I held – so how she uncovered it, I can only speculate. Perhaps she had communed directly with Cerridwen, The Moon Goddess. Anyway – it transpired that Gwendolen had been having her monthly bleedings for most of a year before matters came to a head. She had kept this secret from Blodeuwedd, how I don't know, but it meant that the potion I had wished to administer, never was. That, of course would have been only a temporary measure. Gwendolen's inevitable ultimate demise would still unleash the Demon horde – but it would have given me more time to discover a remedy. I had been labouring non-stop with that in mind but so far, had been unsuccessful.

The crisis was precipitated just after Gwendolen's fourteenth birthday. From time to time work was required on the buildings in our compound. We had a small group of artisans who would normally attend to this. If something major was required, we would sometimes hire outside workers to carry it out. Our community was still expanding and a new accommodation hall was needed. A group of woodworkers was brought in from a nearby village to do the work. This consisted of a Master-Carpenter, five labourers and a young apprentice. This apprentice was perhaps just a little older than Gwendolen. It was he that she set her mind on to father the child she needed for her sacrifice. The workmen had no dealings with the Moonchild. Like most, they regarded her with superstitious dread. But the girl was undoubtedly pretty and the apprentice was young enough to think with his member rather than his brain. Gwendolen worked on him over a period of time. She manipulated him and stoked the fire of his desire for her. His fear of her waned somewhat, or at least transmuted into a heightened sense of sexual titillation. When she judged that the lad's lust sufficiently outweighed his reticence, Gwendolen moved to consummate their liaison.

It was perhaps fortunate, although not for everyone, that this did not go as the Moonchild planned. As Gwendolen surreptitiously led the apprentice-boy into a woodshed, one of the lad's workmates happened by. He was appalled at what he accurately suspected was about to happen and ran to inform his master. The workers were on a break for their mid-day meal. The Master-Carpenter was also horrified. He did not know exactly what Gwendolen was but recognized her as an eldritch being. Sexual congress with such a creature was never less than perilous for any mortal – let alone a callow youth who knew no better. As a group, the artisans hurried to intervene before it was too late. They also feared the wrath of the Druids for such a transgression by one of their number.

I know this happened because much of it was overheard. Two of my brethren were already hurrying in the wake of the workman and a runner had been dispatched to inform me. The Master-Carpenter barged into the woodshed and emerged, seconds later, hauling the shamefaced apprentice by the arm. He loudly berated the youth on his folly as he dragged him out. The lad, no doubt embarrassed, flustered and fearful of punishment, denied stridently that he'd been up to anything untoward. Then Gwendolen emerged from the doorway – frustrated and furious. A small crowd of onlookers were gathering, attracted by the disturbance. The mortified youth turned his venom on the Moonchild, calling her an abomination, a freak and any other insult his untutored mind could come up with. He strenuously denied that he had ever actually intended to lie with her.

Gwendolen was incandescent with rage. Not only had her intention been foiled but the pent up frustrations of years concealing her true nature and living under our constricting regime, boiled over and she lost control. Her inherent character ripped forth as she stood amidst the seven artisans. The workmen convulsed, as every bone in their bodies was snapped and snapped again. They writhed in agony for long moments until death finally stilled their suffering. Seconds later, my two Druids arrived on the scene and suffered the same fate. Gwendolen could well have gone on to massacre the horrified onlookers – but she came to her senses and realised the precariousness of her situation. She knew that I had to be on my way, no doubt accompanied by several powerful Druids. Even she, would have been outmatched. The Moonchild fled. This was her chance for freedom – freedom to pursue her own ends and grow into her full unassailable strength. She ran from Pentref Derwyddon and up onto the wooded slopes of the Hill of Morden.

I arrived to survey the scene of carnage that Gwendolen had left behind. Our compound was in uproar and rife with calls for vengeance. My first task was to calm my flock. I forbade any pursuit of the Moonchild. She would not be difficult to apprehend – though I was the only one that knew this. Years previously, I had placed a mark on Gwendolen - unbeknownst to her. If she ever left the boundaries of Pentref Derwyddon, she would soon succumb to an enchanted sleep. I took my six most senior Druids to my quarters and revealed to them all that I knew of the Moonchild. After nightfall, I went in their company and retrieved the sleeping girl.

I had set upon a course of action. It was at best a temporary solution, which meant that others would have to deal with my unfinished business – though I would try to set some things in train that would hopefully help those who would be faced with the threat of a risen Moonchild. By the time this would come to pass, I and all living things around me would long since have gone to dust. I placed a deeper enchantment on Gwendolen, that would keep her asleep – but still alive – for many, many, many years to come. We took the girl up and bore her to the entrance of the tunnels, delved into the heart of the hill. There, I locked her in, to slumber as the centuries marched on. I knew that, by the nature of the heartrock, she could not break out – even by the use of her powerful magic. With a heavy heart, I returned to Pentref Derwyddon and sent downriver to summon one of our sea-going galleys. When it arrived, late in the night, I ordered it to sail immediately for Gallia. On board, I sent three of my most trusted lieutenants, bearing the magical key to the Morden tunnels. They were to place this in the safekeeping of a Brother Order there.

I was in my ninety-first year when these events occurred. I know now, that I won't see a ninety-second. A wasting sickness came upon me, within weeks of entombing the Moonchild. The two matters had to be connected. For the time left to me, I have sought to uncover something of use but nothing comes. My legacy is not one I am proud of. I have friends among the Fey and they have visited me during my decline. I told them some of the looming threat that the Moonchild posed for future generations. I did not tell them all. Though they were my friends, I do not fully trust the Fey. They certainly command powerful enough magic to challenge Gwendolen – but I doubted they would have the will. The fate of humankind means very little to the Fey. They have their own sense of honour – which I do not share. I did not tell them anything of the chains of magic I had initiated, which I hope will come to fruition in time to empower those who may, one day, face the Moonchild's risen malice.

I write this account to try and inform those wise enough to decipher the words. I will commend the book's keeping to a colony in Iwerddon – with the hope and belief it will find its way to the proper hands. I continue to seek further enlightenment. A short time ago, words came to me – in a language I do not know and which I don't believe is spoken anywhere in my lifetime. I don't know the meaning of these words but I believe they are a form of prophecy. The last thing I will do is transcribe these words into this Codex.

Evil magic turned to good, Will fertilize a Sisterhood, And Seven Sisters shining bright, Shall face the coming of the night, Then one brave Sister will arise, And through Her awful Sacrifice, Shall heal the Rent and close the Veil, So Gwendolen cannot prevail.

Caradoc – Derwyddon Uchel Y Yestre Felyn. (Chief Druid of Strivling.)

Chapter Fifty Seven – The Rosemont Hotel. (Monday 16th June 1980.)

The Rosemont Hotel, just off Dumbarton Road in the west of Glasgow, had seen better days. It was neither very large nor very small, with forty-two rooms spread over three floors, a reception lobby, a public bar, a restaurant and a function suite. The hotel's doors had closed for business over two years ago. It had lain unused and unloved since then, until purchased, at a knock down price by Neil Mac Mannanan – although his name never appeared anywhere in the transaction. Neil himself, along with the Seven Sisters Coven, were in a precarious position. They were threatened from two directions, although both stemmed from the same source. Gwendolen – The Adversary – was risen from her living tomb in the Abbey Craig and now was free in the world. She was aware of The Coven and seemed to see them as a threat. At her behest, The King of The Fey had sent Sealgaire Glas assassins against Neil and Gloria. The assassins had all been killed but there were plenty more of them. It was fair to assume that other members of The Coven could well now be targeted for death.

It seemed wise to find a bolt hole in which to re-group, be safe and consider their options. It turned out, Neil was wealthy enough to finance this. He reasoned that it would be more difficult for the Fey to track them in the midst of many humans, than it would be if they hid somewhere in the wilderness, where there weren't any others to confuse the trail. The dilapidated hotel would fit the bill just fine. It was bigger than they needed but that was alright. The members of The Coven, Ann's children and Jenny's husband, along with Neil, precipitately walked out on their lives and moved to the hotel. It was a drastic action, leaving possessions and jobs and abandoning everything for an uncertain future – but until they could resolve and negate the threats that faced them – it was a matter of survival.

Of the forty-two bedrooms, the group only needed five. Gloria and Neil shared, as did Janet and Michelle, Ruth and Sharon, Jenny and her husband Archie and, of course, Ann and her daughters, Sandra and Karen. They selected the best of the beds and other furnishings from the rest of the rooms, to make these five as comfortable as possible. Neil attended to getting all the utilities turned on, so they had water, electricity and gas. Security was a big consideration. The hotel had its main entrance onto the street at the front. There was a service and delivery door to the rear, which opened onto the narrow lane that ran past the back of the building. The hotel had been built early in the twentieth century and was adjoined on either side to tenement housing from the same period. Gloria used her expertise to install surveillance cameras covering the doors, as well as the street and the lane. Neil, using his own expertise – Fey Magic – set up an alarm system, tuned to the tones of the eleven occupants. Everyone has a unique vibration which the Fey called a tone, as that was how they perceived it. Anyone crossing Neil's boundary, who's tone wasn't recognized, would trigger an alarm. Any intruder Fey in nature, would be met with various lethal and magical booby traps.

Once the group was installed in their new quarters, as safely and comfortably as they could make it, their thoughts had to turn to what to do next. They didn't fully understand why they were carrying the can for the impending Armageddon that seemed to be on the cards but it seemed they were the only game in town. If they did not do something about it, it appeared that the world was doomed – at least as far as humanity was concerned. Whether they wanted to or not was irrelevant. Powerful enemies were set on their destruction – so the only options were to hide away and hope to survive, or fight and destroy the powers that sought their destruction. The first was not really a viable choice. The facts pointed to a demon apocalypse coming, in, perhaps no more than a year's time. The Seven Sisters had all read Neil's translation and transcription of The Codex of Caradoc. Apart from clarifying the origins of their present troubles, it didn't take them much further forward. It more or less told them what they couldn't do rather than what they could. The poem, in English, at the very end, seemed to point to an ultimate victory but the talk of an "awful sacrifice" filled them with dread. The women of the Coven truly considered the others as sisters – bonded perhaps even more strongly than they would have been by blood. They had no doubt that the poem spoke of them. It could mean no other. None of them were prepared to lose even one of their number.

The women were growing ever stronger in magical power – individually but even more so as a group. They were, however, still novices in the magical arts. Their potency was great but their knowledge on how best to use it was very limited. Neil had risked a trip back to the cottage he'd had to abandon after the Sealgaire Glas attack. From it he retrieved his extensive library. There were books of ancient Fey lore, treatises on magic, grimoires and spell books. He himself began studying them and so did Gloria and Ruth. Ruth seemed to be totally absorbed in them and spent hours poring over the grimoires and spell books. Not all were in English and even the ones that were, tended to be in an archaic form. From time to time she'd ask Neil to interpret passages that she found too obscure.

The public bar became the common room of choice but Gloria claimed the function suite as exclusive territory for the Coven. Every evening, unless other matters intervened, the Coven would assemble there to practice and learn techniques and knowledge gleaned from the books. All others were excluded from these sessions, though Neil could feel the power being generated, wherever he was in the building. So far, they didn't have a clue what the way forward might be. The Coven were merely trying to build their muscle to face whatever came along. Neil, however, had decided on one course of action. King Feargas of the Fey must die. Neil had sworn a blood feud against the King, after the monarch had sent the Sealgaire Glas against him. His motives weren't just personal though. He calculated that, whoever inherited the throne, might revoke the agreement the King had made with Gwendolen. Feargas wasn't universally popular amongst his subjects and many would not be happy at his alliance with the dreaded Adversary. Even if the King's successor was not of that mind, there wasn't a clear heir to the throne. Two prominent candidates existed and there would be a lot of political wheeling and dealing before one was chosen. It was even possible that civil war could erupt. Whatever happened, there would be confusion and delay, which should keep the Sealgaire Glas off Neil and the Coven's backs – at least for a time.

There was much research, planning and preparation to be done. In the meantime, the group had been settling in. Jenny's husband, Archie, had been the most flummoxed by the whole situation. He had had no idea of his wife's double life. Mind you, he'd never had any idea about the numerous affairs and flings with younger men that she'd indulged in over the years either. Archie was retired and actually seemed to welcome the change. He'd appointed himself handyman and kept busy with the numerous tasks that required doing around the hotel. The group had taken up residence in the hotel a fortnight ago and things were now more or less in the order they wanted them to be. No-one, apart from Neil, had ventured out since they'd moved in. The others in the group would have to do something about altering their appearance to guard against being recognised. All of them had simply vanished from their previous lives and doubtless the police would be treating them as missing persons. The amount of gruesome and bizarre murders that had taken place in Scotland over the last seven months, would heighten concerns over their safety. In addition, Gloria was a Venatore officer – a role she now accepted she'd never go back to. Nevertheless, her disappearance would have triggered alarm bells in that organisation. They'd be looking for her. Ruth and Janet, who both lived with their parents, had left letters behind, reassuring that they were alright but that would do little to allay the parents' anxiety. The authorities would also be worried over the whereabouts of Ann's two girls. All in all, there were multiple agencies, human and otherwise, who'd be searching for the fugitive group. They couldn't risk being discovered by any of them.

On this particular Monday, Gloria wanted a conversation with Neil. When they were back in their room that evening she said, "Neil, what would you say our relationship is?" He was slightly taken aback by the question. "We're friends and colleagues," he replied. "So, what about the sex?" was her next question. "It's great," he replied. "Then, it's just sex and nothing deeper," Gloria said – and it was more of a statement than a question. "There's nothing wrong with that," Neil said. "I know that humans can attach emotional significance to what is a physical act. It's part of your bonding instinct – primarily for the procreation and raising of offspring. It's not the same for Fey. Our males can consciously withhold active sperm during ejaculation – just as our females can do with their eggs. To the Fey, sex is mainly about pleasure and relaxation. It is not a basis for bonding. We do not really have relationships of that kind."

"So," Gloria went on, "You wouldn't be upset if I had sex with someone else?" "No – of course not," Neil replied. "Why would I?" "Fine," Gloria said, "I just wanted to make sure we were both on the same page. You know it's Ruth's birthday tomorrow?" Neil nodded. "We're planning a surprise party tomorrow evening, Gloria continued. "I know," Neil said. He was always amused that humans chose to celebrate being one year closer to the end of their lives. "Maybe you should think about giving her a birthday treat," Gloria said. "What do you mean?" Neil asked. "I see how you are together," Gloria told him. "The electricity fairly crackles between you. You Fey might not do love but you certainly do lust – and Ruth is deep in lust with you also. Put the poor girl out of her misery. She's in need of a good fuck. Not in my bed though," Gloria pressed on before Neil could say anything, "I draw the line at that. Sort out one of the upstairs rooms and take her there – and while you're at it – you might consider doing the same for Ann." Even with his Fey outlook on life, Neil was amazed. "Are you my pimp now?" he asked in an amused tone. "No," Gloria replied seriously. "I'm simply looking after the well-being of my coven. I need them all at the top of their game. Their lives may depend on it. Ann is a sexual person and it has been a while for her." "Ok," Neil said, "are there any more of the Coven you would like me to service for you?" He said this in a bantering manner but he knew Gloria was being serious. "Not really," Gloria said. "Jenny might welcome a shag too but you'd need to be a bit discreet there. Wouldn't want to upset Archie. He's not as broad minded as we are - though it wouldn't be the first time Jenny as found entertainment elsewhere. You learn things when you meld minds with others." Neil marvelled at what had just happened. Gloria had an ability to surprise him, like no other human he'd ever known. Conversation over, they got into bed and indulged in a long session of mutual pleasure and relaxation.

Chapter Fifty Eight – Gwendolen Y Lleuad. (Monday 16th June 1980.)

Gwendolen surveyed herself in the dressing table mirror. "Looking good for a two thousand year old," she told her reflection and smiled. It hadn't taken her long to acclimatize to this new world. She had absorbed the English language and could speak it perfectly – in whatever regional accent she desired. There was no need for money. Gwendolen just took what she wanted. Shop assistants would give her whatever she chose and immediately forget they had ever done so – no matter the size or value of the item. She was currently living in a luxurious suite in a prestigious London hotel. Gwendolen's magic had matured while she slept and was now far more potent than it had been previously. There was nothing in this world that she could see as a threat to her. There were practitioners of magic around – she sensed them – but none powerful enough to rival her. There was the rag-tag group from near Gwendolen's birthplace but now that she was free, they were beneath her contempt. They were a remnant of that old fart Caradoc and he was long gone.

Gwendolen did indeed look good. Despite her actual great age, she looked and felt like a woman in her mid-twenties. She didn't know how the aging process would affect her now that she was free of Caradoc's enchantment.

Time would tell on that. Gwendolen had discovered the wonders of coloured contact lenses. She now sported a pair of blue ones that concealed her serpent eyes. She was a stunning looking woman and she dressed stylishly in expensive clothes. The joys of sex were another thing Gwendolen had discovered and she'd embraced it wholeheartedly. She had been a virgin prior to her imprisonment. This, she had surrendered, soon after her liberation. The first time had been uncomfortable and somewhat disappointing. Since then, Gwendolen had learned that sexual pleasure depended very much on the calibre of your partner – in terms of the dimensions of their organ, their staying power and their technique. She had become much more discerning in her choice of men. Sex with members of her own gender, was usually much more satisfying than what she experienced with even the best of men. Who knows a woman's body better than another woman? Another woman couldn't make her pregnant though and that was always a consideration.

Gwendolen was in no hurry to conceive. She was enjoying life in this easy and bounteous world and didn't need her demon minions to dominate here. She could have whatever and whoever she desired and no-one could resist her. There was, however, the matter of the Fey. They commanded a great deal of magical power and could be, at least, an irritant in future. Gwendolen had temporarily nullified their threat. Their foolish King had accepted her offer of truce and had allied his people with her against the rogue Fey and his little witchy friends. The threat of the Fey was the only thing which persuaded Gwendolen that activating her demon horde was a necessary step to take. The Fey might one day realise their precarious situation and then they could be dangerous. The Moonchild had not become pregnant yet but was confident that it wouldn't be a problem. So far, the sex had been experimental and for fun. She was, however, well in tune with her own menstrual cycle. She knew exactly the best time to conceive and tonight would be the night. Gwendolen was on her way to a high-roller charity function that evening. There would be plenty of eligible sperm-donors in attendance. She would have fun sampling a few of them, having no problem mixing business with pleasure.

Chapter Fifty Nine – Happy Birthday To You. (Tuesday 17th June 1980.)

Ruth had burned for another sexual encounter with Neil. She had thought that it would inevitably happen but had been chafed with impatience at how long it was taking to occur. To offset her longing and frustration, she had buried herself in research. Most of this was in the grimoires and books of magic from Neil's occult library. She often had to consult him to decipher obscure passages that she found hard to understand. When she was doing this, she could sense Neil's lust for her. Ruth waited for him to initiate a tryst but it hadn't happened yet. She decided that if it didn't happen soon, she'd simply have to take the initiative herself. One book that particularly intrigued Ruth, was a treatise on sex-magic. She could well understand how the power of an orgasm could be used to project potent magical force. This book, Ruth had taken to her room, preferring to keep her interest in it private. If she encountered anything that was difficult to comprehend, she puzzled over it until understanding dawned on her. Ruth never once asked Neil's guidance regarding this particular subject.

Ruth also conducted another form of research. She was very sexually motivated but woefully lacking in experience and knowledge of matters erotic. Ruth didn't know how to learn about this, other than by direct involvement. And then an idea struck her. Through casual conversation, she had come to realise that Ann was probably the most sexually adventurous and experienced of her Coven-mates. Ruth resolved to pick her brains. She was reticent at first but soon found that Ann was more than willing to share with her. They took to going off together when circumstances allowed. They would sit apart from the others and talk. No-one of the others noticed anything strange in this. Although the Coven was a close-knit collective, it was only natural that some friends would be closer than others. Ann talked freely and Ruth was shocked, titillated and amused by turns. Ann's predilection for exhibitionism surprised Ruth. She had never realized that a woman could get pleasure from showing her naked body in public. When she envisioned this afterward, she found herself getting turned on at the thought. It seemed an exciting idea but Ruth doubted that she would ever have the nerve to go through with it. That aspect apart, Ruth learned a great deal from Ann. She couldn't wait to put this into practice. Then her chance came.

Neil had taken Gloria's suggestion to heart, at least as far as Ruth was concerned. He had felt a connection to her, when they'd been together in the Royal Hotel, that he hadn't with any other woman, either Fey or human. This intrigued him but also scared him a little – though he would never admit this, not even to himself. Love was not a Fey characteristic. He did not consider himself capable of it. Friendship and loyalty were things he had experienced and valued. He felt this way about Gloria and indeed all of the Coven. Neil was not without empathy and tried to do the right thing by others whenever he could. His initial sexual approach to Ruth had been undertaken in that vein.

What he had experienced with her had turned out different to what he'd anticipated. It wasn't love but what was it? He had yearned to be with her again but was wary of going there. Gloria had, last night, opened the door for him and he didn't resist any longer.

Neil checked out the rooms on the first floor and selected the third one – room 103. There was not a great deal he could do with it, other than making sure the bedding was fresh and clean but that was fine. The bed was the only thing that mattered anyway. Ruth agreed straight away when Neil asked her to meet him there at two o'clock that afternoon. She was immediately nervous again but it was an excited nervousness. The butterflies in Ruth's stomach were back but there was never any question of her not keeping the assignation. She suspected that the sex she had previously enjoyed with Neil, had been out of the ordinary but she had little in her experience to compare it with. Neil was undoubtedly and exceptional lover. It was unlikely that Ruth would ever meet anyone to equal him – never mind surpass him. She still didn't have any sexy underwear but that didn't bother her at all, this time round. She wasn't planning to be wearing any for very long.

Both Neil and Ruth arrived at room 103 early. Each of them were eager to begin. Neil noted a change in Ruth's energy straight away. She was nervous, to be sure, but there was a resolve about her that he hadn't detected before. Neither of them lost any time in getting naked. The first time they'd been together, Ruth had been diffident, relying on Neil to take the lead. That was not the case this time. Neil was already erect in anticipation of what was to come. Ruth took hold of the stiffened cock and put her other hand on Neils naked chest, gently guiding him back towards the bed. He felt the bed on the back of his legs and allowed Ruth to sit him down on it. Still holding his cock, Ruth knelt down on the floor in front of him. Neil was surprised at this more assertive Ruth. He was even more astonished when she took his hardened cock into her mouth. This was something he had never expected.

Neil was thrown off his game by this unanticipated turn of events. His usual practice in matters of sex, was to anticipate his partners desires and do what was required to maximise her pleasure. This is what aroused him also. He was turned on by seeing and experiencing the woman's sexual gratification and the frenzy which his attentions induced. He was totally unused to being the recipient of erotic ministrations. Strange as it may seem, in all his many carnal liaisons, no woman had ever performed oral sex on him. This was a first. Neil gave himself over to the sensations that now engulfed his manhood. It was bliss.

This action was totally new to Ruth also. She strove to remember everything that Ann had told her. She moved her head up and down Neil's shaft, making sure that it was her lips and not her teeth that enveloped the engorged flesh of his dick. She flicked and caressed his penis with her tongue whilst gently sucking on it. Ruth held Neil's cock in place with the finger and thumb of her left hand at its base. With her right hand, she fondled and petted his balls. Neil prided himself on his sexual control. He had never yet prematurely ejaculated. He would come when it was the right time to come – and not a moment before. Now, however, he lost himself in the sensations Ruth visited on his prick. She increased the frequency and intensity of her actions – growing in confidence that she was doing it right.

As she relaxed into it, Ruth began to enjoy what she was doing. She loved the effect she was having on Neil. She could feel the tension growing in him. He was making inarticulate sounds in the back of his throat and thrusting spasmodically forward with his hips. Then, suddenly, spunk flooded Ruth's mouth as Neil let loose in a paroxysm of sensual abandon. She had been expecting this but the actuality of it, almost threw her. The taste was not unpleasant but she wasn't fond of the texture. Nevertheless, she persevered and swallowed it all down. Ruth didn't stop yet. As per Ann's instructions, she continued to suck and lick, as residual ejaculate seeped from Neil's cock. She made it her business to make sure that not a trace of semen remained on his penis, before she finally sat back on her haunches and looked up into Neil's glazed eyes. It gave her an enormous thrill to see what she saw there.

Ruth climbed onto the bed and Neil pulled himself up beside her. They lay entwined in each other's arms, resting for a little but knowing there was more to come. "Where did you learn to do that?" Neil asked. Ruth saw no reason not to be honest. "I've never done it before," she told him. "Ann coached me what to do." "Well, she's an excellent teacher and you're an even better student," Neil said admiringly. After a moment he went on, "You know, Gloria has suggested that I have sex with Ann – Jenny too. She thinks it would be good for them. How would you feel about that?" Ruth thought for a little and replied, "They are my sisters. Why would I object to them having pleasure? Anything you do with them, or anybody for that matter, won't make what we do together any less special. I already know that you're with Gloria. It doesn't bother me."

Ruth began fondling Neil's dick and it wasn't long before it sprang to life again. "So – how about a birthday fuck?" she asked coquettishly. Neil was far from reluctant. He rolled over on top of Ruth and inserted two fingers into her vagina. She was wet and more than ready. Neil lifted her legs up and supported them with one arm beneath the backs of her knees. He repositioned his body and pushed his granite-hard cock into the slick, warm snugness of her cunt. Neil sighed with pleasure as the soft moist flesh enveloped and tenderly but firmly gripped his phallus. He began to thrust and Ruth matched him stroke for stroke. They began slowly and gently but intensified rapidly until they were plunging away wildly in a fever of erogenous frenzy. The bed was rocking and groaning and Ruth's fingernails, once again, lacerated Neil's back – a fact to which he was totally oblivious until afterwards. Both were vocalizing loudly – mostly incoherencies but Ruth's were laced with obscenities she'd never have uttered under any other circumstances.

Although he was swept up in the passion of the moment, Neil still stayed very much aware of Ruth, her burning need and exactly where she was in her erotic progression. He knew she was very close to orgasm. The tension in her was palpable and escalating rapidly. Then it released in a furious explosion of screaming and vaginal juices. Ruth's fingernails dug deeply into Neil's flesh but he never missed a beat. He continued to pound Ruth's cunt – if anything even harder than before. Neil sensed, rightly, that Ruth was about to come again. Another powerful paroxysm engulfed her but Neil ploughed on regardless. Ruth's eyes were wide and suffused with an animalistic wildness. She was sobbing and ecstatic tears spilled from those wild eyes – though she was totally oblivious to them. Neil perceived that Ruth was about to come for a third time. This was what he was waiting for. As Ruth climaxed again, Neil unleashed his own climactic eruption. This mutual orgasm triggered something Neil had never felt before. A wash of cold, pure power flowed over him. It was not unpleasant but was disconcerting. Although he'd never directly experienced it previously, Neil recognized it from descriptions he'd read. There was more to Ruth than he had ever realised. This was a manifestation of sex-magic – a very potent force indeed.

Chapter Sixty – A Party and How to Change a Tone. (Tuesday 17th June 1980.)

Everybody had been under a lot of stress. The sheer disruption to all their lives, plus the fear of possible attack, had taken its toll. Ruth's birthday party gave everyone a chance to let their hair down and relax. Archie had set up a sound system in the function suite and a copious supply of alcohol had been bought in. There were crisps, salted peanuts and sausage rolls laid out on a table. Everyone was in attendance, including Ann's two young daughters. It didn't take long for the party to get into full swing, not unusual when a group of women were involved. All seven of the adults, as well as the two children, were soon up dancing to the music from Archie's sound system. The only two men present, sat together at a table, drinking and surveying the dancers.

One of the things Neil had asked the Coven to work on, was a way of disguising his tone. He didn't know if this was possible. It was his intention to slip into the Land of the Fey and attempt to assassinate the King. There were plenty of portals he could use to effect entry. That was not a problem. Every living creature had its own unique vibration. The Fey called this their tone, as they literally could hear it. This was something they were very sensitive to. As someone who had been exiled and declared rogue, Neil's tone would have been circulated and widely known. Alarms would be tripped the moment he made use of a portal and he'd be rapidly hunted down, with nowhere to hide. A disguise was required if he was to have any chance of succeeding. Gloria was looking into this but she had other irons in the fire. She was wary of falling into the trap of tunnel vision. They had been guilty of this when they'd focused all their efforts on tracking down Keranrodai – The Harbinger. He was merely a decoy to draw their attention, while The Adversary walked free from her prison unopposed. Gloria was determined not to make that mistake again.

Neil was slightly bored. He liked humans but their parties were kind of tame. At a Fey gathering much more wildness would be in progress by this time. As he watched the dancers and mused, it suddenly struck him how attractive every member of the Coven was. He was a bit surprised that he hadn't noticed this before. Jenny was a bit older but still a good-looking woman. Neil wondered if there was any significance to this. It was a possibility. Magic had all sorts of convoluted and obscure pathways that often, even the direct participants, couldn't discern. Neil smiled wryly. If, as he was inclined to do, he followed Gloria's suggestion regarding Jenny and Ann, he would have had sex with more than half of them. Were they his personal harem or was he simply a sex-toy, to be passed around for their gratification? There was a case to be made for either proposition. Given Neil's Fey morality, neither situation would have bothered him one little bit. He didn't think that either actually pertained though. They were in a unique situation and relationship. It was a weird mish-mash of magical energies and abilities, allied to fear and danger.

They might all be dead in a week – so why not have some fun while they could?

It was while Neil indulged in these cogitations, that Ann left the dancers and approached him. He could see that she was tipsy but not yet fully drunk. "I've just been talking to Gloria," she said. "She suggested that I invite you up to room 103. What do you say?" Neil saw the eagerness in her face. She clearly wanted and perhaps needed this. "Right now?" he asked. "Why not?" Ann answered. "The kids are occupied and I can disappear for a while." "Why not indeed," Neil said. "Let's go then." He got up and the two of them made their way out of the function suite. Neil had already seen Ann's naked body, when he'd helped her perform a steamy striptease to, what she perceived as, a room full of horny men. It had been a stunning sight and he was nothing loath to encounter it at closer quarters. The time had not been right, back then, but he always suspected that he would have sex with Ann at some point. Apparently, tonight was that point.

The Fey metabolism could handle much more alcohol than the human equivalent. Neil had enjoyed several stiff drinks but was, so far, feeling little effect from it. He was somewhat amused at what his role seemed to be in their little community. He wasn't sure if Gloria was trying to make some point – pimping him around to her friends. If she was, he couldn't fathom what it was. Gloria was a tough cookie. Neil liked her and indeed admired her. He also knew that, if he had to choose one exclusive sex partner, (a very human concept) it would be her. Maybe, when all this was over and life settled down, he would re-evaluate his position. Maybe he would go native and ask Gloria to spend the rest of her life with him – exclusively. The trouble was, that he didn't know whether she was only with him because of the situation they had all been forced into. Maybe it was all they had in common – apart from the glorious sex.

Neil gave himself a metaphorical shake as he climbed the stairs with Ann. He was about to have intercourse with a beautiful and experienced woman. It probably wasn't the time to get too philosophical. Living with humanity seemed to be rubbing off on him. They entered room 103. The bedclothes were still in disarray from Neil's earlier bout with Ruth. He sat on the bed and watched as Ann began to undress. He knew her predilections and that she'd enjoy disrobing for him. Ann didn't linger over her performance but still put a lot of art into her undressing. Her body was every bit as ravishing as Neil remembered. Ann was breathing heavily and there was a lustful glint in her eyes. They spoke of a wildness that was almost primal in nature. Relishing Neil's obviously appreciative scrutiny of her nakedness, Ann glided slowly over towards him. She pushed him forcefully back onto the bed and unbuckled his belt, before jerking his trousers and underwear down to his knees, freeing his erect cock to spring into view.

Ann climbed onto the bed and straddled Neil. She took hold of his penis and deftly inserted it into her cunt. Ann began to gyrate, sensually rocking slowly back and forward as she did so. Neil propped himself up slightly on his elbows, so he could have a better view of her performance – and it was a performance – an erotic, entrancing display of the female form in titillating motion. For a time, Ann moved gracefully and in a measured fashion, savouring the feel of Neil's hardness inside her. Her clitoris rubbed gently against his flesh, sending delicious sensations through her lower body. His gaze upon her uncovered body soon began to inflame Ann's passion. Her graceful, balletic performance began to spiral rapidly into something much wilder and frenetic. Ann bucked and writhed – growing more and more frenzied by the second. She was gasping an ululating cry as she rode Neil, ever harder and more fiercely. He thought her magnificent – a force of nature. Then, with a rising scream, Ann climaxed. Her body went rigid and then convulsed as Neil's cock and balls were drenched, for a second time that day, by forcefully ejaculated vaginal fluids. This triggered his own orgasm and he pumped fluids spasmodically in the other direction. Ann collapsed on top of him, covering his face in wet, grateful kisses. He didn't feel he deserved any gratitude. All he'd done was lay there and watch. Ann had done everything else. Nevertheless, Ann was satiated and Neil was happy.

Ten minutes or so later, when they re-entered the function suite, the dancers seemed to be taking a temporary break. They were sitting at tables and drinking, chatting away happily. There were a few knowing smiles as the pair joined them. Neil noticed that Gloria and Ruth were at a separate table, deep in what seemed like an earnest conversation. Then, an obviously popular song came on the sound system and the women found it time to dance again. Gloria didn't join them. Instead, she came over to sit beside Neil. "How was Ann?" she asked in a seemingly light tone. "None of your business," Neil replied, somewhat sourly. "Ok grumpy," she said. "I only asked. Anyway, Ruth has come up with a possible way to solve a couple of our problems – including altering your tone." "Don't tell me," Neil said. "Sex-magic?" "Yes. How did you know?" Gloria asked. "I felt the effects of it earlier," was Neil's reply. "Oh. Well we've got some more research to do and maybe a few days more to prepare for it. But yes, that's what we're considering," Gloria told him. Neil resigned himself that if sex-magic was to be attempted, it would almost inevitably involve him. He didn't know exactly what it would entail but he would likely be shagging again. He wondered who it would be this time.

Chapter Sixty One – Can Rape Be Fun?. (Tuesday 17th June 1980.)

No test was needed. Gwendolen was pregnant and she knew she was. The previous evening, she'd had three disappointing and unfruitful sexual encounters in the toilets and carpark of the Gala event. It wasn't until she had returned to her own hotel and seduced a young night-porter that she'd met with success. The sex was still disappointing but his seed was strong. Because of her eldritch nature, Gwendolen's term would be much shorter than that of an ordinary mortal.

There were things to do in preparation for the birth and subsequent sacrifice. She required acolytes to assist in the ritual. There was a practicing coven who operated in and around London's Highgate Cemetery. Gwendolen's sources told her that this was a traditional group, numbering thirteen, who held their Hexensabbat monthly, on the night of the full moon. She intended to hijack this congregation and dispose of their leader. Gwendolen herself, would be the thirteenth witch, presiding over the others. They would come with her to the appointed place and serve in the rite that confirmed her as Queen of The Moon Demons. The full moon was over a week away but Gwendolen decided to check out the cemetery, partially because she was feeling elated and restless – and partially because she wanted to see if there was anything to be learned about her future minions that would make subjugating them easier.

It was a warm evening with a gusty wind. Gwendolen waited until after dark before going to Highgate. The gates were, of course, locked but that was no barrier to the Moonchild. She simply pushed them and they swung easily open. Gwendolen was aware of the two men watching her and sensed their evil intent. They obviously saw nothing strange in her opening the gates – probably thinking that they'd been unlocked all along. Gwendolen was intrigued. She wondered how rape would feel. She didn't need the men's sperm, being already pregnant. If she hadn't been, she would have had no problem if conception had come by this circumstance. How the baby got there was of no importance, as long as it got there. The Moonchild knew that the men couldn't harm her. Nor could they damage the child she now carried. For her own entertainment, Gwendolen decided to let matters play out. She would act the part of a defenceless female and see what transpired.

The men stalked Gwendolen, foolishly imagining that she didn't know exactly what they were doing. Gradually and stealthily they moved in on her. In a secluded part of the cemetery they pounced. The men rushed the woman and tackled her to the ground. One of them had a knife that he held to Gwendolen's throat, having first made sure that she'd seen it. "Behave yourself darling and we'll all have a good time," the man with the knife said gruffly. "Or struggle a bit," the other interjected. "I enjoy some violence with my shagging. It turns me well on." Gwendolen considered her options. Should she act scared and submissive – or should she be scrappy and fight back? She decided on the latter. A bit of violence turned her on as well.

Both Gwendolen's assailants were big men, easily able to subdue a normal woman of her build and have their way with her. She writhed and struggled, as if in fear and panic and the men responded, working together to pin her to the ground. One of them reached under her skirt and ripped off Gwendolen's underwear. The one with the knife kept it at her throat but used his other hand to tear open her blouse. Pushing up her bra he exposing her tits, he roughly seized her right breast and squeezed it cruelly hard. Gwendolen writhed around violently and got her right hand free. She raked her fingernails down the face of the man who'd pulled off her panties, drawing blood and eliciting an obscenity from him. The man's response was rapid and brutal. He punched Gwendolen very hard on the mouth, drawing blood in retaliation. Gwendolen went very still and lay as if resigned to her fate. While the guy with the knife held her still, the other one positioned himself between her legs and coarsely rammed his cock up her cunt.

The man between Gwendolen's legs, pumped her viciously and pitilessly. This was beginning to get promising, Gwendolen thought but was almost immediately disappointed. The man violently climaxed and emptied his balls inside her. As he was in the throes of his orgasm, the man slapped Gwendolen forcefully across the face. She was annoyed – not by the slap but by the premature ending of his efforts. She had barely began to get warmed up. Gwendolen had had enough. She didn't hold out any hope of the second man being more competent than the first. With merely a thought, Gwendolen threw both men off her and sat up. The men were confused, having no idea what had just happened. Gwendolen projected another thought and snapped the neck of the man who had menaced her with the knife. She wasn't letting the other man off so easy. First she broke both his legs and both his arms. Then she crushed his balls beyond repair – he didn't know how to use them properly anyway. Gwendolen magically restored her damaged clothing and then departed – leaving the surviving man to scream in agony interspersed with terrified sobbing. She smiled to herself. Rape *could* be fun after all.

Chapter Sixty Two – Altered Images. (Saturday 21st June 1980.)

Nothing much happened in the days following Ruth's party although Neil noticed that the Coven were spending more time at their nightly closed doors sessions in the function room. There was one talking point though. On Wednesday night, a report was shown on television with a report looking for information on missing persons. It had featured photographs of all the Coven members apart from Gloria and Sharon. Archie's picture had been there also along with Sandra and Karen, Ann's kids. The report said that Jenny, Michelle and Ruth all worked in some capacity at Riverdale Day Centre in Stirling and that all the women had been associated with the series of grisly murders perpetrated by Garry Wallace and Morgan Jones at the end of 1979 and the beginning of 1980. Gloria wasn't mentioned at all. As a Venatore officer, that organization would be conducting their own private investigation. Sharon was unknown to anyone in this country

None of the fugitives, apart from Neil, had left the building since they moved to live in the hotel. They were beginning to get a bit stir crazy but this nationwide exposition of their faces complicated any change in their status. Neil was sent out to do some shopping, for which Gloria had given him a list. This included hair-dye, wigs, scissors and several pairs of sunglasses, in adult and children's sizes. They were about to undertake a mass make-over. Only Ann had long hair. Michelle cut this short for her and then they dyed it from auburn to blond. The other women chose to use wigs which were longer in style. Janet going from blond to black, Ruth from black to red, Jenny from grey to black and Michelle from brown to blond. Sandra and Karen's hair had been long, like their mum's. They too went short and blond. Archie also used a wig, going from bald to black, although his was less than convincing. He thought the best option for him was to wear a hat. They still planned to limit their outdoor exposure but hoped that their disguises would give a layer of security when they did venture out.

Other than that, the group was doing little other than passing time. Their options for being proactive were almost nil. Sharon was a talented and powerful seer. She considered questing for signs and perhaps a location for the Adversary but decided against, fearing that Gwendolen would track her back to their hideaway. The group did put effort into structuring the day for Ann's children. They were obviously missing a big chunk of education. The group members made use of their various individual expertise to home-school the girls. Neil wanted to introduce them to the rudiments of magic but Ann was adamant in refusing this – they were far too young she asserted.

Fortunately, everyone rubbed along well enough with each other. There were no personality clashes. Apart from the Coven's alone time, they decided to have a gathering once a week, at which they'd all got together to chat and have a social drink. All that would change soon. That evening, after the makeover, Gloria informed Neil that they were just about ready to proceed with the sex-magic ritual. She asked if he was willing to participate and he assented – having been expecting it. Gloria told him that there was some preparatory work still to be done and some details to be ironed out but they should be ready to go on the coming Wednesday evening. She wouldn't discuss any details just yet but promised he'd be fully briefed before the event. With that he'd have to be satisfied. Maybe he was just a sex-toy after all.

Chapter Sixty Three – Come Together. (Wednesday 25th June 1980.)

Neil walked into the darkened function suite. He was naked – as were the seven women who awaited him there. Only the middle of the room was lit. A circle of twenty-one large candles mounted in tall candlesticks provided the only illumination. Inside that circle, stood another circle – this one, of naked women. The seventh woman, Sharon, sat on a sheepskin rug, in the middle of the concentric rings. She was orientated on a north/south axis, with her feet to the south. Behind her, at the north end of the axis, Ruth held a small hand drum and a wooden stick to beat it with. The drum belonged to Sharon but Ruth would be presiding over the ritual this evening. In addition to the drum and stick, Ruth held a paper cup – as did all her sisters. Neil was carrying one too. The cups contained a small measure of a carefully brewed potion. Ruth had concocted this over a period of two days. It was mildly soporific but its main purpose was to help everyone participating in the ceremony enter a strong and enduring mind meld.

Neil approached from the south. On tables arranged around the concentric circles, seven incense sticks poured a heady perfume into the atmosphere. When Gloria had told Neil what was required in this particular sex-magic ritual, she asked if he could fulfill the requirements. Confident in his Fey heritage and his personal prowess, he had replied, "Of course." Now he was faced with the reality, he wasn't so sure. Could he even achieve arousal under these circumstances? If Neil couldn't get hard, the whole thing was a bust. He had never failed in that respect previously but there was always a first time. Perhaps the array of delectable female flesh on display would help. It was a remarkable sight. The flickering candlelight seemed to enhance the view rather than obscuring it. The intended purpose of this pagan sacrament was twofold. The first was, obviously, to temporarily effect a change in Neil's tone – enabling him to enter the Land of The Fey undetected and attempt to kill the King. If it worked, it would give him a week, or at the outside, eight days, to get in and out again before it wore off. The second objective, was to help Sharon to target the Adversary, spy on her and withdraw, without revealing her own location. That was why Sharon would be Neil's vessel this night.

Neil walked across the dance-floor and stopped just outside the circle of naked witches. Ruth raised her paper cup to her lips and everyone else followed suit. She paused for a moment and then drank the potion down in one swallow. Simultaneously, the others did the same, before throwing the empty cups aside. Ruth readied the drum and drumstick. She gave one single beat and Neil stepped into the circle, while Sharon lay back on the sheepskin – along the north/south axis. After a pause of a few seconds, Ruth struck the drum again. Sharon opened her legs whilst pulling her knees up and placing her feet flat on the rug. It was an enticing sight. Neil's worry over performance fright vanished. His cock began to stiffen. Some time back, Ann had told Neil how she felt when exposing herself naked to the lustful sight of men. She had described feeling their gaze, almost as a physical touch on her flesh. He understood this now. The eyes of every woman in the room were drawn to his engorged penis and he experienced this as a sensual tingling caress. His erection, already rigid, hardened another notch or two.

Ruth struck the drum again. In response, Neil knelt down and positioned himself between Sharon's legs. He held position there, while the sexual tension in the room grew and thickened. Another drumbeat and Neil pushed his cock home. A collective sigh escaped the circle of spectators – as if they themselves had just been penetrated. Neil held there immobile until Ruth began to sound out a slow rhythm on the drum. He began to move, thrusting and withdrawing in time with Ruth's tempo. Neil's strokes were long – pushing his dick fully in and then pulling it out to just before the point where it would spring free of its enveloping warm wetness. The surrounding women chanted in time to the rhythm of the drum. There were no words to this – only a throaty sound like that of a woman in the early moments of sexual congress.

The chanting intensified as the mind-meld took full effect. For once, Neil was part of this and it blew him away. His mind was bonded with every one of the women and they with him – as they were with each other also. It was the truest form of intimacy imaginable and – given the context in which it was occurring – the most erotic. Although he only physically penetrated one woman, he was, in effect, fucking each and every one of them. The ritual required that Neil and Sharon should climax in unison. Normally, Neil wouldn't have found this a challenge. It was kind of his thing, after all. This situation was different though. He was precluded from employing any of the techniques he'd customarily use to induce orgasm in his partner. He had to be governed by Ruth's rhythmic drumming. Sharon would come, only through his perseverance and endurance. Again, this wouldn't have worried Neil, under other circumstances. His sexual control was normally impeccable – but the sheer overload of eroticism he was currently experiencing, threatened to blow that away. Every fibre of him was crying out for the release of ejaculation. Neil burned to pour his cum into Sharon's welcoming pussy – and by proxy, into the moist cunt of every woman in the place.

Ruth increased the speed of her rhythm and Neil responded. Sharon, who'd been lying inert up till then, began to writhe and moan. She rocked her hips, meeting Neil's thrusts with thrusts of their own. The chant from the witch's circle also grew in speed and intensity. It took on the tone of a lascivious wanton moan, as their arousal burgeoned into something stronger and more insistent. Ruth was escalating her drumming speed at a faster rate now. The feeling in the room was growing wilder and edging towards frenzy. In his peripheral vision, Neil became conscious that the watching witches seemed unable to stand still. They too were now writhing and panting – their vocalisations getting louder and more feverish. Ruth's drumming rate was very fast and insistent now. Neil had lost himself in the group mind and carnal compulsion. He pistoned away in a spaced-out frenzy, while Sharon bucked and screamed beneath him.

The atmosphere in the room was frenetic. Everyone was held fast, in the grip of a furious maelstrom of sexual intensity. The pressure grew and grew till it seemed like it couldn't get more acute and compelling – and then it did. It felt that there wasn't much more they could take. The experience was exhilarating, transcendental and terrifying. Neil reached a peak and could go no further. He had to release and did so – and then became engulfed in the most mind-blowing mass orgasm that swept all of them away in a tsunami of pure erotic ecstasy. For an indeterminate period of time, every participant lost sense of themselves. Many of the women, totally transported, stood astride puddles of vaginal fluids, even though some of them had never experienced such a response before. Neil had not had any control over his climax but neither had Sharon. The ritual had governed that their orgasms would happen simultaneously and trigger the mass reaction amongst Sharon's sisterhood. The energy released was massive and immeasurable.

Time passed and people began to come back to themselves. Everyone was shaky. Neil and Sharon still lay entwined on the sheepskin rug. They were aware but neither yet had the energy to disentangle themselves. Ruth had been hard hit also. She sat dazedly on the floor, with the drum lying on her lap. The rest of the women staggered to find seats and sit down before they fell down. Meanwhile, in faraway London, Gwendolen Y Lleuad was engaged in a delicious naked romp with a pretty little blond called Felicity, when a cold bolt of unrecognized energy shot through her. For a second or two she was held immobile and helpless. The interval passed soon enough but Gwendolen was disconcerted. She hadn't believed that anyone in this world had the power to affect her in any way. Perhaps she'd have to re-evaluate that opinion. The Moonchild was concerned but not overly worried. She still had supreme confidence in her own powers but some caution would be advisable.

Back in The Rosemont Hotel, two hours after the ritual, the Sisterhood and Neil gathered in the public bar so that Sharon could update them on what she'd seen at the point of orgasm. Neil was packed and ready to go. His time was short and he planned to leave immediately on conclusion of this meeting. The atmosphere was a bit surreal. Everyone was still a bit spaced-out after the emotional and intensely sexual experience earlier. It felt that nobody had any secrets from each other anymore. They'd stood together, naked in body and – even more revealingly – in mind also. It wasn't possible to go back to how it was before. Nobody felt any shame, as such but they had shared a tremendously intimate occasion and it had changed their dynamic. Before they went to meet the others, Neil gave Gloria a manila folder. He told her that it contained pass-codes and instructions on how to access his many bank accounts. When she asked him why, he told her that he might not return from his mission to the Land of The Fey. The group would need access to this money in order to continue to function. They had no other means of supporting themselves. Gloria was touched by this gesture. She realised that, for a Fey, this was a very selfless act. Not so much for the money itself but for the thought behind it. Fey were not none for empathy and consideration for others. She already liked Neil but now she liked him even more.

Sharon didn't have a great deal to tell them but what she did have, was dynamite. The Moonchild was currently in London, was already pregnant and would give birth much sooner than a normal woman. It would take place under the full moon on the 24th September – just about three months away. Not only that but Gwendolen would travel to the Abbey Craig, the site of her former prison, in order to have the baby – and carry out her obscene sacrifice. Time was running out fast and they still didn't have a clue what to do about it. "We're fucked," Gloria thought to herself, "And not in a good way" – though she didn't voice this out loud. It was clear, however, that all her friends were thinking the same thing.

Chapter Sixty Four – Return to The Land of The Fey.

Neil had lost the best part of a day and a half, simply in travelling. He would like to have used a portal which came out near the royal palace but those would certainly be guarded. Instead, he'd driven for five hours into the north of England. The portal there was obscure and gave transit to one far from the King's residence. It was unlikely to be watched – at least not constantly. Neil's calculated risk succeeded. He effected entry to his Homeland, safely and undetected. He was confident that his tone had been altered and would not set any alarms ringing. His problem was the distance he now had to travel. Under normal circumstances, it would be about a two day trek. Despite his disguised tone, he still had to travel surreptitiously. Someone could still recognize him. Neil was under no illusions regarding his chances of getting clear, if and when he killed the King. This was most likely a suicide mission.

Things were not good back at The Rosemont Hotel. Matters were rushing towards a disastrous conclusion. Neil had considered dropping his trip back to his Homeland. Although there were other good reasons for assassinating the King, he had to admit that a large part of his mission was fueled by a thirst for vengeance. Feargas had sent Sealgaire Glas to kill Neil and Gloria. By Neil's Fey code, this instituted a blood feud. Given what Sharon had uncovered, regarding The Adversary, he wondered if he should forego revenge and concentrate on helping Gloria's Coven find a way to negate Gwendolen's malignancy. Perhaps he knew, with a deep conviction, that their position was hopeless. He also admitted to himself, that he was peripheral to this whole affair. The Seven Sisters were centre stage. Neil was merely a bit-part player, useful at times but not integral to the Coven's work. If any way could be found to thwart the Moonchild's ambitions, it would be by the talented and mystically empowered members of the Coven. They had seemed to come from nowhere. Their magic had been acquired through a variety of unlikely sources and had blended into a collective body that amplified their power many fold. Perhaps it was their destiny to win this uneven conflict and save the world – a world that didn't even know it needed saving – and a world that would be totally oblivious to their efforts after the event. Caradoc's prophecy suggested this might, in fact, come to pass. Whatever the outcome, it didn't depend on Neil but on Gloria and her Sisters.

Neil focused his mind on the task in hand. He urgently required transport and a suitable disguise – and he had an idea where to get both. The Sealgaire Glas had certain routes they rode in patrol. The portal Neil had come through, was on one such route and would be visited very day or two. Neil secreted himself overlooking the path which the patrol would take. There would be no more than two Sealgaire Glas riding this sector, as it was considered a low risk area. Because of that, they were liable to be fairly relaxed and less than fully alert. It was Neil's hope that the riders would look upon their patrol as nothing more than a pleasant jaunt through beautiful countryside. The countryside was indeed beautiful. Neil savoured his surroundings. Whichever way things turned out here – and even if he survived it – this was almost certainly the last time he'd be here. Neil was happy with his life among the humans but his Homeland was stunning. The flowers were more varied, more vibrant and their perfume headier than back in the human world. The sun seemed warmer and the breezes sweeter. Neil sighed. He had made his choices and would abide by them. His only regret was never being able to experience this natural perfection again. He would have liked to have let Gloria see it. Humans were not specifically prohibited from visiting but life here could be hazardous for mortals. There was much they wouldn't understand here and could fall into deadly danger quite easily.

Neil needed clothing and he needed a Sealgaire Glas horse. The horses in The Land of The Fey were swift – much swifter than anything in the human world. The horses of the Sealgaire Glas were the swiftest of the swift. Neil needed such a mount to traverse the distance to the King's palace, speedily enough to carry out his mission – so he waited and watched. Neil waited and watched for a long time. Late into the evening, two horsemen appeared. They were Sealgaire Glas. Neil readied his bow. This was the only distance weapon he had brought with him. He was, in fact, an accomplished marksman with firearms but chose the bow instead. He was enough of a traditionalist to feel that a gun was not the correct weapon with which to pursue a blood feud. Anyway, he was deadly with a bow – as also were the Sealgaire Glas. Neil waited his moment and then stood up to fire. His second arrow was in flight before the first one had even hit its target. The two unwary hunters never even knew what hit them. Both fell dead from their saddles.

The superbly trained horses were not the least spooked by the sudden loss of their riders. They just stood there patiently while Neil approached them. The first thing he did was secure one of the horses to a tree, in case something should cause them to bolt and leave him on foot. Then he surveyed the two dead hunters, selecting the one nearest his own size. He stripped this one of his uniform and put it on himself. All the while, Neil was revising his plan. His original intention had been to hide somewhere close to the King's palace and try to take a shot at him when he came out into his garden or on some other business. Neil realised though, that the two slain hunters would soon be missed. When the bodies were found, the realm would be put on a state of high alert and his task would become much harder. The very fact that two Sealgaire Glas were missing would cause alarm, even if the bodies weren't found. Neil calculated, if he left now and rode hard through the night, he'd reach the palace just before dawn, when the guards were at their most tired and least attentive. Sometimes, a bold stroke could carry luck with it. He resolved to be bold.

Quickly hiding the bodies, Neil set one horse free and mounted the other one. The dead hunters were not well concealed but they were at least out of sight to casual passersby. Darkness was beginning to fall as Neil set his horse's head towards the palace and urged it into a gallop. These steeds were, not only fleet of foot but were bred for tremendous endurance as well. Neil had no doubt the horse would carry him at speed to his destination. Full night fell as they flew across the land. It was never completely dark in The Land of The Fey. The stars shone brightly and lit the way well enough to allow for no slackening in Neil's speed. His calculation proved accurate and the palace came into sight about half an hour before the sun came up. The guards on the gate were well used to the comings and goings of the Sealgaire Glas. Assassination was something that probably never even entered their thinking. Who would want to kill the King? Dressed in the livery of the King's elite hunters and with his hood pulled up, Neil was wearily waved through. His altered tone did not alert the sentinels to his identity. They did not recognize it, of course, but that was not a cause for concern.

Neil dismounted in the courtyard. He did not waste time stabling the horse but immediately entered the building. His course was set now and he was committed. Only decisive speed and a great deal of luck, would bring Neil's bold thrust to a successful conclusion. At this hour, the palace corridors were empty. That would not last. Neil strode on. Stealth would not serve him at all now. Neil turned the final corner and there ahead was the King's door. In front of it, two sentries stood on watch. They came alert as soon as Neil appeared. They weren't alarmed but were watchful. Part of the Sealgaire Glas attire was a small pouch, often used for the carrying of dispatches. Neil had removed this from his belt and was holding it aloft in his left hand as he advanced on the sentries. The guards would be expecting to take charge of any message and then convey it to the King.

Neil had his bow slung over his back, as the Sealgaire Glas always did when riding. He still had room though, to draw Clayfansolas – his magical sword which was invisible until drawn. Many Fey had such weapons, so the sentries would be aware that Neil might well be armed that way – but they had no reason to be suspicious. Neil held out the pouch and the guard to his left reached out to take it. They did not recognize his tone but in a place where there were so many, it did not alarm them. Had it been Neil's true tone – one that had been proscribed by the King – it would have registered with them immediately. As the guard reached forward, Neil drew his blade and, in the same motion, crashed it down to split the hapless sentries skull. Before the other one could react, Neil swept Clayfansolas back handed and took off his head.

Now was the time for stealth but speed was still also essential. King Feargas was strong in magic and could still save himself if roused. Swiftly and silently, Neil slipped into the bedchamber. The King lay sleeping alone in the massive bed. Neil recognized his tone. There was no time to delay. Neil crossed soundlessly to the bed. He didn't risk waking the King, though he would have liked him to know who was taking his life. Neil took his sword in both hands and plunged it down into the King's chest. Just as the blade descended, the

King's eyes flew open but he was too late. Neil took his life and the blood feud was satisfied – although unlikely to be finished. Revenge would inevitably be sought against Neil himself and any of his allies. So be it.

Such a personage as King Feargas, could not be killed quietly. The escape of energy released by his violent death, would be sensed throughout the palace. No sooner had that thought come to Neil, than alarm bells began to loudly peal. If Neil hoped to escape, he had to move quickly while confusion still reigned. Walking quickly but being careful not to run, Neil headed for the nearest way out. There were shouts of alarm and the sound of racing footsteps but he managed to slip through the door before being spotted. His exit brought him out adjacent to the stables. Neil slipped into the building and selected a horse. Bareback and without a bridle he mounted the beast and urged it into motion. Horse and rider exploded from the stable and across the courtyard. The gate guards leapt clear to avoid being trampled and Neil galloped past them. In a flash he was through the gate and out into the countryside. He was away but not yet clear. Urging his mount onwards, Neil stayed as low as he could. Just as he thought that, miraculously, he was going to escape, a Sealgaire Glas arrow winged through the early-morning air and skewered him in the back.

Chapter Sixty Five – Bananas Are Not The Only Fruit. (Thursday 26th June 1980)

Sharon and Ruth had been left physically and emotionally drained by the ritual the previous night. All the women had been joined in the ceremony but those two had borne a greater burden than the others. Sharon had been the vessel, taking Neil's cock and semen directly into her body. The sheer passion that had engulfed her was overwhelming – not to say surprising. She had not expected it. Of all the women who could have been selected for that role, she was probably the most unsuitable. Sharon had agreed reluctantly to fulfill that function because she was a seer and they needed information on The Adversary. She thought of it as "taking one for the team". Under normal circumstances, Sharon, as the saying went, batted for the other team. Men – no matter how pretty – were not to her taste. The sheer erotic power generated by the Coven, (not to mention Neil) had fired up Sharon's own responses and they bore little cause and effect to what was actually being done to her body. She could only describe and reconcile it to herself, as a transcendental occurrence.

Ruth, on the other hand, was experiencing a burgeoning sexual liberation, after having been repressed since she first discovered that parts of her body could be stimulated to give pleasure. Neil had opened up the joys of sex to her and she found him very much to her taste. Ruth was well aware of her inexperience and was avid to learn more. That's why she had become fascinated by sex-magic and delved deeply into it. That, in turn, paved the way for last night's ritual – which had achieved what it set out to achieve – dispiriting as some of that was. Ruth had presided over the rites, acting as a conduit for the avalanche of erotic passion that was generated. It had been an exhilarating, white-knuckle, ecstatic and super-orgasmic experience, which required complete surrender of herself to the communal libido. Both women were completely wrung out and the hangover lasted well into the next day.

Ruth and Sharon became roommates, more or less by default. Everyone else had somebody they wanted to share with. The two young women got on well though. At twenty-five, Sharon was a few years older than Ruth. Although she was the most recent addition to the Sisterhood, the Irishwoman had lived longer with the world of the occult than any of them. Recruited as a child, she'd been raised and trained in the traditions of the Druids. Her innate abilities as a seer had been developed and honed to the maximum. Sharon was more knowledgeable than Ruth but in some respects, her social development was even less than her's. Ruth had led a fairly sheltered life. Sexually, she had been inhibited by a traumatic experience with an older cousin. She'd never had a normal girl/boy relationship. Sharon had realised quite young that she was lesbian. She had experimented with heterosexual sex, so her bout with Neil hadn't been her first. She had soon realised that it wasn't for her though. Sharon had never had a steady girlfriend but had had several steamy and fleeting encounters.

That Thursday had been uneventful. Everyone was still feeling the effects of the previous evening – and no-one had a clue how they should proceed. Ruth and Sharon had retired to their room after the communal evening meal. Both were still slightly amped up by the residual energy from the sex-ritual. Each girl was lying abed on her back. For a while, they lay in silence and then Ruth spoke.

"Caradoc calls Gwendolen the Moonchild. Why's that? What does she have to do with the moon?"

"I don't know. I don't think Caradoc knew either."

"Don't Druids have a lot to do with the moon?"

"Yes. Many of our rituals and observances depend on the phases of the moon."

"Isn't there anything you can do to find a way to fight Gwendolen?"

"There's only one thing that might be powerful enough. I've never seen it done but I've heard about it. It's called "Drawing down the Moon". It is usually carried out by a High Priestess. The Moon Goddess is called down to Earth and possesses the body of the High Priestess. I don't think there's anyone alive nowadays with the power or knowledge to do it."

"Pity. That might have helped."

The women lay in silence for another little while. They had gotten into their night-clothes earlier. Ruth wore a cotton nightdress while Sharon had on an oversize Tee-shirt. After a minute or two, Ruth spoke again. "You know," she said, "I've been studying this really old book on sex-magic. That's how I learned about last night's ritual." "Oh," Sharon replied. "Well," Ruth went on. "There's this fairly obscure section about the goddess Cerridwen. She's the Moon Goddess. Anyway – it took me a while to decipher it all. There's a sex-magic ritual to consult with her." "Oh," Sharon said again. "Maybe that could be useful but we'd need to wait for Neil to get back." "No," Ruth told her. "This is a much more intimate ritual and – it's the Moon Goddess – so no male can be involved." "Oh," said Sharon for the third time. "Are you coming on to me, Ruth?" Ruth was blushing as she said, "Yes I am – but what I said was true. There really is a ritual. I don't think I'm lesbian – at least not totally. I enjoy sex with Neil. But – I've been thinking about it a lot – thinking about you – thinking about having sex with you – and I've been getting excited about it – but I don't know how to do it – it's just my imagination – but the idea turns me on." Sharon said nothing for a moment or two – and then, "Come on over here then and I'll see if I can teach you. I think you might enjoy it."

Chapter Sixty Six – A Hostile Takeover. (Saturday 28th June 1980)

It was midnight and the moon was riding high in the sky. Only a few fluffy clouds floated in the air. The Highgate Coven was in full session. Twelve naked witches stood in a circle around their naked High Priestess. She – Magrid by name – though that was not how she was known in her everyday life, stood in the centre of the circle. She was bedaubed in the blood of the black cockerel she had just sacrificed. This coven was the real deal. They may not be as powerful as some occult practitioners but they had sufficient witchcraft that all the members had very comfortable lifestyles and bad things happened to anyone who crossed them. Some had even died in quite horrible circumstances. The Coven held their Sabbats every full-moon in Highgate Cemetery. They took steps to ensure that they were never disturbed at their rites. So it was with some astonishment that they saw a lone, ash-blond woman. stride into the midst of their circle.

The woman addressed the shocked witches. "Greetings sisters," she said. "Apologies for gatecrashing your sweet little Sabbat." Magrid erupted in fury. She advanced towards the interloper but suddenly found herself unable to move even her little finger. As she stood in frustrated fury and a fast blossoming fear, the woman spoke again. "Let me introduce myself. My name is Gwendolen and I am the Moonchild, Queen of Demons. I see myself as an arch-villain and as such, I require minions. You, my dear sisters, are now those minions. The appointments are not optional. We have mischief to perform and mayhem to sow. On the third full moon from this one, I will give birth and summon my demonic minions. Until then, you are my new playmates. We will have much, much fun and you will taste power like you never had before. When we finish here, you will get dressed and come away with me. You will leave everything and everyone behind – but don't be sad. This is a blessing I'm bestowing on you and you will be exalted among my subjects. There's a new world coming. Be glad you're on the right side of it."

None of the naked women uttered a sound. "Now," Gwendolen said, "If you want to live – kneel to me – *now*!" Within a few seconds, all the women were down on their knees – all except Magrid, who still couldn't move. The subservient witches were utterly cowed. They could sense the raw power emanating from Gwendolen and were afraid. The Moonchild turned her attention to the rigidly paralysed Magrid. "You didn't kneel," she said, in mock surprise. Magrid's fear had grown into full-blown terror and it showed in her eyes. Gwendolen pretended to be considering the situation. After a moment or two she spoke again. "Such an auspicious occasion should be marked by a blood sacrifice. It must be a worthy one, given the momentous nature of our destiny. I judge that your former leader, pitiful as she is, will be sufficient for this purpose."

Gwendolen focused her attention on Magrid. The woman's skin began to flay from her body. It started at her head and peeled all the way down to her feet. It was agony but Magrid could not even achieve the release of a scream. She stood there like an anatomical dummy, displaying blood vessels, sinew, bones and muscles. Gwendolen kept her pinned there, alive, for fully five minutes as she processed around the circle looking each of the kneeling witches in the eye. She was not wearing her contact lenses, so they saw fully the serpent in her gaze. Her circuit complete, Gwendolen turned back to Magrid and the grotesque manikin simply disintegrated. Her intestines spilled out and blood vessels shed their contents on the ground. The tortured woman collapsed in a gruesome, gory mess of bone, blood and viscera – finally released to death. Gwendolen was satisfied her credentials had been well established with the terrified witches. She surveyed them imperiously and said, "Get dressed. It's time to go."

Chapter Sixty Seven – A Problem For The Venatores. (Monday 30th June 1980)

Major Tom Beresford sat in front of the table in a plush conference room at the Home Office in London. Three men in grey suits were seated on the other side of the table. "So Beresford," said the man in the middle. "You have a rogue Venatore officer." "With respect sir," Beresford replied, "Technically speaking, Captain Garcia is not one of ours. She belongs to the Spanish Branch, although she had been seconded to us for a time." "Stop trying to be a politician, Beresford," the middle man rebuked. "Garcia has gone off the rails in the U.K. She's your responsibility. I've read your report. So, update us." "Very well sir," Beresford responded. "Garcia went off the radar on the 17th of May. No-one has heard from her since. The alarm wasn't raised though, until the 1st of June when she failed to turn up for duty at her home office. For a time she had been monitoring a strange phenomenon identified in some of the women who had been involved in the Koldunya case. They seemed to have been infected by some of the pernicious magic that had been visited on them. Given the source of this magic, I was highly suspicious of it. I could only see it progressing in a negative direction. I had, in fact, pencilled in four of these women for possible termination. It seems my judgement was accurate. These women and another who'd also been associated with the case, have since vanished also."

"Do you have actual evidence that these women are in cahoots with Garcia?" the middle man enquired. "Could something else have happened to them?" "We don't have anything concrete, as such," was Beresford's reply. "But Garcia was apparently trying to mould the women into some kind of coven. We have the testimony of her former apprentice to confirm this. We also know that Garcia had involved the Fey, Neil Mac Mannanan, in an official Venatore investigation – the death of a young woman in Kirkcaldy. This was not officially authorised. This particular Fey had also appeared briefly during the Koldunya affair, having had dealings with the other woman in Garcia's group, one Ann Graham – the girlfriend of Garry Wallace – the male accomplice of Koldunya. There is little doubt that this group were involved in the series of deaths in Fife, beginning with the one in Kirkcaldy that I've just mentioned. What role they played in this, is unclear. It ended, after we discovered the body of a goblin-like creature on the beach of a small coastal town called Leven. He had been shot in the head multiple times with a combination of silver and iron bullets. Several of our radio handsets had gone missing during this time from a storage facility in Glasgow. Only a Venatore officer could have had access to this. We believe that Garcia took them so she could monitor our communications. We've had to totally revise all our frequencies and install scramblers to guard against this."

"All very well, Beresford," the man in the grey suit said. "All of this is in your report. Has there been any progress?" "Not as such sir. We believe that the group must have found a bolt-hole somewhere in which to hunker down. I've got a team examining any recent property sales and transfers in Scotland, to see if anything shows up. They may, of course, already have been in possession of such a place or indeed have moved away from Scotland – but it's a starting point. We have also circulated photographs and descriptions of all the fugitives to our operatives and have people on the streets looking for them. The civil police have been alerted too and there was an appeal put out on television just recently. I'm afraid, there's not much more we can do at present – not until some kind of incident occurs anyway. Incidentally, we have one active surveillance in progress. We identified one likely property that changed ownership recently. It's a hotel in Glasgow. We've been unable to establish who the new owner is and that's suspicious in itself. We only started surveillance last night. All the windows are covered by curtains but lights have been seen shining through – so there's someone inside. So far, no-one has gone in or come out. I'm travelling north directly after this meeting. We're going to force an entry, early tomorrow morning. We can't afford to sit around too long. This way, we'll find out for definite, one way or the other.

The man in the grey suit, who'd done all the talking, did not look pleased. "I want your full attention on this," he said. "The future of the Venatores is on the line here – not to mention your own. I expect you to keep us fully informed You are authorised to use deadly force in this matter but make sure you have found the right people. The termination order has already been signed and you can pick it up from my secretary on your way out. And Beresford – You've already fumbled the ball on this one. Make sure you don't drop it. Now go and sort it out." Beresford was a bit miffed. He didn't think that the present situation was down to any negligence on his behalf – but any argument would have been pointless. He simply nodded his head and left. There was work to be done.

Chapter Sixty Eight – Group Dynamics. (Monday 30th June 1980)

Gloria was weary, worried and frustrated. Neil had not yet returned, though all might still be alright with him. The longer he was gone, the less likely it was that he would come back at all. As a group, they were no nearer to finding a way to tackle the Moonchild. Despite all their research into Neil's ancient books of lore, a solution remained elusive. The one avenue which looked viable was a binding spell. It could be used to hold Gwendolen in check but she was very powerful and Gloria doubted whether even the combined strength of the Coven carried enough juice to overcome her. Nevertheless, it was the only idea they'd come up with – so they bent their efforts to preparing for it. Each night, at the Sisterhood's closed-door session, they melded their minds together and tried to build up their occult muscle. It was, at least, something to focus on.

There was something else going on in the group, that Gloria couldn't quite put her finger on. There was a subtle change happening in the Coven's energy. She'd always felt herself the focal point of their efforts but this seemed to be shifting. No-one was challenging her for leadership, as such. She just sensed a re-distribution in the balance of power. Never having been part of a coven before, Gloria didn't know if this was a normal state of affairs in such groups. It was probably to be expected in a nascent entity like the Seven Sisters was. The majority of members were new to magic and all of them were developing at their own rates. It was probably only natural that there'd be periods of adjustment as the equilibrium settled into new configurations. Gloria also acknowledged internally that she was seeing herself as a failure. She had always been confident in her own abilities but now felt that her leadership had failed. All they were doing was hiding away and doing nothing, while a torrent rushed upon them. It was perhaps this perception of failure that was making her feel insecure.

There was undoubtedly something going on between Ruth and Sharon. In such a close-knit group, it was impossible to keep such a thing secret. Not that it was necessarily anyone else's business. Gloria was aware that Sharon was gay but she hadn't thought Ruth was. Mind you, Ruth had been coming on in leaps and bounds. She had certainly come into her own in recent weeks. Perhaps a further awakening was also happening in her sexuality. Gloria knew that Ruth's power and development had been undergoing, what she thought of as, a growth-spurt. Gloria worried that Ruth might outstrip and outgrow the others and pull away from the group. She felt a bit ashamed by this thought. Ruth was the sweetest of them all and had never exhibited any sign of an inflated ego. Gloria felt she was losing it. She needed to get a grip or she'd be no use to anyone.

Many of Gloria's misgivings were merely a reflection of the Coven's psyche. Everyone was, to a greater or lesser degree, fearful, frustrated and out of ideas. Perhaps Ruth was the least affected by this. She felt herself on the brink of something – a breakthrough that would light the way forward. It almost certainly had to do with Cerridwen, The Moon Goddess. Ruth was almost ready to broach the subject of the new ritual she'd been researching to the wider group. Some of her research had been practical in nature and practiced with Sharon – and it had been amazing. The things Sharon had done to her with tongue, lips, teeth and fingers had been truly awesome. Ruth had been realistic enough to acknowledge that no human male lover could take her to the sexual heights that Neil had. She'd since discovered that a human female one could. She, herself, had learned quickly and was now imparting as much pleasure as she was receiving. Just last night, she and Sharon had reached peaks of mutual ecstasy that she hadn't thought possible.

Ruth was convinced that the ritual, known simply as "The Rite of The Goddess" or "The Sapphic Moon Circle", would provide them with knowledge and perhaps tools with which to combat the threat of Gwendolen. There were some stumbling blocks though. Firstly, the ritual had to take place outdoors and, like many such, under a full moon. Secondly, there had to be a third active participant. In the previous sex-magic ritual, Sharon, although lesbian, had been roused to sexual frenzy, ostensibly by heterosexual intercourse. What had actually happened was, that the group arousal had overwhelmed Sharon's own sensibilities and carried her away. For The Rite of The Goddess to work, all three participants required to achieve genuine sexual ecstasy. Ruth had no idea which of the other five women would be capable of that. Nevertheless, she intended to raise the subject after their group exercise this evening – only to be thwarted by, of all people, Sharon.

The Coven had entered their mind-meld, concentrating on the binding spell they hoped to deploy against Gwendolen. They had used something similar to hold Keranrodai immobile before killing him. This spell was meant to augment that power, to deal with the much more dangerous and potent Moonchild. Killing her was not, unfortunately, an option. Their only hope seemed to be holding the fearsome Adversary in some form of stasis, preventing her from fulfilling her disastrous destiny. At best, this was an unsatisfactory and temporary solution – but it seemed to be the only one on the table. At the end of each session, they had gotten into the habit of channeling their communal power to Sharon, in the hope of spying some more on Gwendolen. The Moonchild had been well off the radar since that brief glimpse of her on Wednesday evening. Tonight proved no different. Gwendolen was keeping herself cloaked from prying eyes – but something else caught Sharon's roving sight. "The hotel's being watched," she told the group. "There's two people stationed at the front and two at the back. They are Venatores – and their mood is hostile."

Chapter Sixty Nine – Time To Check Out . (Tuesday 1st July 1980)

The group's impending discovery and possible apprehension by the Venatores, was an added complication but one that Gloria felt qualified to deal with. This was logistics and tactics – which she'd been trained for and had lots of practical experience in. Gloria had to formulate an extrication plan – and quickly. For the first time in a while, she felt in command, despite the fraught nature of the situation. The first thing Gloria did, was post a watcher at both the front and rear of the building. They were told to stay out of sight and give warning should there be any attempt to rush the hotel. The chance of being tracked down was always a possibility but they hadn't expected it to happen so soon. The Venatores did have extensive resources but there had to be an element of blind luck in this.

Gloria had no illusions about the benevolence of her former employers. When she had been reporting to them, regarding the magic she'd detected in Garry Wallace's previous victims, Gloria had not been totally forthcoming. Knowing Beresford's approach to his work, she had tended to downplay the extent of what was happening in Stirling. He had shown no concern for the aftercare of the women, following a traumatic and bewildering experience for them. Beresford was a ruthless careerist and Gloria considered him a sociopath, with no empathy for anyone else. If he saw the women as any kind of threat, he would have no compunction applying for a termination order –

and would likely succeed in getting it. She also reckoned that her own disappearance would be viewed in the most unfavourable light. In Beresford's eyes, she would be a traitor and a rogue operative. This would colour the authorities' view of her also. She would be hunted down, arrested and, most likely, terminated without trial.

They hadn't really considered what to do in situation like they found themselves in now. That would probably been addressed in time but the speed of their discovery was a surprise. The hotel's characteristics, which made it a secure hideaway, also made it a bit of a trap. There was only one way in at the front and one at the rear, making it easily defensible but also difficult to escape. The Coven were strong in magics but the Venatore operatives would have warding against witchcraft – though there was some doubt about whether what the Sisterhood did was, in fact, witchcraft. It felt different somehow but Gloria didn't want to risk finding out – at least not in these circumstances. Escape was the objective and Gloria put her mind to it now.

Everyone had appearance altering disguises but Gloria didn't trust in them. Neil's Fey ability to go "unseen" would be very useful right now but he had not yet returned and possibly never would. As far as Gloria could see, there were a few alternatives to get clear of the hotel. They could simply walk out one or both of the doors and make a break for it. The Venatores were not yet there in great numbers but they'd have guns and possible authorisation to use deadly force. It would be risky. Gloria and Sharon both had pistols of their own but Sharon wasn't combat trained or experienced. They would be outgunned and casualties would be almost certain. Alternatively, they could either go up or down. Gloria knew there were cellars, though nobody had explored them yet. The hotel was an old construction and possibly there was access to the cellars of the adjoining tenements on either side. Failing that, they might be able to escape across the roofs of the adjacent buildings.

It was just after midnight in the early hours of Tuesday morning. Gloria asked Michelle and Janet to check out the cellars, while Ruth and Sharon were sent upstairs to do the same with the attic. Gloria herself stayed on the ground floor, in case her marksmanship was needed. An hour or so later, the group, apart from Ann and Archie, who were on watching duty at the windows, assembled in the function suite. There was no way out, neither up nor down. The walls in the cellars were too thick to do anything with and a similar situation applied to the attic. There was access to the roof but traversing the rooftops, slanting as they were, would be too dangerous – besides, anyone escaping that way would be easily seen from across the street.

They had ascertained that the Venatores at the front of the hotel were most likely in a dark grey Transit van, parked across the street, a little way up from the door. The ones at the back hadn't yet been spotted. As a precaution, the group had parked three cars a few streets away in case of emergency. They just hadn't counted on being bottled up in the hotel. That was a grievous oversight. The members of the Coven were still unclear about their powers and what abilities they actually had. Maybe they could simply storm their way out the front door. There were only two Venatores there. The situation might not remain that way for much longer. Was it time to grasp the nettle and go for it – while they still could? After a terse discussion and a show of hands, they took the decision to go now. A quick plan was cobbled together. The Coven members would link hands in a circle around Archie and Ann's daughters. The Coven would merge their individual consciousnesses and try to project a defensive shell around them. They would exit the front door of the hotel in this formation and make their way to the escape cars. If the Venatores tried to intervene, they would be dealt with. The officers themselves might have protective warding against witchcraft but their vehicle didn't. Keeping the mind-meld intact whilst on the move, would be difficult but it would protect them from Venatore bullets – at least that was the hope. Meanwhile, unknown to the Sisterhood, Beresford was less than an hour away, with a squad of twelve of his top firearms officers.

The group loaded up as many of the reference books into satchels as they could. Then they propped the front doors open and formed up their formation in the lobby. It was a bit of a clunky plan but time was passing and Gloria was apprehensive. She had no doubt regarding her status with her former employers. The radio silence from the Venatores pointed to them discovering that she'd purloined some of their radios and altering their frequencies to exclude her from listening in. She had switched through the channels to try and find the one they were now using but there were a limited number available. The Venatores had obviously done a major revamp of their communications. Gloria was also uneasy at the speed with which they had been located. They could well be rushing upon the Sisterhood, right now, in overwhelming force. That outcome could turn out very bloody indeed. Gloria wanted out of there as quickly as possible. She worried about just how much

Beresford knew. Perhaps she was being unnecessarily spooked but her instincts told her differently.

In the Transit van, Officer Miller came alert when the hotel's doors were pushed open. He quickly shook his partner, Officer Kemp, awake. It had been her turn for some shuteye. Then he spoke rapidly into his radio. "Attention, Group Leader, hotel doors have been wedged open. Looks like someone's getting ready to come out. Advise please." Beresford responded immediately. "Detain whoever emerges until I get there. We're about half an hour out. If it proves to be our fugitives – shoot to kill. Officers Quinn and Somerville – be ready to come to the front if required to support Miller and Kemp. But stay alert, in case this is a diversion." A few seconds later, the group, in their formation exited the building and turned left along the pavement. Miller spoke again, "They've left the building. I'm confident it's them – though they've made some attempts to alter their appearance. As expected, there are children with them." Beresford rapped back. "Take them out. Quinn and Somerville get round there quickly. Shoot to kill." "But the children," Miller protested. "You have your orders," Beresford replied forcefully, "Now – get on with it."

Miller and Kemp grabbed the automatic rifles that hung in clips on the van's walls and exited the vehicle. The two operatives knew Garcia. They'd worked with her and had liked her but they were soldiers in an unconventional war. So – despite the presence of two young children, orders were orders. They opened fire – but their bullets had no effect. The Coven's shield was holding. Gloria hadn't been sure the Venatores would try to intercept them. She thought they might simply try to put a discreet tail on the group. This over the top show of force was shocking and smacked of mindless hatred and desperation. Beresford's influence was very much in evidence. There was a narrow passageway up ahead, which led between two low Victorian midden buildings. She intended to take the group through this and magically collapse the middens to foil any pursuit. They never got that far.

Everyone was, understandably, alarmed at the gunfire. The noise was overwhelming. Archie looked back, in alarm. Unfortunately, as he did so, he stepped too close to one of Ann's daughters. His foot entangled with hers and she tripped. Not watching where he was going, Archie stumbled over her and fell. Given the group's tight formation, inevitably, those following tripped and fell also. Their hands came apart and the shield began to fail. It didn't collapse straight off but began to fade very rapidly. There was no time to re-establish the mind-meld. Any second now, the bullets would begin to bite. Everyone sensed it. Ruth reacted quickest. She was one, at the rear of the group, who had fallen. Spinning round on her knees, Ruth flicked her right hand towards the Venatores. Their guns immediately exploded in mid-shot. Hot, jagged shards flew in all directions, killing Officer Miller instantly and severely injuring Kemp. Fortunately for the Coven, the shield still had enough juice left in it to protect them.

Ruth scrambled to her feet, just as a white Transit screeched round the corner and hurtled towards them – obviously, the other two Venatores. Ruth stood, with her feet apart and thrust both hands towards the speeding vehicle. An invisible and irresistible force rushed out and battered into the Transit, bringing it to a sudden dead stop. The entire front of the van crumpled all the way back through the cab, crushing and mangling the two occupants inside into bloody, lifeless messes. Everyone was stunned by the sudden onset of violence and the gory, dramatic and abrupt conclusion it had been brought to. The children were in tears and Ann was trying to soothe them. Gloria took control. "Let's get going," she said loudly. "There'll be time enough later to recover from what's happened. There'll be more Venatores on the way and someone will definitely have called the police after that disturbance. We need to get clear quickly." Gloria ushered them into motion, reflecting on the power Ruth had just displayed. Did they all harbour such abilities? If so – they had little to fear from any human challengers. Gwendolen, however, was another story.

Chapter Seventy – Ladies In Black . (Tuesday 1st July 1980)

Gwendolen had acquired a high-cabbed Ford Transit minibus. It was originally yellow and belonged to a local council. The Moonchild had transformed it, magically, into a glossy, gleaming black. The vehicle was a twelve-seater – ideal to accommodate her new coven, who numbered that amount exactly. Gwendolen was, in many respects, still a child emotionally – and a petulant child at that. She had had to hide and repress her natural power and inclinations under the stern eyes of the Druids, led by that prick, Caradoc. Her resentment still burned bright. The Druids dressed in white robes, so Gwendolen decided that her colour would be black – therefore that's what she and all her followers would wear. She had made up her mind to indulge her each and every whim. No-one would be allowed to deny her ever again. Presently, her power was immense – but very soon, it would be irresistible.

Gwendolen was bringing her recently press-ganged acolytes, which she called, Fy Noson Ddu (My Black Night), on a leisurely progress northwards. Currently, they'd commandeered an entire floor of a swanky Manchester hotel. The whole group was gathered in Gwendolen's plush suite for a pep-talk and exposition of their duties and obligations. "Tomorrow," she told them, "We'll all be going shopping. The merchants will give you everything you desire – free of any price. You will select clothing, any style or fashion that takes your fancy. All of it will be black. From now on, you will wear nothing but that colour. Clothes, shoes, handbags and even underwear – must now be black. Now, I'm not saying that this is a strict rule. That would make it sound special. It's not. All my rules are strict. Any transgression – even the first – will result in a very painful and horrible death. Just remember your former leader and how she left this world. Know also, that I don't need all of you for my purposes. So, I will have no compunction in disposing of any who do not give me total devotion and obedience."

Gwendolen, in fact, only needed two attendants, with magical aptitude, to help her give birth and enact the ensuing ritual. She continued her monologue. "In a few weeks' time, I will come into my full power. Until then, we will get to know each other and you will be further instructed in your duties and privileges – but we will have fun doing it. When I summon my demon army, I intend to subjugate humanity, not exterminate it. Humans are so entertaining to fuck with – sometimes literally. You will come into supernatural powers that you can't even imagine just now. Anything you desire, you will simply have to take. Consider yourselves blessed. As my trusted lieutenants, the world and everything in it, is yours. You can see the copious amounts of alcohol and food that I've had brought up. Tonight – we will eat, get drunk and have multiple sexual liaisons. I intend to indulge my every whim. You will learn to do the same. From now on, your watchword is depravity."

Most, if not all, the conscripted women, thought Gwendolen quite mad – but they had seen her power and were afraid. They didn't know how things would work out but survival demanded that they do as they were told.

Chapter Seventy One – Spying On The Enemy. (Saturday 5th July 1980)

Gloria and the gang were back in Neil's cottage in the Ochil Hills. Conditions were a bit cramped but, for the time being, there was no alternative. The mood was subdued and beaten down. All of them, but particularly Gloria and Ruth, were sorrowful regarding Neil. He had been gone for over a week now, and no-one expected to ever see him again. The women, through no choice of their own, had been pitted against a formidable foe – one that they couldn't kill, even if they could find a way to do so. As far as they knew, Gwendolen's death would precipitate the very disaster they were trying to prevent. There seemed to be no light at the end of the tunnel and despondency was rife. The Sisterhood were defeated in mind and spirit. This was not a situation that Gloria would allow to persist. She was a fighter and resolved to find a way to go down fighting – if they were to go down at all.

They were not totally cut off in the cottage. Neil had installed a television and it was on much of the time. An item on the news had piqued Gloria's curiosity. It was a sensational enough story in its own right. Twenty-seven patrons had died in an incident at a Manchester nightclub, on Friday evening. Information was sketchy and confused. The initial reports had spoken of a riot but gave no rationale for the extremely high death-toll. Something very much out of the ordinary had occurred. Later television reports became much more guarded and Gloria detected the hand of Venatore news management – an example being the low profile, media wise, that had been afforded to their recent run in with the Venatores in Glasgow. Perhaps she was being paranoid but this Manchester incident smacked strongly of a supernatural incident – and one that the Venatores had their teeth into already.

The Coven had made a couple of half-hearted attempts, through Sharon, to find out what Gwendolen was up to and where she was. The Moonchild seemed to be cloaking herself and they were unsuccessful. The one certainty they seemed to have, was that Gwendolen would make her way to the Abbey Craig, near Stirling, with the intent of giving birth there under the full moon on 24th September. The Coven could wait and seek to confront her at that time – or they could try to disrupt her progress and stop her reaching that destination at that time. Perhaps that would make a difference – but to accomplish it, they'd have to locate their nemesis. Gloria suggested a new approach. This episode in Manchester might provide them with a focus they hadn't had up till now. Gloria's gut told her that the Moonchild's fingerprints were all over this incident. Gwendolen could cloak herself but ordinary mortals couldn't. Boosted by the mind-meld of her Sisters, Sharon would quest for and try to latch on to the memory of someone who'd been in the nightclub during last evening's mayhem.

It took some time and patience but eventually Sharon found what she was looking for. She used her power as a seer to look through the eyes of a young woman who had survived the massacre. As she watched, Sharon described what she was seeing and hearing to the rest of the Coven. "I'm in a large, busy room. There's loud music and flashing lights. Everyone's dancing and look like they're having a good time. I see a group of women that have all come in together. There's maybe about a dozen of them. They're noticeable because they're all dressed in black and a few of them are a bit older than you might expect at a place like this. Some of them are quite attractive but one of them stands out above the rest. She's a stunning blond and the others seem to be fawning all over her. She certainly appears to be the leader of the pack. I only saw her briefly before but I've no doubt it's Gwendolen. It seems she's found some friends."

Nothing out of the ordinary happened for some time. It was a disadvantage of this form of seeing that Sharon could only follow where her host had looked at the time. The music played on and the dancers continued to gyrate. Sharon continued her commentary. "There's a sudden stampede of panicked looking dancers, obviously trying to get away from something that's going down on the dancefloor. My host can't see what it is but bouncers are converging from the edges of the dancefloor. Wow! One of their heads has just exploded. There's blood, bone and brains flying everywhere. There's a total stampede happening now. The screams are drowning out the music, loud as it is. My host is being pushed and jostled. She's screaming too and trying to fight her way through the crowd. I presume she's heading for an exit. Another heads just exploded – but I can't see who it is. Now – some force has just battered half a dozen or so people and splattered them all over a wall, just to my right. They're all horribly mangled and must be dead. My host is through a door and outside. She was lucky, being close to an exit when this all broke out. There are still screams and ominous crashes coming from the hall."

There was not a lot more of value to be gleaned from this host. The one item of note was a black minibus that had been carelessly left right in front of the club's front door. It was not in any of the parking slots and looked out of place. People were milling about looking either stunned or totally terrified. It was a strain for Sharon to maintain contact, so she let it drop. She'd seen enough to know that the attack had been supernatural in nature and orchestrated by the Moonchild. It looked like she had already embarked on her reign of terror – even before she had control of her demon horde.

The group discussed what Sharon had told them, while she rested from her efforts. It was informative but didn't give them a great deal to work with. After a few minutes, Sharon made a suggestion. She had got a good look at one of the women in black. Gwendolen was probably cloaking herself but that didn't mean all her companions were. With the woman's face to guide her, Sharon could try to latch onto her. The Coven joined hands once again and concentrated on merging their magics into the group consciousness. Once the mind-meld was established, they channeled their power through Sharon. She concentrated on visualizing the woman's face that she'd seen in her earlier expedition. After a few minutes, Sharon informed them of success. She signalled to the others and they relaxed once more.

Sharon made her report. "The woman's name is Elaine Westwater," she said. "She's quite young – just twenty. She's a practicing witch with a coven in London that meets at the Highgate Cemetery. The woman is new to this – she's only been involved for a few months – and she's totally terrified. Gwendolen has more or less kidnapped the coven after brutally killing their leader. They don't know exactly what her intentions are but she seems to want them to assist at some ritual in a few months' time. I think we can assume it's the one at the full moon on the Abbey Craig. Some of the coven are getting on board with Gwendolen – they see opportunities in following her – but the majority are simply scared stiff. They will do as she tells them, simply out of fear. The black minibus I spoke about earlier is theirs. It's how they're getting around. That's about all I can get for the moment – but now that I've found this Elaine once, it should be easier to acquire her again. She could be like our spy in the camp.

The Coven members discussed the information that Sharon had gleaned and speculated what use, if any, it could be put to. It wasn't immediately clear but they were pleased that they at least had some kind of handle on what the Moonchild was up to. After some discussion, Ruth spoke up. "There's something I think we might try," she said, glancing at Sharon – who gave a nod of assent. "Sharon and I have been working on something," Ruth went on, blushing a little. "Yes, we noticed," Gloria interjected. There were a few good-natured sniggers around the circle and Ruth blushed even more brightly. The others were now well aware that the two young women had been indulging in certain nocturnal activities together. Gloria had been worried about Ruth and was keeping a watchful eye on her. Early on Tuesday morning, the Coven's youngest member, had killed three – or possibly four – Venatore officers. Taking a human life was not a trivial matter and Gloria was worried that Ruth would be beset by overwhelming guilt. So far – no such reaction had been detectable.

Ruth took a deep breath and plunged into her explanation. "We know that Gwendolen's power is seemingly connected to the Moon. She's called the Moonchild, after all. We don't know enough about her and that means we don't know how to beat her. Maybe if we could consult someone that knows the Moon and Gwendolen's connection to it – then we might discover a way to fight her. The situation's getting kind of desperate and time's running out. As you know, I've been studying sex-magic. We've all seen how powerful that can be. The last ritual did everything we required of it." Ruth's voice caught in her throat as she thought of Neil's role in that venture. She felt his absence very sharply.

Ruth steadied herself again and went on, "Anyway, there's another sex-magic ritual that I've been looking into. It's designed to allow the participants to commune with the Moon Goddess, Cerridwen. The rite is called "The Sapphic Moon Circle" in the book I'm studying. It's different from the last ritual. All the celebrants need to be female. It requires three women to take part and it must be enacted out in the open, under the Full Moon. There's not many Full Moons left before Gwendolen is due to give birth – so, if we're going to attempt it, it'll have to be soon. Sharon and I are obviously willing to take part – but we'll need another volunteer – but not just anyone will do. All three women need to be able to achieve genuine sexual arousal and climax, solely through the actions of other women."

Ruth paused, a bit embarrassed before she continued. "If one of you volunteers, we'd need to experiment and practice before the actual ritual – to make sure that everyone was suitable." She trailed off, not knowing how her suggestion was being taken. There was silence for a few moments. Then Janet spoke up. "I'll give it a try," she said.

Chapter Seventy Two – Hanging By A Thread . (Saturday 5th July 1980)

Tom Beresford was under pressure. He had expected the debacle in Glasgow on Tuesday morning to finish him. Somewhat perversely, the atrocity at the Dauphine Club in Manchester had kept him in a job. Beresford was awaiting a summons to the Home Office, where his resignation would no doubt be required. Fortunately, the Minister had a busy schedule and then the attack at the nightclub had shifted the focus to there. It was seen as an emergency and there was no-one, other than Beresford, with the seniority and experience to handle such a situation. Ironically, Gloria Garcia would have been the only candidate who had enough familiarity with the U.K. Venatores to have taken his place.

It had become quickly apparent that something uncanny had happened at the nightclub and the Venatores had been notified. Beresford had immediately taken command of the investigation. He was worried. With two major operations in progress, his forces were overstretched. Four of his top operatives had died in Glasgow, which didn't help. Perhaps reinforcements would have to be requested from sister organisations in Continental Europe. Beresford was in Manchester. He had seen the bodies, read witness statements and even interviewed some himself. He'd hoped that, somehow, Garcia and her crew had been involved. His initial investigations had dashed that hope. Supernatural forces had been wielded here, but by a group that had hitherto been unknown.

The most recurrent theme amongst witnesses was the group, most often estimated at about a dozen, of women, all dressed in black who had entered the club en masse. It was the fact that they had made their entrance as a solid group, that made them noticeable. One or two witnesses commented on the ease with which these women got served at the crowded bar, where often patrons could have a frustrating time waiting for the bar staff to get round to them. The women in black were attended to as soon as they approached the bar. One witness wondered if they were visiting celebrities, though he didn't recognize any of them. He also noted that no money ever changed hands when drinks were being served. Beresford was convinced that this mysterious group was central to the incident.

As to the episode itself, Beresford could discern no obvious motivation for it. In one witness's account, it started when a fight broke out on the dancefloor. She said that the bouncers in The Dauphine were very efficient. Normally, trouble was snuffed out before it really got started. The stewards were moving in to quell this disturbance, when one of their heads burst open in an explosion of gore and other cranial tissues. Then all hell broke loose. More skulls blew open and people were being hurled with bone-shattering force against walls and even up to the ceiling. Understandably, panic bloomed in an instant. There was a frantic and chaotic stampede, as people sought escape from the terrifying forces that were being unleashed on the dancefloor. It was noted that the only people who didn't join in the desperate dash for the exits, were the aforesaid women in black. They were later seen leaving the club, boarding a black minibus and driving off, before the police had arrived. At the wheel, had been a blond woman, described as being stunningly good looking.

Whoever this group were, they hadn't appeared on the radar before. They obviously commanded eldritch powers but their motivation was obscure. It all seemed so pointless. Could it simply be violence for the sake of violence. That was not unknown amongst evil-doers – who seemed to get a buzz out of terrifying people and killing innocents in all sorts of ghastly ways. Whatever the reasons for their actions, this group had to be found and eradicated swiftly. There was no doubt in Beresford's mind, that they were the perpetrators of this atrocity. Everything pointed to it. His gut, as well as his logical analysis told him this was so. He had put out an alert to find the black minibus. It had been found, abandoned, further north in Newcastle. So far, no-one had been discovered who'd seen the women leaving it. Beresford put out a further alert, to apprehend any group of women seen dressed in black. They might, of course, have changed their attire – but should such a band be discovered, agents were warned to exercise extreme caution and be prepared to use deadly force.

Chapter Seventy Three – Go Forth And Make Me Proud . (Sunday 6th July 1980)

Elaine Westwater and Linda Latimer approached the church. They were in Carlisle on an assignment set by Gwendolen. The night before, she had gathered her minions once again in her hotel room – this time in Edinburgh. She was not best pleased with them. "I'm disappointed," she told them. "Disappointing me is second only to disobeying me – but – as this is new to you, I'll let it pass this one time. Last night, at the dancing place, not one of you took a hand in the proceedings. You just stood and goggled while I spread all the mayhem. I've given each and every one of you a boost to any magical power you already possessed. This came directly from my own reservoir – yet you signally failed to use it. That is not good enough. It made me doubt the wisdom of choosing you for greatness. How can you know what you can achieve, if you never test your abilities? I fear that you may not have the mindset required of the roles I have in mind for you."

Gwendolen paused and swept the others with a withering glare. "It's never a good thing," she went on, "to make me doubt my own wisdom. I might well react badly to that. Anyway – I'm going to give you a chance to redeem yourselves. It's time for my little birds to fly the nest. You will all be paired up in teams of two and I'll allot each team a target. I expect you to hit each target with maximum destruction and loss of life. Use your initiative and make it spectacular. You will all reconvene here one week from tonight. In that time, as well as hitting your allotted target, I expect other adventures and debauchery to have taken place. I have imbued you all with powers that will give you great scope. Use them. Anything you want, will be given to you by shopkeepers, innkeepers and merchants. They will happily comply with your desires and have no memory of it afterwards. Learn to take advantage of this. Show me that you can be the oppressors I need you to be.

There will be hunters seeking you. Some of you may fall foul of them. Some of you may even be killed. Believe me – that is a more desirable fate than you'll suffer as a result of disappointing me. This is a test of your survival skills also. You may be called on to indulge in mortal combat and subterfuge. You are not permitted to change your clothing from black at any time. You must always proclaim who you are and who you represent. Oh – by the way – I'd advise against anyone thinking that, because you are out of my sight, that you can sneak back to your old life. I can find you wherever you go – and my vengeance will be terrible – not only against you, but against your loved ones also. So, gather round and I'll give you your assignments."

Elaine and Linda had been paired together and given The Sacred Heart Church as the focus of their murderous intent. Gwendolen explained that she had suffered strictures at the hands of the Druids. There were none of that order left on which to wreak revenge – so she would substitute the Catholic Church in their place. Its authoritarian priests and sheeplike followers reminded her of the cult of the Druids and made them eminently eligible to be attacked. The Sacred Heart had been chosen more or less at random. It was in the preferred geographical area and well-enough attended for a strike to be significant. That was all the Moonchild required. This was, after all, merely a test of her acolytes' mettle and a small overture to the greater works she had planned.

Elaine and Linda were not sure how they should proceed in this matter. Collapsing the building on its worshipping congregation would be effective enough, a feat they were confident they could achieve, but it wouldn't signify more than a simple tragedy to the general public. Gwendolen was demanding more than that. The two women discussed their options. They decided that they would seize control of the occupants during the 11.30 Mass on Sunday morning. This was the best attended Mass of the weekend. They had no doubt that they had the power to subdue the congregation and hold them in thrall while they enacted their atrocities. The priest, and then a few of his flock, would be slaughtered, one at a time, in inventive and messy ways. Then a more general carnage would ensue – using Gwendolen's methods from The Dauphine Club. A small group – half a dozen or so – would be allowed to live, so that they could tell the tale of the horrors that had taken place. Elaine and Linda agreed that Gwendolen should be satisfied by this. Then they would party their time away, with possibly a few more gory deaths thrown in, until it was time to report back to their leader.

The Church of The Sacred Heart was a traditionally styled building of medium size for its type. Built of stone, it had stained glass windows down both sides and on the wall at the altar end. At 11.45, Elaine and Linda entered through the door at the rear of the building. They strode, side by side, up the central aisle. The priest, wearing a green vestment with a large golden cross emblazoned on its back, was doing something at the altar, facing away from his congregation. He was being attended by two altar-boys, dressed in a black garment overlaid by a white one. A few heads turned to watch the women's progress as they paraded up the passageway. Elaine reckoned there might be anything up to a hundred worshippers present. The women stopped in front of the altar rail. Linda turned to face the congregation and Elaine seized control of the priest, from a distance of about ten feet away. Using her magic, she levitated him a couple of feet above the floor and turned him round to face his flock. At the same moment, Linda threw both her arms upwards and out to the sides. Every pane of stained glass shattered with a crash and the pieces fell, to scatter noisily on the ground.

There were gasps of astonishment and many screams of alarm from the startled congregation. Several people stood up, preparatory to fleeing. Linda thrust them back down onto their pews and slammed all the doors shut with a thunderous boom. The priest hung helpless in mid-air, his face registering disbelief and terror. Linda's voice rang out, "Remain in your seats. Nobody is to move. Any attempt to leave will be punished severely." She was a tall, striking blond with piercing brown eyes. Elaine was also fair-haired but more petite and pretty. They stood there, dominating the church and confident in their power. It was time for them to put their savagely gory plan into action. The priest would be first to suffer. They intended to pull off, first his arms and then his legs, to leave him bleeding to death in agony whilst suspended in front of the altar. As the priest died, a few of the congregation would be selected for various horrible individual manglings. The finale would be when the witches unleashed a maelstrom of death and destruction on the main body of the congregation. Then Elaine and Linda would make their exit, leaving behind a few shattered survivors to tell the world what had passed inside the church that morning. Even Gwendolen's exacting standards should be satisfied with that bloodbath.

A pretty, dark-haired woman, sitting in the front row, stood up. Linda turned her attention to her and tried to slam the woman violently back into her seat. Nothing happened. In her peripheral vision, Linda saw some others getting to their feet. Neither she nor Elaine could fathom what was happening. They could still feel their power fizzing inside themselves – but it seemed to have no effect on the women. The first woman who'd stood up spoke. "We are the Seven Sisters," the woman said. "We've been watching you Elaine. When you fell in with Gwendolen's plans, you signed your own death-warrant. Your career of evil is over." The two black clad witches collapsed to the floor, their hearts crushed within their bodies. As the priest fell to the ground unhurt, the seven Coven members left their pews and amidst the church-goers bemused chatter, departed the building.

Chapter Seventy Four – A Venatore Score . (Monday 7th July 1980)

A new alert went out to all Venatore agents. Beresford had concentrated his existing forces in the North of England and the Scottish Borders. It seemed to be where the new menace was active at the moment. Beresford had rushed north to interview witnesses at the church in Carlisle. It was obvious to him that the two black-clad aggressors were members of the same group that had attacked the nightclub in Manchester. He also came to the conclusion that it was Garcia and her associates who had foiled whatever nastiness would have transpired, had they not been there. This was an interesting development and one that required some thought.

Beresford's new alert came from the incident in Carlisle. If his agents encountered, even two black-attired women together, they were to be treated as suspects and detained. This was caveated by the warning that any such women were possibly powerful witches and were likely to be very dangerous. Once again, deadly force was authorised. Beresford was puzzled by the women's' persistence in wearing readily identifiable clothing. True – other women wore black – but it still made them stand out, especially when they were in a group – even one as small as two. Perhaps it had some kind of cultish significance. He obviously didn't know of Gwendolen's perverse nature and her intention to weed out the less able of her minions.

Officers Jim Morton and Jim Gardner were patrolling Newcastle city centre when they saw two women dressed in black, strolling through the Haymarket Bus Station. In accordance with standing orders, the two Jims approached the women and showed them their Venatore IDs. At first, the women reacted calmly enough, but when the Venatores informed them they were being detained, they went on the attack. Luckily for Gardner and Morton, the witches were unaware of the warding against witchcraft that protected all front-line Venatore Officers. The agents felt a cold blast as a percussion spell blew past them, doing no harm. They had to react quickly, before the women realised that direct action against them was futile but other objects could be launched against them.

It was a volatile situation – but one with which the Venatores had more experience. It was a life or death confrontation. The women obviously commanded great power. If they figured out how to best use it, the agents were as good as dead. Neither woman had ever been in such direct conflict before. All the harmful things they'd perpetrated on others previously, had been done at a distance. The Venatores therefore reacted quicker and they did so to deadly effect. They both drew their guns, and, as mandated by Beresford, shot the women dead. Beresford himself had mixed feelings when he received his agents' reports. He was pleased that two of the mysterious and murderous group had been taken out – and that his officers were unharmed. He would have loved, however, to interrogate the two renegade women but subduing anyone with the formidable potency that these two had, was not an easy thing to do. The Venatores were working on a couple of devices that might help in that respect but they weren't ready for production yet. At the moment, dealing out summary execution was the only viable option. At least, Beresford consoled himself, that was four of the black-clad women taken out of the picture. Now, they just had to find and destroy the rest of them.

Chapter Seventy Five – At Home With The Coven . (Friday 11th July 1980)

Janet had never been terribly motivated by sex. Sometimes, with Garry, it had been quite good but she never felt the earth move. That was different to what was happening now. Janet, like all the women, had been caught up in the energy of the sex ritual they'd carried out – but other than that, her sex-life was non-existent. This didn't bother her in the slightest. She had felt no amorous interest in anyone – male or female. In fact, as far as she could remember, Janet had never ever been attracted to a member of her own gender. What Ruth and Sharon were doing to her now, was altering her perception totally. This was the first time they'd been able to procure the private use of a bedroom. The full moon was just over a fortnight away and Ruth was keen to enact "The Sapphic Moon Circle" on that night. She was convinced that a consultation with the Moon Goddess would give them an edge in their conflict with Gwendolen. For this ritual to succeed, it required the efforts of three enthusiastic female participants. Today was Janet's initiation into the mysteries and joys of lesbian lovemaking. She found that it was very much to her taste. Who better than a woman to know the workings of another woman's body?

Most of the other members of the Coven were working on preparations for the ritual too – but in a possibly less direct way. Gloria was tending to the potion that was a pre-requisite for the ceremony. She was stirring it and keeping it simmering away – making sure it never came to the boil, which would ruin it. Gloria had jumped at the chance of direct action last Sunday. She had felt it would be good for morale and would strike a blow against Gwendolen – not to mention, saving innocent lives. It had shown that they had the strength to defeat the Moonchild's followers – albeit that the odds had been seven to two, they had still prevailed. Gloria figured that it had been worth the risk of travelling to Carlisle. It was frustrating that they couldn't have gone after others of Gwendolen's group but without a focal point to concentrate on, Sharon had been unable to track any of them down. Still – any small victory was better than none. It had cheered them all up but time was rapidly running out – and that dampened her mood.

Ann and Jenny were busy cutting and sewing special robes that the three participants would wear in the initial part of the ceremony. They were made of black cloth with a large, white full moon stitched onto the back and a smaller version placed over the left breast. The two women chatted away happily as they worked. It was good to have something to occupy their minds. Sandra and Karen, Ann's daughters, sat together on the floor, working on arithmetic problems their mother had set them. It was a constricting existence for the two youngsters. Fears over security, meant that they were rarely allowed outside. The girls never complained though. Like all the rest, they simply tried to make the best of the situation. Archie, with no defined role, was sitting watching television, while the last of the group, Michelle, was at the dormer window in the attic, keeping lookout. Archie had already turned the sound up on the television a couple of times, to mask the noises coming from the bedroom.

Gloria had been keeping an eye on the tv news, to try to discover what atrocities had been committed by the other pairs Gwendolen had sent out. On Monday, something of note had happened on a train following its departure from Darlington Station. There had initially been a vague story of multiple fatalities and then it slipped off the bulletins altogether for a while, before reappearing and being reported as a tragic derailment. Strangely, no pictures or film of the accident site were shown. The death toll had been estimated at over seventy. Gloria had immediately detected Government news management, probably orchestrated by Beresford. Then, on Wednesday, nearly one hundred people had died on a plane at Manchester Airport, ostensibly as the result of a tainted oxygen supply, despite the fact that the aircraft was still on the ground.

These two incidents, happening so close together, had shocked the nation. Gloria was convinced that they were the handiwork of the Moonchild's followers and that there were probably other catastrophes, that had been quashed before the media got hold of them. As it happened, Gloria was premature in her assessment. A bulletin came on the television that Archie was watching, reporting an explosion at a petrochemical plant near Falkirk. There were believed to be several fatalities and many injured. This third disaster seemed to bear the imprint of Gwendolen's devotees. This left one pair of saboteurs unaccounted for, but so far, their exploits had not reached the media. As the women broke off their activities to watch the news, Michelle dashed into the room, to warn that an unknown car was fast approaching up the single-track road that led only to the cottage and nowhere else.

Chapter Seventy Six – Showdown At The Northern Britannia. (Friday 11th July 1980)

The Venatores were swamped. They hadn't been designed to deal with the sheer volume of supernatural incidents and deaths that were happening right now. The organisation just didn't have the manpower. Even Tom Beresford, who had great confidence in his own abilities, was beginning to doubt that he could deal with this new terror group. They were prolific and relentless. Their endgame seemed to be unguessable. If Beresford had had a way of contacting

Gloria Garcia, he would have reached out to her for much needed help. As it was, he'd put out a desperate plea to Venatore divisions in Europe for much needed back-up. Things were looking bleak – but then, they got a break. Beresford had put out a new directive to his beleaguered troops. "Do not engage anyone you suspect are members of the "Women in Black". Instead, follow and observe them. See if you can discover their base." This approach had quickly borne fruit.

It started with a puzzle. Two butchered bodies were discovered in the precincts of Durham Cathedral, in the North of England. They looked like they could well be members of The Women in Black. Who had killed them, was a mystery. Beresford's best guess was Garcia or some of her group. He had dispatched two of his overstretched teams to investigate. On their way driving across country, one of the teams had spotted another two possible suspects, travelling in a red Austin Princess with a black roof. When they reported this back to Beresford, he had pulled them from their assignment and told them to tail the pair of women but not to engage. It would be difficult not to be discovered by the suspects whilst doing this but, fortunately, the women seemed totally oblivious – so much so that the Venatores began to smell a rat. Nevertheless, they continued their operation and followed the women all the way to Edinburgh.

The women stopped outside The Northern Britannia Hotel, near Waverley Station in Edinburgh. They left the car where it was and went inside. When they hadn't come back after an hour, the Venatore agents followed them into the building. At reception, no-one could tell them anything about the black-clad women – but they did discover that the entire top floor had been taken over, though there was no record of by who. The agents returned to their car and reported in. As they sat there, another two women dressed in black, parked a grey Volkswagen Beetle behind the Austin Princess and entered the hotel. Officer Thomson, the senior of the two, voiced his misgivings to Beresford. He felt that it smacked of a set-up. It had been too coincidental that they'd encountered the first two women at random and then were able to follow them with ease. Thomson worried that the whole thing might be a trap.

Beresford took note of the officer's fears but he'd just been informed of the explosion near Falkirk. This could not be allowed to continue – assuming, which he did, that the latest incident was down to this blood-soaked group. Besides – Beresford had faith in his own abilities and judgement. If he'd been honest with himself, he'd have admitted that his thought process was coloured by quite a bit of desperation. Even if it was a trap, which he considered to be unlikely, he would go in with overwhelming force. Beresford told the two agents to hold their position and wait for him. He was coming north. Then he ordered all of his remaining front-line officers to Edinburgh. This could be a big break and the opportunity had to be seized. Flying by the seat of his pants was very much Tom Beresford's style and it hadn't let him down yet.

While he was waiting for his full force to assemble, Beresford took steps to confirm the actual presence of his quarry in the hotel and to scope out their position. He found out that the mystery guests made extensive use of room service. So, when they sent down for more booze, a Venatore agent took the place of a porter to deliver it. He returned to report. The group were assembled in the "Walter Scott" suite and it was indeed the women in black. There were seven of them, all drinking and relaxed. They did not seem to be expecting any trouble. This allayed any doubts Beresford might have had that a trap was planned. He could end this menace in one fell swoop. The agent reported that one of the women appeared to be pregnant, even though she seemed to be drinking just as heavily as the rest.

The plan was simple. Using a passkey, a squad would enter the suite and kill everyone they found inside. Beresford would deal with the aftermath in due course. Given the situation, he now had an embarrassment of riches. He had almost forty, well trained and well-armed operatives in attendance. Nowhere near that number would be required. In fact, he'd be hard-pressed to even get them all into the suite at the one time. Once set in motion, the whole operation should only take a couple of minutes. Beresford determined that a squad of ten, armed with automatic assault weapons, would be more than adequate for the job. He, himself, would not be going in with the initial assault. There were better trained, younger and more expendable agents to fulfill that role. Beresford would wait in the corridor with a second, back-up squad. The rest of his force, he dispersed through the hotel, covering entrances and stairways – in case more of the occult group showed up.

Gwendolen was indeed relaxed and enjoying herself. Humans were so easy to manipulate. She had lost half her minions, when she'd sent them forth into the world. This was expected. Gwendolen still had more than she needed for her purposes and these were the best of the bunch. It gratified her also that none had tried to flee. Two she had lost to the coven she'd become aware of while she was still imprisoned. This did not qualify them as a genuine threat. It had taken all seven of them to overcome a pair of the Moonchild's weakest.

Another two had been killed in a chance encounter with the Venatores. This brought that organisation onto Gwendolen's radar. They were even less of a threat than the Coven. Nevertheless, she intended to obliterate both the Coven and the Venatores. The former, would present themselves soon enough for destruction. The latter, she had enticed in – and they'd taken the bait. Gwendolen's attention had been elsewhere when her last two followers had been slain. She didn't know who'd done that – but she was unconcerned. The Druids were long gone and the Fey were neutralized. There was nothing in this world that could rival her, even before she had her army of demons at her beck and call. Now that the unworthy had been weeded from her followers, it was time for some fun.

The Venatore hit squad stood in the corridor outside the Walter Scott Suite door. They had made their way there in utmost silence. All weapons had been checked and they were ready to go. The ten members of the entry team got themselves in order and they were all set. Beresford, standing off to the side with the six reserves, gave a hand signal and the team leader inserted the key into the lock and opened the door. The squad shuffled through quickly and then the chatter of automatic gunfire erupted. It came to an abrupt end, to be replaced by screaming – only it didn't sound like women doing the screaming. There was some banging and thumping and then everything went uncannily silent. Beresford hesitated a second or two. He couldn't imagine what was going on but there was nothing else for it. Beresford ordered the reserves into the suite and crowded in behind them.

The sight that met their eyes was pure carnage. Body parts littered the floor and blood was everywhere. The women in black sat there drinking nonchalantly, totally ignoring the slaughterhouse scene all around them. The Venatore officers were stunned – and then they recovered themselves and opened fire. They sprayed the women with automatic fire but not one bullet hit its mark. There seemed to be an invisible barrier protecting them. The screaming commenced again as Venatore officers began being ripped apart. Arms, legs and then heads were torn off and scattered amongst the debris already on the floor. Beresford stood transfixed for a couple of seconds and then he too was ripped apart and died screaming.

Chapter Seventy Seven – Back From The Dead. (Friday 11th July 1980)

The women's consternation, at the unknown car approaching the cottage, turned to joy when they saw who was driving. It was Neil. Everyone had given him up as dead. His venture into The Land of The Fey had always smacked of a suicide mission. They also knew that his temporary altered tone would last no longer than a week at the outside – and now, more than a fortnight later, he was back. As the car had approached, Gloria had hammered three times on the bedroom door, to alert the three women inside that something was happening. A few minutes later, they joined the others, to find Neil sitting in the living room. Ruth rushed to him and embraced him with joyous enthusiasm, causing him to wince with pain but still return her hug with a smile on his face.

Jenny put the kettle on and everyone settled down to hear Neil's story. He'd gone first to the hotel in Glasgow, but finding it abandoned, had rightly guessed he'd find them at the cottage. He told them how he'd killed the Fey King through a mixture of opportunism and sheer blind luck. He'd almost made a clean getaway on horseback but had been hit and seriously injured by a Fey arrow. Neil had managed to stay on his horse. He had galloped towards the nearest portal back to the world of the humans, growing weaker by the minute. The sound of pursuit behind him, spurred Neil on, but the pain and loss of blood, eventually proved too much for him and he tumbled from the saddle to the ground.

Neil had still been conscious, when the pursuers reached him. He had looked up to see his cousin, Brigid, and five of her retinue surrounding him. Brigid was the Sherriff of Domhan Anduine – the human lands in Scotland that encompassed Stirling – a post previously held by Neil himself. There was no love lost between the cousins. Neil had resigned himself to his fate. Brigid was royally appointed by King Feargas himself and apprehending his assassin would be a real feather in her cap. At that point, Neil had passed out. When he awoke, Neil found himself, not in a dungeon cell like he expected, but in a soft, comfortable bed. His wound had been treated and bandaged. A little while later, a physician had come to see him and gave him medicine to take. When the physician had left, Brigid came in and explained her strange reaction to apprehending him.

Brigid had a claim to the vacant throne of Talavnafey – The Land of The Fey. She intended to press that claim. Having her cousin as the assassin of the late King could be an embarrassment to her. It would be used by her competitors to claim that she was somehow implicated in the dire deed. Brigid had decided that an anonymous assassin would suit her ends better than turning in her cousin and confirming his guilt. She had been quite frank in telling him, that the only reason she was leaving him alive was that a secretly buried body could someday be discovered – and subsequent questions asked. Brigid had chosen to conceal him while he recuperated somewhat. As soon as he was fit enough to be moved, she would spirit him back to the human world – with the warning that if he ever came back, she would not again be so merciful.

This had been what had happened. Neil had re-entered this realm early this morning. It had been at a portal across country from the one he had used to get in. The Fey who had escorted him was sympathetic. As they parted, he informed Neil that there were two of Gwendolen's followers bent on nefarious business in nearby Durham. Neil had "borrowed" a car from a supermarket carpark and driven to Durham. He had quickly located the tones of the two women in black and had moved in on them. The women were strong in magic but they were still human. Neil had entered their minds but could discern nothing. There was a block placed there and it had to be the work of the Adversary. It was strong enough that the women were able to break free of Neil's control and he'd had no choice but to draw sword and kill them. Now he had come home. He was not yet fully recovered but was on the mend. Now he wanted the women to tell him what had happened at the hotel and how things stood with them now. There was much to tell him.

Chapter Seventy Eight – Time To Hunker Down. (Friday 11th July 1980)

Gwendolen Y Lleuad and her six women in black left the charnel house of The Walter Scott Suite and made their way down through the big hotel. On their journey they encountered and killed ten more Venatore agents. Gwendolen was much more merciful with these slayings – contenting herself with merely snapping their necks. Despite being parked in a restricted area, the Volkswagen and Austin Princess were where they'd been left. Neither had received even as much as a parking ticket. There would be no problems with the vehicles being identified or followed. Gwendolen had put an enchantment on them that rendered them unnoticeable. The women got into the cars and drove away from the mayhem of The Northern Britannia.

The Golf Hotel near The King's Park in Stirling, was much less opulent than their usual venues, but that was the women's destination. Gwendolen had enjoyed her little indulgences. The violence, destruction and general nastiness had been unnecessary, other than to meet Gwendolen's childish whims. Now, she required a time of preparation – a time to get ready for her coming ascension. It would be boring but she'd endure it. There was no need though, to avoid alcohol, despite the fact that her pregnancy would be progressing ever more quickly. The baby didn't have to be born healthy. It was destined to live less than an hour anyway.

Chapter Seventy Nine – The Sapphic Moon Circle. (Sunday 27th July 1980)

The day had come. Tonight was the night of the full moon. Tonight, the ritual of The Sapphic Moon Circle would be enacted. Ruth, Sharon and Janet had been preparing and rehearsing extensively. A special unguent had been blended and a special potion brewed. Ceremonial robes had been made, with pockets to accommodate the necessary ritual accoutrements. A small clearing, set among trees high in the Ochil Hills, had been selected as the venue and the ground prepared. It was about fifteen minutes' walk from the cottage and suitably isolated. Only the three participants would be present. There could be no distractions.

It was a clear night and warm, which was fortunate, considering the nudity that would be involved. The three celebrants left the cottage just before eleven at night. They had waited for it to get dark and for the moon to ride high. The women were wearing only their ceremonial black robes with the moon emblazoned on the back and over the left breast. They were all nervous and excited. Ruth, in particular, had high hopes for the outcome of this ritual. All the women of the Coven were also hopeful, though not overly optimistic. They were desperate for some way to combat and stymie Gwendolen's intentions. In two months' time, the Moonchild would give birth and – if things went as she planned – she would come into her full power as the Queen of The Demons and it would be the end for humanity as it now was. Killing Gwendolen, if that was even possible, would unleash a maybe even worse outcome. The ritual of The Sapphic Moon Circle, was a last despairing throw of the dice. The Coven needed something – anything – to give them a glimmer of hope.

Ruth led the procession up the hillside, followed, in single-file, by Sharon and Janet. They went in silence – focusing their minds on what was to come. The moon shone down on them, lighting the way. After a time, the women reached the clearing. Earlier in the day, wood had been laid for a small fire in the centre of the clearing. It had been soaked in a special oil, which would make it burn with a bright silvery flame. Ruth reached into the pocket of her robe and brought out a box of matches. Striking a match, she put it to the wood and the fire sprung to life. As the flames grew higher, each woman took a flask from her robe and drank down the liquid inside. They replaced the empty flasks in their pockets and stood for a moment in quiet contemplation.

Ruth was the first to move. She brought out a small tub and screwed off the lid. It was filled with a creamy silver paste. Going to Janet, Ruth opened her friend's robe and pushed it from her shoulders. It fell to the ground, leaving her totally naked. Ruth dipped two fingers into the unguent and anointed both of Janet's nipples. She then did the same to the little pink pearl of Janet's clitoris. Immediately those three sensitive spots began to tingle. Janet took the tub from Ruth and went to enact the same procedure on Sharon, who then, in turn, ministered to Ruth. Sharon laid down the tub and the three naked young women went to stand around the fire. They joined hands and began to move. Three times, the women circled around the fire clockwise and then three times counter-clockwise, before three more in the first direction. All the while, the tingling in their anointed parts grew in intensity – bringing about a delicious sexual arousal.

The potion they'd drank was taking effect also. It warmed the lower parts of their abdomens and stimulated a fire in their groins. Although they were no longer in motion, the women were finding it impossible to stand still. They writhed where they stood and vaginal juices began to flow freely. It was time. Sharon and Janet let go of each other's hands. With Ruth in the middle, hand in hand with the other two, they walked away from the fire. The women all moved apart. Ruth lay down on the cool grass, lying on her left side. She was bent forward, forming a crescent. Janet lay down next – behind Ruth. She rested her head between Ruth's thighs, with her mouth in easy reach of her cunt. Sharon adopted the same position between Janet's legs and they closed the circle with Ruth's mouth in close proximity to Sharon's vagina. The circle was complete.

The women were already in a high state of sexual excitement – and now they went to work on each other. Tongues probed, lips caressed and teeth nibbled. Fingers searched, delved and manipulated. The fire in the women's loins was fanned quickly to a furnace. They writhed and moaned, giving and taking pleasure, but never breaking contact. Ruth was the first to reach climax. She came spasmodically and then continued to come. One orgasm would run its course and then blossom directly into the next one. Soon, Janet and Sharon were in the same state of orgasmic ecstasy. The circle fizzed and popped with erotic energy as the women squirmed and thrashed in paroxysms of sheer erogenous, mind-blowing frenzy.

Ruth began to feel herself drifting away – though she continued to be fully aware of the ministrations Janet was lavishing on her pussy and of the smell taste and feel of Sharon's wet cunt on her mouth nose and tongue. While all that carried on, a part of her consciousness slipped through to another plane altogether. A beautiful woman materialized in front of her eyes. The woman was tall, with flowing red hair. She wore a long blue dress and behind her head was a silver glowing disc. It reminded Ruth of the halos she'd seen in old representations of Christian saints.

"Welcome, Ruth of The Seven Sisters," the woman said – though her lips never moved. "I am Cerridwen. I know what troubles you – so listen now to what I say. You have all made a mistake. You believe that Gwendolen of the Maetae is *the* Moonchild. She is not. She is *a* Moonchild. There are others – of which you are one. I am neither good nor evil. I simply – Am. Some mortals are born with an affinity to me. These are the Moonchildren. I do not create them but I will succour any of them who cry to me for help. I have already done so for Gwendolen and now I will do so for you. She is stronger than you and was able to connect with me directly. You are less strong – but you have used what resources you have wisely. It's been a long time since anyone has performed the Moon Circle. I congratulate you.

There are cosmic forces – ever in conflict – that even a Goddess, such as I, do not fully understand. Some of these forces brought about the conjunctions that enabled Gwendolen to be the creature that she is. Other, conflicting forces, allowed Caradoc the Druid to put her in stasis until someone capable of opposing her could be brought forth. In human terms, these machinations take a long time – but finally here you are. Now – listen well. Here is what you must do if you wish to stop Gwendolen achieving her destiny.

There is an item – let us call it the Moonstone. This you must have in hand when you confront Gwendolen. Finding the Moonstone is not straight forward. It will only reveal itself when Gwendolen commences her Ritual of Becoming. You must be ready to seize it quickly as soon as it appears. That is why your friends of The Seven Sisters have been endowed with great magic. Only they have the power to hold her in check while you retrieve the Moonstone and hurry to face her before she completes the sacrifice of her child. Look for it on the night of the full moon in September. It will lie in the grounds that was once the dwelling of Caradoc the Druid. You will have no doubts of where and what it is, when you see it. Now – here is what you must do." Cerridwen then described what needed to be done and Ruth's heart quailed within her.

The three women came to a final explosive orgasm and collapsed where they lay. They were physically and mentally exhausted. It was a long time before any of them was able to move and it took days for them to fully recover. Ruth now knew what lay before her and she was sore afraid.

Chapter Eighty – A Time Of Peace. (Sunday 27th July to September 23rd 1980)

When the three women eventually staggered back to the cottage, Ruth recounted her vision – all except the last part. She knew that if she told them how it had to end, they'd be horrified and refuse to let her do it. She wasn't sure herself that she could actually go through with it. Any opposition and her resolve would crumble and all would be lost. Ruth determined to keep the matter secret and steel herself for what was to come. She would let her sisters believe that the mere presence of the Moonstone would be enough to foil Gwendolen.

Everyone was relieved that a solution seemed to have been found, even though they would have to go up against Gwendolen and her black clad followers. Neil was suspicious. Knowing eldritch matters as he did, he thought it all sounded a bit too easy. Nevertheless, he held his peace. If Ruth wanted to share, she would. As it was, there was no place for Neil in the confrontation that was to come. It was all in the hands of Gloria and her sisters. He had to trust in his female friends – and he did – but still he fretted.

After things settled down a bit, Neil phoned around his contacts. It gave him something to do. That is how he learned about the massacre at the Northern Britannia Hotel. The British Venatores were all but wiped out. Gloria was shocked when he told her. She'd worked with most of the dead. None of the story had leaked to the general public but it was well known in the security community. Britain now had no effective force to combat any supernatural threats – and there were more of them than people would ever guess. Fortunately, most of these were low-level, unlike the one that the Coven currently faced.

The group decided to move back to the Rosemont Hotel. There would be little danger now from the Venatores and the cottage was very cramped for space. They could return to the cottage on the eve of Gwendolen's ritual. The civilian police would still be on the lookout for them as missing persons but it was unlikely that the Venatores had shared any information with them. It was not their normal practice. They rested up for one more day, to let the women who'd taken part in the Moon Circle recover a bit, and then they set off in a convoy of three cars and drove to the Rosemont.

Back at the hotel, the group soon fell into a comfortable routine. The Coven still met most evenings, to practice and perfect their mind-meld and exercise their magical muscle. But it was far from all work and no play. They all came together for convivial communal meals. There were spontaneous gatherings, warmed by the consumption of alcohol. Neil, once again, shared a bed with Gloria – and he had several visits to room 103. Ann was his most frequent companion. Ruth only went with him a couple of times. She found that Sharon was more than adequate for her sexual needs. Quite often, Janet would join them for a pleasurable threesome. She had discovered that sex with her own gender was very much more to her taste than the messy fumblings of a man. On one occasion, Neil had a memorable liaison with Jenny in room 103. He was Fey and felt no guilt at screwing a married woman. He also learned a few things at the hands, lips and cunt of Jenny. She was an older woman but admirably accomplished.

There was much laughter and camaraderie. There was much love and companionship. It was an idyllic interlude – but it couldn't last. As September progressed, the mood became more subdued and introverted. Ruth, in particular, became very withdrawn, which was not at all like her. Tension was understandable. A battle was coming and its outcome was by no means certain. The days ticked off, ever more slowly it seemed but the 23rd still arrived all to soon. It was time to head back to the cottage and get ready for the following day.

Chapter Eighty One – The Hour Approaches. (Wednesday 24th September 1980)

The day was dull and overcast and this mirrored the mood amongst the Seven Sisters. All of them were apprehensive about what lay before them in the coming evening. Win or lose, it would be a testing and dangerous time. There were many unknowns. Not the least of these was, where exactly would Gwendolen's ritual take place. They knew it was to be on the Abbey Craig – but this covered a large area – much of it covered in trees. Finding the site, in time to intervene, could prove problematic. The timing of the intervention was critical also. It could not happen before the ceremony commenced. Otherwise the Moonstone would not be revealed. Neither could it be left too late, as Ruth needed time to retrieve the Moonstone and get to the ritual site before Gwendolen completed it. There were many imponderables. The only certainty that the Coven had, was total faith in their sisters. Come what may, they would stick together. They would not let each other down.

Although tonight's burden would fall squarely on the women of the Seven Sisters, a role had been found for Neil, who had been feeling sidelined and ineffectual. They would marry technology to magic. Neil would use his Fey senses to locate Gwendolen's presence. He would then communicate this to Gloria via the Venatore radios that they still had. Neil would then take up position on the Abbey Craig cliff, overlooking the ruins of Cambuskenneth Abbey. The Abbey had been built on the ground where once Caradoc's Druid compound had stood – and where Ruth was to find the Moonstone. Neil would endeavour to alert her to its location quickly, when it put in an appearance. Ruth would have the other Venatore radio they possessed. It was unclear whether anyone other than Ruth would be able to detect the item, but it was worth trying. Neil's Fey senses might prove equal to the task.

Gwendolen was fizzing with barely suppressed excitement. The last two months of minimal activity – and thus minimal fun – had awakened echoes in her of her time under the strict tutelage of the Druids. This had done little to enhance her mood. Soon though, all restraints would be off. She could do whatever she pleased and none could stop her. Already Gwendolen was planning and relishing the anticipation of her future exploits. She had no maternal feelings for the child she was soon to bring forth. It was merely a means to an end. Besides – her pregnancy had made her enormous and she hated it. She looked forward to having her perfect body back. Tonight's full moon was known as the Harvest Moon. It was also a Super-Moon, meaning it would appear larger than normal. Gwendolen saw these facts as good omens. Soon, she would be reaping her own glorious harvest.

As the day wore on, the cloud began to dissipate and it grew brighter. At eight o'clock, the Coven, apart from Ruth, got into their cars and drove the few miles to the Abbey Craig. They parked at its foot in the carpark for the Wallace Monument. The monument was closed by this time and the carpark was empty. Night was drawing in and darkness was falling. Neil drove Ruth to Cambuskenneth Abbey and dropped her off there. He then took himself up onto the Craig and melted in amongst the trees. When a Fey doesn't want to be seen, they are very hard to detect.

Gwendolen and her group were already on the hill. They had been making preparations for the night's ritual. The site chosen was a wide clearing near the summit – coincidentally the same one in which the witch Koldunya had initiated Garry Wallace, last winter. A three foot deep ditch had been dug measuring about six feet square. The women had filled this with chopped wood and had then drenched it with gallons of an oil on which enchantments had been placed. A pair of ropes had been suspended from the bough of a tree from which Gwendolen could support herself as she squatted to deliver her baby. Her labour was starting, so it wouldn't be long now.

Chapter Eighty Two – Endgame. (Wednesday 24th September 1980)

The moon hung huge and golden in the sky, as Gwendolen expelled her baby into the waiting arms of one of her black-clad minions. She herself, was stark naked. At that very moment, the wood in the pit burst into vivid red flames, that lit the surrounding trees in a lurid glow. Also on that instant, Neil spotted a ghostly silver radiance amongst the ruins of Cambuskenneth Abbey. It had to be the Moonstone. He got on the radio to Ruth but she'd already seen it and was on her way towards it. It had been a night of anguish for the young woman – and it didn't promise to get any better – just the opposite, in fact. She didn't understand why all this had landed on her head. There were only two choices available to her and neither one was good. But – if truth be told, there wasn't actually a choice at all. Her conscience would only let her do one thing. Apart from a still standing bell tower, the ruins of the Abbey were at foundation level. They were no obstacle to Ruth, as she ran to retrieve the Moonstone.

Gloria had been waiting for word from Neil that the Moonstone was in evidence. The Coven had taken up position earlier, concealed within the trees on the edge of the clearing. Now they stepped forward and advanced into the clearing in line abreast. Gwendolen was on her feet with the baby in her arms, Her attendants had tended to what had to be done and handed the child to her. Two of them had then carried out the ceremony of anointing with oil that was called for in the ritual. Gwendoln had glanced down at the little boy and saw that he had his mother's eyes. This elicited no emotional response whatsoever. She looked up and smiled icily. "So you've decided to stop skulking and show yourselves," she said. "I see one of you has had the wisdom to absent herself. Well – this is where your pathetic little band finds its doom." Gwendolen gestured to her acolytes. "Kill them now." She ordered. The women in black moved forward to do Gwendolen's bidding and were promptly blown asunder. Bits of them rained down and pattered onto the grass.

Ruth reached the Moonstone where it lay beside the line of grey foundation stones for some ancient abbey building. The object was about the size and shape of a tennis ball and it glowed with a pearlescent silver light. It was this aura that had shown Ruth where it lay. She had no idea where it had come from or whether it had lain where it was, invisible and unseen through the ages. There was no time for speculation right now, nor was there any point. She bent to pick it up. The orb was surprisingly heavy. It was smooth to the touch and unusually cold. Ruth scooped it up and turned to run towards the nearby roadway. She didn't know how long her sisters could delay Gwendolen. She had to hurry.

"Impressive," said Gwendolen sardonically. "But no matter. I no longer need them. I'll just have to deal with you myself. I was merely giving them the chance to shine." She bent her mind to obliterating the six mortals who faced her. Had any of the women been outside the mind-meld, each and every one of them would have been ripped apart – but their resolve held. They all felt a painful tugging at every joint but their communal strength managed to resist. The pressure on them didn't relent though. They had to maintain their group defiance. If even one of them lost concentration, they were all dead. The Coven, in their turn, projected power, intended to hold the Moonchild in stasis. It worked – but only partially. Gwendolen was about thirty paces from the firepit. All she had to do was deposit her newborn into those flames and it was all over. Slowly she edged towards it as the Coven tried to hold her back. It was at a snail's pace, but she was getting there. Sweat was pouring down the faces of Gloria and her companions. The strain on them was immense. Gwendolen was very, very strong – but still they held on, as best they could.

Neil had scrambled down the footpath to where he'd left his car. He'd set off at a sprint as soon as the Moonstone appeared. He got to his car and slammed it into motion. Quickly, he caught up to where Ruth was running along the road and called for her to get in. She did so and Neill accelerated away. He drove round the foot of the Abbey Craig and up to the narrow road which led to the summit. This was not usually used for motor traffic but Neil threw the car up it anyway. He sped upwards and then slewed the car onto the grass and through to the clearing. With a glance, Gwendolen killed the engine, but Ruth was already where she needed to be.

The Coven were losing the battle of wills – and they knew it – but still they clung tenaciously on. Gwendolen was more than halfway to the fire when Ruth arrived. The moment she brought the Moonstone into view, Gwendolen stopped moving. She was puzzled but not yet too worried. This intervention was unexpected bur she'd soon figure it out. Gwendolen was still supremely confident in her own power. She would ultimately prevail.

Now that it came to it, Ruth was strangely calm. She knew what she had to do and was at peace with it. Purposefully Ruth walked towards the firepit. As she got closer to it, Gloria suddenly divined her intention. The words of Caradoc's prophetic poem sprang into her mind – especially the bit about an "awful sacrifice". The others twigged seconds later. The Coven broke their mind-meld but fortunately Gwendolen was realising what was afoot and turned her attention to Ruth. Her friends started forward to try and intercept Ruth, but she froze them all with a wave of her hand. Gwendolen also found out she'd lost the ability to move.

At that moment, Ruth had come into her own. She was untouchable. As she walked towards her painful death, Ruth recalled Cerridwen's words. "Gwendolen is stronger than you – so your sacrifice must be stronger than her's. She acts out of selfishness – so you must act out of love." And Ruth was acting out of love – love of her sisters – that they might live and that their world might go on. Without hesitation Ruth stepped into the firepit and the flames engulfed her.

Ruth's hold broken, anguished screams erupted from her friends and several of them collapsed to their knees in despair. Gloria was upbraiding herself. She should have known. She should have done something to stop this – but now it was too late. The flames flared brighter around Ruth – but something strange was happening. As she stood there amidst the leaping flames, none of them seemed to have any effect on her. Then Gwendolen began to scream hideously. Their eyes were drawn to her and a fearsome sight greeted them. Her body was being consumed as if it was she who stood amidst the flames. She writhed in agony as her flesh was eaten away. The baby too wailed – but briefly, as his little body also succumbed to the invisible flames. The fire continued to do its work, even after Gwendolen screamed no more. At length there was nothing left of her or her short-lived child. At that moment, the fire in the pit died and Ruth stood there in a daze but very much alive.

The other women ran to her and engulfed her in hugs and kisses. Neil also ran across the clearing and joined in. Ruth was totally perplexed. She felt herself growing weak at the knees. She was absolutely stunned – dazed to still be alive. "That wasn't supposed to happen," she kept repeating in a small voice. The Moonstone was gone. Her friends gently moved Ruth from the dead firepit. There were so many questions. Gwendolen was undoubtedly dead. Did that mean they'd failed and that literal pandemonium would be unleashed on the earth. A soft voice drew their attention. "That Moonchild is gone and this one remains." They turned to see an ethereally beautiful woman with long red hair and a silvery moon-disk behind her head. Ruth knew her immediately as Cerridwen. "You had to believe that your death was imminent," the woman continued though her lips didn't move. "Had you not done so – then there would have been no sense of sacrifice – and Gwendolen would have prevailed. You believed that you were committing the ultimate sacrifice. That is powerful magic. It was the concept of loving sacrifice, rather than the actuality of it that mattered. You are brave and true, Ruth of The Seven Sisters. Your actions have banished the demons and the rent is sealed. The Moonstone absorbed Gwendolen's essence and that of her son. It has taken them to the Demon Realm where she will rule as Queen, far from the world of humans. Live and be happy." With that, Cerridwen faded from view and left the Seven Sisters with their Fey friend Neil, standing beneath the golden moonlight, amidst the mangled remains of the women in black. It was over – and the Coven survived.

Printed in Great Britain
by Amazon